Praise for #1 *New York Times* bestselling author Linda Lael Miller

"Linda Lael Miller creates vibrant characters and stories I defy you to forget."

—#1 *New York Times* bestselling author
Debbie Macomber

"Miller has found a perfect niche with charming western romances and cowboys who will set readers' hearts aflutter."

—*RT Book Reviews*

"Miller tugs at the heartstrings as few authors can."

—*Publishers Weekly*

Praise for *New York Times* bestselling author B.J. Daniels

"[B.J.] Daniels is truly an expert at Western romantic suspense."

—*RT Book Reviews*

"B.J. Daniels delivers it all in *Mountain Sheriff*—warm, wonderful characters, tightly woven, page-turning intrigue and passionate romance."

—*RT Book Reviews*

The daughter of a town marshal, **Linda Lael Miller** is a *New York Times* bestselling author of more than one hundred historical and contemporary novels. Linda's books have hit #1 on the *New York Times* bestseller list seven times. Raised in Northport, Washington, she now lives in Spokane, Washington. Visit her website at lindalaelmiller.com.

New York Times and *USA TODAY* bestselling author **B.J. Daniels** lives in Montana with her husband, Parker, and three springer spaniels. When not writing, she quilts, boats and plays tennis. Contact her at bjdaniels.com, on Facebook, Facebook.com/pages/bj-daniels, or Twitter, @bjdanielsauthor.

#1 *New York Times* Bestselling Author

LINDA LAEL MILLER

THE McKETTRICK WAY

WITHDRAWN

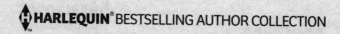
HARLEQUIN® BESTSELLING AUTHOR COLLECTION

ISBN-13: 978-0-373-01044-8

The McKettrick Way
Copyright © 2016 by Harlequin Books S.A.

The publisher acknowledges the copyright holders of the individual works as follows:

The McKettrick Way
Copyright © 2007 by Linda Lael Miller

Mountain Sheriff
Copyright © 2003 by Barbara Heinlein

Recycling programs
for this product may
not exist in your area.

This edition published by arrangement with Harlequin Books S.A.

For questions and comments about the quality of this book, please contact us at CustomerService@Harlequin.com.

HARLEQUIN®
www.Harlequin.com

Printed in U.S.A.

CONTENTS

THE McKETTRICK WAY

Linda Lael Miller

In memory of my dad, Grady "Skip" Lael.
Happy trails, cowboy.

CHAPTER ONE

BRAD O'BALLIVAN OPENED the driver's-side door of the waiting pickup truck, tossed his guitar case inside and turned to wave a farewell to the pilot and crew of the private jet he hoped never to ride in again.

A chilly fall wind slashed across the broad, lonesome clearing, rippling the fading grass, and he raised the collar of his denim jacket against it. Pulled his hat down a little lower over his eyes.

He was home.

Something inside him resonated to the Arizona high country, and more particularly to Stone Creek Ranch, like one prong of a perfectly balanced tuning fork. The sensation was peculiar to the place—he'd never felt it in his sprawling lakeside mansion outside Nashville, on the periphery of a town called Hendersonville, or at the villa in Mexico, or any of the other fancy digs where he'd hung his hat over the years since he'd turned his back on the spread—and so much more—to sing for his supper.

His grin was slightly ironic as he stood by the truck and watched the jet soar back into the sky. His retirement from the country music scene, at the age of thirty-five and the height of his success, had caused quite a media stir. He'd sold the jet and the big houses and most of what was in them, and given away the rest, except for the guitar and the clothes he was wearing. And he knew he'd never regret it.

He was through with that life. And once an O'Ballivan was through with something, that was the end of it.

The jet left a trail across the sky, faded to a silver spark, and disappeared.

Brad was about to climb into the truck and head for the ranch house, start coming to terms with things there, when he spotted a familiar battered gray Suburban jostling and gear-grinding its way over the rough road that had never really evolved beyond its beginnings as an old-time cattle trail.

He took off his hat, even though the wind nipped at the edges of his ears, and waited, partly eager, partly resigned.

The old Chevy came to a chortling stop a few inches from the toes of his boots, throwing up a cloud of red-brown dust, and his sister Olivia shut the big engine down and jumped out to round the hood and stride right up to him.

"You're back," Olivia said, sounding nonplussed. The eldest of Brad's three younger sisters, at twenty-nine, she'd never quite forgiven him for leaving home—much less getting famous. Practical to the bone, she was small, with short, glossy dark hair and eyes the color of a brand-new pair of jeans, and just as starchy. Olivia was low-woman-on-the-totem-pole at a thriving veterinary practice in the nearby town of Stone Creek, specializing in large animals, and Brad knew she spent most of her workdays in a barn someplace, or out on the range, with one arm shoved up where the sun didn't shine, turning a crossways calf or colt.

"I'm delighted to see you, too, Doc," Brad answered dryly.

With an exasperated little cry, Olivia sprang off the soles of her worn-out boots to throw her arms around his neck, knocking his hat clear off his head in the process. She hugged him tight, and when she drew back, there were tears on her dirt-smudged cheeks, and she sniffled self-consciously.

"If this is some kind of publicity stunt," Livie said, once she'd rallied a little, "I'm never going to forgive you." She bent to retrieve his hat, handed it over.

God, she was proud. She'd let him pay for her education, but returned every other check he or his accountant sent with the words *NO THANKS* scrawled across the front in thick black capitals.

Brad chuckled, threw the hat into the pickup, to rest on top of the guitar case. "It's no stunt," he replied. "I'm back for good. Ready to 'take hold and count for something,' as Big John used to say."

The mention of their late grandfather caused a poignant and not entirely comfortable silence to fall between them. Brad had been on a concert tour when the old man died of a massive coronary six months before, and he'd barely made it back to Stone Creek in time for the funeral. Worse, he'd had to leave again right after the services, in order to make a sold-out show in Chicago. The large infusions of cash he'd pumped into the home place over the years did little to assuage his guilt.

How much money is enough? How famous do you have to be? Big John had asked, in his kindly but irascible way, not once but a hundred times. *Come home, damn it. I need you. Your little sisters need you. And God knows, Stone Creek Ranch needs you.*

Shoving a hand through his light brown hair, in need of trimming as always, Brad thrust out a sigh and scanned the surrounding countryside. "That old stallion still running loose out here, or did the wolves and the barbed wire finally get him?" he asked, raw where the memories of his grandfather chafed against his mind, and in sore need of a distraction.

Livie probably wasn't fooled by the dodge, but she was gracious enough to grant Brad a little space to recover in, and he appreciated that. "We get a glimpse of Ransom every once in a while," she replied, and a little pucker of worry formed between her eyebrows. "Always off on the horizon somewhere, keeping his distance."

Brad laid a hand on his sister's shoulder. She'd been fascinated with the legendary wild stallion since she was little. First sighted in the late nineteenth century and called King's Ransom because that was what he was probably worth, the animal was black and shiny as wet ink, and so elusive that some people maintained he wasn't flesh and blood at all, but spirit, a myth believed for so long that thought itself had made him real. The less fanciful maintained that Ransom was one in a long succession of stallions, all descended from that first mysterious sire. Brad stood squarely in this camp, as Big John had, but he wasn't so sure Livie took the same rational view.

"They're trying to trap him," she said now, tears glistening in her eyes. "They want to pen him up. Get samples of his DNA. Turn him out to stud, so they can sell his babies."

"Who's trying to trap him, Liv?" Brad asked gently. It was cold, he was hungry, and setting foot in the old ranch house, without Big John there to greet him, was a thing to get past.

"Never mind," Livie said, bucking up a little. Setting her jaw. "You wouldn't be interested."

There was no point in arguing with Olivia O'Ballivan, DVM, when she got that look on her face. "Thanks for bringing my truck out here," Brad said. "And for coming to meet me."

"I didn't bring the truck," Livie replied. Some people would have taken the credit, but Liv was half again too stubborn to admit to a kindness she hadn't committed, let alone one she considered unwarranted. "Ashley and Melissa did that. They're probably at the ranch house right now, hanging streamers or putting up a Welcome Home, Brad banner or something. And I only came out here because I saw that jet and figured it was some damn movie star, buzzing the deer."

Brad had one leg inside the truck, ready to hoist himself into the driver's seat. "That's a problem around here?" he asked, with a wry half grin. "Movie stars buzzing deer in Lear jets?"

"It happens in Montana all the time," Livie insisted, plainly incensed. She felt just as strongly about snowmobiles and other off-road vehicles.

Brad reached down, touched the tip of her nose with one index finger. "This isn't Montana, shortstop," he pointed out. "See you at home?"

"Another time," Livie said, not giving an inch. "After all the hoopla dies down."

Inwardly, Brad groaned. He wasn't up for hoopla, or any kind of celebration Ashley and Melissa, their twin sisters, might have cooked up in honor of his re-

turn. Classic between-a-rock-and-a-hard-place stuff—
he couldn't hurt their feelings, either.

"Tell me they're not planning a party," he pleaded.

Livie relented, but only slightly. One side of her
mouth quirked up in a smile. "You're in luck, Mr. Mul-
tiple Grammy Winner. There's a McKettrick baby
shower going on over in Indian Rock as we speak,
and practically the whole county's there."

The name McKettrick unsettled Brad even more
than the prospect of going home to banners, streamers
and a collection of grinning neighbors, friends and sisters. "Not Meg," he muttered, and then blushed, since
he hadn't intended to say the words out loud.

Livie's smile intensified, the way it did when she
had a solid hand at gin rummy and was fixing to go
out and stick him with a lot of aces and face cards. She
shook her head. "Meg's back in Indian Rock for good,
rumor has it, and she's still single," she assured him.
"Her sister Sierra's the one having a baby."

In a belated and obviously fruitless attempt to hide
his relief at this news, Brad shut the truck door between
himself and Livie and, since the keys were waiting in
the ignition, started up the rig.

Looking smug, Livie waved cheerily, climbed back
into the Suburban and drove off, literally in a cloud
of dust.

Brad sat waiting for it to settle.

The feelings took a little longer.

"GO HAUNT SOMEBODY ELSE!" Meg McKettrick whispered to the ghost cowboy riding languidly in the passenger seat of her Blazer, as she drove past Sierra's new
house, on the outskirts of Indian Rock, for at least the

third time. Both sides of the road were jammed with cars, and if she didn't find a parking place soon, she'd be late for the baby shower. If not the actual *baby*. "Pick on Keegan—or Jesse—or Rance—*anybody* but me!"

"They don't need haunting," he said mildly. He looked nothing like the august, craggy-faced, white-haired figure in his portraits, grudgingly posed for late in his long and vigorous life. No, Angus McKettrick had come back in his prime, square-jaw handsome, broad shouldered, his hair thick and golden brown, his eyes intensely blue, at ease in the charm he'd passed down to generations of male descendants.

Still flustered, Meg found a gap between a Lexus and a minivan, wedged the Blazer into it, and turned off the ignition with a twist of one wrist. Tight-tipped, she jumped out of the rig, jerked open the back door, and reached for the festively wrapped package on the seat. "I've got news for you," she sputtered. "*I* don't need haunting, either!"

Angus, who looked to Meg as substantial and "real" as anybody she'd ever encountered, got out and stood on his side of the Blazer, stretching. "So you say," he answered, in a lazy drawl. "All of *them* are married, starting families of their own. Carrying on the Mc-Kettrick name."

"Thanks for the reminder," Meg bit out, in the terse undertone she reserved for arguments with her great-great-however-many-greats grandfather. Clutching the gift she'd bought for Travis and Sierra's baby, she shouldered both the back and driver's doors shut.

"In my day," Angus said easily, "you'd have been an old maid."

"Hello?" Meg replied, without moving her mouth.

Over her long association with Angus McKettrick—
which went back to her earliest childhood memories—
she'd developed her own brand of ventriloquism, so
other people, who couldn't see him, wouldn't think
she was talking to herself. "This *isn't* 'your day.' It's
mine. Twenty-first century, all the way. Women don't
define themselves by whether they're married or not."
She paused, sucked in a calming breath. "Here's an
idea—why don't you wait in the car? Or, better yet,
go ride some happy trail."

Angus kept pace with her as she crossed the road,
clomping along in his perpetually muddy boots. As always, he wore a long, cape-shouldered canvas coat over
a rough-spun shirt of butternut cotton and denim trou-
sers that weren't quite jeans. The handle of his ever-
present pistol, a long-barreled Colt .45, made a bulge
behind his right coat pocket. He wore a hat only when
there was a threat of rain, and since the early-October
weather was mild, he was bareheaded that evening.

"It might be your testy nature that's the problem,"
Angus ruminated. "You're downright pricklish, that's
what you are. A woman ought to have a little sass to
her, to spice things up a mite. You've got more than
your share, though, and it ain't becoming."

Meg ignored him, and the bad grammar he always affected when he wanted to impart folksy wisdom, as she tromped up the front steps, shuffling the
bulky package in her arms to jab at the doorbell. *Here
comes your nineteenth noncommittal yellow layette,*
she thought, wishing she'd opted for the sterling baby
rattles instead. If Sierra and Travis knew the sex of
their unborn child, they weren't telling, which made
shopping even more of a pain than normal.

The door swung open and Eve, Meg and Sierra's mother, stood frowning in the chasm. "It's about time you got here," she said, pulling Meg inside. Then, in a whisper, "Is he with you?"

"Of course he is," Meg answered, as her mother peered past her shoulder, searching in vain for Angus. "He never misses a family gathering."

Eve sniffed, straightened her elegant shoulders. "You're late," she said. "Sierra will be here any minute!"

"It's not as if she's going to be surprised, Mom," Meg said, setting the present atop a mountain of others of a suspiciously similar size and shape. "There must be a hundred cars parked out there."

Eve shut the door smartly and then, before Meg could shrug out of her navy blue peacoat, gripped her firmly by the shoulders. "You've lost weight," she accused. "And there are dark circles under your eyes. Aren't you sleeping well?"

"I'm fine," Meg insisted. And she *was* fine—for an old maid.

Angus, never one to be daunted by a little thing like a closed door, materialized just behind Eve, looked around at his assembled brood with pleased amazement. The place was jammed with McKettrick cousins, their wives and husbands, their growing families.

Something tightened in the pit of Meg's stomach.

"Nonsense," Eve said. "If you could have gotten away with it, you would have stayed home today, wandering around that old house in your pajamas, with no makeup on and your hair sticking out in every direction."

It was true, but beside the point. With Eve Mc-

Kettrick for a mother, Meg couldn't get away with much of anything. "I'm here," she said. "Give me a break, will you?"

She pulled off her coat, handed it to Eve, and sidled into the nearest group, a small band of women. Meg, who had spent all her childhood summers in Indian Rock, didn't recognize any of them.

"It's all over the tabloids," remarked a tall, thin woman wearing a lot of jewelry. "Brad O'Ballivan is in rehab again."

Meg caught her breath at the name, and nearly dropped the cup of punch someone shoved into her hands.

"Nonsense," a second woman replied. "Last week those rags were reporting that he'd been abducted by aliens."

"He's handsome enough to have fans on other planets," observed a third, sighing wistfully.

Meg tried to ease out of the circle, but it had closed around her. She felt dizzy.

"My cousin Evelyn works at the post office over in Stone Creek," said yet another woman, with authority. "According to her, Brad's fan mail is being forwarded to the family ranch, just outside of town. He's not in rehab, and he's not on another planet. He's *home*. Evelyn says they'll have to build a second barn just to hold all those letters."

Meg smiled rigidly, but on the inside, she was scrambling for balance.

Suddenly, woman #1 focused on her. "You used to date Brad O'Ballivan, didn't you, Meg?"

"That—that was a long time ago," Meg said as graciously as she could, given that she was right in the middle of a panic attack. "We were just kids, and it was a summer thing—" Frantically, she calculated the distance between Indian Rock and Stone Creek—a mere forty miles. Not nearly far enough.

"I'm sure Meg has dated a lot of famous people," one of the other women said. "Working for McKettrickCo the way she did, flying all over the place in the company jet—"

"Brad wasn't famous when I knew him," Meg said lamely.

"You must miss your old life," someone else commented.

While it was true that Meg was having some trouble shifting from full throttle to a comparative standstill, since the family conglomerate had gone public a few months before, and her job as an executive vice president had gone with it, she *didn't* miss the meetings and the sixty-hour workweeks all that much. Money certainly wasn't a problem; she had a trust fund, as well as a personal investment portfolio thicker than the Los Angeles phone book.

A stir at the front door saved her from commenting.

Sierra came in, looking baffled.

"Surprise!" the crowd shouted as one.

The surprise is on me, Meg thought bleakly. *Brad O'Ballivan is back.*

BRAD SHOVED THE truck into gear and drove to the bottom of the hill, where the road forked. Turn left, and he'd be home in five minutes. Turn right, and he was headed for Indian Rock.

He had no damn business going to Indian Rock.

He had nothing to say to Meg McKettrick, and if

he never set eyes on the woman again, it would be two weeks too soon.

He turned right.

He couldn't have said why.

He just drove.

At one point, needing noise, he switched on the truck radio, fiddled with the dial until he found a country-western station. A recording of his own voice filled the cab of the pickup, thundering from all the speakers.

He'd written that ballad for Meg.

He turned the dial to Off.

Almost simultaneously, his cell phone jangled in the pocket of his jacket; he considered ignoring it—there were a number of people he didn't want to talk to—but suppose it was one of his sisters calling? Suppose they needed help?

He flipped the phone open, not taking his eyes off the curvy mountain road to check the caller ID panel first. "O'Ballivan," he said.

"Have you come to your senses yet?" demanded his manager, Phil Meadowbrook. "Shall I tell you again just *how much* money those people in Vegas are offering? They're willing to build you your own *theater,* for God's sake. This is a three-year gig—"

"Phil?" Brad broke in.

"Say yes," Phil pleaded.

"I'm retired."

"You're thirty-five," Phil argued. "*Nobody* retires at thirty-five!"

"We've already had this conversation, Phil."

"Don't hang up!"

Brad, who'd been about to thumb the off button, sighed.

"What the hell are you going to do in Stone Creek, Arizona?" Phil demanded. "Herd cattle? Sing to your horse? Think of the money, Brad. Think of the women, throwing their underwear at your feet—"

"I've been working real hard to repress that image," Brad said. "Thanks a lot for the reminder."

"Okay, forget the underwear," Phil shot back, without missing a beat. "But think of the money!"

"I've already got more of that than I need, Phil, and so do you, so spare me the riff where your grandchildren are homeless waifs picking through garbage behind the supermarket."

"I've used that one, huh?" Phil asked.

"Oh, yeah," Brad answered.

"What are you doing, right this moment?"

"I'm headed for the Dixie Dog Drive-In."

"The *what?*"

"Goodbye, Phil."

"What are you going to do at the Dixie-Whatever Drive-In that you couldn't do in Music City? Or Vegas?"

"You wouldn't understand," Brad said. "And I can't say I blame you, because I don't really understand it myself."

Back in the day, he and Meg used to meet at the Dixie Dog, by tacit agreement, when either of them had been away. It had been some kind of universe-thing, purely intuitive. He guessed he wanted to see if it still worked—and he'd be damned if he'd try to explain that to Phil.

"Look," Phil said, revving up for another sales pitch, "I can't put these casino people off forever. You're riding high right now, but things are bound to cool off. I've got to tell them *something*—"

"Tell them 'thanks, but no thanks,'" Brad suggested. This time, he broke the connection.

Phil, being Phil, tried to call twice before he finally gave up.

Passing familiar landmarks, Brad told himself he ought to turn around. The old days were gone, things had ended badly between him and Meg anyhow, and she wasn't going to be at the Dixie Dog.

He kept driving.

He went by the Welcome To Indian Rock sign, and the Roadhouse, a popular beer-and-burger stop for truckers, tourists and locals, and was glad to see the place was still open. He slowed for Main Street, smiled as he passed Cora's Curl and Twirl, squinted at the bookshop next door. That was new.

He frowned. Things changed, places changed.

What if the Dixie Dog had closed down?

What if it was boarded up, with litter and sagebrush tumbling through a deserted parking lot?

And what the hell did it matter, anyhow?

Brad shoved a hand through his hair. Maybe Phil and everybody else was right—maybe he was crazy to turn down the Vegas deal. Maybe he *would* end up sitting in the barn, serenading a bunch of horses.

He rounded a bend, and there was the Dixie Dog, still open. Its big neon sign, a giant hot dog, was all lit up and going through its corny sequence—first it was covered in red squiggles of light, meant to suggest catsup, and then yellow, for mustard. There were a few cars lined up in the drive-through lane, a few more in the parking lot.

Brad pulled into one of the slots next to a speaker and rolled down the truck window.

"Welcome to the Dixie Dog Drive-In," a youthful female voice chirped over the bad wiring. "What can I get you today?"

Brad hadn't thought that far, but he was starved. He peered at the light-up menu box under the chunky metal speaker. Then the obvious choice struck him and he said, "I'll take a Dixie Dog," he said. "Hold the chili and onions."

"Coming right up" was the cheerful response. "Anything to drink?"

"Chocolate shake," he decided. "Extra thick."

His cell phone rang again.

He ignored it again.

The girl thanked him and roller-skated out with the order about five minutes later.

When she wheeled up to the driver's-side window, smiling, her eyes went wide with recognition, and she dropped the tray with a clatter.

Silently, Brad swore. Damn if he hadn't forgotten he was famous.

The girl, a skinny thing wearing too much eye makeup, immediately started to cry. "I'm sorry!" she sobbed, squatting to gather up the mess.

"It's okay," Brad answered quietly, leaning to look down at her, catching a glimpse of her plastic name tag. "It's okay, Mandy. No harm done."

"I'll get you another dog and a shake right away, Mr. O'Ballivan!"

"Mandy?"

She stared up at him pitifully, sniffling. Thanks to

the copious tears, most of the goop on her eyes had slid south. "Yes?"

"When you go back inside, could you not mention seeing me?"

"But you're Brad O'Ballivan!"

"Yeah," he answered, suppressing a sigh. "I know."

She was standing up again by then, the tray of gathered debris clasped in both hands. She seemed to sway a little on her rollers. "Meeting you is just about the most important thing that's ever happened to me in my whole entire *life*. I don't know if I could keep it a secret even if I tried!"

Brad leaned his head against the back of the truck seat and closed his eyes. "Not forever, Mandy," he said. "Just long enough for me to eat a Dixie Dog in peace."

She rolled a little closer. "You wouldn't happen to have a picture you could autograph for me, would you?"

"Not with me," Brad answered. There were boxes of publicity pictures in storage, along with the requisite T-shirts, slick concert programs and other souvenirs commonly sold on the road. He never carried them, much to Phil's annoyance.

"You could sign this napkin, though," Mandy said. "It's only got a little chocolate on the corner."

Brad took the paper napkin, and her order pen, and scrawled his name. Handed both items back through the window.

"Now I can tell my grandchildren I spilled your lunch all over the pavement at the Dixie Dog Drive-In, and here's my proof." Mandy beamed, waggling the chocolate-stained napkin.

"Just imagine," Brad said. The slight irony in his tone was wasted on Mandy, which was probably a good thing.

"I won't tell anybody I saw you until you drive away," Mandy said with eager resolve. "I *think* I can last that long."

"That would be good," Brad told her.

She turned and whizzed back toward the side entrance to the Dixie Dog.

Brad waited, marveling that he hadn't considered incidents like this one before he'd decided to come back home. In retrospect, it seemed shortsighted, to say the least, but the truth was, he'd expected to be— Brad O'Ballivan.

Presently, Mandy skated back out again, and this time, she managed to hold on to the tray.

"I didn't tell a soul!" she whispered. "But Heather and Darlene *both* asked me why my mascara was all smeared." Efficiently, she hooked the tray onto the bottom edge of the window.

Brad extended payment, but Mandy shook her head.

"The boss said it's on the house, since I dumped your first order on the ground."

He smiled. "Okay, then. Thanks."

Mandy retreated, and Brad was just reaching for the food when a bright red Blazer whipped into the space beside his. The driver's-side door sprang open, crashing into the metal speaker, and somebody got out, in a hurry.

Something quickened inside Brad.

And in the next moment, Meg McKettrick was

standing practically on his running board, her blue eyes blazing.

Brad grinned. "I guess you're not over me after all," he said.

CHAPTER TWO

AFTER SIERRA HAD opened all her shower presents, and cake and punch had been served, Meg had felt the old, familiar tug in the middle of her solar plexus and headed straight for the Dixie Dog Drive-In. Now that she was there, standing next to a truck and all but nose to nose with Brad O'Ballivan through the open window, she didn't know what to do—or say.

Angus poked her from behind, and she flinched.

"Speak up," her dead ancestor prodded.

"Stay out of this," she answered, without thinking.

Puzzlement showed in Brad's affably handsome face. "Huh?"

"Never mind," Meg said. She took a step back, straightened. "And I am *so* over you."

Brad grinned. "Damned if it didn't work," he marveled. He climbed out of the truck to stand facing Meg, ducking around the tray hooked to the door. His dark-blond hair was artfully rumpled, and his clothes were downright ordinary.

"*What* worked?" Meg demanded, even though she knew.

Laughter sparked in his blue-green eyes, along with considerable pain, and he didn't bother to comment.

"What are you doing here?" she asked.

Brad spread his hands. Hands that had once played

Meg's body as skillfully as any guitar. Oh, yes. Brad O'Ballivan knew how to set all the chords vibrating.

"Free country," he said. "Or has Indian Rock finally seceded from the Union with the ranch house on the Triple M for a capitol?"

Since she felt a strong urge to bolt for the Blazer and lay rubber getting out of the Dixie Dog's parking lot, Meg planted her feet and hoisted her chin. *McKettricks,* she reminded herself silently, *don't run.*

"I heard you were in rehab," she said, hoping to get under his hide.

"That's a nasty rumor," Brad replied cheerfully.

"How about the two ex-wives and that scandal with the actress?"

His grin, insouciant in the first place, merely widened. "Unfortunately, I can't deny the two ex-wives," he said. "As for the actress—well, it all depends on whether you believe her version or mine. Have you been following my career, Meg McKettrick?"

Meg reddened.

"Tell him the truth," Angus counseled. "You never forgot him."

"No," Meg said, addressing both Brad *and* Angus.

Brad looked unconvinced. He was probably just egotistical enough to think she logged onto his Web site regularly, bought all his albums and read every tabloid article about him that she could get her hands on. Which she did, but that was *not* the point.

"You're still the best-looking woman I've ever laid eyes on," he said. "That hasn't changed, anyhow."

"I'm not a member of your fan club, O'Ballivan," Meg informed him. "So hold the insincere flattery, okay?"

One corner of his mouth tilted upward in a half grin, but his eyes were sad. He glanced back toward the truck, then met Meg's gaze again. "I don't flatter anybody," Brad said. Then he sighed. "I guess I'd better get back to Stone Creek."

Something in his tone piqued Meg's interest.

Who was she kidding?

Everything about him piqued her interest. As much as she didn't want that to be true, it was.

"I was sorry to hear about Big John's passing," she said. She almost touched his arm, but managed to catch herself just short of it. If she laid a hand on Brad O'Ballivan, who knew what would happen?

"Thanks," he replied.

A girl on roller skates wheeled out of the drive-in to collect the tray from the window edge of Brad's truck, her cheeks pink with carefully restrained excitement. "I might have said something to Heather and Darleen," the teenager confessed, after a curious glance at Meg. "About you being who you are and the autograph and everything."

Brad muttered something.

The girl skated away.

"I've gotta go," Brad told Meg, looking toward the drive-in. Numerous faces were pressed against the glass door; in another minute, there would probably be a stampede. "I don't suppose we could have dinner together or something? Maybe tomorrow night? There are—well, there are some things I'd like to say to you."

"Say yes," Angus told her.

"I don't think that would be a good idea," Meg said.

"A drink, then? There's a redneck bar in Stone Creek—"

"Don't be such a damned prig," Angus protested, nudging her again.

"I'm not a prig."

Brad frowned, threw another nervous look toward the drive-in and all those grinning faces. "I never said you were," he replied.

"I wasn't—" Meg paused, bit her lower lip. *I wasn't talking to you. No, siree, I was talking to Angus Mc-Kettrick's ghost.* "Okay," she agreed, to cover her lapse. "I guess one drink couldn't do any harm."

Brad climbed into his truck. The door of the drive-in crashed open, and the adoring hordes poured out, screaming with delight.

"Go!" Meg told him.

"Six o'clock tomorrow night," Brad reminded her. He backed the truck out, made a narrow turn to avoid running over the approaching herd of admirers and peeled out of the lot.

Meg turned to the disappointed fans. "Brad O'Ballivan," she said diplomatically, "has left the building."

Nobody got the joke.

THE SUN WAS SETTING, red-gold shot through with purple, when Brad crested the last hill before home and looked down on Stone Creek Ranch for the first time since his grandfather's funeral. The creek coursed, silvery-blue, through the middle of the land. The barn and the main house, built by Sam O'Ballivan's own hands and shored up by every generation to follow, stood as sturdy and imposing as ever. Once, there had been two houses on the place, but the one belonging to Major John Blackstone, the original landowner, had been torn down long ago. Now a copse of oak trees stood where the major had lived, surrounding a few old graves.

Big John was buried there, by special dispensation from the Arizona state government.

A lump formed in Brad's throat. *You see that I'm laid to rest with the old-timers when the bell tolls,* Big John had told him once. *Not in that cemetery in town.*

It had taken some doing, but Brad had made it happen.

He wanted to head straight for Big John's final resting place, pay his respects first thing, but there was a cluster of cars parked in front of the ranch house. His sisters were waiting to welcome him home.

Brad blinked a couple of times, rubbed his eyes with a thumb and forefinger, and headed for the house.

Time to face the proverbial music.

MEG DROVE SLOWLY back to the Triple M, going the long way to pass the main ranch house, Angus's old stomping grounds, in the vain hope that he would decide to haunt it for a while, instead of her. A descendant of Angus's eldest son, Holt, and daughter-in-law Lorelei, Meg called their place home.

As they bumped across the creek bridge, Angus assessed the large log structure, added onto over the years, and well-maintained.

Though close, all the McKettricks were proud of their particular branch of the family tree. Keegan, who occupied the main house now, along with his wife, Molly, daughter, Devon, and young son, Lucas, could trace his lineage back to Kade, another of Angus's four sons.

Rance, along with his daughters, was Rafe's prog-

eny. He and the girls and his bride, Emma, lived in the
grandly rustic structure on the other side of the creek
from Keegan's place.

Finally, there was Jesse. He was Jeb's descendant,
and resided, when he wasn't off somewhere participating in a rodeo or a poker tournament, in the house
Jeb had built for his wife, Chloe, high on a hill on
the southwestern section of the ranch. Jesse was happily married to a hometown girl, the former Cheyenne
Bridges, and like Keegan's Molly and Rance's Emma,
Cheyenne was expecting a baby.

Everybody, it seemed to Meg, was expecting a baby.

Except her, of course.

She bit her lower lip.

"I bet if you got yourself pregnant by that singing
cowboy," Angus observed, "he'd have the decency to
make an honest woman out of you."

Angus had an uncanny ability to tap into Meg's
wavelength; though he swore he couldn't read her
mind, she wondered sometimes.

"Great idea," she scoffed. "And for your information, I *am* an honest woman."

Keegan was just coming out of the barn as Meg
passed; he smiled and waved. She tooted the Blazer's
horn in greeting.

"He sure looks like Kade," Angus said. "Jesse looks
like Jeb, and Rance looks like Rafe." He sighed. "It
sure makes me lonesome for my boys."

Meg felt a grudging sympathy for Angus. He'd ruined a lot of dates, being an almost constant companion, but she loved him. "Why can't you be where they
are?" she asked softly. "Wherever that is."

"I've got to see to you," he answered. "You're the last holdout."

"I'd be all right, Angus," she said. She'd asked him about the afterlife, but all he'd ever been willing to say was that there was no such thing as dying, just a change of perspective. Time wasn't linear, he claimed, but simultaneous. The "whole ball of string," as he put it, was happening at once—past, present and future. Some of the experiences the women in her family, including herself and Sierra, had had up at Holt's house lent credence to the theory.

Sierra claimed that, before her marriage to Travis and the subsequent move to the new semi-mansion in town, she and her young son, Liam, had shared the old house with a previous generation of McKettricks— Doss and Hannah and a little boy called Tobias. Sierra had offered journals and photograph albums as proof, and Meg had to admit, her half sister made a compelling case.

Still, and for all that she'd been keeping company with a benevolent ghost since she was little, Meg was a left-brain type.

When Angus didn't comment on her insistence that she'd get along fine if he went on to the great roundup in the sky, or whatever, Meg tried again. "Look," she said gently, "when I was little, and Sierra disappeared, and Mom was so frantic to find her that she couldn't take care of me, I really needed you. But I'm a grown woman now, Angus. I'm independent. I have a life."

Out of the corner of her eye, she saw Angus's jaw tighten. "That Hank Breslin," he said, "was no good for Eve. No better than *your* father was. Every time the right man came along, she was so busy cozying up to the *wrong* one that she didn't even notice what was right in front of her."

Hank Breslin was Sierra's father. He'd kidnapped Sierra, only two years old at the time, when Eve served him with divorce papers, and raised her in Mexico. For a variety of reasons, Eve hadn't reconnected with her lost daughter until recently. Meg's own father, about whom she knew little, had died in an accident a month before she was born. Nobody liked to talk about him— even his name was a mystery.

"And you think I'll make the same mistakes my mother did?" Meg said.

"Hell," Angus said, sparing her a reluctant grin, "right now, even a *mistake* would be progress."

"With all due respect," Meg replied, "having you around all the time is not exactly conducive to romance."

They started the long climb uphill, headed for the house that now belonged to her and Sierra. Meg had always loved that house—it had been a refuge for her, full of cousins. Looking back, she wondered why, given that Eve had rarely accompanied her on those summer visits, had instead left her daughter in the care of a succession of nannies and, later, aunts and uncles.

Sierra's kidnapping had been a traumatic event, for certain, but the problems Eve had subsequently developed because of it had left Meg relatively unmarked. She hadn't been lonely as a child, mainly because of Angus.

"I'll stay clear tomorrow night, when you go to Stone Creek for that drink," Angus said.

"You like Brad."

"Always did. Liked Travis, too. 'Course, I knew he was meant for your sister, that they'd meet up in time."

Meg and Sierra's husband, Travis, were old friends. They'd tried to get something going, convinced they were perfect for each other, but it hadn't worked. Now that Travis and Sierra were together, and ecstatically happy, Meg was glad.

"Don't get your hopes up," she said. "About Brad and me, I mean."

Angus didn't reply. He appeared to be deep in thought. Or maybe as he looked out at the surrounding countryside, he was remembering his youth, when he'd staked a claim to this land and held it with blood and sweat and sheer McKettrick stubbornness.

"You must have known the O'Ballivans," Meg reflected, musing. Like her own family, Brad's had been pioneers in this part of Arizona.

"I was older than dirt by the time Sam O'Ballivan brought his bride, Maddie, up from Haven. Might have seen them once or twice. But I knew Major Blackstone, all right." Angus smiled at some memory. "He and I used to arm wrestle sometimes, in the card room back of Jolene Bell's Saloon, when we couldn't best each other at poker."

"Who won?" Meg asked, smiling slightly at the image.

"Same as the poker," Angus answered with a sigh. "We'd always come out about even. He'd win half the time, me the other half."

The house came in sight, the barn towering nearby. Angus's expression took on a wistful aspect.

"When you're here," Meg ventured, "can you see Doss and Hannah and Tobias? Talk to them?"

"No," Angus said flatly.

"Why not?" Meg persisted, even though she knew Angus didn't want to pursue the subject.

"Because they're not dead," he said. "They're just on the other side, like my boys."

"Well, I'm not dead, either," Meg said reasonably. She refrained from adding that she could have shown him their graves, up in the McKettrick cemetery. Shown him his own, for that matter. It would have been unkind, of course, but there was another reason for her reluctance, too. In some version of that cemetery, given what he'd told her about time, there was surely a headstone with *her* name on it.

"You wouldn't understand," Angus told her. He always said that, when she tried to find out how it was for him, where he went when he wasn't following her around.

"Try me," she said.

He vanished.

Resigned, Meg pulled up in front of the garage, added onto the original house sometime in the 1950s, and equipped with an automatic door opener, and pushed the button so she could drive in.

She half expected to find Angus sitting at the kitchen table when she went into the house, but he wasn't there.

What she needed, she decided, was a cup of tea.

She got Lorelei's teapot out of the built-in china cabinet and set it firmly on the counter. The piece was legendary in the family; it had a way of moving back to the cupboard of its own volition, from the table or the counter, and vice versa.

Meg filled the electric kettle at the sink and plugged it in to heat.

Tea was not going to cure what ailed her.

Brad O'Ballivan was back.

Compared to that, ghosts, the mysteries of time and space, and teleporting teapots seemed downright mundane.

And she'd agreed, like a fool, to meet him in Stone Creek for a drink. What had she been thinking?

Standing there in her kitchen, Meg leaned against the counter and folded her arms, waiting for the tea water to boil. Brad had hurt her so badly, she'd thought she'd never recover. For years after he'd dumped her to go to Nashville, she'd barely been able to come back to Indian Rock, and when she had, she'd driven straight to the Dixie Dog, against her will, sat in some rental car, and cried like an idiot.

There are some things I'd like to say to you, Brad had told her, that very day.

"What things?" she asked now, aloud.

The teakettle whistled.

She unplugged it, measured loose orange pekoe into Lorelei's pot and poured steaming water over it.

It was just a drink, Meg reminded herself. An innocent drink.

She should call Brad, cancel gracefully.

Or, better yet, she could just stand him up. Not show up at all. Just as he'd done to her, way back when, when she'd loved him with all her heart and soul, when she'd believed he meant to make a place for her in his busy, exciting life.

Musing, Meg laid a hand to her lower abdomen.

She'd stopped believing in a lot of things when Brad O'Ballivan ditched her.

Maybe he wanted to apologize.

She gave a teary snort of laughter.

And maybe he really had fans on other planets.

A rap at the back door made her start. Angus? He never knocked—he just appeared. Usually at the most inconvenient possible time.

Meg went to the door, peered through the old, thick panes of greenish glass, saw Travis Reid looming on the other side. She wrestled with the lock and let him in.

"I'm here on reconnaissance," he announced, taking off his cowboy hat and hanging it on the peg next to the door. "Sierra's worried about you, and so is Eve."

Meg put a hand to her forehead. She'd left the baby shower abruptly to go meet Brad at the Dixie Dog Drive-In. "I'm sorry," she said, stepping back so Travis could come inside. "I'm all right, really. You shouldn't have come all the way out here—"

"Eve tried your cell—which is evidently off—and Sierra left three or four messages on voice mail," he said with a nod toward the kitchen telephone. "Consider yourself fortunate that I got here before they called out the National Guard."

Meg laughed, closed the door against the chilly October twilight, and watched as Travis took off his sheepskin-lined coat and hung it next to the hat. "I was just feeling a little—overwhelmed."

"Overwhelmed?" She'd been *possessed*.

Travis went to the telephone, punched in a sequence of numbers and waited. "Hi, honey," he said presently, when Sierra answered. "Meg's alive and well. No armed intruders. No bloody accident. She was just—overwhelmed."

"Tell her I'll call her later," Meg said. "Mom, too."

"She'll call you later," Travis repeated dutifully. "Eve, too." He listened again, promised to pick up a gallon of milk and a loaf of bread on the way home and hung up.

Knowing Travis wasn't fond of tea, Meg offered him a cup of instant coffee, instead.

He accepted, taking a seat at the table where generations of McKettricks, from Holt and Lorelei on down, had taken their meals. "What's really going on, Meg?" he asked quietly, watching her as she poured herself some tea and joined him.

"What makes you think anything is going on?"

"I know you. We tried to fall in love, remember?"

"Brad O'Ballivan's back," she said.

Travis nodded. "And this means—?"

"Nothing," Meg answered, much too quickly. "It means nothing. I just—"

Travis settled back in his chair, folded his arms, and waited.

"Okay, it was a shock," Meg admitted. She sat up a little straighter. "But you already knew."

"Jesse told me."

"And nobody thought to mention it to me?"

"I guess we assumed you'd talked to Brad."

"Why would I do that?"

"Because—" Travis paused, looked uncomfortable. "It's no secret that the two of you had a thing going, Meg. Indian Rock and Stone Creek are small places, forty miles apart. Things get around."

Meg's face burned. She'd thought, she'd truly believed, that no one on earth knew Brad had broken her heart. She'd pretended it didn't matter that he'd left town so abruptly. Even laughed about it. Gone on to finish college, thrown herself into that first entry-level job at McKettrickCo. Dated other men, including the then-single Travis.

And she hadn't fooled anyone.

"Are you going to see him again?"

Meg pressed the tips of her fingers hard into her closed eyes. Nodded. Then shook her head from side to side.

Travis chuckled. "Make a decision, Meg," he said.

"We're supposed to have a drink together tomorrow night, at a cowboy bar in Stone Creek. I don't know why I said I'd meet him—after all this time, what do we have to say to each other?"

"'How've ya been?'" Travis suggested.

"I *know* how he's been—rich and famous, married twice, busy building a reputation that makes Jesse's look tame," she said. "I, on the other hand, have been a workaholic. Period."

"Aren't you being a little hard on yourself? Not to mention Brad?" A grin quirked the corner of Travis's mouth. "Comparing him to *Jesse?*"

Jesse had been a wild man, if a good-hearted, well-intentioned one, until he'd met up with Cheyenne Bridges. When he'd fallen, he'd fallen hard, and for the duration, the way bad boys so often do.

"Maybe Brad's changed," Travis said.

"Maybe not," Meg countered.

"Well, I guess you *could* leave town for a while. Stay out of his way." Travis was trying hard not to smile. "Volunteer for a space mission or something."

"I am *not* going to run," Meg said. "I've always wanted to live right here, on this ranch, in this house. Besides, I intend to be here when the baby comes."

Travis's face softened at the mention of the impending birth. Until Sierra came along, Meg hadn't thought he'd ever settle down. He'd had his share of demons to overcome, not the least of which was the tragic death of his younger brother. Travis had blamed himself for what happened to Brody. "Good," he said. "But what do you actually *do* here? You're used to the fast lane, Meg."

"I take care of the horses," she said.

"That takes, what—two hours a day? According to Eve, you spend most of your time in your pajamas. She thinks you're depressed."

"Well, I'm not," Meg said. "I'm just—catching up on my rest."

"Okay," Travis said, drawing out the word.

"I'm not drinking alone and I'm not watching soap operas," Meg said. "I'm vegging. It's a concept my mother doesn't understand."

"She loves you, Meg. She's worried. She's not the enemy."

"I wish she'd go back to Texas."

"Wish away. She's not going anywhere, with a grandchild coming."

At least Eve hadn't taken up residence on the ranch; that was some comfort. She lived in a small suite at the only hotel in Indian Rock, and kept herself busy shopping, day trading on her laptop and spoiling Liam.

Oh, yes. And nagging Meg.

Travis finished his coffee, carried his cup to the

sink, rinsed it out. After hesitating for a few moments, he said, "It's this thing about seeing Angus's ghost. She thinks you're obsessed."

Meg made a soft, strangled sound of frustration.

"It's not that she doesn't believe you," Travis added.

"She just thinks I'm a little crazy."

"No," Travis said. "Nobody thinks that."

"But I should get a life, as the saying goes?"

"It would be a good idea, don't you think?"

"Go home. Your pregnant wife needs a gallon of milk and a loaf of bread."

Travis went to the door, put on his coat, took his hat from the hook. "What do *you* need, Meg? That's the question."

"Not Brad O'Ballivan, that's for sure."

Travis grinned again. Set his hat on his head and turned the doorknob. "Did I mention him?" he asked lightly.

Meg glared at him.

"See you," Travis said. And then he was gone.

"He puts me in mind of that O'Ballivan fella," Angus announced, nearly startling Meg out of her skin.

She turned to see him standing over by the china cabinet. Was it her imagination, or did he look a little older than he had that afternoon?

"Jesse looks like Jeb. Rance looks like Rafe. Keegan looks like Kade. You're seeing things, Angus."

"Have it your way," Angus said.

Like any McKettrick had ever said *that* and meant it.

"What's for supper?"

"What do you care? You never eat."

"Neither do you. You're starting to look like a bag of bones."

"If I were you, I wouldn't make comments about bones. Being dead and all, I mean."

"The problem with you young people is, you have no respect for your elders."

Meg sighed, got up from her chair at the table, stomped over to the refrigerator and selected a boxed dinner from the stack in the freezer. The box was coated with frost.

"I'm sorry," Meg said. "Is that a hint of silver I see at your temples?"

Self-consciously, Angus shifted his weight from one booted foot to the other. "If I'm going gray," he scowled, "it's on account of you. None of my boys ever gave me half as much trouble as you, or my Katie, either. And they were plum full of the dickens, all of them."

Meg's heart pinched. Katie was Angus's youngest child, and his only daughter. He rarely mentioned her, since she'd caused some kind of scandal by eloping on her wedding day—with someone other than the groom. Although she and Angus had eventually reconciled, he'd been on his deathbed at the time.

"I'm *all right,* Angus," she told him. "You can go. Really."

"You eat food that could be used to drive railroad spikes into hard ground. You don't have a husband. You rattle around in this old house like some—ghost. I'm not leaving until I know you'll be happy."

"I'm happy *now.*"

Angus walked over to her, the heels of his boots thumping on the plank floor, took the frozen dinner out of her hands, and carried it to the trash compactor. Dropped it inside.

"Damn fool contraption," he muttered.

"That was my supper," Meg objected.

"Cook something," Angus said. "Get out a skillet. Dump some lard into it. Fry up a chicken." He paused, regarded her darkly. "You *do* know how to cook, don't you?"

CHAPTER THREE

JOLENE'S, BUILT ON the site of the old saloon and brothel where Angus McKettrick and Major John Blackstone used to arm wrestle, among other things, was dimly lit and practically empty. Meg paused on the threshold, letting her eyes adjust and wishing she'd listened to her instincts and cancelled; now there would be no turning back.

Brad was standing by the jukebox, the colored lights flashing across the planes of his face. Having heard the door open, he turned his head slightly to acknowledge her arrival with a nod and a wisp of a grin.

"Where is everybody?" she asked. Except for the bartender, she and Brad were alone.

"Staying clear," Brad said. "I promised a free concert in the high school gym if we could have Jolene's to ourselves for a couple of hours."

Meg nearly fled. If it hadn't been against the Mc-Kettrick code, as inherent to her being as her DNA, she would have given in to the urge and called it good judgment.

"Have a seat," Brad said, drawing back a chair at one of the tables. Nothing in the whole tavern matched, not even the bar stools, and every stick of furniture was scarred and scratched. Jolene's was a hangout for honky-tonk angels; the winged variety would surely have given the place a wide berth.

"What'll it be?" the bartender asked. He was a squat man, wearing a muscle shirt and a lot of tattoos. With his handlebar mustache, he might have been from Angus's era, instead of the present day.

Brad ordered a cola as Meg forced herself across the room to take the chair he offered.

Maybe, she thought, as she asked for an iced tea, the rumors were true, and Brad was fresh out of rehab.

The bartender served the drinks and quietly left the saloon, via a back door.

Brad, meanwhile, turned his own chair around and sat astraddle it, with his arms resting across the back. He wore jeans, a white shirt open at the throat and boots, and if he hadn't been so breathtakingly handsome, he'd have looked like any cowboy, in any number of scruffy little redneck bars scattered all over Arizona.

Meg eyed his drink, since doing that seemed slightly less dangerous than looking straight into his face, and when he chuckled, she felt her cheeks turn warm.

Pride made her meet his gaze. "What?" she asked, running damp palms along the thighs of her oldest pair of jeans. She'd made a point of *not* dressing up for the encounter—no perfume, and only a little mascara and lip gloss. War paint, Angus called it. Her favorite ghost had an opinion on everything, it seemed, but at least he'd honored his promise not to horn in on this interlude, or whatever it was, with Brad.

"Don't believe everything you read," Brad said easily, settling back in his chair. "Not about me, anyway."

"Who says I've been reading about you?"

"Come on, Meg. You expected me to drink Jack

Daniel's straight from the bottle. That's hype—part of the bad-boy image. My manager cooked it up."

Meg huffed out a sigh. "You haven't been to rehab?"

He grinned. "Nope. Never trashed a hotel room, spent a weekend in jail, or any of the rest of the stuff Phil wanted everybody to believe about me."

"Really?"

"Really." Brad pushed back his chair, returned to the jukebox, and dropped a few coins in the slot. An old Johnny Cash ballad poured softly into the otherwise silent bar.

Meg took a swig of her iced tea, in a vain effort to steady her nerves. She was no teetotaler, but when she drove, she didn't drink. Ever. Right about then, though, she wished she'd hired a car and driver so she could get sloshed enough to forget that being alone with Brad O'Ballivan was like having her most sensitive nerves bared to a cold wind.

He started in her direction, then stopped in the middle of the floor, which was strewn with sawdust and peanut shells. Held out a hand to her.

Meg went to him, just the way she'd gone to the Dixie Dog Drive-In the day before. Automatically.

He drew her into his arms, holding her close but easy, and they danced without moving their feet.

As the song ended, Brad propped his chin on top of Meg's head and sighed. "I've missed you," he said.

Meg came to her senses.

Finally.

She pulled back far enough to look up into his face. "Don't go there," she warned.

"We can't just pretend the past didn't happen, Meg," he reasoned quietly.

"Yes, we can," she argued. "Millions of people do it, every day. It's called denial, and it has its place in the scheme of things."

"Still a McKettrick," Brad said, sorrow lurking behind the humor in his blue eyes. "If I said the moon was round, you'd call it square."

She poked at his chest with an index finger. "Still an O'Ballivan," she accused. "Thinking you've got to explain the shape of the moon, as if I couldn't see it for myself."

The jukebox in Jolene's was an antique; it still played 45s. Now a record flopped audibly onto the turntable, and the needle scratched its way into Willie Nelson's version of "Georgia."

Meg stiffened, wanting to pull away.

Brad's arms, resting loosely around her waist, tightened slightly.

Over the years, the McKettricks and the O'Ballivans, owning the two biggest ranches in the area, had been friendly rivals. The families were equally proud and equally stubborn—they'd had to be, to survive the ups and downs of raising cattle for more than a century. Even when they were close, Meg and Brad had always identified strongly with their heritages.

Meg swallowed. "Why did you come back?" she asked, without intending to speak at all.

"To settle some things," Brad answered. They were swaying to the music again, though the soles of their boots were still rooted to the floor. "And you're at the top of my list, Meg McKettrick."

"You're at the top of mine, too," Meg retorted. "But I don't think we're talking about the same kind of list."

He laughed. God, how she'd missed that sound. How

she'd missed the heat and substance of him, and the sun-dried laundry smell of his skin and hair...

Stop, she told herself. She was acting like some smitten fan or something.

"You bought me an engagement ring," she blurted, without intending to do anything of the kind. "We were supposed to elope. And then you got on a bus and went to Nashville and married what's-her-name!"

"I was stupid," Brad said. "And scared."

"No," Meg replied, fighting back furious tears. "You were *ambitious.* And of course the bride's father owned a recording company—"

Brad closed his eyes for a moment. A muscle bunched in his cheek. "Valerie," he said miserably. "Her name was Valerie."

"Do you really think I give a damn what her name was?"

"Yeah," he answered. "I do."

"Well, you're wrong!"

"That must be why you look like you want to club me to the ground with the nearest blunt object."

"I got over you like that!" Meg told him, snapping her fingers. But a tear slipped down her cheek, spoiling the whole effect.

Brad brushed it away gently with the side of one thumb. "Meg," he said. "I'm so sorry."

"Oh, that changes everything!" Meg scoffed. She tried to move away from him again, but he still wouldn't let her go.

One corner of his mouth tilted up in a forlorn effort at a grin. "You'll feel a lot better if you forgive me." He curved the fingers of his right hand under her chin, lifted. "For old times' sake?" he cajoled. "For the nights when we went skinny-dipping in the pond behind your house on the Triple M? For the nights we—"

"No," Meg interrupted, fairly smothering as the memories wrapped themselves around her. "You don't deserve to be forgiven."

"You're right," Brad agreed. "I don't. But that's the thing about forgiveness. It's all about grace, isn't it? It's supposed to be undeserved."

"Great logic if you're on the *receiving* end!"

"I had my reasons, Meg."

"Yeah. You wanted bright lights and big money. Oh, and fast women."

Brad's jaw tightened, but his eyes were bleak. "I couldn't have married you, Meg."

"Pardon my confusion. You gave me an engagement ring and proposed!"

"I wasn't thinking." He looked away, faced her again with visible effort. "You had a trust fund. I had a mortgage and a pile of bills. I laid awake nights, sweating blood, thinking the bank would foreclose at any minute. I couldn't dump that in your lap."

Meg's mouth dropped open. She'd known the O'Ballivans weren't rich, at least, not like the McKettricks were, but she'd never imagined, even once, that Stone Creek Ranch was in danger of being lost.

"They wanted that land," Brad went on. "The bankers, I mean. They already had the plans drawn up for a housing development."

"I didn't know—I would have helped—"

"Sure," Brad said. "You'd have helped. And I'd never have been able to look you in the face again. I had one chance, Meg. Valerie's dad had heard my demo and he was willing to give me an audition. A fifteen-minute slot in his busy day. I tried to tell you—"

Meg closed her eyes for a moment, remembering. Brad had told her he wanted to postpone the wedding until after his trip to Nashville. He'd promised to come back for her. She'd been furious and hurt—and keeping a secret of her own—and they'd argued....

She swallowed painfully. "You didn't call. You didn't write—"

"When I got to Nashville, I had a used bus ticket and a guitar. If I'd called, it would have been collect, and I wasn't *about* to do that. I started half a dozen letters, but they all sounded like the lyrics to bad songs. I went to the library a couple of times, to send you an e-mail, but beyond 'how are you?' I just flat-out didn't know what to say."

"So you just hooked up with Valerie?"

"It wasn't like that."

"I'm assuming she was a rich kid, just like me? I guess you didn't mind if *she* saved the old homestead with a chunk of her trust fund."

Brad's jawline tightened. "*I* saved the ranch," he said. "Most of the money from my first record contract went to paying down the mortgage, and it was still a struggle until I scored a major hit." He paused, obviously remembering the much leaner days before he could fill the biggest stadiums in the country with devoted fans, swaying to his music in the darkness, holding flickering lighters aloft in tribute. "I didn't love Valerie, and she didn't love me. She was a rich kid, all right. Spoiled and lonesome, neglected in the ways rich kids so often are, and she was in big trouble. She'd gotten herself pregnant by some married guy who wanted nothing to do with her. She figured her dad would kill her if he found out, and given his temper, I tended to agree. So I married her."

Meg made her way back to the table and sank into her chair. "There was...a baby?"

"She miscarried. We divorced amicably, after trying to make it work for a couple of years. She's married to a dentist now, and really happy. Four kids, at last count." Brad joined Meg at the table. "Do you want to hear about the second marriage?"

"I don't think I'm up to that," Meg said weakly.

Brad's hand closed over hers. "Me, either," he replied. He ducked his head, in a familiar way that tugged at Meg's heart, to catch her eye. "You all right?"

"Just a little shaken up, that's all."

"How about some supper?"

"They serve supper here? At Jolene's?"

Brad chuckled. "Down the road, at the Steakhouse. You can't miss it—it's right next to the sign that says, Welcome To Stone Creek, Arizona, Home Of Brad O'Ballivan."

"Braggart," Meg said, grateful that the conversation had taken a lighter turn.

He grinned engagingly. "Stone Creek has always been the home of Brad O'Ballivan," he said. "It just seems to mean more now than it did when I left that first time."

"You'll be mobbed," Meg warned.

"The whole town could show up at the Steakhouse, and it wouldn't be enough to make a mob."

"Okay," Meg agreed. "But you're buying."

Brad laughed. "Fair enough," he said.

Then he got up from his chair and summoned the

bartender, who'd evidently been cooling his heels in a storeroom or office.

The floor felt oddly spongy beneath Meg's feet, and she was light-headed enough to wonder if there'd been some alcohol in that iced tea after all.

THE STEAKHOUSE, UNLIKE JOLENE'S, was jumping. People called out to Brad when he came in, and young girls pointed and giggled, but most of them had been at the welcome party Ashley and Melissa had thrown for him on the ranch the night before, so some of the novelty of his being back in town had worn off.

Meg drew some glances, though—all of them admiring, with varying degrees of curiosity mixed in. Even in jeans, boots and a plain woolen coat over a white blouse, she looked like what she was—a McKettrick with a trust fund and an impressive track record as a top-level executive. When McKettrickCo had gone public, Brad had been surprised when she didn't turn up immediately as the CEO of some corporation. Instead, she'd come home to hibernate on the Triple M, and he wondered why.

He wondered lots of things about Meg McKettrick.

With luck, he'd have a chance to find out everything he wanted to know.

Like whether she still laughed in her sleep and ate cereal with yogurt instead of milk and arched her back like a gymnast when she climaxed.

Since the Steakhouse was no place to think about Meg having one of her noisy orgasms, Brad tried to put the image out of his mind. It merely shifted to another part of his anatomy.

They were shown to a booth right away, and given

menus and glasses of water with the obligatory slices of fresh lemon rafting on top of the ice.

Brad ordered a steak, Meg a Caesar salad.

The waitress went away, albeit reluctantly.

"Okay," Brad said, "it's my turn to ask questions. Why did you quit working after you left McKettrickCo?"

Meg smiled, but she looked a little flushed, and he could tell by her eyes that she was busy in there, sorting things and putting them in their proper places. "I didn't need the money. And I've always wanted to live full-time on the Triple M, like Jesse and Rance and Keegan. When I spent summers there, as a child, the only way I could deal with leaving in the fall to go back to school was to promise myself that one day I'd come home to stay."

"You love it that much?" Given his own attachment to Stone Creek Ranch, Brad could understand, but at the same time, the knowledge troubled him a little, too. "What do you do all day?"

Her mouth quirked in a way that made Brad want to kiss her. And do a few other things, too. "You sound like my mother," she said. "I take care of the horses, ride sometimes—"

He nodded. Waited.

She didn't finish the sentence.

"You never married." He hadn't meant to say that. Hadn't meant to let on that he'd kept track of her all these years, mostly on the Internet, but through his sisters, too.

She shook her head. "Almost," she said. "Once. It didn't work out."

Brad leaned forward, intrigued and feeling pretty

damn territorial, too. "Who was the unlucky guy? He must have been a real jackass."

"You," she replied sweetly, and then laughed at the expression on his face.

He started to speak, then gulped the words down, sure they'd come out sounding as stupid as the question he'd just asked.

"I've dated a lot of men," Meg said.

The orgasm image returned, but this time, he wasn't Meg's partner. It was some other guy bringing her to one of her long, exquisite, clawing, shouting, bucking climaxes, not him. He frowned.

"Maybe we shouldn't talk about my love life," she suggested.

"Maybe not," Brad agreed.

"Not that I exactly have one."

Brad felt immeasurably better. "That makes two of us."

Meg looked unconvinced. Even squirmed a little on the vinyl seat.

"What?" Brad prompted, enjoying the play of emotions on her face. He and Meg weren't on good terms—too soon for that—but it was a hopeful sign that she'd met him at Jolene's and then agreed to supper on top of it.

"I saw that article in *People* magazine. 'The Cowboy with the Most Notches on His Bedpost,' I think it was called?"

"I thought we weren't going to talk about our love lives. And would you mind keeping your voice down?"

"We agreed not to talk about *mine,* if I remember correctly, which, as I told you, is nonexistent. And to avoid the subject of your second wife—at least, for now."

"There have been women," Brad said. "But that bed-post thing was all Phil's idea. Publicity stuff."

The food arrived.

"Not that I care if you carve notches on your bed-post," Meg said decisively, once the waitress had left again.

"Right," Brad replied, serious on the outside, grinning on the inside.

"Where is this Phil person from, anyway?" Meg asked, mildly disgruntled, her fork poised in midair over her salad. "Seems to me he has a pretty skewed idea on the whole cowboy mystique. Rehab. Trashing hotel rooms. The notch thing."

"There's a 'cowboy mystique'?"

"You know there is. Honor, integrity, courage—those are the things being a cowboy is all about."

Brad sighed. Meg was a stickler for detail; good thing she hadn't gone to law school, like she'd once planned. She probably would have represented his second ex-wife in the divorce and stripped his stock portfolio clean. "I tried. Phil works freestyle, and he sure knew how to pack the concert halls."

Meg pointed the fork at him. "*You* packed the concert halls, Brad. You and your music."

"You like my music?" It was a shy question; he hadn't quite dared to ask if she liked *him* as well. He knew too well what the answer might be.

"It's…nice," she said.

Nice? Half a dozen Grammies and CMT awards, weeks at number one on every chart that mattered, and she thought his music was "nice"?

Whatever she thought, Brad finally concluded, that was all she was going to give up, and he had to be satisfied with it.

For now.

He started on the steak, but he hadn't eaten more than two bites when there was a fuss at the entrance to the restaurant and Livie came storming in, striding right to his table.

Sparing a nod for Meg, Brad's sister turned immediately to him. "He's hurt," she said. Her clothes were covered with straw and a few things that would have upset the health department, being that she was in a place where food was being served to the general public.

"Who's hurt?" Brad asked calmly, sliding out of the booth to stand.

"Ransom," she answered, near tears. "He got himself cut up in a tangle of rusty barbed wire. I'd spotted him with binoculars, but before I could get there to help, he'd torn free and headed for the hills. He's hurt bad, and I'm not going to be able to get to him in the Suburban—we need to saddle up and go after him."

"Liv," Brad said carefully, "it's dark out."

"He's *bleeding,* and probably weak. The wolves could take him down!" At the thought of that, Livie's eyes glistened with moisture. "If you won't help, I'll go by myself."

Distractedly, Brad pulled out his wallet and threw down the money for the dinner he and Meg hadn't gotten a chance to finish.

Meg was on her feet, the salad forgotten. "Count me in, Olivia," she said. "That is, if you've got an extra horse and some gear. I could go back out to the Triple

M for Banshee, but by the time I hitched up the trailer, loaded him and gathered the tack—"

"You can ride Cinnamon," Olivia told Meg, after sizing her up as to whether she'd be a help or a hindrance on the trail. "It'll be cold and dark up there in the high country," she added. "Could be a long, uncomfortable night."

"No room service?" Meg quipped.

Livie spared her a smile, but when she turned to Brad again, her blue eyes were full of obstinate challenge. "Are you going or not—cowboy?"

"Hell, yes, I'm going," Brad said. Riding a horse was a thing you never forgot how to do, but it had been a while since he'd been in the saddle, and that meant he'd be groaning-sore before this adventure was over. "What about the stock on the Triple M, Meg? Who's going to feed your horses, if this takes all night?"

"They're good till morning," Meg answered. "If I'm not back by then, I'll ask Jesse or Rance or Keegan to check on them."

Livie led the caravan in her Suburban, with Brad following in his truck, and Meg right behind, in the Blazer. He was worried about Ransom, and about Livie's obsession with the animal, but there was one bright spot in the whole thing.

He was going to get to spend the night with Meg McKettrick, albeit on the hard, half-frozen ground, and the least he could do, as a gentleman, was share his sleeping bag—and his body warmth.

"RIGHT SMART OF you to go along," Angus commented, appearing in the passenger seat of Meg's rig. "There might be some hope for you yet."

Meg answered without moving her mouth, just in case Brad happened to glance into his rearview mirror and catch her talking to nobody. "I thought you were giving me some elbow room on this one," she said.

"Don't worry," Angus replied. "If you go to bed down with him or something like that, I'll skedaddle."

"I'm not going to 'bed down' with Brad O'Ballivan."

Angus sighed. Adjusted his sweat-stained cowboy hat. Since he usually didn't wear one, Meg read it as a sign bad weather was on its way. "Might be a good thing if you did. Only way to snag some men."

"I will not dignify that remark with a reply," Meg said, flooring the gas pedal to keep up with Brad, now that they were out on the open road, where the speed limit was higher. She'd never actually been to Stone Creek Ranch, but she knew where it was. Knew all about King's Ransom, too. Her cousin Jesse, practically a horse-whisperer, claimed the animal was nothing more than a legend, pieced together around a hundred campfires, over as many years, after all the lesser tales had been told.

Meg wanted to see for herself.

Wanted to help Olivia, whom she'd always liked but barely knew.

Spending the night on a mountain with Brad O'Ballivan didn't enter into the decision at all. Much.

"Is he real?" she asked. "The horse, I mean?"

Angus adjusted his hat again. "Sure he is," he said, his voice quiet, but gruff. Sometimes a look came into his eyes, a sort of hunger for the old days and the old ways.

"Is there anything you can do to help us find him?"

Angus shook his head. "You've got to do that your-selves, you and the singing cowboy and the girl."

"Olivia is not a girl. She's a grown woman and a veterinarian."

"She's a snippet," Angus said. "But there's fire in her. That O'Ballivan blood runs hot as coffee brewed on a cookstove in hell. She needs a man, though. The knot in *her* lasso is way too tight."

"I hope that reference wasn't sexual," Meg said stiffly, "because I do *not* need to be carrying on that type of conversation with my dead multi-great grand-father."

"It makes me feel old when you talk about me like I helped Moses carry the commandments down off the mountain," Angus complained. "I was young once, you know. Sired four strapping sons and a daughter by three different women—Ellie, Georgia and Con-cepcion. And I'm not dead, neither. Just…different."

Olivia had stopped suddenly for a gate up ahead, and Meg nearly rear-ended Brad before she got the Blazer reined in.

"Different as in dead," Meg said, watching through the windshield, in the glow of her headlights, as Brad got out of his truck and strode back to speak to her, leaving the driver's-side door gaping behind him.

He didn't look angry—just earnest.

"If you want to ride with me," he said when Meg had buzzed down her window, "fine. But if you're plan-ning to drive this rig up into the bed of my truck, you might want to wait until I park it in a hole and lower the tailgate."

"Sorry," Meg said after making a face.

Brad shook his head and went back to his truck. By

then, Olivia had the gate open, and he drove ahead onto an unpaved road winding upward between the juniper and Joshua trees clinging to the red dirt of the hillside.

"What was that about?" Meg mused, following Brad and Olivia's vehicles through the gap and not really addressing Angus, who answered, nonetheless.

"Guess he's prideful about the paint on that fancy jitney of his," he said. "Didn't want you denting up his buggy."

Meg didn't comment. Angus was full of the nineteenth-century equivalent of "woman driver" stories, and she didn't care to hear any of them.

They topped a rise, Olivia still in the lead, and dipped down into what was probably a broad valley, given what little Meg knew about the landscape on Stone Creek Ranch. Lights glimmered off to the right, revealing a good-size house and a barn.

Meg was about to ask if Angus had ever visited the ranch when he suddenly vanished.

She shut off the Blazer, got out and followed Brad and Olivia toward the barn. She wished it hadn't been so dark—it would have been interesting to see the place in the daylight.

Inside the barn, which was as big as any of the ones on the Triple M and boasted all the modern conveniences, Olivia and Brad were already saddling horses.

"That's Cinnamon over there," Olivia said with a nod to a tall chestnut in the stall across the wide breezeway from the one she was standing in, busily preparing a palomino to ride. "His gear's in the tack room, third saddle rack on the right."

Meg didn't hesitate, as she suspected Olivia had expected her to do, but found the tack room and Cinnamon's gear, and lugged it back to his stall. Brad and his sister were already mounted and waiting at the end of the breezeway when Meg led the gelding out, however.

"Need a boost?" Brad asked, in a teasing drawl, saddle leather creaking as he shifted to step down from the big paint he was riding and help Meg mount up.

Cinnamon was a big fella, taller by several hands than any of the horses in Meg's barn, but she'd been riding since she was in diapers, and she didn't need a boost from a "singing cowboy," as Angus described Brad.

"I can do it," she replied, straining to grip the saddle horn and get a foot into the high stirrup. It was going to be a stretch.

In the next instant, she felt two strong hands pushing on her backside, hoisting her easily onto Cinnamon's broad back.

Thanks, Angus, she said silently.

CHAPTER FOUR

IT WAS A purely crazy thing to do, setting out on horse-back, in the dark, for the high plains and meadows and secret canyons of Stone Creek Ranch, in search of a legendary stallion determined not to be found. It had been way too long since she'd done anything like it, Meg reflected, as she rode behind Olivia and Brad, on the borrowed horse called Cinnamon.

Olivia had brought a few veterinary supplies along, packed in saddle bags, and while Meg was sure Ransom, wounded or not, would elude them, she couldn't help admiring the kind of commitment it took to set out on the journey anyway. Olivia O'Ballivan was a woman with a cause and for that, Meg envied her a little.

The moon was three-quarters full, and lit their way, but the trail grew steadily narrower as they climbed, and the mountainside was steep and rocky. One misstep on the part of a distracted horse and both animal and rider would plunge hundreds of feet into an abyss of shadow, to their very certain and very painful deaths.

When the trail widened into what appeared, in the thin wash of moonlight, to be a clearing, Meg let out her breath, sat a little less tensely in the saddle, loosened her grip on Cinnamon's reins. Brad drew up his own mount to wait for her, while Olivia and her horse shot forward, intent on their mission.

"Do you think we'll find him?" Meg asked. "Ransom, I mean?"

"No," Brad answered, unequivocally. "But Livie was bound to try. I came to look out for her."

Meg hadn't noticed the rifle in the scabbard fixed to Brad's saddle before, back at the O'Ballivan barn, but it stood out in sharp relief now, the polished wooden stock glowing in a silvery flash of moonlight. He must have seen her eyes widen; he patted the scabbard as he met her gaze.

"You're expecting to shoot something?" Meg ventured. She'd been around guns all her life—they were plentiful on the Triple M—but that didn't mean she liked them.

"Only if I have to," Brad said, casting a glance in the direction Olivia had gone. He nudged his horse into motion, and Cinnamon automatically kept pace, the two geldings moving at an easy trot.

"What would constitute having to?" Meg asked.

"Wolves," Brad answered.

Meg was familiar with the wolf controversy—environmentalists and animal activists on the one side, ranchers on the other. She wanted to know where Brad stood on the subject. He was well-known for his love of all things finned, feathered and furry—but that might have been part of his carefully constructed persona, like the notched bedpost and the trashed hotel rooms.

"You wouldn't just pick them off, would you? Wolves, I mean?"

"Of course not," Brad replied. "But wolves are predators, and Livie's not wrong to be concerned that they'll track Ransom and take him down if they catch the blood-scent from his wounds."

A chill trickled down Meg's spine, like a splash of cold water, setting her shivering. Like Brad, she came from a long line of cattle ranchers, and while she allowed that wolves had a place in the ecological scheme of things, like every other creature on earth, she didn't romanticize them. They were not misunderstood *dogs*, as so many people seemed to think, but hunters, savagely brutal and utterly ruthless, and no one who'd ever seen what they did to their prey would credit them with nobility.

"Sharks with legs," she mused aloud. "That's what Rance calls them."

Brad nodded, but didn't reply. They were gaining on Olivia now; she was still a ways ahead, and had dismounted to look at something on the ground.

Both Brad and Meg sped up to reach her.

By the time they arrived, Olivia's saddlebags were open beside her, and she was holding a syringe up to the light. Because of the darkness, and the movements of the horses, a few moments passed before Meg focused on the animal Olivia was treating.

A dog lay bloody and quivering on its side.

Brad was off his horse before Meg broke the spell of shock that had descended over her and dismounted, too. Her stomach rolled when she got a better look at the dog; the poor creature, surely a stray, had run afoul of either a wolf or coyote pack, and it was purely a miracle that he'd survived.

Meg's eyes burned.

Brad crouched next to the dog, opposite Olivia, and stroked the animal with a gentleness that altered something deep down inside Meg, causing a grinding sensation, like the shift of tectonic plates far beneath the earth.

"Can he make it?" he asked Olivia.

"I'm not sure," Olivia replied. "At the very least, he needs stitches." She injected the contents of the syringe into the animal's ruff. "I sedated him. Give the medicine a few minutes to work, and then we'll take him back to the clinic in Stone Creek."

"What about the horse?" Meg asked, feeling helpless, a bystander with no way to help. She wasn't used to it. "What about Ransom?"

Olivia's eyes were bleak with sorrow when she looked up at Meg. She was a veterinarian; she couldn't abandon the wounded dog, or put him to sleep because it would be more convenient than transporting him back to town, where he could be properly cared for. But worry for the stallion would prey on her mind, just the same.

"I'll look for him tomorrow," Olivia said. "In the daylight."

Brad reached across the dog, laid a hand on his sister's shoulder. "He's been surviving on his own for a long time, Liv," he assured her. "Ransom will be all right."

Olivia bit her lower lip, nodded. "Get one of the sleeping bags, will you?" she said.

Brad nodded and went to unfasten the bedroll from behind his saddle. They were miles from town, or any ranch house.

"How did a dog get all the way out here?" Meg asked, mostly because the silence was too painful.

"He's probably a stray," Olivia answered, between soothing murmurs to the dog. "Somebody might have dumped him, too, down on the highway. A lot of people think dogs and cats can survive on their own—hunt and all that nonsense."

Meg drew closer to the dog, crouched to touch his head. He appeared to be some kind of Lab-retriever mix, though it was hard to tell, given that his coat was saturated with blood. He wore no collar, but that didn't mean he didn't have a microchip—and if he did, Olivia would be able to identify him immediately, once she got him to the clinic. Though from the looks of him, he'd be lucky to make it that far.

Brad returned with the sleeping bag, unfurling it. "Okay to move him now?" he asked Olivia.

Olivia nodded, and she and Meg sort of helped each other to their feet. "You mount up," Olivia told Brad. "And we'll lift him."

Brad whistled softly for his horse, which trotted obediently to his side, gathered the dangling reins, and swung up into the saddle.

Meg and Olivia bundled the dog, now mercifully unconscious, in the sleeping bag and, together, hoisted him high enough so Brad could take him into his arms. They all rode slowly back down the trail, Brad holding that dog as tenderly as he would an injured child, and not a word was spoken the whole way.

When they got back to the ranch house, where Olivia's Suburban was parked, Brad loaded the dog into the rear of the vehicle.

"I'll stay and put the horses away," Meg told him. "You'd better go into town with Olivia and help her get him inside the clinic."

Brad nodded. "Thanks," he said gruffly.

Olivia gave Meg an appreciative glance before

scrambling into the back of the Suburban to ride with the patient, ambulance-style. Brad got behind the wheel.

Once they'd driven off, Meg gathered the trio of horses and led them into the barn. There, in the breezeway, she removed their saddles and other tack and let the animals show her which stalls were their own. She checked their hooves for stones, made sure their automatic waterers were working, and gave them each a flake of hay. All the while, her thoughts were with Brad, and the stray dog lying in the back of Olivia's rig.

A part of her wanted to get into the Blazer and head straight for Stone Creek, and the veterinary clinic where Olivia worked, but she knew she'd just be in the way. Brad could provide muscle and moral support, if not medical skills, but Meg had nothing to offer.

With the O'Ballivans' horses attended to, she fired up the Blazer and headed back toward Indian Rock. She covered the miles between Stone Creek Ranch and the Triple M in a daze, and was a little startled to find herself at home when she pulled up in front of the garage door.

Leaving the Blazer in the driveway, Meg went into the barn to look in on Banshee and the four other horses who resided there. On the Triple M, horses were continually rotated between her place, Jesse's, Rance's and Keegan's, depending on what was best for the animals. Now they blinked at her, sleepily surprised by a late-night visit, and she paused to stroke each one of their long faces before starting for the house.

Angus fell into step with her as she crossed the side yard, headed for the back door.

"The stallion's all right," he informed her. "Holed up in one of the little canyons, nursing his wounds."

"I thought you said you couldn't help find him," Meg said, stopping to stare up at her ancestor in the moonlight.

"Turned out I was wrong," Angus drawled. His hat was gone; the bad weather he'd probably been expecting hadn't materialized.

"Mark the calendar," Meg teased. "I just heard a McKettrick admit to being wrong about something."

Angus grinned, waited on the small, open back porch while she unlocked the kitchen door. In his day, locks hadn't been necessary. Now the houses on the Triple M were no more immune to the rising crime rate than anyplace else.

"I've been wrong about plenty in my life," Angus said. "For one thing, I was wrong to leave Holt behind in Texas, after his mother died. He was just a baby, and God knows what I'd have done with him on the trail between there and the Arizona Territory, but I should have brought him, nonetheless. Raised him with Rafe and Kade and Jeb."

Intrigued, Meg opened the door, flipped on the kitchen lights and stepped inside. All of this was ancient family history to her, but to Angus, it was immediate stuff. "What else were you wrong about?" she asked, removing her coat and hanging it on the peg next to the door, then going to the sink to wash her hands.

Angus took a seat at the head of the table. In this house, it would have been Holt's place, but Angus was in the habit of taking the lead, even in small things.

"I ever tell you I had a brother?" he asked.

Meg, about to brew a pot of tea, stopped and stared

at him, stunned out of her fatigue. "No," she said. "You didn't." The McKettricks were raised on legend and lore, cut their teeth on it; the brother came as news. "Are you telling me there could be a whole other branch of the family out there?"

"Josiah got on fine with the ladies," Angus reminisced. "It would be my guess his tribe is as big as mine."

Meg forgot all about the tea-brewing. She made her way to the table and sat down heavily on the bench, gaping at Angus.

"Don't fret about it," he said. "They'd have no claim on this ranch, or any of the take from that McKettrickCo outfit."

Meg blinked, still trying to assimilate the revelation. "No one has *ever* mentioned that you had a brother," she said. "In all the diaries, all the letters, all the photographs—"

"They wouldn't have said anything about Josiah," Angus told her, evidently referring to his sons and their many descendants. "They never knew he existed."

"Why not?"

"Because he and I had a falling-out, and I didn't want anything to do with him after that. He felt the same way."

"Why bring it up now—after a century and a half?"

Angus shifted uncomfortably in his chair and, for a moment, his jawline hardened. "One of them's about to land on your doorstep," he said after a long, molar-grinding silence. "I figured you ought to be warned."

"*Warned?* Is this person a serial killer or a crook or something?"

"No," Angus said. "He's a lawyer. And that's damn near as bad."

"As a family, we haven't exactly kept a low profile for the last hundred or so years," Meg said slowly. "If Josiah has as many descendants as you do, why haven't any of them contacted us? It's not as if McKettrick is a common name, after all."

"Josiah took another name," Angus allowed, after more jaw-clamping. "That's what we got into it about, him and me."

"Why would he do that?" Meg asked.

Angus fixed her with a glare. Clearly, even after all the time that passed, he hadn't forgiven Josiah for changing his name and for whatever had prompted him to do that.

"He went to sea, when he was hardly more than a boy," Angus said. "When he came back home to Texas, years later, he was calling himself by another handle and running from the law. Hinted that he'd been a pirate."

"A *pirate?*"

"Left Ma and me to get by on our own, after Pa died," Angus recalled bitterly, looking through Meg to some long-ago reality. "Rode out before they'd finished shoveling dirt into Pa's grave. I ran down the road after him—he was riding a big buckskin horse—but he didn't even look back."

Tentatively, Meg reached out to touch Angus's arm. Clearly, Josiah had been the elder brother, and Angus a lot younger. He'd adored Josiah McKettrick—that much was plain—and his leaving had been a defining event in Angus's life. So defining, in fact, that he'd never acknowledged the other man's existence.

Angus bristled. "It was a long time ago," he said.

"What name did he go by?" Meg asked. She knew she wasn't going to sleep, for worrying about the injured dog and the stallion, and planned to spend the rest of the night at the computer, searching on Google for members of the heretofore unknown Josiah-side of the family.

"I don't rightly recall," Angus said glumly.

Meg knew he was lying. She also knew he wasn't going to tell her his brother's assumed name.

She got up again, went back to brewing tea.

Angus sat brooding in silence, and the phone rang just as Meg was pouring boiling water over the loose tea leaves in the bottom of Lorelei's pot.

Glancing at the caller ID panel, she saw no name, just an unfamiliar number with a 615 area code.

"Hello?"

"He's going to recover," Brad said.

Tears rushed to Meg's eyes, and her throat constricted. He was referring to the dog, of course. And using the cell phone he'd carried when he still lived in Tennessee. "Thank God," she managed to say. "Did Olivia operate?"

"No need," Brad answered. "Once she'd taken X-rays and run a scan, she knew there were no internal injuries. He's pretty torn up—looks like a baseball with all those stitches—but he'll be okay."

"Was there a microchip?"

"Yeah," Brad said after a charged silence. "But the phone number's no longer in service. Livie ran an internet search and found out the original owner died six months ago. Who knows where Willie's been in the meantime."

"Willie?"

"The dog," Brad explained. "That's his name. Willie."

"What's going to happen to Willie now?"

"He'll be at the clinic for a while," Brad said. "He's in pretty bad shape. Livie will try to find out if anybody adopted him after his owner died, but we're not holding out a lot of hope on that score."

"He'll go to the pound? When he's well enough to leave the clinic?"

"No," Brad answered. He sounded as tired as Meg felt. "If nobody has a prior claim on him, he'll come to live with me. I could use a friend—and so could he." He paused. "I hope I didn't wake you or anything."

"I was still up," Meg said, glancing in Angus's direction only to find that he'd disappeared again.

"Good," Brad replied.

A silence fell between them. Meg knew there was something else Brad wanted to say, and that she'd want to hear it. So she waited.

"I'm riding up into the high country again first thing in the morning," he finally said. "Looking for Ransom. I was wondering if—well—it's probably a stupid idea, but—"

Meg waited, resisting an urge to rush in and finish the sentence for him.

"Would you like to go along? Livie has a full schedule tomorrow—one of the other vets is out sick—and she wants to keep an eye on Willie, too. She's going to obsess about this horse until I can tell her he's fine, so I'm going to find him if I can."

"I'd like to go," Meg said. "What time are you leaving the ranch?"

"Soon as the sun's up," Brad answered. "You're sure? The country's pretty rough up there."

"If you can handle rough country, O'Ballivan, so can I."

He chuckled. "Okay, McKettrick," he said.

Meg found herself smiling. "I'll be there by 6:00 a.m., unless that's too early. Shall I bring my own horse?"

"Six is about right," Brad said. "Don't go to the trouble of trailering another horse—you can ride Cinnamon. Dress warm, though. And bring whatever gear you'd need if we had to spend the night for some reason."

Alone in her kitchen, Meg blushed. "See you in the morning," she said.

"'Night," Brad replied.

"Good night," Meg responded—long after Brad had hung up.

Giving up on the tea and, at least for that night, researching Josiah McKettrick, and having decided she needed to at least *try* to sleep, since tomorrow would be an eventful day, Meg locked up, shut off the lights and went upstairs to her room.

After getting out a pair of thermal pajamas, she took a long shower in the main bathroom across the hall, brushed her teeth, tamed her wet hair as best she could and went to bed.

Far from tossing and turning, as she'd half expected, she dropped into an immediate, consuming slumber, so deep she remembered none of her dreams.

Waking, she dressed quickly, in jeans and a sweatshirt, over a set of long underwear, made of some miraculous microfiber and bought for skiing, and finished off her ensemble with two pairs of socks and her sturdiest pair of boots. She shoved toothpaste, a brush and a small tube of moisturizer into a plastic storage bag, rolled up a blanket, tied it tightly with twine from the kitchen junk drawer and breakfasted on toast and coffee.

She called Jesse on her cell phone as she climbed into the Blazer, after feeding Banshee and the others. Cheyenne, Jesse's wife, answered on the second ring.

"Hi, it's Meg. Is Jesse around?"

"Sleeping," Cheyenne said, yawning audibly.

"I woke you up," Meg said, embarrassed.

"Jesse's the lay-abed in this family," Cheyenne responded warmly. "I've been up since four. Is anything wrong, Meg? Sierra and the baby—?"

"They're fine, as far as I know," Meg said, anxious to reassure Cheyenne and, at the same time, very glad she'd gotten Jesse's wife instead of Jesse himself. He'd look after her horses if she asked, but he'd want to know where she was going, and if she replied that she and Brad O'Ballivan were riding off into the sunrise together, he'd tease her unmercifully. "Look, Cheyenne, I need a favor. I'm going on a—on a trail ride with a friend, and I'll probably be back tonight, but—"

"Would this 'friend' be the famous Brad O'Ballivan?"

"Yes," Meg said, but reluctantly, backing out of the driveway and turning the Blazer around to head for Stone Creek. It was still dark, but the first pinkish gold rays of sunlight were rimming the eastern hills. "Cheyenne, will you ask Jesse to check on my horses if he doesn't hear from me by six or so tonight?"

"Of course," Cheyenne said. "So you're going riding

with Brad, and it might turn into an overnight thing. Hmmmmm—"

"It isn't anything romantic," Meg said. "I'm just helping him look for a stallion that might be hurt, that's all."

"I see," Cheyenne said sweetly.

"Just out of curiosity, what made you jump to the conclusion that the friend I mentioned was Brad?"

"It's all over town that you and country music's baddest bad boy met up at the Dixie Dog Drive-In the other day."

"Oh, great," Meg breathed. "I guess that means Jesse knows, then. And Rance and Keegan."

Cheyenne laughed softly, but when she spoke, her voice was full of concern. "Rance and Jesse are all for finding Brad and punching his lights out for hurting you so badly all those years ago, but Keegan is the voice of reason. He says give Brad a week to prove himself, *then* punch his lights out."

"The McKettrick way," Meg said. Her cousins were as protective as brothers would have been, and she loved them. But in terms of her social life, they weren't any more help than Angus had been.

"We'll talk later," Cheyenne said practically. "You're probably driving."

"Thanks, Chey," Meg answered.

When she got to Stone Creek Ranch, Brad came out of the house to greet her. He was dressed for the trail in jeans, boots, a work shirt and a medium-weight leather coat.

Meg's breath caught at the sight of him, and she was glad of the mechanics of parking and shutting off the

Blazer, because it gave her a few moments to gather her composure.

Normally, she was unflappable.

She'd handled some of the toughest negotiations during her career with McKettrickCo, without so much as a flutter of nerves, but there was something about Brad that erased all the years she'd spent developing a thick skin and a poker face.

He opened the Blazer door before she was quite ready to face him.

"Hungry?" he asked.

"I had toast and coffee at home," Meg answered.

"That'll never hold you till lunch," he said. "Come on inside. I've got some *real* food on the stove."

"Okay," Meg said, because short of sitting stubbornly in the car, she couldn't think of a way to avoid accepting his invitation.

The O'Ballivan house, like the ones on the Triple M, was large and rustic, and it exuded a sense of rich history. The porch wrapped around the whole front of the structure, and the back door was on the side nearest the barn. Meg followed Brad up the porch steps in front and around to another entrance.

The kitchen was big, and except for the wooden floors, which looked venerable, the room showed no trace of the old days. The countertops were granite, the cupboards gleamed, and the appliances were ultramodern, as were the furnishings.

Meg felt strangely let down by the sheer glamour of the place. All the kitchens on the Triple M had been modernized, of course, but in all cases, the original wood-burning stoves had been incorporated, and the tables all dated back to Holt, Rafe, Kade and Jeb's time, if not Angus's.

If Brad noticed her reaction, he didn't mention it. He dished up an omelet for her, and poured her a cup of coffee.

"You cook?" Meg teased, washing her hands at the gleaming stainless steel sink.

"I'm a fair hand in a kitchen," Brad replied modestly. "Dig in. I'll go saddle the horses while you eat."

Meg nodded, sat down and tackled the omelet.

It was delicious, and so was the coffee, but she felt uncomfortable sitting alone in that kitchen, as fancy as it was. She kept wondering what Maddie O'Ballivan would think, if she could see it, or even Brad's mother. Surely if things had been as difficult financially as Brad had let on the night before, at Jolene's, the renovations were fairly recent.

Having eaten as much as she could, Meg rinsed her plate, stuck it into the dishwasher, along with her fork and coffee cup, and hurried to the back door. Brad was out in front of the barn, the big paint ready to ride, tightening the cinch on Cinnamon's saddle. He picked her rolled blanket up off the ground and tied it on behind.

"Not much gear," he said. "Do you know how cold it gets up there?"

"I'll be fine," Meg said.

Brad merely shook his head. His own horse was restless, and the rifle was in evidence, too, looking ominous in the worn scabbard.

"That's quite a kitchen," Meg said as Brad gave her a leg up onto Cinnamon's back.

"Big John said it was a waste of money," Brad recalled, smiling to himself as he mounted up. "That was my granddad."

Meg knew who Big John O'Ballivan was—everybody in the county did—but she didn't point that out. If Brad wanted to talk about his family, to pass the time, that was fine with Meg. She nudged Cinnamon to keep pace with Brad's horse as they crossed a pasture, headed for the hills beyond.

"He raised you and your sisters, didn't he?" she asked, though she knew that, too.

"Yes," Brad said, and the set of his jaw reminded her of the way Angus's had looked, when he told her about his estranged brother.

Meg's curiosity spiked, but she didn't indulge it. "I take it Willie's still on the mend?"

Brad's grin was as dazzling as the coming sunrise would be. "Olivia called just before you showed up," he said with a nod. "Willie's going to be fine. In a week or two, I'll bring him home."

Remembering the way Brad had handled the dog, with such gentleness and such strength, Meg felt a pinch in the center of her heart. "You plan on staying, then?"

He tossed her a thoughtful look. "I plan on staying," he confirmed. "I told you that, didn't I?"

You also told me we'd get married and you'd love me forever.

"You told me," she said.

"Would this be a good time to tell you about my second wife?"

Meg considered, then shook her head, smiling a little. "Probably not."

"Okay," Brad said, "then how about my sisters?"

"Good idea." Meg had known Olivia slightly, but there was a set of twins in the family, too. She'd never met them.

"Olivia has a thing for animals, as you can see. She needs to get married and channel some of that energy into having a family of her own, but she's got a cussed streak and runs off every man who manages to get close to her. Ashley and Melissa—the twins—are fraternal. Ashley's pretty down-home—she runs a bed-and-breakfast in Stone Creek. Melissa's clerking in a law office in Flagstaff."

"You're close to them?"

"Yes," Brad said, expelling a long breath. "And, no. Olivia resents my leaving home—I can't seem to get it through her head that we wouldn't have *had* a home if I hadn't gone to Nashville. The twins are ten years younger than I am, and seem to see me more as a visiting celebrity than their big brother."

"When Olivia needed help," Meg reminded him, "she came to you. So maybe she doesn't resent you as much as you think she does." There was something really different about Olivia O'Ballivan, Meg thought, looking back over the night before, but she couldn't quite figure out what it was.

"I hope you're right," Brad said. "It's fine to love animals—I'm real fond of them myself. But Olivia carries it to a whole new place. So much so that there's no room in her life for much of anything—or anybody—else."

"She's a veterinarian, Brad," Meg said reasonably. "It's natural that animals are her passion."

"To the exclusion of everything else?" Brad asked.

"She'll be fine," Meg said. "When Olivia meets the right man, she'll make room for him. Just wait and see."

Brad looked unconvinced. He raised his chin and said, "If we're going to find that horse, we'd better move a little faster."

Meg nodded in agreement and Cinnamon fell in behind Brad's gelding as they started the twisting, perilous climb up the mountainside.

CHAPTER FIVE

LOOKING FOR THAT wild stallion was a fool's errand, and Brad knew it. As he'd told Meg, his primary reason for undertaking the quest was to keep Olivia from doing it. Now he wondered how many times, during his long absence, his little sister had climbed this mountain alone, at all hours of the day and night, and in all seasons of the year.

The thought made him shudder.

The country above Stone Creek was as rugged as it had ever been. Wolves, coyotes and even javelinas were plentiful, as were rattlesnakes. There were deep crevices in the red earth, some of them hidden by brush, and they'd swallowed many a hapless hiker. But the worst threat was probably the weather—at that elevation, blizzards could strike literally without warning, even in July and August. It was October now, and that only increased the danger.

Meg, shivering in her too-light coat, rode along beside him without complaint. Being a McKettrick, he thought, with a sad smile turned entirely inward, she'd freeze to death before she'd admit she was cold.

Inviting her along had been a purely selfish act, and Brad regretted it. Too many things could happen, most of them bad.

They'd been traveling for an hour or so when he

stopped alongside a creek to rest the horses. High banks on either side sheltered them from the wind, and Meg got a chance to warm up.

Brad opened his saddlebags and brought out a long-sleeved thermal shirt, extended it to Meg. She hesitated a moment—that damnable McKettrick pride again—then took the shirt and pulled it on, right over the top of her coat.

The effect was comically unglamorous.

"Where's a Starbucks when you need one?" she joked.

Brad grinned. "There's an old line shack up the trail a ways," he told her. "Big John always kept it stocked with supplies, in case a hiker got stranded and needed shelter. It's not Starbucks, but I'll probably be able to rustle up a pot of coffee and some lunch. If you don't mind the survivalist packaging."

Meg's relief was visible, though she wouldn't have expressed it verbally, Brad knew. "We didn't need to bring the blankets and other gear then," she reasoned. "If there's a line shack, I mean."

"You've been living in the five-star lane for too long," Brad replied, but the jibe was a gentle one. "A while back, some hunters were trespassing on this land—Big John posted No Hunting signs years ago—and a snowstorm came up. They were found, dead of exposure, about fifty feet from the shack."

She shivered. "I remember," she said, and for a moment, her blue eyes looked almost haunted. The story had been a gruesome one, and she obviously *did* remember—all too clearly.

"We're not all that far from the ranch," Brad said. "It would probably be best if I took you back."

Meg's gaze widened, and grew more serious. "And you'd turn right around and come back up here to look for Ransom?"

"Yes," Brad answered, resigned.

"Alone."

He nodded. Once, Big John would have made the journey with him. Now there was no one.

"I'm staying," Meg said and shifted slightly, as if planting her feet. "You *invited* me to come along, in case you've forgotten."

"I shouldn't have. If anything happened to you—"

"I'm a big girl, Brad," she interrupted.

He looked her over, and—as always—liked what he saw. Liked it so much that his throat tightened and he had a hard time swallowing so he could hold up his end of the conversation. "You probably weigh a hundred and thirty pounds wrapped in a blanket and dunked into a lake. And despite your illustrious heritage, you're no match for a pack of wolves, a sudden blizzard, or a chasm that reaches halfway to China."

"If you can do it," Meg said, "*I* can do it."

Brad shoved a hand through his hair, exasperated even though he knew it was his own fault that Meg was in danger. After all, he *had* asked her to come along, half hoping the two of them would end up sharing a sleeping bag.

What the hell had he been thinking?

The pertinent question, he decided, was what had he been thinking *with*—not his brain, certainly.

"We'd better get moving again," she told him, when he didn't speak. Before they'd left the ranch, he'd given her a pair of binoculars on a neck strap; now she pulled them out from under the donated undershirt, her coat, and whatever was beneath that. "We have a horse to find."

Brad nodded, cupped his hands to give her a leg up onto Cinnamon's back. She paused for a moment, deciding, before setting her left foot in the stirrup of his palms.

"This is a tall horse," she said, a little flushed.

"We should have named him Stilts instead of Cinnamon," Brad allowed, amused. Meg, like the rest of her cousins, had virtually grown up on horseback, as had he and Olivia and the twins. She'd interpret even the smallest courtesy—the offer of a boost, for instance— as an affront to her riding skills.

Forty-five minutes later, Meg, using the binoculars, spotted Ransom on the crest of a rocky rise.

"There he is!" she whispered, awed. "Wait till I tell Jesse he's real!"

After a few seconds, she lifted the binoculars off her neck by the strap and handed them across to Brad.

Brad drew in a breath, struck by the magnificence of the stallion, the defiance and barely restrained power. A moment or so passed before he thought to scan the horse for wounds. It was hard to tell, given the distance, even with binoculars, but Ransom wasn't limping, and Brad didn't see any blood. He could report to Olivia, in all honesty, that the object of her equine obsession was holding his own.

Before lowering the binoculars, Brad swept them across the top of that rise, and that was when he saw the two mares. He chuckled. Ransom had himself a harem, then.

He watched them a while, then gave the binoculars back to Meg, with a cheerful, "He has company."

Meg's face glowed. "They're beautiful," she whispered, as if afraid to startle the horses and send them fleeing, though they were well over a mile away, by Brad's estimation. "And Ransom. He knows we're here, Brad. It's almost as if he wanted to let us see that he's all right."

Brad raised his coat collar against a chilly breeze and wished he'd worn his hat. He'd considered it that morning, but it had seemed like an affectation, a way of asserting that he was still a cowboy, by his own standards if not those of the McKettricks. "He knows," he agreed finally, "but it's more likely that he's taunting us. Catch-me-if-you-can. That's what he'd say if he could talk."

Meg's entire face was glowing. In fact, Brad figured if he could strip all those clothes off her, that glow would come right through her skin and be enough to warm him until he died of old age.

"How about that coffee?" she said, grinning.

AFTER SEEING BRAD'S kitchen on Stone Creek Ranch, Meg had expected the "line shack" to be a fancy log A-frame with a Jacuzzi and Internet service. It was an actual *shack,* though, made of weathered board. There was a lean-to on one side, to shelter the horses, but no barn, with hay stored inside. Brad gave the animals grain from a sealed metal bin, and filled two water buckets for them from a rusty old pump outside.

Meg might have gone inside and started the fire, so they could brew the promised coffee, but she was mesmerized, watching Brad. It was as though the two of them had somehow gone back in time, back to when

all the earlier McKettricks and O'Ballivans were still
in the prime of their lives.

Once, there had been several shacks like that one
on the Triple M, far from the barns and bunkhouses.
Ranch hands, riding the far-flung fence lines, or just
traveling overland for some reason, used to spend the
night in them, take refuge there when the weather
was bad. Eventually, those tiny buildings had become
hazards, rather than havens, and they'd been knocked
down and burned.

"Pretty decrepit," Brad said, leading the way into
the shack.

Things skittered inside, and the smell of the place
was faintly musty, but Brad soon had a good fire going
in the ancient potbellied stove. There was no furniture
at all, but shelves, made of old wooden crates stacked
on top of each other, held cups, food in airtight silver
packets, cans of coffee.

The whole place was about the size of Meg's downstairs powder room on the Triple M.

"I'd offer you a chair," Brad said, grinning, "but obviously there aren't any. Make yourself at home while I
rinse out these cups at the pump and fill the coffeepot."

Meg examined the plank floor, sat down cross-
legged, and reveled in the warmth beginning to
emanate from the wood-burning stove. The shack, in-
adequate as it was, offered a welcome respite from the
cold wind outside. The hunters Brad had mentioned
probably wouldn't have died if they'd been able to reach
it. She remembered the news story; the facts had been
bitter and brutal.

Like Stone Creek Ranch, the Triple M was posted,
and hunting wasn't allowed. Still, people trespassed

constantly, and Rance, Keegan and Jesse enforced the
boundaries—mostly in a peaceful way. Just the winter before, though, Jesse had caught two men running
deer with snowmobiles on the high meadow above his
house, and he'd scared them off with a rifle shot aimed
at the sky. Later, he'd tracked the pair to a tavern in
Indian Rock—strangers to the area, they'd laughed
at his warning—and put both of them in the hospital.
He might have killed them, in fact, if Keegan hadn't
gotten wind of the fight and come to break it up, and
even with his help, it took the local marshal, Wyatt
Terp, his deputy, and half the clientele in the bar to get
Jesse off the second snowmobiler. He'd already pul-
verized the first one.

There was talk about filing assault charges against
Jesse, and later it was rumored that there might be law-
suits, but nothing ever came of either. Meg, along with
everybody else in Indian Rock, doubted the snowmo-
bilers would ever set foot in town again, let alone on
the Triple M.

But there was always, as Keegan liked to say, a fresh
supply of idiots.

Brad came in with the cups and the full coffeepot,
shoving the door closed behind him with one shoulder. Again, Meg had a sense of having stepped right
out of the twenty-first century and into the nineteenth.

Despite cracks between the board walls, the shack
was warm.

Brad set the coffeepot on the stove, measured
ground beans into it from a can, and left it to boil,
cowboy-style. No basket, no filter.

Then he emptied two of the crates being used as

cupboards and dragged them over in front of the stove, so he and Meg could sit on them.

Overhead, thunder rolled across the sky, loud as a freight train.

Meg stiffened. "Rain?"

"Snow," Brad said. "I saw a few flakes drift past while I was outside. Soon as we've warmed up a little and fortified ourselves with caffeine and some grub, we'd better make for the low country."

Had there been any windows, Meg would have gotten up to look out of one of them. She could open the door a crack, but the thought of being buffeted by the rising wind stopped her.

By reflex, she scrambled to extract her cell phone from her coat pocket, flipped it open.

"No service," she murmured.

"I know," Brad said, smiling a little as he rose off the crate he'd been sitting on to add wood to the stove. Fortunately, there seemed to be an adequate supply of that. "I tried to call Olivia and let her know Ransom was still king of the hill a few minutes ago. Nothing."

Another round of thunder rattled the roof, and out in the lean-to, the horses fussed in alarm.

"Be right back," Brad said, heading for the door.

When he returned, he had a bedroll and Meg's pitifully insufficient blanket with him. And the horses were quiet.

"Just in case," he said when Meg's gaze landed, alarmed, on the overnight gear. "It's snowing pretty hard."

Meg, feeling foolish for sitting on her backside while Brad had been tending to the horses and fetching their gear inside, stood to lift the lid off the coffeepot and peek inside. The water was about to boil, but it would be a few minutes before the grounds settled to the bottom and they could drink the stuff.

"Relax, Meg," Brad said quietly. "There's still a chance the snow will ease up before dark."

At once tantalized and full of dread at the prospect of spending the night alone in a line shack with Brad O'Ballivan, Meg paced back and forth in front of the stove.

She knew what would happen if they stayed.

She'd known when she accepted Brad's invitation. Known when she set out for Stone Creek Ranch before dawn.

And he probably had, too.

She shoved both hands into her hair and paced faster.

"Meg," Brad said, sitting leisurely on his upended crate, *"relax."*

"You knew," she accused, stopping to shake a finger at him. "You knew we'd be stuck here!"

"So did you," Brad replied, unruffled.

Meg went to the door, wrenched it open and looked out, oblivious to the cold. The snow was coming down so hard and so fast that she couldn't see the pine trees towering less than a hundred yards from where she stood.

Attempting to travel under those conditions would be suicide.

Brad came and helped her shut the door again.

On the other side of the wall, in the lean-to, the horses made no sound.

Meg was standing too close to Brad, no question about it. But when she tried to move, she couldn't.

They looked into each other's eyes.

The very atmosphere zinged around them.

If Brad had kissed her then, she wouldn't have had the will to do anything but kiss him right back, but he didn't. "I'd better get some drinking water," he said, turning away and reaching for a bucket. "While I can still find my way back from the pump."

He went out.

Meg, needing something to do, pushed the coffee-pot to the back of the stove so it wouldn't boil over and then examined a few of the food packets, evidently designed for post-apocalyptic dinner parties. The expiration dates were fifty years in the future.

"Spaghetti à la the Starship Enterprise," she muttered. There was Beef Wellington, too, and even meat loaf. At least they wouldn't starve.

Not right away, anyhow.

They'd starve *slowly.*

If they didn't freeze to death first.

Meg tried her cell phone again.

Still no service.

It was just as well, she supposed. Cheyenne knew her approximate location. Jesse would feed her horses, and if her absence was protracted, he and Keegan and Rance were sure to come looking for her. In the meantime, though, there would be a lot of room for speculation about what might be going on up there in the high country. And Jesse wouldn't miss a chance to tease her about it.

She was still holding the phone when Brad came in again, carrying a bucket full of water. He looked so cold that Meg almost went to put her arms around him.

Instead, she poured him a cup of hot coffee, still

chewy with grounds, and handed it to him as soon as he'd set the bucket down.

"I don't suppose there's a generator," she said because the shack was darkening, even though it wasn't noon yet, and by nightfall, she wouldn't be able to see the proverbial hand in front of her face.

He favored her with a tilted grin. "Just a couple of battery-operated lamps and a few candles. We'll want to conserve the batteries, of course."

"Of course," Meg said, and smiled determinedly, hoping that would distract Brad from the little quaver in her voice.

"We don't have to make love," Brad said, lingering by the stove and taking slow, appreciative sips from his coffee. "Just because we're alone in a remote line shack during what may be the snowstorm of the century."

"You are not making me feel better."

That grin again. It was saucy, but it had a wistful element. "Am I making you feel *something?*"

"Nothing discernible," Meg lied. In truth, all her nerves felt supercharged, and her body was remembering, against strict orders from her mind, the weight and warmth of Brad's hands, caressing her bare skin.

"I used to be pretty good at it. Making you feel things, that is."

"Brad," Meg said, "don't."

"Okay," he said.

Meg was relieved, but at the same time, she wished he hadn't given up quite so easily.

"You wanted coffee," Brad remarked. "Have some."

Meg filled a cup for herself. Scooted her crate an inch or two farther from Brad's and sat down.

The shadows deepened and the shack seemed to

grow even smaller than it was, pressing her and Brad closer together. And then closer still.

"This," Meg said, inspired by desperation, "would be a good time to talk about your second wife. Since we've been putting it off for a while."

Brad chuckled, fished in his saddlebags, now lying on the floor at his feet, and brought out a deck of cards. "I was thinking more along the lines of gin rummy," he said.

"What was her name again?"

"What was whose name?"

"Your second wife."

"Oh, her."

"Yeah, her."

"Cynthia. Her name is Cynthia. And I don't want to talk about her right now. Either we reminisce, or we play gin rummy, or—"

Meg squirmed. "Gin rummy," she said decisively. "There is no reason at all to bring up the subject of sex."

"Did I?"

"Did you what?"

"Did I bring up the subject of sex?"

"Not exactly," Meg said, embarrassed.

Brad grinned. "We'll get to that," he said. "Sooner or later."

Meg swallowed so much coffee in the next gulp that she nearly choked.

"There are some things I've been wondering about," Brad said easily, watching her over the rim of his metal coffee mug. His eyes smoldered with lazy blue heat.

Outside, the snow-thunder crashed again, but the horses didn't react. They'd probably already settled down for the night, snug in their furry hides and their lean-to.

"I'm hungry," Meg said, reaching for one of the food packets.

Brad went on as though she hadn't spoken at all. "Do you still like to eat cereal with yogurt instead of milk?"

Meg swallowed. "Yes."

"Do you still laugh in your sleep?"

"I—I suppose."

"Do you still arch your back like a bucking horse when you climax?"

Meg's face felt hotter than the old stove, which rocked a little with the heat inside it, crimson blazes glowing through the cracks. "What kind of question is that?"

"A personal one, I admit," Brad said. He might have passed for a choirboy, so innocent was his expression, but his eyes gave him away. They had the old glint of easy confidence in them. He knew he could have her anyplace and anytime he wanted—he was just biding his time. "I'll know soon enough, I guess."

"No," she said.

"No?" He raised an eyebrow.

"No, I don't arch my back when I—I don't arch my back."

"Hmmmm," Brad said. "Why not?"

Because I don't have sex, Meg almost answered, but in the last, teetering fraction of a second, she realized she didn't want to admit that. Not to Brad, the man with all the notches on his bedpost.

"You haven't been sleeping with anybody?" he asked.

"I didn't say that," Meg replied, keeping her distance, mainly because she wanted so much to take Brad's coffee from his hand, set it aside, straddle his thighs and let him work his slow, thorough magic. Peeling away her outer garments, kissing and caressing everything he uncovered.

"Nobody who could make you arch your back?"

Meg was suffused with aching, needy misery. She'd been in fairly close proximity to Brad all morning, and managed to keep her perspective, but now they were alone in a remote shack, and he'd already begun to seduce her. Without so much as a kiss, or a touch of his hand. With Brad O'Ballivan, even gin rummy would qualify as foreplay.

"Something like that," she said. It was a lame answer, and way too honest, but she'd figured if she tossed his ego a bone, the way she might have done to get past a junkyard dog, she'd get a chance to diffuse the invisible but almost palpable charge sparking between them.

"I came across one of Maddie's diaries a few years ago," Brad said, still stripping her with his eyes. Maddie, of course, was his ancestress—Sam O'Ballivan's wife. "She mentioned this line shack several times. She and Sam spent a night here, once, and conceived a child."

That statement should have quelled Meg's passion— unlike Sam and Maddie, she and Brad weren't married, weren't in love. She wasn't using any form of birth control, since there hadn't been a man in her life for nearly a year, and intuition told her that for all Brad's preparations, Brad hadn't brought any condoms along.

Yet, the mention of a baby opened a gash of yearning within Meg, a great, jagged tearing so deep and so dark and so raw that she nearly doubled over with the pain of it.

"Are you all right?" Brad asked, on his feet quickly, taking her elbows in his hands, looking down into her face.

She said nothing. She couldn't have spoken for anything, not in that precise moment.

"What?" Brad prompted, looking worried.

She couldn't tell him that she'd wanted a baby so badly she'd made arrangements with a fertility specialist on several occasions, always losing her courage at the last moment. That she'd almost reached the point of sleeping with strangers, hoping to get pregnant.

In the end, she hadn't been able to go through with that, either.

She'd never known her own father. Oh, she'd lacked for nothing, being a McKettrick. Nothing except the merest acquaintance with the man who'd sired her. He was so anonymous, in fact, that Eve had occasionally referred to him, not knowing Meg was listening, as "the sperm donor."

She wanted more for her own son or daughter. Granted, the baby's father didn't have to be involved in their day-to-day life, or pay child support, or much of anything else. But he had to have a face and a name, so Meg could show her child a photograph, at some point in time, and say, "This is your daddy."

"Meg?" Brad's hands tightened a little on her elbows.

"Panic attack," she managed to gasp.

He pressed her down onto one of the crates, ladled some water from the bucket he'd braved the elements to fill at the pump outside, and held it to her lips.

She sipped.

"Do you need to take a pill or something?"

Meg shook her head.

He dragged the second crate closer, and sat facing her, so their knees touched. "Since when do you get panic attacks?" he asked.

Tears stung Meg's eyes. She rocked a little, hugging herself, and Brad steadied the ladle in her hands, raised it to her mouth again.

She sipped, more slowly this time, and Brad set it aside when she was finished.

"Meg," he repeated. "The panic attacks?"

It only happens when I suddenly realize I want to have a certain man's baby more than I want anything in the world. And when that certain man turns out to be you.

"It's a freak thing," she said. "I've never had one before."

Brad raised an eyebrow—he'd always been perceptive. It was one of the qualities that made him a good songwriter, for example. "I mentioned that Sam and Maddie conceived a child in this line shack, and you started hyperventilating." He leaned forward a little, took both Meg's hands gently in his. "I remember how much you wanted kids when we were together," he mused. "And now your sister is having a baby."

Meg's heart wedged itself into her windpipe. She'd wanted a baby, all right. And she'd conceived one, with Brad, and miscarried soon after he left for Nashville. Not even her mother had known.

She nodded.

Brad stroked the side of her cheek with the backs of his fingers, offering her comfort. She'd never told him about the pregnancy—she'd been saving the news for their wedding night—but now she knew she would have no choice, if they got involved again.

"I'm not jealous of Sierra," she said, anxious to make that clear. "I'm happy for her and Travis."

"I know," Brad said. He drew her from her crate onto his lap; she straddled his thighs. But beyond that, the gesture wasn't sexual. He simply held her, one hand gently pressing her head to his shoulder.

After a little deep breathing, in order to calm herself, Meg straightened and gazed into Brad's face.

"Suppose we had sex," she said softly. Tentatively. "And I conceived a child. How would you react?"

"Well," Brad said after pondering the idea with an expression of wistful amusement on his face, "I guess that would depend on a couple of things." He kissed her neck, lightly. Nibbled briefly at her earlobe.

A hot shudder went through Meg. "Like what?"

"Like whether we were going to raise the baby together or not," Brad replied, still nibbling. When Meg stiffened slightly, he drew back to look into her face again. "What?"

"I was sort of thinking I could just be a single mother," Meg said.

She was off Brad's thighs and plunked down on her crate again so quickly that it almost took her breath away.

"And my part would be what?" he demanded. "Keep my distance? Go on about my business? What, Meg?"

"You have your career—"

"I don't have my career. That part of my life is over. I've told you that."

"You're young, Brad. You're very talented. It's inevitable that you'll want to sing again."

"I don't have to be in a concert hall or a recording studio to sing," he said tersely. "I mean to live on Stone Creek Ranch for good, and any child of *mine* is going to grow up there."

Meg stood her ground. After all, she was a McKettrick. "Any child of *mine* is going to grow up on the Triple M."

"Then I guess we'd better not make a baby," Brad replied. He got up off the crate, went to the stove and refilled his coffee cup.

"Look," Meg said more gently, "we can just let the subject drop. I'm sorry I brought it up at all—I just got a little emotional there for a moment and—"

Brad didn't answer.

They were stuck in a cabin together, at least overnight, and maybe longer. They had to get along, or they'd both go crazy.

She retrieved the pack of cards from the floor, where Brad had set them earlier. "Bet I can take you, O'Ballivan," she said, waggling the box from side to side. "Gin rummy, five-card stud, go fish—name your poison."

He laughed, and the tension was broken—the overt kind, anyway. There was an underground river of the stuff, coursing silently beneath their feet. "Go fish?"

"Lately, I've played a lot of cards—with my nephew, Liam. That's his favorite."

Brad chose rummy. Set a third crate between them for a table top. "You think you can take me, huh?" he challenged. And the look in his eyes, as he dealt the first hand, said *he* planned on doing the taking—and the cards didn't have a thing to do with it.

CHAPTER SIX

IT WAS A wonder to Brad that he could sit there in the middle of that line shack, playing gin rummy with Meg McKettrick, when practically all he'd thought about since coming home to Stone Creek was bedding down with her. She'd practically invited him to father her baby, too.

Whatever his reservations might be where her insistence on raising the child alone was concerned, and on the Triple M to boot, he sure wouldn't have minded the *process* of conceiving it.

So why wasn't he on top of her at that very moment?

He studied his cards solemnly—Meg was going to win this hand, as she had the last half dozen—and pondered the situation. The wind howled around the shack like a million shrieking banshees determined to drive them both out into the freezing cold, making the walls shake. And the light was going, too, even though it wasn't noon yet.

"Play," Meg said impatiently, a spark of mischievous triumph—and something else—dancing in her eyes.

"If I didn't know better," Brad said ruefully, "I'd think you'd stacked the deck. You're going to lay down all your cards and set me again, aren't you?"

She grinned, looking at him coyly over the fan of

cards. Even batting her eyelashes. "There's only one way to find out," she teased.

A cowboy's geisha, Brad thought. Later, when he was alone at the ranch, he'd tinker around with the idea, maybe make a song out of it. He might have retired from recording and life on the road, but he knew he'd always make music.

Resigned, he drew a card from the stack, couldn't use it, and tossed it away.

Meg's whole being seemed to twinkle as she took his discard, incorporated it into a grand slam of a run and went out with a flourish, spreading the cards across the top of the crate.

"McKettrick luck," she said, beaming.

On impulse, Brad put down his cards, leaned across the crate between them and kissed Meg lightly on the mouth. She tensed at first, then responded, giving a little groan when he used his tongue.

Her arms slipped around his shoulders.

He wanted with everything in him to shove cards and crate aside, lay her down, then and there, and have her.

Whoa, he told himself. *Easy. Don't scare her off.*

There were tears in her eyes when she drew back from his kiss, sniffled once, and blinked, as though surprised to find herself alone with him, in the eye of the storm.

Like most men, Brad was always unsettled when a woman cried. He felt an urgent need to rectify whatever was wrong, and at the same time, knew he couldn't.

Meg swabbed at her cheeks with the back of one hand, straightened her proud McKettrick spine.

"What's the matter?" Brad asked.

"Nothing," Meg answered, averting her gaze.

"You're lying."

"Just hedging a little," she said, trying hard to smile and falling short. "It was like the old days, that's all. The kiss I mean. It brought up a lot of feelings."

"Would it help if I told you I felt the same way?"

"Not really," she said. A thoughtful look came into those fabulous, fathomless eyes of hers.

Brad slid the crate to one side and leaned in close, filled with peculiar suspense. He had to know what was going on in her head. "What?"

"Lots of people have sex," she told him, "without anybody getting pregnant."

"The reverse is also true," he felt honor-bound to say. "Far as I know, making love still causes babies."

"Making love," Meg said, "is not necessarily the same thing as having sex."

Brad cleared his throat, still walking on figurative eggshells. "True," he said very cautiously. Was she messing with him? Setting him up for a rebuff? Meg wasn't a particularly vengeful person, at least as far as he knew, but he'd hurt her badly all those busy years ago. Maybe she wanted to get back at him a little.

"What I have in mind," she told him decisively, "is *sex,* as opposed to making love." A pause. "Of course."

"Of course," he agreed. Hope fluttered in his chest, like a bird flexing its wings and rising, windborne, off a high tree branch. At the same time, he felt stung— Meg was making it clear that any intimacy they might enjoy during this brief time-out-of-time would be strictly for physical gratification. Frenetic coupling of bodies, an emotion-free zone.

Since beggars couldn't be choosers, he was willing

to bargain, but the disturbing truth was, he wanted more from Meg than a noncommittal quickie. She wasn't, after all, a groupie to be groped and taken in the back of some tour bus, then forgotten.

She squinted at him, catching something in his expression. "This bothers you?" she asked.

He tried to smile. "If you want to have sex, Mc-Kettrick, I'm definitely game. It's just that—"

"What?"

"It might not be a good idea." Was he crazy? Here was the most beautiful woman he'd ever seen, essentially offering herself to him—and he was leaning on the brake lever?

"Okay," she said, and she looked hurt, uncomfortable, suddenly shy.

And that was his undoing. All his noble reluctance went right out the door.

He pulled her onto his lap again.

She hesitated, then wrapped both arms around his neck.

"Are you sure?" he asked her quietly, gruffly. "We're taking a chance here, Meg. We *could* conceive a child—"

The idea filled him with desperate jubilation, strangely mingled with sorrow.

"We could," she agreed, her eyes shining, dark with sultry heat, despite the chill seeping in between the cracks in the plain board walls.

He cupped her chin in his hand, made her look into his face. "Fair warning, McKettrick. If there's a baby, I'm not going to be an anonymous father, content to cut a check once a month and go on about my business as if it had never happened."

She studied him. "You're serious."

He nodded.

"I'll take that chance," she decided, after a few moments of deliberation.

He kissed her again, deeply this time, and when their mouths parted, she looked as dazed as he felt. Once, during a rehearsal before a concert, he'd gotten a shock from an electric guitar with a frayed chord. The jolt he'd taken, kissing Meg just now, made the first experience seem tame.

She was straddling him, and even through their jeans, the insides of her thighs, squeezing against his hips, seemed to sear his skin. She squirmed against his erection, making him groan.

Never in his life had Brad wanted a bed as badly as he did at that moment. It wasn't right to lay Meg down on a couple of sleeping bags, on that cold floor.

But even as he was thinking these disjointed thoughts, he was pulling her shirt up, slipping his hands beneath all that fabric, stroking her bare ribs.

She shivered deliciously, closed her eyes, threw her head back.

"Cold?" Brad asked, worried.

"Anything but," she murmured.

"You're sure?"

"Absolutely sure," Meg said.

He found the catch on her bra, opened it. Cupped both hands beneath her full, warm breasts.

She moaned as he chafed her nipples gently, using the sides of his thumbs.

And that was when they heard the deafening and unmistakable *thwup-thwup-thwup* of helicopter blades, directly above the roof of the line shack.

MEG LOOKED UP, disbelieving. Jesse, Rance, or Keegan—or all three. Who else would take a chopper up in weather like that?

Out in the lean-to, the horses whinnied in panic. The walls of the cabin shook as Meg jumped to her feet and righted her bra in almost the same motion. *"Damn!"* she sputtered furiously.

"That had better not be Phil," Brad said ominously. He was standing, too, his gaze fixed on the trembling ceiling.

Meg smoothed her hair, straightened her clothes. "Phil?"

"My manager," Brad reminded her.

"We should be so lucky," Meg yelled, straining to be heard over the sound of the blades. "It's my cousins!"

They both went to the door and peered out, heedless of the blasting cold, made worse by the downdraft from the chopper, Meg ducking under Brad's left arm to see.

Sure enough, the McKettrickCo helicopter, a relic of the corporation days, was settling to the ground, bouncing on its runners in the deepening snow.

"I'll be damned," Brad said with a grin of what looked like rueful admiration, forcing the door shut against the icy wind. At the last second, Meg saw two figures moving toward them at a half crouch.

"I'll kill them," Meg said.

The door rattled on its hinges at the first knock.

Meg stood back while Brad opened it again.

Jesse came through first, followed by Keegan. They wore Western hats pulled low over their faces, leather coats thickly lined with sheep's wool, and attitudes.

"I tried to stop them," Angus said, appearing at Meg's elbow.

"Good job," Meg scoffed, under her breath, without moving her lips.

Angus spread his hands. "They're McKettricks," he reminded her, as though that explained every mystery in the universe, from spontaneous human combustion to the Bermuda Triangle.

"Are you crazy?" Meg demanded of her cousins, storming forward to stand toe-to-toe with Jesse, who was tight-jawed, casting suspicious glances at Brad. "You could have been killed, taking the copter up in a blizzard!"

Brad, by contrast, hoisted the coffeepot off the stove, grinning wryly, and not entirely in a friendly way. "Coffee?" he asked.

Jesse scowled at him.

"Don't mind if I do," Keegan said, pulling off his heavy leather gloves. He tossed Meg a sympathetic glance in the meantime, one that said, *Don't blame me. I'm just here to keep an eye on Jesse.*

Brad found another cup and, without bothering to wipe it out, filled it and handed it to Keegan. "It's good to see you again," he said with a sort of charged affability, but underlying his tone was an unspoken, *Not.*

"I'll just bet," Jesse said, whipping off his hat. His dark blond hair looked rumpled, as though he'd been shoving a hand through it at regular intervals.

"Jesse," Keegan warned quietly.

Meg stood nearly on tiptoe, her nose almost touching Jesse's, her eyes narrowed to slits. "What the *hell* are you doing here?"

Jesse wasn't about to back down, his stance made that clear, and neither was Meg. Classic McKettrick standoff.

Keegan, used to the family dynamics, and the most diplomatic member of the current generation, eased an arm between them, holding his mug of hot coffee carefully in the other. "To your corners," he said easily, forcing them both to take a step back.

Jesse gave Brad a scathing look—once, they'd been friends—and turned to face Meg again. "I might ask you the same question," he countered. "What the hell are *you* doing here? With *him?*"

Brad cleared his throat, folded his arms. Waited. He looked amused—the expression in his eyes notwithstanding.

"That, Jesse McKettrick," Meg seethed, "is my own business!"

"We came," Keegan interceded, still unruffled but, in his own way, as watchful as Jesse was, "because Cheyenne told us you were up here on horseback. When we got word of the blizzard, we were worried."

Meg threw her arms out, slapped them back against her sides. "Obviously, I'm all right," she said. "Safe and sound."

"I don't know about that," Jesse said, taking Brad's measure again.

A muscle bunched in Brad's jaw, but he didn't speak.

"Get your stuff, if you have any," Jesse told Meg. "We're leaving." He turned to Brad again, added reluctantly, "You'd better come with us. This storm is going to get a lot worse before it gets better."

"Can't leave the horses," Brad said.

Meg was annoyed. Her cousins had landed a helicopter in front of the line shack, in the middle of a blinding whiteout, determined to carry her out bodily if they had to, and all he could think about was the horses?

"I'll stay and ride out with you," Jesse told Brad. Whatever his issues with Brad might be, he was a rancher, born and bred. And a rancher never left a horse stranded, whether it was his own or someone else's, if he had any choice in the matter. His blue eyes sliced to Meg's face. "Keegan will get you back to the Triple M."

"Suppose I don't want to go?"

"Better decide," Keegan put in. "This storm is picking up steam as we speak. Another fifteen or twenty minutes, and the four of us will be bunking in here until spring."

Meg searched Jesse's face, glanced at Brad.

He wasn't going to express an opinion one way or the other, apparently, and that galled her. She knew it wasn't cowardice—Brad had never been afraid of a brawl, with her rowdy cousins or anybody else. Which probably meant he was relieved to get out of a sticky situation.

Color flared in her cheeks.

"I'll get my coat," she said, glaring at Brad. Still hoping he'd stop her, send Jesse and Keegan packing.

But he didn't.

She scrambled into her coat with jamming motions of her fists, and got stuck in the lining of one sleeve.

"Call Olivia," Brad said, watching her struggle, one corner of his mouth tilted slightly upward in a bemused smile. "Let her know I'm okay."

Meg nodded once, angrily, and let Keegan shuffle her out into the impossible cold to the waiting helicopter.

"Smooth," Brad remarked, studying Jesse, shutting the door behind Meg and Keegan and offering a brief, silent prayer for their safety. Flying in this weather was a major risk, but if anybody was up to the job, it was Keegan. His father had been a pilot, and all three of the McKettrick boys were as skilled at the controls of a plane or a copter as they were on the back of a horse.

A little of the air went out of Jesse, but not much. "We'd better ride," he said, "if we're going to make it out of here before dark."

"What'd you think I was going to do, Jesse?" Brad asked evenly, reaching for the poker, opening the stove door to bank the fire. "Rape her?"

Jesse thrust a hand through his hair. "It wasn't that," he said, but grudgingly. "Until we spotted the smoke from the line shack chimney, we thought the two of you might still be out there someplace, in a whole lot of trouble."

"You couldn't have just turned the copter toward the Triple M and left well enough alone?" He hadn't shown it in front of Meg, but Brad was about an inch off Jesse. Meg wasn't a kid, and if she'd needed protection, he would have provided it.

Jesse's eyes shot blue fire. "Maybe Meg's ready to forget what you did to her, but I'm not," he said. "She put on a good show back then, but inside, she was a shipwreck. Especially after the miscarriage."

For Brad, the whole world came to a screeching, spark-throwing stop in the space of an instant.

What miscarriage?

"Uh-oh," Jesse said.

It was literally all Brad could do not to get Jesse by the lapels and drag an answer out of him. He even took a step toward the door, meaning to stop Meg from leaving, but the copter was already lifting off, shaking the shack, setting the horses to fretting again.

"There—was—a baby?"

"Let's go get those horses ready for a hard ride," Jesse said, averting his gaze. Clearly, he'd assumed Meg had told Brad about the child. Now Jesse was the picture of regret.

"Tell me," Brad pressed.

"You'll have to talk to Meg," Jesse answered, putting his hat on again and squaring his shoulders to go back out into the cold and around to the lean-to. "I've already said more than I should have."

"It was mine?"

Jesse reddened. Yanked up the collar of his heavy coat. "*Of course* it was yours," he said indignantly. "Meg's not the type to play that kind of game."

Brad put on his own coat and yanked on some gloves. He felt strangely apart from himself, as though his spirit had somehow gotten out of step with his body.

Meg had been pregnant when he caught that bus to Nashville.

He knew in his bones it was true.

If he'd been anything but a stupid, ambitious kid, he'd have known it then. By the fragile light in her eyes. By the way she'd touched his arm, as if to get his attention so she could say something important, then drawn back, trembling a little.

He'd still have gone to Nashville—he'd had to, to save Stone Creek from the bankers and developers. But he'd have sent for Meg first thing, swallowed his pride whole if he had to, or thumbed it back to Arizona to be with her.

Tentatively, Jesse laid a hand on Brad's shoulder. Withdrew it again.

After securing the line shack as best they could, they left, made their way to the fitful horses, saddled them in silence.

THE ROAR OF the copter's engine and the whipping of the blades made conversation impossible without a headset, and Meg refused to put hers on.

Keegan concentrated on working the controls, keeping a close watch on the instrument panel. The blizzard had intensified; they were literally flying blind.

Presently, though, visibility increased, and Meg relaxed a little.

Keegan must have been watching her out of the corner of his eye, because he reached over and patted her lightly on the arm. Picked up the second headset and nudged her until she took it, put on the earphones, adjusted the mic.

"I can't believe you did this," she said.

Keegan grinned. His voice echoed through the headset. "Rule number one," he said. "Never leave another McKettrick stuck in a blizzard."

Meg huffed out a sigh. "I was perfectly all right!"

"Maybe," Keegan replied, banking to the northwest, in the direction of the Triple M. "But we didn't have any way of knowing that. Switch on your cell phone. You'll find we left at least half a dozen messages on your voice mail, trying to find out if you were okay."

"What if they don't make it out of that storm?" Meg fretted. Before, she'd just been furious. Now, with a little perspective, she was suddenly assailed by worries, on all sides. The fear was worse than the anger. "What if the horses get lost?"

"Brad knows the trail," Keegan assured her, "and Jesse could ride out of hell if he had to. If they don't show up in a few hours, I'll come back looking for them."

"You're not invincible, you know," Meg said tersely. "Even if you *are* a McKettrick."

"I'll do what I have to do," he told her. "Are you and Brad—well—back on?"

"That is patently none of your affair."

Keegan's grin was damnably endearing. "When has that ever stopped me?"

"No," Meg said, beaten. "We are *not* 'back on.' I was just helping him look for Ransom, that's all."

"Ransom? The stallion?"

"Yes."

"He's real?"

"I've seen him with my own eyes."

"You decided to go chasing a wild horse in the middle of a blizzard?"

"It wasn't snowing when we left Stone Creek Ranch," Meg said, feeling defensive.

"Know what I think?"

"No, but I'm afraid you're going to tell me."

Keegan's grin widened, took on a wicked aspect. "You wanted to sleep with Brad. He wanted to sleep with you. And I use the word *sleep* advisedly. Both of you knew snow's a real possibility in the high country, year-round. And there's the old line shack, handy as hell."

"*So* none of your business. And who do you think you are, Dr. Phil?"

Keegan chuckled, shook his head once. "It probably won't help," he told her, "but if we'd known we were interrupting a tryst, we'd have stayed clear."

"We were *playing gin rummy*."

"Whatever."

Meg folded her arms and wriggled deeper into the cold leather seat. "Keegan, I don't have to convince you. And I definitely don't have to explain."

"You're absolutely right. You don't."

By then, they were out of the snow, gliding through a golden autumn afternoon. They passed over the town of Stone Creek, continued in the direction of Indian Rock.

Meg didn't say another word until Keegan set the copter down in the pasture behind her barn, the downdraft making the long grass ripple like an ocean.

"Thanks for the ride," she said tersely, waiting for the blades to slow so she could get out without having her head cut off. "I'd invite you in, but right now, I am seriously pissed off, and the less I see of any of my male relatives, you included, the better."

Keegan cocked a thumb at her. "Got it," he said. "And for the record, I don't give a rat's ass if you're pissed off."

Meg reached across and slugged him in the upper arm, hard, but she laughed a little as she did it. Shook her head. "Goodbye!" she yelled, tossing the headset into his lap.

Keegan signaled her to keep her head down, and watched as she pushed open the door of the copter and leaped to the ground.

Ducking, she headed for the house.

Angus was standing in the kitchen when she let herself in, looking apologetic.

"Thanks a heap for the help," Meg said.

"There's not much I can do with folks who can't see or hear me," Angus replied.

"I get all the luck," Meg answered, pulling off her coat and flinging it in the direction of the hook beside the door.

Angus looked solemn. "You've got trouble," he said.

Meg tensed, instantly alarmed. She'd ridden home from the mountaintop in relative comfort, but the trip would be dangerous on horseback, even for men who'd literally grown up in the saddle. "Jesse and Brad are okay, aren't they?"

"They'll be fine," Angus assured her. "A couple of shots of good whiskey'll fix 'em right up."

"Then what are you talking about?"

"You'll find out soon enough."

"Do you have to be so damned cryptic?"

Angus's grin was reminiscent of Keegan's. "I'm not cryptic," he said. "I can get around just fine."

"Very funny."

He chuckled.

Frazzled, Meg blurted, "First you tell me about your long-lost brother, and how some unknown McKettrick is about to show up. Then you say I've got trouble. Spill it, Angus!"

He sobered. "Jesse let the cat out of the bag. And that's all I'm going to say."

Meg froze. She had only one deep, dark secret, and Jesse couldn't have let it slip because he didn't know what it was.

Did he?

She put one hand to her mouth.

Angus patted her shoulder. "You'd better go out to the barn and feed the horses early. You might be too busy later on."

Meg stared at her ancestor. "Angus McKettrick—"

He vanished.

Typical man.

Meg placed the promised call to Olivia O'Ballivan, got her voice mail and left a message. Next, she started a pot of coffee, then picked her coat up off the floor, put it back on and went out to tend to the livestock.

The work helped to ease her anxiety, but not all that much.

All the while, she was wondering if Jesse had found out about the baby somehow, if he'd told Brad.

You've got trouble, Angus had said, and the words echoed in her mind.

She finished her chores and returned to the house, shedding her coat again and washing her hands at the sink before pouring herself a mug of fresh coffee. She considered lacing it with a generous dollop of Jack Daniel's, to get the chill out of her bones, then shoved the bottle back in the cupboard, unopened.

If Jesse and Brad didn't get home, Keegan wouldn't be the only one to go out looking for them.

She reached for the telephone, dialed Cheyenne's cell number.

"I'm sorry," Cheyenne said immediately, not bothering with a hello. "When I passed your message on to Jesse, about checking on your horses if you didn't call before nightfall, he wanted to know where you'd gone." She paused. "And I told him."

Meg pressed the back of one hand to her forehead

and closed her eyes for a moment. If a certain pair of stubborn cowboys got lost in that blizzard, or if Jesse had, as Angus put it, "let the cat out of the bag," the embarrassing scene at the line shack would be the least of her problems.

"There's a big storm in the high country," she said quietly, "and Jesse and Brad are on horseback. Let me know when Jesse gets back, will you?"

Cheyenne drew in an audible breath. "Oh, my God," she whispered. "They're riding in a *blizzard?*"

"Jesse can handle it," Meg said. "And so can Brad. Just the same, I'll rest easier when I know they're home."

Cheyenne didn't answer for a long time. "I'll call," she promised, but she sounded distracted. No doubt she was thinking the same thing Meg was, that it had been reckless enough, flying into a snowstorm in a helicopter. Taking a treacherous trail down off the mountain was even worse.

Meg spoke a few reassuring words, though they sounded hollow even to her, and she and Cheyenne said goodbye.

At loose ends, Meg took her coffee to the study at the front of the house and logged onto the computer. Ran a search on the name Josiah McKettrick, though her mind wasn't on genealogical detective work, and she started over a dozen times.

In the kitchen, she heated a can of soup and ate it mechanically, never tasting a bite. After that, she read for a couple of hours, then she took a long, hot bath, put on clean sweats and padded downstairs again, thinking she'd watch some television. She was trying to focus on a rerun of *Dog the Bounty Hunter* when she heard a car door slam outside.

Boot heels thundered up the front steps.

And then a fist hammered at the heavy wooden door.

"Meg!" Brad yelled. "Open up! *Now!*"

CHAPTER SEVEN

BRAD LOOKED CRAZED, standing there on Meg's doorstep. She moved to step out of his way, but before she could, he advanced on her, backing her into the entryway. Kicking the door shut behind him with a hard motion of one foot.

He hadn't stopped to change clothes after the long, cold ride down out of the hills, and he was soaked to the skin. He'd lost his gloves somewhere, and there was a faintly bluish cast to his taut lips.

"Why didn't you tell me about the baby?" he demanded, shaking an index finger under Meg's nose when she collided with the wall behind her, next to Holt and Lorelei's grandfather clock. The ponderous tick-tock seemed to reverberate throughout the known universe.

Meg's worst fears were confirmed in that moment. Jesse *had* known about her pregnancy and subsequent miscarriage—and he'd let it slip to Brad.

"Calm down," she said, recovering a little.

Brad gripped her shoulders. If he'd been anyone other than exactly who he was, Meg might have feared for her safety. But this was Brad O'Ballivan. Sure, he'd crushed her heart, but he wasn't going to hurt her physically, she knew that. It was one of the few absolutes.

"Was there a child?"

Meg bit her lower lip. She'd always known she'd have to tell him if they crossed paths again, but she hadn't wanted it to be like this. "Yes," she whispered, that one word scraping her throat raw.

"My baby?"

She felt a sting of indignation, hot as venom, but it passed quickly. "Yes."

"Why didn't you tell me?"

Meg straightened her spine, lifted her chin a notch. "You were in Nashville," she said. "You didn't write. You didn't call. I guess I didn't think you'd be interested."

The blue fury in Brad's eyes dulled visibly; he let go of her shoulders, but didn't step back. She felt cornered, overshadowed—but still not threatened. Oddly, it was more like being shielded, even protected.

He shoved a hand through his hair. "How could I not be interested, Meg?" he rasped bleakly. "You were carrying our baby."

Slowly, Meg put her palms to his cheeks. "I miscarried a few weeks after you left," she said gently. "It wasn't meant to be."

Moisture glinted in his eyes, and that familiar muscle bunched just above his jawline. "Still—"

"Go upstairs and take a hot shower," Meg told him. "I'll fix you something to eat, and we'll talk."

Brad tensed again, then relaxed, though only slightly. Nodded.

"Travis left some clothes behind when he and Sierra moved to town," she went on, when he didn't speak. "I'll get them for you."

With that, she led the way up the stairs, along the hallway to the main bathroom. After pushing the door open and waiting for Brad to enter, she went on to the master bedroom, pulled an old pair of jeans and a long-sleeved T-shirt from a bureau drawer.

Brad was already in the shower when she returned, naked behind the steamy glass door, but clearly visible.

Swallowing a rush of lust, Meg set the folded garments on the lid of the toilet seat, placed a folded towel on top of them and slipped out.

She was cooking scrambled eggs when Brad came down the back stairs fifteen minutes later, barefoot, his hair towel-rumpled, wearing Travis's clothes. Without comment, Meg poured a cup of fresh coffee and held it out to him.

He took it, after a moment's hesitation, and sipped cautiously.

Meg was relieved to see that the hot shower had restored his normal color. Before, he'd been ominously pale.

"Sit down," she said quietly.

He pulled out Holt's chair and sat, watching her as she turned to the stove again. Even with her back turned to him, she could feel his gaze boring into the space between her shoulder blades.

"What happened?" he asked, after a few moments.

She looked back at him briefly before scraping the eggs onto a waiting plate. Didn't speak.

"The miscarriage," he prompted grimly. "What made it happen?"

With a pang, Meg realized he thought it might have been his fault somehow, her losing their baby. Because he'd gone to Nashville, or because of the fight they'd had before he left.

She'd suffered her own share of guilt over the years,

wondering if she could have done something differently, prevented the tragedy. She didn't want Brad to go through the same agony.

"There was no specific incident," she said softly. "I was pregnant, and then I wasn't. It happens, Brad. And it's not always possible to know why."

Brad absorbed that, took another sip of his coffee. "You should have told me."

"I didn't tell anyone," Meg said. "Not even my mother."

"Then how did Jesse know?"

Now that she'd had time to think, the answer was obvious. Jesse had been the one to take her to the hospital that long-ago night. She'd told him it was just a bad case of cramps, but he'd either put two and two together on his own or overheard the nurses and doctors talking.

"He was with me," she said.

"He was, and I *wasn't*," Brad answered.

She set the plate of scrambled eggs in front of him, along with two slices of buttered toast and some silverware. "It wouldn't have changed anything," she said. "Your being there, I mean. I'd still have lost the baby, Brad."

He closed his eyes briefly, like someone taking a hard punch to the solar plexus, determined not to fight back.

"You should have told me," he insisted.

She gave the plate a little push toward him and, reluctantly, he picked up his fork, began to eat. "We've been over that," she said, sitting down on the bench next to the table, angled to face Brad. "What good would it have done?"

"I could have—helped."

"How?"

He sighed. "You went through it alone. That isn't right."

"Lots of things aren't 'right' in this world," Meg reasoned quietly. "A person just has to—cope."

"The McKettrick way," Brad said without admiration. "Some people would call that being bullheaded, not coping."

She propped an elbow on the tabletop, cupped her chin in her hand, and watched as he continued to down the scrambled eggs. "I'd do the same thing all over again," she confessed. "It was hard, but I toughed it out."

"Alone."

"Alone," Meg agreed.

"It must have been a lot worse than 'hard.' You were only nineteen."

"So were you," she said.

"Why didn't you tell your mother?"

Meg didn't have to reflect on that one. From the day Hank Breslin had snatched Sierra and vanished, Eve had been hit by problem after problem—a serious accident, in which she'd been severely injured, subsequent addictions to painkillers and alcohol, all the challenges of steering McKettrickCo through a lot of corporate white water.

"She'd been through enough," she replied simply. Brad's question had been rhetorical—he'd known the McKettrick history all along.

"She'd have strung me up by my thumbs," Brad said. And though he tried to smile, he didn't quite make it. He was still in shock.

"Probably," Meg said.

He'd finished the food, shoved his plate away. "Where do we go from here?" he asked.

"I don't know," she said. "Maybe nowhere."

He moved to take her hand, but withdrew just short of touching her. Scraped back his chair to stand and carry the remains of his meal to the sink. Set the plate and silverware down with a thunk.

"Was our baby a boy or a girl?" he asked gruffly, standing with his back to her.

She saw the tension in his broad shoulders as he awaited her answer. "I didn't ask," she said. "I guess I didn't want to know. And it was probably too early to tell, anyway. I was only a few weeks into the pregnancy."

He turned, at last, to face her, but kept his distance, leaning back against the counter, folding his arms. "Do you ever think about what it would be like if he or she had survived?"

All the time, she thought.

"No," she lied.

"Right," he said, clearly not believing her.

"I'm—I'm sorry, Brad. That you had to find out from someone else, I mean."

"But not for deceiving me in the first place?"

Meg bristled. "I didn't deceive you."

"What do you call it?"

"You were *gone.* You had things to do. If I'd dragged you back here, you wouldn't have gotten your big chance. You would have hated me for that."

At last, he crossed to her, took her chin in his hand. "I couldn't hate you, Meg," he said gravely, choking a little on the words. "Not ever."

For a few moments, they just stared at each other in silence.

Brad was the first to speak again. "I'd better get back to the ranch." Another rueful attempt at a grin. "It's been a bitch of a day."

"Stay," Meg heard herself say. She wasn't thinking of leading Brad to her bed—not *exclusively* of that, anyhow. He'd just ridden miles through a blizzard on horseback, he'd taken a chill in the process, and the knowledge that he'd fathered a child was painfully new.

He was silent, perhaps at a loss.

"You shouldn't be alone," Meg said. *And neither should I.*

She knew what would happen if he stayed, of course. And she knew it was likely to be a mistake. They'd become strangers to each other over the years apart, living such different lives. It was too soon to run where angels feared to tread.

But she needed him that night, needed him to hold her, if nothing else.

And his need was just as great.

He grinned, though wanly. "How do we know your cousins won't land on the roof in a helicopter?" he asked.

"We don't," Meg said, and sighed. "They meant well, you know."

"Sure they did," he agreed wryly. "They were out to save your virtue."

Meg stood, went to Brad, slipped her arms around his middle. It seemed such a natural thing to do, and yet, at the same time, it was a breathtaking risk. "Stay," she said again.

He held her a little closer, propped his chin on top

of her head. Stroked the length of her back with his hands. "Those who don't learn from history," he said, "are condemned to repeat it."

Meg rested her head against his shoulder, breathed in the scent of him. Felt herself softening against the hard heat of his body.

And the telephone rang.

"It might be important," Brad said, setting Meg away from him a little, when she didn't jump to answer.

She picked up without checking the ID panel. "Hello."

"Jesse's home," Cheyenne said, honoring her earlier promise to let Meg know when he returned. "He's half-frozen. I poured a hot toddy down him and put him to bed."

"Thanks for calling, Chey," Meg replied.

"You're all right?" Cheyenne asked shyly.

Wondering how much Jesse had told his wife when he got home, Meg replied that she was fine.

"He told me he and Keegan barged in on you and Brad, up in the mountains somewhere," Cheyenne went on. "I'm sorry, Meg. Maybe I should have kept my mouth shut, but I heard a report of the blizzard on the radio and I—well—I guess I panicked a little."

"Everything's all right, Cheyenne. Really."

"He's there, isn't he? Brad, I mean. He's with you, right now."

"Since I'd rather not have a midnight visit from my cousins," Meg said, "I'm admitting nothing."

Cheyenne giggled. "My lips are zipped. Want to have lunch tomorrow?"

"That sounds good," Meg answered, smiling. Brad

was standing behind her by then, sliding his hands under the front of her sweatshirt, stopping just short of her bare breasts. She fought to keep her voice even, her breathing normal. "Good night, Cheyenne."

"I'll meet you in town, at Lucky's Bar and Grill at noon," Cheyenne said. "Call me if you're still in bed or anything like that, and we'll reschedule."

Brad tweaked lightly at Meg's nipples; she swallowed a gasp of pleasure. "See you there," she replied, and hung up quickly.

Brad turned Meg around, gave her a knee-melting kiss and then swept her up into his arms. Carried her to the back stairs.

She directed him to the very bed Holt and Lorelei had shared as man and wife.

He laid her down on the deep, cushy mattress, a shadow figure rimmed in light from the hallway behind him. She couldn't see his face, but she felt his gaze on her, gentle and hungry and so hot it seared her.

Afraid honor might get the better of him, Meg wriggled out of her sweatpants, pulled the top off over her head. Planning to sleep in the well-worn favorites, she hadn't bothered to put on a bra and panties after her bath earlier. Now she was completely naked. Utterly vulnerable.

Brad made a low, barely audible sound, rested one knee on the mattress beside her.

"Hold me," she whispered, and traces of an old song ran through her mind.

Help me make it through the night...

He stripped, maneuvered Meg so she was under the covers and joined her. The feel of him against her, solid and warm and all man, sent an electric rush of dizziness through her, pervading every cell.

She wrapped her arms around his neck and clung—she who never allowed herself to cling to anyone or anything except her own fierce pride.

A long, delicious time passed, without words, without caresses—only the holding.

The decision that there would be no foreplay was a tacit one.

The wanting was too great.

Brad nudged Meg's legs apart gently, settled between them, his erection pressing against her lower belly like a length of steel, heated in a forge.

She moaned and arched her back slightly, seeking him.

He took her with a single long, slow, smooth stroke, nestling into her depths. Held himself still as she gasped in wordless welcome.

He kissed her eyelids.

She squirmed beneath him.

He kissed her cheekbones.

Craving friction, desperate for it, Meg tried to move her hips, but he had her pinned, heavily, delectably, to the bed.

She whimpered.

He nibbled at her earlobes, one and then the other.

She ran her hands urgently up and down his back.

He tasted her neck.

She pleaded.

He withdrew, thrust again, but slowly.

She said his name.

He plunged deep.

And Meg came apart in his arms, raising herself

high. Clawing, now at his back, now at the bedclothes, surrendering with a long, continuous, keening moan.

The climax was ferocious, but it was only a prelude to what would follow, and knowing that only increased Meg's need. Her body merged with Brad's, fused to it at the most elemental level, and the instant he began to move upon her she was lost again.

Even as she exploded, like a shattering star, she was aware of his phenomenal self-control, but when she reached her peak, he gave in. She reveled in the flex of his powerful body, the ragged, half groan, half shout of his release. Felt the warmth of his seed spilling inside her—and prayed it would take root.

Finally, he collapsed beside her, his face buried between her neck and the curve of her shoulder, his arms and legs still clenched around her, loosening by small, nearly imperceptible shivers.

Instinctively, Meg tilted her pelvis slightly backward, cradling the warmth.

A long while later, when both their breathing had returned to normal, or some semblance of that, Brad lifted his head. Touched his nose to hers. Started to speak, then thrust out a sigh, instead.

Meg threaded her fingers through his hair. Turned her head so she could kiss his chin.

"Guess you just earned another notch for the bedpost," she said.

He chuckled. "Yeah," he said. "Except this is *your* bed, McKettrick. *You* seduced *me.* I want that on record. Either way, since it's obviously an antique, carving the thing up probably wouldn't be the best idea."

"We're going to regret this in the morning, you know," she told him.

"That's then," he murmured, nibbling at her neck again. "This is now."

"Um-hmm," Meg said. She wanted *now* to last forever.

"I kept expecting a helicopter."

Meg laughed. "Me, too."

Brad lifted his head again, and in the moonlight she could see the smile in his eyes. "Know what?"

"What?"

"I'm glad it happened this way. In a real bed, and not the floor of some old line shack." He kissed her, very lightly. "Although I would have settled for anything I could get."

She pretended to slug him.

He laughed.

She felt him hardening against her, pressed against the outside of her right thigh. Stretching, he found the switch on the bedside lamp and turned it, spilling light over her. The glow of it seemed to seep into her skin, golden. Or was it the other way around? Was *she* the one shining, instead of the lamp?

"God," Brad whispered, "you *are* beautiful."

A tigress before, now Meg felt shy. Turned her head to one side, closed her eyes.

Brad caressed her breasts, her stomach and abdomen and the tops of her thighs; his touch so light, so gentle, that it made her breath catch in her throat.

"Look at me," he said.

She met his eyes. "The light," she protested weakly.

He slid his fingers between the moist curls at the juncture of her thighs. "So beautiful," he said.

She gasped as he made slow, sweet circles, deliberately exciting her. "Brad—"

"What?"

She was conscious of the softness of her belly; knew her breasts weren't as firm and high as he remembered. She wanted more of his lovemaking, and still more, but under the cover of darkness and finely woven sheets and the heirloom quilt Lorelei McKettrick had stitched with her own hands, so many years before. "The *light*."

He made no move to flip the switch off again, but continued to stroke her, watching her responses. When he slipped his fingers inside her, found her G-spot and plied it expertly, she stopped worrying about the light and became a part of it.

WHILE MEG SLEPT, Brad slipped out of bed, pulled his borrowed clothes back on and retrieved his own from the bathroom where he'd showered earlier. Sat on the edge of the big claw-foot bathtub to pull on his socks and boots, still damp from his ride down the mountainside with Jesse.

Downstairs, he found the old-fashioned thermostat and turned it up. Dusty heat whooshed from the vents. In the kitchen he switched on the lights, filled and set the coffeemaker. Maybe these small courtesies would make up for his leaving before Meg woke up.

He found a pencil and a memo pad over by the phone, planning to scribble a note, but nothing suitable came to mind, at least not right away.

"Thanks" would be inappropriate.

"Goodbye" sounded too blunt.

Only a jerk would write "See you around."

"I'll call you later"? Too cavalier.

Finally, he settled on, "Horses to feed."

Four of his songs had won Grammies, and all he

could come up with was "horses to feed"? He was slipping.

He paused, stood looking up at the ceiling for a few moments, wanting nothing so much as to go back upstairs, crawl in bed with Meg again and make love to her.

Again.

But she'd said they were going to have regrets in the morning, and he didn't want to see those regrets on her face. The two of them would make bumbling excuses, never quite meeting each other's eyes.

And Brad knew he couldn't handle that.

So he left.

MEG STOOD IN her warm kitchen, bundled in a terry-cloth bathrobe and surrounded by the aroma of freshly brewed coffee, peering at the note Brad had left.

Horses to feed.

"The man's a poet," she said out loud.

"Do you think it took?" Angus asked.

Meg whirled to find him standing just behind her, almost at her elbow. "You scared me!" she accused, one hand pressed to her heart, which felt as though it might scramble up her esophagus to the back of her throat.

"Sorry," Angus said, though there was nothing the least bit contrite about his tone or his expression.

"Do I think *what* took?" Meg had barely sputtered the words when the awful realization struck her: Angus was asking if she thought she'd gotten pregnant, which meant—

Oh, God.

"Tell me you weren't here!"

"What do you take me for?" Angus snapped. "Of *course* I wasn't!"

Meg swallowed. Flushed to the roots of her hair. "But you knew—"

"I saw that singing cowboy leave just before sunup," came the taciturn reply. Now Angus was blushing, too. "Wasn't too hard to guess the rest."

"Will you stop calling him 'that singing cowboy'? He has a name. It's Brad O'Ballivan."

"I know that," Angus said. "But he's a fair hand with a horse, and he croons a decent tune. To my way of thinking, that makes him a singing cowboy."

Meg gave him a look, padded to the refrigerator, jerked open the door and rummaged around for something that might constitute breakfast. She'd cooked the last of the eggs for Brad, and the remaining choices were severely limited. Three green olives floating in a jar, some withered cheese, the arthritic remains of last week's takeout pizza and a carton of baking soda.

"Food doesn't just appear in an icebox, you know," Angus announced. "In my day, you had to hunt it down, or grow it in a garden, or harvest it from a field."

"Yes, and you probably walked ten miles to and from school," Meg said irritably, "uphill both ways."

She was starving. She'd have to hit the drive-through in town, then pick up some groceries. All that before her lunch with Cheyenne.

"I never went to school," Angus replied seriously, not getting the joke. "My ma taught me to read from the Good Book. I learned the rest on my own."

Meg sighed as an answer, shoved the splayed fingers of one hand through her tangled hair. Although she'd been disappointed at first to wake up and find

Brad gone, now she was glad he couldn't see her. She looked like—well—a woman who had been having howling, sweaty-sheet sex half the night.

She started for the stairs.

"Make yourself at home," she told Angus, wondering if he'd catch the irony in her tone. For him, "home" was the Great Beyond, or the main ranch house down by the creek.

When she came down again half an hour later, showered and dressed in jeans and a lightweight blue sweater, he was sitting in Holt's chair, waiting for her.

"You ever think about wearing a dress or a skirt?" he asked, frowning.

Meg let that pass. "I've got some errands to run. See you later."

The telephone rang.

Brad?

She checked the caller ID panel.

Her mother.

"Voice mail will pick up," she told Angus.

"Answer it," Angus said sternly.

Meg reached for the receiver. "Hello, Mom. I was just on my way out the door—"

"You'd better sit down," Eve told her.

The pit of Meg's stomach pitched. "Why? Mom, is Sierra all right? Nothing's happened to Liam—"

"Both of them are fine. It's nothing like that."

Meg let out her breath. Leaned against the kitchen counter for support. "What, then?"

"Your father contacted me this morning. He wants to see you."

Meg's knees almost gave out. She'd never met her father, never spoken to him on the telephone or received so much as a birthday or Christmas card from him. She wasn't even sure what his name was—he used so many aliases.

"Meg?"

"I'm here," Meg said. "I don't want to see him."

"I knew I should have talked to you in person," Eve sighed. "But I was so alarmed—"

"Mother, did you hear what I just said? I don't want to see my father."

"He claims he's dying."

"Well, I'm sincerely sorry to hear that, but I still don't want anything to do with him."

"Meg—"

"I mean it, Mother. He's been a nonentity in my life. What could he possibly have to say to me now, after all this time?"

"I don't know," Eve replied.

"And if he wanted to talk to me, why did he call you?" The moment the question left her mouth, Meg wished she hadn't asked it.

"I think he's afraid."

"But he wasn't afraid of you?"

"He's past that, I think," Eve said. She'd been downright secretive on the subject of Meg's father from the first. Now, suddenly, she seemed to be urging Meg to make contact with him. What was going on? "Listen, why don't you stop by the hotel, and I'll make you some breakfast. We'll talk."

"Mom—"

"Blueberry pancakes. Maple-cured bacon. Your favorites."

"All right," Meg said, because as shaken as she was,

she could have eaten the proverbial horse. "I'll be there in twenty minutes."

"Good," Eve replied, a little smugly, Meg thought. She was used to getting her way. After all, for almost thirty years, when Eve McKettrick said "jump," everybody reached for a vaulting pole.

"Are you going to ride shotgun?" Meg asked Angus after she'd hung up.

"I wouldn't miss this for anything," Angus said with relish.

Less than half an hour later, Meg was knocking on the front door of her mother's hotel suite.

When it opened, a man stood looking down at her, his expression uncertain and at the same time hopeful. She saw her own features reflected in the shape of his face, the set of his shoulders, the curve of his mouth.

"Hello, Meg," said her long-lost father.

CHAPTER EIGHT

AFTER THE HORSES had been fed, Brad turned them out to pasture for the day and made his way not into the big, lonely house, but to the copse of trees where Big John was buried. The old man's simple marker looked painfully new, amid the chipped and moss-covered stone crosses marking the graves of other, earlier O'Ballivans and Blackstones.

Brad had meant to visit the small private cemetery first thing, but between one thing and another, he hadn't managed it until now.

Standing there, in the shade of trees already shedding gold and crimson and rust-colored leaves, he moved to take off his hat, remembered that he wasn't wearing one and crouched to brush a scattering of fallen foliage from the now-sunken mound.

About time you showed up, he heard Big John O'Ballivan's booming voice observe, echoing through the channels of his mind.

Brad gave a lopsided, rueful grin. His eyes smarted, so he blinked a couple of times. "I'm here, old man," he answered hoarsely. "And I mean to stay. Look after the girls and the place. That ought to make you happy."

There was no reply from his grandfather, not even in his head.

But Brad felt like talking, so he did.

"I'm seeing Meg McKettrick again," he said. "Turns out I got her pregnant, back when we were kids, and she lost the baby. I never knew about it until yesterday."

Had Big John been there in the flesh, there'd have been a lecture coming. Brad would have welcomed that, even though the old man could peel off a strip of hide when he was riled.

One more reason why you should have stayed here and attended to business, Big John would have said. And that would have been just the warm-up.

"You never understood," Brad went on, just as if the old man *had* spoken. "We were going to lose Stone Creek Ranch. Maybe you weren't able to face that, but I had to. Everything Sam and Maddie and the ones who came after did to hold on to this place would have been for nothing."

The McKettricks would have stepped in if he'd asked for help, Brad knew that. Meg herself, probably her mother, too. Contrary as that Triple M bunch was, they'd bailed more than one neighbor out of financial trouble, saved dozens of smaller farms and ranches when beef prices bottomed out and things got tough. Even after all this time, though, the thought of going to them with his hat in his hands made the back of Brad's throat scald.

Although the ground was hard, wet and cold, he sat, cross-legged, gazing upon his grandfather's grave through a misty haze. He'd paid a high price for his pride, big, fancy career notwithstanding.

He'd lost the years he might have spent with Meg, the other children that might have come along. He hadn't been around when Big John needed him, and his sisters, though they were all educated, independent women, had been mere girls when he left. Sure, Big John had loved and protected them, in his gruff way, but that didn't excuse *his* absence. He should have been their big brother.

Caught up in these thoughts, and all the emotions they engendered, Brad heard the approaching rig, but didn't look around. Heard the engine shut off, the door slam.

"Hey," Olivia said softly from just behind him.

"Hey," he replied, not ready to look back and meet his sister's gaze.

"Willie's better. I've got him in the truck."

Brad blinked again. "That's good," he said. "Guess I'd better go to town and get him some dog food and stuff."

"I brought everything he needs," Livie said, her voice quiet. She came and sat down beside Brad. "Missing Big John?"

"Every day," Brad admitted. Their mother had hit the road when the twins were barely walking, and their dad had died a year later, herding spooked cattle in a lightning storm. Big John had stepped up to raise four young grandchildren without a word of complaint.

"Me, too," Livie replied softly. "You ever wonder where our mom ended up?"

Brad knew where Della O'Ballivan was—living in a trailer park outside of Independence, Missouri, with the latest in a long line of drunken boyfriends—but he'd never shared that information with his sisters. The story, brought to him by the private detective he'd hired on the proceeds from his first hit record, wasn't a pretty one.

"No," he said in all honesty. "I never wonder." He'd

gone to see Della, once he'd learned her whereabouts. She'd been sloshed and more interested in his stardom, and how it might benefit her, than getting to know him. Ironically, she'd refused the help he *had* offered—immediate admission to one of the best treatment centers in the world—standing there in a tattered housecoat and scruffy slippers, with lipstick stains in the deep smoker's lines surrounding her mouth. She hadn't even asked about her daughters or the husband she'd left behind.

"She's probably dead," Livie said with a sigh.

Since Della's existence couldn't be called living, Brad agreed. "Probably," he replied. Except for periodic requests for a check, which were handled by his accountant, Brad never heard from their mother.

"It's why I don't want to get married, you know," Livie confided. "Because I might be like her. Just get on a bus one day and leave."

Just get on a bus one day and leave.

Like he'd done to Meg, Brad reflected, hurting. Maybe he was more like Della than he'd ever want to admit aloud.

"You'd never do that," he told his sister.

"I used to think she'd come home," Livie went on sadly. "To see me play Mary in the Christmas program at church, or when I got that award for my 4-H project, back in sixth grade."

Brad slipped an arm around Livie's shoulders, felt them trembling a little, squeezed. His reaction had been different from Livie's—if Della had come back, especially after their dad was killed, he'd have spit in her face.

"And you figure if you got married and had kids,

you'd just up and leave them? Miss all the Christmas plays and the 4-H projects?"

"I remember her, Brad," Livie said. "Just the lilac smell of her, and that she was pretty, but I remember. She used to sing a lot, hanging clothes out on the line and things like that. She read me stories. And then she was—well—just *gone*. I could never make sense of it. I always figured I must have done something really bad—"

"The flaw was in her, Livie, not you."

"That's the thing about flaws like that. You never know where they're going to show up. Mom probably didn't expect to abandon us."

Brad didn't agree, but he couldn't say so without revealing way too much. The Della he knew was an unmedicated bipolar with a penchant for gin, light on the tonic water. She'd probably married Jim O'Ballivan on a manic high, and decided to hit the road on a low—or vice versa. It was a miracle, by Brad's calculations, that she'd stayed on Stone Creek Ranch as long as she had, far from the bright lights and big-town bars, where a practicing drunk might enjoy a degree of anonymity.

Coupled with things Big John had said about his daughter-in-law, "man to man" and in strictest confidence, that she'd hidden bottles around the place and slept with ranch hands when there were any around, Brad had few illusions about her morals.

Livie got to her feet, dusting off her jeans as she rose, and Brad immediately did the same.

"I'd better get Willie settled in," she said. "I've got a barn full of sick cows to see to, down the road at the Iversons' place."

"Anything serious?" Brad asked, as Livie headed

for the Suburban parked next to his truck, and he kept pace. "The cows, I mean?"

"Some kind of a fever," Livie answered, looking worried. "I drew some random blood samples the last time I was there, and sent them to the university lab in Tempe for analysis. Nothing anybody's ever seen before."

"Contagious?"

Livie sighed. Her small shoulders slumped a little, under the weight of her life's calling, and not for the first time, Brad wished she'd gone into a less stressful occupation than veterinary medicine.

"Possibly," she said.

Brad waited politely until she'd climbed into the Suburban—Willie was curled comfortably in the backseat, in a nest of old blankets—then got behind the wheel of his truck to follow her to the house.

There, he was annoyed to see a black stretch limo waiting, motor purring.

Phil.

Muttering a curse, Brad did his best to ignore the obvious, got out of the truck and strode to Livie's Suburban to hoist Willie out of the backseat and carry him into the house. Livie was on his heels, arms full of rudimentary dog equipment, but she cast a few curious glances toward the stretch.

They entered through the kitchen door. Olivia set the dog bed down in a sunny corner, and Brad carefully lowered Willie onto it.

"Who's in the big car?" Livie asked.

"Probably Phil Meadowbrook," Brad said a little tersely.

"Your manager?" Livie's eyes were wary. She was

probably thinking Phil would make an offer Brad couldn't refuse, and he'd leave again.

"*Former* manager."

Willie, his hide crisscrossed with pink shaved strips and stitches, looked up at Brad with luminous, trusting eyes.

Livie was watching him, too. There was something bruised about her expression. She knew him better than Willie did.

"We need you around, Brad," she said at great cost to her pride. "Not just the twins and me, but the whole community. If the Iversons have to put down all those cows, they'll go under. They're already in debt up to their eyeballs—last year, Mrs. Iverson had a bout with breast cancer, and they didn't have insurance."

Brad's jaw tightened, and so did the pit of his stomach. "I'll write a check," he said.

Livie caught hold of his forearm. *"No,"* she said with a vehemence that set him back on his heels a little. "That would make them feel like charity cases. They're good, decent people, Brad."

"Then what do you want me to do?" Half Brad's attention was on the conversation, the other half on the distant closing of the limo door, so he'd probably sounded abrupt.

"Put on a concert," Livie said. "There are half a dozen other families around Stone Creek in similar situations. Divvy up the proceeds, and that will spare everybody's dignity."

Brad frowned down at his sister. "How long has *that* plan been brewing in your busy little head, Dr. Livie?"

She smiled. "Ever since you raised all that money

for the animals displaced during Hurricane Katrina," she said.

A knock sounded at the outside door.

Phil's big schnoz was pressed to the screen.

"Gotta go," Livie said. She squatted to give Willie a goodbye pat and ducked out of the kitchen, headed for the front.

"Can I come in?" Phil asked plaintively.

"Would it make a difference if I said no?" Brad shot back.

The screen door creaked open. "Of course not," Phil said, smiling broadly. "I came all the way from New Jersey to talk some sense into your head."

"I could have saved you the trip," Brad answered. "I'm not going to Vegas. I'm not going *anywhere*." He liked Phil, but after the events of the past twenty-four hours, he was something the worse for wear. With his chores done and the overdue visit to Big John's grave behind him, he'd planned to eat something, take a hot shower and fall face-first into his unmade bed.

"Who said anything about Vegas?" Phil asked, the picture of innocent affront. "Maybe I want to deliver a big fat royalty check or something like that."

"And maybe you're full of crap," Brad countered. "I just *got* a 'big, fat royalty check,' according to my accountant. He's fit to be tied because the recording company promised to parcel the money out over at least fifteen years, and it came in a lump sum instead. Says the taxes are going to eat me alive."

Phil sniffled, pretended to wipe tears from his eyes. "Cry me a river, Mr. Country Music," he said. "I belong to the you-can-never-be-too-rich school of thought. Until my niece suffered that bout with anorexia—thank

God she recovered—I thought you could never be too thin, either, but that theory's down the swirler."

Brad said nothing.

"What happened to that dog?" Phil asked, after giving Willie the eyeball.

"He was attacked by coyotes—or maybe wolves."

Livie had lugged in a bag of kibble and a couple of bowls, along with the bed Willie was lounging on now, and she'd set two prescription bottles on the counter, too, though Brad hadn't noticed them until now. He busied himself with reading the labels.

"Why anybody'd want to live in a place where a thing like that is even remotely possible, even if he *is* a dog," Phil marveled, "is beyond me."

Willie was to have one of each pill—an antibiotic and a painkiller—morning and night. With food.

"A lot of things are beyond you, Phil," Brad said, figuring Olivia must have dosed the dog that morning before leaving the clinic, which meant the medication could wait until suppertime.

"He's pretty torn up. Wouldn't have happened in Music City, to a dog *or* a man."

"Evidently," Brad said, still distracted, "you've repressed the gory memories of my second divorce."

Phil chuckled. "You could give all that extra royalty money you're so worried about to good ole Cynthia," he suggested. "Write it off as an extra settlement and let *her* worry about the taxes."

"You're just full of wisdom today. Something else, too."

Uninvited, Phil drew back a chair at the table and sank into it, one hand pressed dramatically to his heart.

"Phew," he sighed. "The old ticker ain't what it used to be."

"Right," Brad said. "I was there for the celebration after your last cardiology workup, remember? You probably have a better heart than I do, so spare me the sympathy plays."

"You have a heart?" Phil countered, raising his bushy gray eyebrows almost to his thinning hairline. Even with plugs, the carpet looked pretty sparse. Phil's pate always reminded Brad of the dolls his sisters had had when they were little, sprouting shocks of hair out of holes in neat little rows. "Couldn't prove it by me."

"Whatever," Brad said, dipping one of Willie's bowls into the kibble bag, then setting it down, full, where the dog could reach it without getting off his bed. He followed up by filling the other bowl with tap water. Then, on second thought, he dumped that and poured the bottled kind, instead.

"This is something big," Phil said. "That's why I came in person."

"If I let you tell me, will you leave?" By then, Brad was plundering the fridge for the makings of breakfast.

"Got any kosher sausage in there?" the older man asked.

"Sorry," Brad answered. He'd come up with something if Phil stayed, since he couldn't eat in front of the man, but he was still hoping for a speedy departure.

Next, he'd be hanging up a stocking on Christmas Eve, setting out an empty basket the night before Easter.

"Big opportunity," Phil continued. "Very, very big."

"I don't care."

"You don't care? This is a *movie*, Brad. The lead.

A *feature,* too. A big Western with cattle and wagons and a cast of dozens. And you won't even have to sing."

"No."

"Two years ago, even a year ago, you would have *killed* for a chance like this!"

"That was then," Brad said, flashing back to the night before, when he'd said practically the same thing to Meg, "and this is now."

"I've got the script in the car. In my briefcase. Solid gold, Brad. It might even be Oscar material."

"Phil," Brad said, turning from the fridge with the makings of a serious omelet in his hands, "what part of 'no' is eluding you? Would it be the *N,* or the *O?*"

"But you'd get to play an *outlaw,* trying to go straight."

"Phil."

"You're really serious about this retirement thing, aren't you?" Phil sounded stunned. Aggrieved. And petulant. "In a year—hell, in *six months*—when you've got all this down-home stuff out of your system, you'll wish you'd listened to me!"

"I listened, Phil. Do you want an omelet?"

"Do I *want an omelet?* Hell, no! I want you to make a damned *movie!*"

"Not gonna happen, Phil."

Phil was suddenly super-alert, like a predator who's just spotted dinner on the hoof. "It's some woman, isn't it?"

Again, he flashed on Meg. The way she'd felt, silky and slick, against him. The way she'd scratched at his back and called his name…

"Maybe," he admitted.

"Do I need to remind you that your romantic history isn't exactly going to inspire a new line of Hallmark valentines?"

Brad sighed. Got out the skillet and set it on the stove. Willie gave him a sidelong look of commiseration from the dog bed.

"If you won't eat an omelet," Brad told Phil, "leave."

"That pretty little thing who sneaked out of here when I came to the door—was that her?"

"That was my sister," Brad said.

Phil raised himself laboriously to his feet, like he was ninety-seven instead of seventy-seven, and all that would save him from a painful and rapid descent into the grave all but yawning at the tips of his gleaming shoes was Brad's signature on a movie contract. "Well, whoever this woman is, I'd like her name. Maybe *she* can get you to see reason."

That made Brad smile. Meg made him see galaxies colliding. Once or twice, during the night, he'd almost seen God. But reason?

Nope.

He plopped a dollop of butter into the skillet.

Phil made a huffy exit, slamming the screen door behind him.

Willie gave a low whine.

"You're right," Brad told the dog. "He'll probably be back."

MEG STOOD AS if frozen in the hallway of Indian Rock's only hotel, wanting to turn and run, but too stunned to move.

She'd just gathered the impetus to flee when her father stuck a hand out. "Ted Ledger," he said, by way of introduction. "Come in and meet your sister, Meg."

Her sister?

It was that, added to a desire to commit matricide, that brought Meg over the threshold and into her mother's simply furnished, elegantly rustic suite.

Eve was nowhere in sight, the coward. But a little girl, ten or twelve years old, sat stiffly on the couch, hands folded in her lap. She was blond and blue-eyed, clad in cheap discount-store jeans and a floral shirt with ruffles, and the look on her face was one of terrified defiance.

"Hello," Meg said, forcing the words past her heart, which was beating in her throat.

The marvelous blue eyes narrowed.

"Carly," said Ted Ledger, "say hello."

"Hello," Carly complied grudgingly.

Looking at the child, Meg couldn't help thinking that the baby she'd lost would have been about this same age, if it hadn't been for the miscarriage.

She straightened her spine. Turned to the father who hadn't cared enough to send her so much as an e-mail, let alone be part of her life. "Where is my mother?" she asked evenly.

"Hiding out," Ledger said with a wisp of a grin. In his youth, he'd probably been handsome. Now he was thin and gray-haired, with dark shadows under his pale blue eyes.

Carly looked Meg over again and jutted out her chin. "I don't want to live with her," she said. "She probably doesn't need a kid hanging around anyhow."

"Go in the kitchen," Ledger told the child.

To Meg's surprise, Carly obeyed.

"Live with me?" Meg echoed in a whisper.

"It's that or foster care," Ledger said. "Sit down."

Meg sat, not because her father had asked her to, but because all the starch had gone out of her knees. Questions battered at the back of her throat, like balls springing from a pitching machine.

Where have you been?

Why didn't you ever call?

If I kill my mother, could a dream-team get me off without prison time?

"I know this is sudden," Ted Ledger said, perching on the edge of the white velvet wingback chair Eve had had sent from her mansion in San Antonio, to make the place more "homey."

"But the situation is desperate. *I'm* desperate."

Meg tried to swallow, but couldn't. Her mouth was too dry, and her esophagus had closed up. "I don't believe this," she croaked.

"Your mother and I agreed, long ago," Ledger went on, "that it would be best if I stayed out of your life. That's why she never brought you to visit me."

"Visit you?"

"I was in prison, Meg. For embezzlement."

"From McKettrickCo," Meg mused aloud, startled, but at the same time realizing that she'd known all along, on some half-conscious level.

"I told you he was a waste of hair and hide," Angus said. He stood over by the fake fireplace, one arm resting on the mantelpiece.

Meg took care to ignore him, not to so much as glance in his direction, though she could see him out of the corner of one eye. He was in old-man mode today, white-headed and wrinkled and John Wayne—tough, but dressed for the trail.

"Yes," Ledger replied. "Your mother saw that there was no scandal—easier to do in those days, before the media came into its own. I went to jail. She went on with her life."

"Where does Carly fit in?"

Ledger's smile was soft and sad. "While I was inside, I got religion, as they say. When I was released, I found a job, met a woman, got married. We had Carly. Then, three years ago, Sarah—my wife—was killed in a car accident. Things went downhill from there—I was diagnosed last month."

Tears burned in Meg's eyes, but they weren't for Ledger, or even for Sarah. They were for Carly. Although she'd grown up in a different financial situation, with all the stability that came with simply being a McKettrick, she knew what the child must be going through.

"You don't have any other family? Perhaps Sarah's people—"

Ledger shook his head. "There's no one. Your mother has generously agreed to pay my medical bills and arrange for a decent burial, but I'll be lucky if I live six weeks. And once I'm gone, Carly will be alone."

Meg pressed her fingertips to her temples and breathed slowly and deeply. "Maybe Mom could—"

"She's past the age to raise a twelve-year-old," Ledger interrupted.

He leaned forward slightly in his chair, rested his elbows on his knees, intertwined his fingers and let his hands dangle. "Meg, you don't owe me a damn thing. I was no kind of father, and I'm not pretending I was. But Carly is your half sister. She's got your blood in her veins. And she doesn't have anybody else."

Meg closed her eyes, trying to imagine herself raising a resentful, grieving preadolescent girl. As much as she'd longed for her own child, nothing had prepared her for this.

"She won't go to foster care," she said. "Mother would never allow it."

"Boarding school, then," Ledger replied. "Carly would hate that. Probably run away. She needs a real home. Love. Somebody young enough to steer her safely through her teens, at least."

"You heard her," Meg said. "She doesn't want to live with me."

"She doesn't know what she wants, except for me to have a miraculous recovery, and that isn't going to happen. I can't ask you to do this for me, Meg—I've got no right to ask anything of you—but I can ask you to do it for Carly."

The room seemed to tilt. From the kitchen, Meg heard her mother's voice, and Carly's. What were they talking about in there?

"Okay," Meg heard herself say.

Ledger's once-handsome face lit with a smile of relief and what looked like sincere gratitude. "You'll do it? You'll look after your sister?"

My sister.

"Yes," Meg said. On the outside, she probably looked calm. On the inside, she was shaking. "What happens now?"

"I go into the hospital for pain control. Carly goes home with you for a few days. When—and if—I get out, she'll come back to stay with me."

Meg nodded, her mind racing, groping, grasping

for some handhold on an entirely new, entirely unexpected situation.

"We've got a room downstairs," Ledger said, rising painfully from the chair. "Carly and I will leave you alone with Eve for a little while."

Over by the fireplace, Angus scowled, powerful arms folded across his chest. Fortunately, he didn't say anything, because Meg would have told him to shut up if he had.

Her father left, Carly trailing after him.

Eve stepped into the kitchen doorway the moment they'd gone.

Angus vanished.

"Nice work, Mom," Meg said, still too shaken to stand up. Since a murder would be hard to pull off sitting down, her mother was off the hook. Temporarily.

"She's about the same age as your baby would have been," Eve said. "It's fate."

Meg's mouth fell open.

"Of course I knew," Eve told her, venturing as far as the white velvet chair and perching gracefully on the edge of its cushion. "I'm your mother."

Meg closed her mouth. Tightly.

Eve's eyes were on the door through which Ted Ledger and Carly had just passed. "I loved him," she said. "But when he admitted stealing all that money, there was nothing I could do to keep him out of prison. We divorced after his conviction, and he asked me not to tell you where he was."

Meg sagged back in her own chair, still dizzy. Still speechless.

"She's a beautiful child," Eve said, referring, of

course, to Carly. "You looked just like her, at that age. It's uncanny, really."

"She's bound to have a lot of problems," Meg managed.

"Of course she will. She lost her mother, and now her father is at death's door. But she has you, Meg. That makes her lucky, in spite of everything else."

"I haven't the faintest idea how to raise a child," Meg pointed out.

"Nobody does, when they start out," Eve reasoned. "Children don't come with a handbook, you know."

Suddenly, Meg remembered the lunch she had scheduled with Cheyenne, the groceries she'd intended to buy. Instantaneous motherhood hadn't been on her to-do list for the day.

She imagined making a call to Cheyenne. *Gotta postpone lunch. You see, I just gave birth to a twelve-year-old in my mother's living room.*

"I had plans," she said lamely.

"Didn't we all?" Eve countered.

"There's no food in my refrigerator."

"Supermarket's right down the road."

"Where have they been living? What kind of life has she had, up to now?"

"A hard one, I would imagine. Ted's something of a drifter—I suspect they've been living out of that old car he drives. He claims he homeschooled her, but knowing Ted, that probably means she knows how to read a racing form and calculate the odds of winning at Powerball."

"Great," Meg said, but something motherly was stirring inside her, something hopeful and brave and very,

very fragile. "Can I count on you for help, or just the usual interference?"

Eve laughed. "Both," she said.

Meg found her purse, fumbled for her cell phone, dialed Cheyenne's number.

It was something of a relief that she got her friend's voice mail.

"This is Meg," she said. "I can't make it for lunch. How about a rain check?"

CHAPTER NINE

MEG MOVED THROUGH the supermarket like a robot, programmed to take things off the shelves and drop them into the cart. When she got home and started putting away her groceries, she was surprised by some of the things she'd bought. There were ingredients for actual meals, not just things she could nuke in the microwave or eat right out of the box or bag.

She was brewing coffee when a knock sounded at the back door.

Glancing over, she saw her cousin Rance through the little panes of glass and gestured for him to come in. Tall and dark-haired, he looked as though he'd just come off a nineteenth-century cattle drive, in his battered boots, old jeans and Western-cut shirt. Favoring her with a lopsided grin, he removed his hat and hung it on one of the pegs next to the door.

"Heard you had a little shock this morning," he said.

Meg shook her head. She'd never gotten over how fast word got around in a place like Indian Rock. Then again, maybe Eve had called Rance, thinking Meg might need emotional support. "You could say that," she replied. "Who told you?"

Rance proceeded to the coffeemaker, which was still doing its steaming and gurgling number, took a mug down from the cupboard above and filled it, heedless of the brew dripping, fragrant and sizzling, onto the base. Of course, being a man, he didn't bother to wipe up the overflow.

"Eve," he said, confirming her suspicions.

Meg, not usually a neatnik, made a big deal of paper-toweling up the spill around the bottom of the coffeemaker. "It's no emergency, Rance," she told him.

He looked ruefully amused. "Your dad walks into your life after something like thirty years and it's not an emergency?"

"I suppose Mom told you about Carly."

Rance nodded. Ushered Meg to a seat at the table, set down his coffee mug and went back to pour a cup for her, messing up the counter all over again. "Twelve years old, something of an attitude," he confirmed, giving her the cup and then sitting astride the bench. "And coming to live with you. Is that going to screw up your love life?"

"I don't *have* a love life," Meg said. Sure, she'd spent the night tangling sheets with Brad O'Ballivan but, one, primal sex didn't constitute a relationship and, two, it was none of Rance's business anyway.

"Whatever," Rance said. "The point is, you've got a kid to raise, and she's a handful, by all accounts. I'm no authority on bringing up kids, but I do have two daughters. I'll do what I can to help, Meg, and so will Emma."

Rance's girls, Maeve and Rianna, were like nieces to Meg, and so was Keegan's Devon. While they were all younger than Carly, they would be eager to include her in the family, and it was comforting to know that.

"Thanks," Meg said as her eyes misted over.

"You can do this," Rance told her.

"I don't seem to have a choice. Carly is my half sister, there's no one else, and blood is blood."

"If there's one concept a hardheaded McKettrick can comprehend right away, it's that."

"I don't know as we're all that hardheaded," Angus put in, after materializing behind Rance in the middle of the kitchen.

Meg didn't glance up, nor did she answer. She was close to Rance, Jesse and Keegan—always had been—but she'd never told them she saw Angus, dead since the early twentieth century, on a regular basis. Her mother knew, having overheard Meg talking to him, long after the age of entertaining imaginary playmates had passed, and for all the problems Eve had suffered after Sierra's kidnapping, she'd given her remaining daughter one inestimable gift. She'd believed her.

You're not the type to see things, Eve had said after Meg reluctantly explained. *If you say Angus McKettrick is here, then he is.*

Remembering, Meg felt a swell of love for her mother, despite an equal measure of annoyance.

"I'd better get back to punching cattle," Rance said, finishing his coffee and swinging a leg over the bench to stand. With winter coming on, he and his hired men were rounding up strays in the hills and driving the whole bunch down to the lower pastures. "If you need a hand over here, with the girl or anything else, you let me know."

Meg grinned up at him. He'd taken time out of a busy day to come over and check on her in person, and she appreciated that. "Once Carly's had a little time to settle in, we'll introduce her to Maeve and Rianna and

Devon. I don't think she's got a clue what it's like to be part of a family like ours."

Rance laid a work-calloused hand on Meg's shoulder as he passed, carrying his empty coffee mug to the sink, then crossing to take his hat down from the peg. "Probably not," he agreed. "But she'll find out soon enough."

With that, Rance left again.

Meg turned to acknowledge Angus. "We *are* hardheaded," she told him. "Every last one of us."

"I'd rather call it 'persistent,'" Angus imparted.

"Your decision," Meg responded, getting up to dispose of her own coffee cup then heading for the backstairs. She didn't know when Carly would be arriving, but it was time to get a room ready for her. That meant changing sheets, opening windows to air the place out and equipping the guest bathroom with necessities like clean towels, a toothbrush and paste, shampoo and the like.

She'd barely finished, and returned to the kitchen to slap together a hasty lunch, when an old car rattled up alongside the house, backfired and shut down. As Meg watched from the window, Ted Ledger got out, keeping one hand to the car for balance as he rounded it, and leaned in on the opposite side, no doubt trying to persuade a reluctant Carly to alight.

Meg hurried outside.

By the time she reached the car, Carly was standing with a beat-up backpack dangling from one hand, staring at the barn.

"Do you have horses?" she asked.

Hallelujah, Meg thought. *Common ground.*

"Yes," she said, smiling.

"I hate horses," Carly said. "They smell and step on people."

Ted passed Meg a beleaguered look over the top of the old station wagon, his eyes pleading for patience.

"You do not," he said to Carly. Then, to Meg, "She's just being difficult."

Duh, Meg thought, but in spite of all her absent-father issues, she felt a pang of sympathy for the man. He was terminally ill, probably broke, and trying to find a place for his younger daughter to make the softest possible landing.

Meg figured it would be a fiery crash instead, complete with explosions, but she also knew she was up to the challenge. Mostly, that is. And with a lot of help from Rance, Keegan, Jesse and Sierra.

Oh, yeah. She'd be calling in her markers, all right. *Code-blue, calling all McKettricks.*

"I'm not staying unless my dad can stay, too," Carly announced, standing her ground, there in the gravel of the upper driveway, knuckles white where she gripped the backpack.

Meg hadn't considered this development, though she supposed she should have. She forced herself to meet Ted's gaze, saw both resignation and hope in his eyes when she did.

"It's a big house," she heard herself say. "Plenty of room."

Rance's earlier question echoed in her mind. *Is that going to screw up your love life?*

There'd be no more overnight visits from Brad, at least not in the immediate future. To Meg, that was both a relief—things were moving too fast on that front—and a problem. Her body was still reverberating with the pleasure Brad had awakened in her, and already craving more.

"Okay," Carly said, moving a little closer to Ted. The two of them bumped shoulders in unspoken communication, and Meg felt a brief and unexpected stab of envy.

Meg tried to carry Ted's suitcase inside, but he wouldn't allow that. Manly pride, she supposed.

Angus watched from the back steps as the three of them trailed toward the house, Meg in the lead, Ted following and Carly straggling at the rear.

"She's a good kid," Angus said.

Meg gave him a look but said nothing.

Just walking into the house seemed to wear Ted out, and as soon as Carly had been installed in her room, he expressed a need to lie down. Meg showed him to the space generations of McKettrick women—she being an exception—had done their sewing.

There was only a daybed, and Meg hadn't changed the sheets, but Ted waved away her offer to spruce up the room a little. She went out, closing the door behind her, and heard the bedsprings groan as if he'd collapsed onto them.

Carly's door was shut. Meg paused outside it, on her way to the rear stairway, considered knocking and decided to leave the poor kid alone, let her adjust to new and strange surroundings.

Downstairs, Meg went back to what she'd been doing when Ted and Carly arrived. She made a couple of extra sandwiches, just in case, wolfed one down with a glass of milk and eyeballed the phone.

Was Brad going to call, or was last night just another slam-bam to him? And if he *did* call, what exactly was she going to say?

WILLIE WAS SURPRISINGLY AMBULATORY, considering what
he'd been through. When Brad came out of the upstairs
bathroom, having showered and pulled on a pair of
boxer-briefs and nothing else, the dog was waiting in
the hall. Climbing the stairs must have been an ordeal,
but he'd done it.

"You need to go outside, boy?" Brad asked. When
Big John's health had started to decline, Brad had
wanted to install an elevator, so the old man wouldn't
have to manage a lot of steps, but he'd met with the
usual response.

An elevator? Big John had scoffed. *Boy, all that fine
Nashville livin' is goin' to your head.*

Now, with an injured dog on his hands, Brad wished
he'd overridden his grandfather's protests.

He moved to lift Willie, intending to carry him
downstairs and out the kitchen door to the grassy side
yard, but a whimper from the dog foiled that idea. Carefully, the two of them made the descent, Willie stopping every few steps to rest, panting.

The whole process was painful to watch.

Reaching the kitchen at last, Brad opened the back
door and waited as Willie labored outside, found a
place in the grass after copious sniffing and did his
business.

Once he was back inside, Brad decided another trip
up the stairway was out of the question. He moved Willie's new dog bed into a small downstairs guest room,
threw back the comforter on one of the twin-sized beds
and fell onto it, face-first.

"WHO'S THE OLD MAN?" Carly asked, startling Meg,
who had been running more searches on Josiah Mc-

Kettrick on the computer in the study, for more reasons than one.

"What old man?" Meg retorted pleasantly, turning in the chair to see her half sister standing in the big double doorway, looking much younger than twelve in a faded and somewhat frayed sleep shirt with a cartoon bear on the front.

"This house," Carly said implacably, "is haunted."

"It's been around a long time," Meg hedged, still smiling. "Lots of history here. Are you hungry?"

"Only if you've got the stuff to make grilled-cheese sandwiches," Carly said. She was in the gawky stage, but one day, she'd be gorgeous. Meg didn't see the resemblance Eve had commented on earlier, but if there was one, it was cause to feel flattered.

"I've got the stuff," Meg assured her, rising from her chair.

"I can do it myself," Carly said.

"Maybe we could talk a little," Meg replied.

"Or not," Carly answered, with a note of dismissal that sounded false.

Meg followed the woman-child to the kitchen, earning herself a few scathing backward glances in the process.

Efficiently, Carly opened the fridge, helped herself to a package of cheese and proceeded to the counter. Meg supplied bread and a butter dish and a skillet, but that was all the assistance Carly was willing to accept.

"Can you cook?" Meg asked, hoping to get some kind of dialogue going.

Carly shrugged one thin shoulder. Her feet were bare and a tiny tattoo of some kind of flower blos-

somed just above one ankle bone. "Dad's hopeless at
it, so I learned."

"I see," Meg said, wondering what could have possessed her father to let a child get a tattoo, and if it
had hurt much, getting poked with all those needles.

"You don't see," Carly said, skillfully preparing her
sandwich, everything in her bearing warning Meg to
keep her distance.

"What makes you say that?"

Another shrug.

"Carly?"

The girl's back, turned to Meg as she laid the sandwich in the skillet and adjusted the gas stove burner
beneath, stiffened. "Don't ask me a bunch of questions,
okay? Don't ask how it was, living on the road, or if
I miss my mother, or what it's like knowing my dad
is going to die. Just leave me be, and we'll get along
all right."

"There's one question I have to ask," Meg said.

Carly tossed her another short, over-the-shoulder
glower. "What?"

"Did it hurt a lot, getting that tattoo?"

Suddenly, a smile broke over Carly's face, and it
changed everything about her. "Yes."

"Why did you do it?"

"That's *two* questions," Carly pointed out. "You
said one."

"Was it because your friends got tattoos?"

Carly's smile faded, and she averted her attention again, spatula in hand, ready to turn her grilled-
cheese sandwich when it was just right. "I don't have
any friends," she said. "We moved around too much.

And I didn't need them anyhow. Me and Dad—that was enough."

Meg's eyes burned.

"I got the tattoo," Carly said, catching Meg off-guard, "because my mom had one just like it, in the same place. It's a yellow rose—because Dad always called her his yellow rose of Texas."

Meg's throat went tight. How was she going to help this child face the loss of not one parent, but two? Sister or not, she was a stranger to Carly.

The phone rang.

Carly, being closest, picked up the receiver, peered at the caller ID panel, and went wide-eyed. *"Brad O'Ballivan?"* she whispered reverently, padding across the kitchen to give Meg the phone. *"The* Brad O'Ballivan?"

Meg choked out a laugh. Well, well, well. Carly was a fan. Just the opening Meg needed to establish some kind of bond, however tenuous, with her newly discovered kid sister. *"The* Brad O'Ballivan," she said before thumbing the talk button. "Hello?"

Brad's answer was an expansive yawn. Evidently, he'd either just awakened or he'd gone to bed early. Either way, the images playing in Meg's mind were scintillating ones, and they soon rippled into other parts of her anatomy, like tiny tsunamis boiling under her skin.

"Willie's home," he said finally.

Carly was staring at Meg. "I have all his CDs," she said.

"That's good," Meg answered.

"We ought to celebrate," Brad went on. "I grill a mean steak. Six-thirty, my place?"

"Only if you have a couple of spares," Meg said. "I have company."

The smell of scorching sandwich billowed from the stove.

Carly didn't move.

"Company?" Brad asked sleepily, with another yawn.

Meg pictured him scantily clothed, if he was wearing anything at all, with an attractive case of bed head. And she blushed to catch herself thinking lascivious thoughts with a twelve-year-old in the same room. "It's a lot to explain over the phone," she said diplomatically, gesturing to Carly to rescue the sandwich, which she finally did.

"The more the merrier," Brad said. "Whoever they are, bring them."

"We'll be there," Meg said.

Carly pushed the skillet off the burner and waved ineffectually at the smoke.

Meg said goodbye to Brad and hung up the phone.

"We're going to *Brad O'Ballivan's house?*" Carly blurted. *"For real?"*

"For real," Meg said. "If your dad feels up to it."

"He's your dad, too," Carly allowed. "And he likes Brad's music. We listen to it in the car all the time."

Meg let the part about Ted Ledger being her dad pass. He'd been her sire, not her father. "Let's let him rest," she said, taking over the grilled cheese operation and feeling glad when Carly didn't protest, or try to elbow her aside.

"How long have you known him?" Carly demanded, almost breathless.

It was a moment before Meg realized the girl was

talking about Brad, not Ted, so muddled were her thoughts. "Since junior high," she said.

"What's he like?"

"He's nice," Meg said carefully, slicing cheese, reaching for the butter dish and then the bread bag.

"'Nice'?" Carly looked not only skeptical, but a little disappointed. "He trashes hotel rooms. He pushed a famous actress into a swimming pool at a big Hollywood party—"

"I think that's mostly hype," Meg said, hoping the kid hadn't heard the notches-in-the-bedpost stuff. She started the new sandwich in a fresh skillet and carried the first one to the sink. When she glanced Carly's way, she was surprised and touched to see she'd taken a seat on the bench next to the table.

"Do you think he'd autograph my CDs?"

"I'd say there was a fairly good chance he will, yes." She turned the sandwich, got out a china plate, poured a glass of milk.

Carly glowed with anticipation. "If I had any friends," she said, "I'd call them all and tell them I get to meet Brad O'Ballivan *in the flesh*."

And what flesh it was, Meg thought, and blushed again. "Once you start school," she said, "you'll have all kinds of friends. Plus, there are some kids in the family around your age."

"It's not my family," Carly said, stiffening again.

"Of course it is," Meg argued, but cautiously, scooping a letter-perfect grilled-cheese sandwich onto a plate and presenting it to Carly with a flourish, along with the milk. She wished Angus had been there, to see her cooking. "You and I are sisters. I'm a McKettrick. So that means you're related to them, too, if only by association."

"I hate milk," Carly said.

"Brad drinks it," Meg replied lightly.

Carly reached for the glass, took a sip. Pondered the taste, and then took another. "You see him, too," the child observed. "The old man, I mean."

Before Meg could come up with an answer, Angus reappeared.

"I'm not that old," he protested.

"Yes, you are," Carly argued, looking right at him. "You must be a hundred, and that's *old*."

Meg's mouth fell open.

"I *told* you I could see him," Carly said with a touch of smugness.

Angus laughed. "I'll be damned," he marveled.

Carly's brow furrowed. "Are you a ghost?"

"Not really," Angus said.

"What are you, then?"

"Just a person, like you. I'm from another time, that's all."

No big deal. I just step from one century to another at will. Anybody could do it.

Meg watched the exchange in amazement, speechless. Ever since she'd started seeing Angus, way back in her nursery days, she'd wished for one other person—just one—who could see him, too. Being different from other people was a lonely thing.

"When my dad dies, will he still be around?"

Angus approached the table, drew back Holt's chair, and sat down. His manner was gruff and gentle, at the same time, and Meg's throat tightened again, recalling all the times he'd comforted her, in his grave, deep-voiced way. "That's a question I can't rightly answer," he said solemnly. "But I can tell you that folks don't really die, in the way you probably think of it. They're just in another place, that's all."

Carly blinked, obviously trying hard not to cry. "I'm going to miss him something awful," she said very softly.

Angus covered the child's small hand with one of his big, work-worn paws. There was such a rough tenderness in the gesture that Meg's throat closed up even more, and her eyes scalded.

"It's a fact of life, missing folks when they go away," Angus said. "You've got Meg, here, though." He nodded his head slightly, in her direction, but didn't look away from Carly's face. "She'll do right by you. It's the McKettrick way, taking care of your own."

"But I'm not a McKettrick," Carly said.

"You could be if you wanted to," Angus reasoned. "You're not a Ledger, either, are you?"

"We've changed our name so many times," the child admitted, her eyes round and sad and a little hungry as she studied Angus, "I don't remember who I am."

"Then you might as well be a McKettrick as not," Angus said.

Carly's gaze slid to Meg, swung away again. "I'm not going to forget my dad," she said.

"Nobody expects you to do that," Angus replied. "Thing is, you've got a long life ahead of you, and it'll be a lot easier with a family to take your part when the trail gets rugged."

Upstairs, a door opened, then closed again.

"Your pa," Angus told Carly, lowering his voice a little, "is real worried about you being all right, once he's gone. You could put his mind at ease a bit, if you'd give Meg a chance to act like a big sister."

Carly bit her lower lip, then nodded. "I wish you wouldn't go away," she said. "But I know you're going to." She paused, and Meg grappled with the sudden knowledge that it was true—one day soon, Angus would vanish, for good. "If you see my mom—her name is Rose—will you tell her I've got a tattoo just like hers?"

"I surely will," Angus promised.

"And you'll look out for my dad, too?"

Angus nodded, his eyes misty. It was a phenom-enon Meg had never seen before, even at family fu-nerals. Then he ruffled Carly's hair and vanished just as Ted came down the stairs, moving slowly, holding tightly to the rail.

It was all Meg could do not to rush to his aid.

"Hungry?" she asked moderately.

"I could eat," Ted volunteered, looking at Carly. His whole face softened as he gazed at his younger child.

It made Meg wonder if he'd ever missed *her,* during all those years away.

As if he'd heard her thoughts, her father turned to her. "You turned out real well," he said after clearing his throat. "Your mom did a good job, raising you. But, then, Eve was always competent."

"We're going to meet Brad O'Ballivan," Carly said.

"Get out," Ted teased, a faint twinkle shining in his eyes. "We're not, either."

"Yes, we are," Carly insisted. "Meg knows him. He just called here. Meg says he might autograph my CDs."

Ted grinned, made his way to the table and sank into

the chair Angus had occupied until moments before. Spent a few moments recovering from the exertion of descending the stairs and crossing the room.

Meg served up the extra sandwiches she'd made earlier, struggling all the while with a lot of tangled emotions. Carly could see Angus. Ted Ledger might be a total stranger, but he was Meg's father, and he was dying.

Last but certainly not least, Brad was back in her life, and there were bound to be complications.

A strange combination of grief, joy and anticipation pushed at the inside walls of Meg's heart.

THEY ARRIVED RIGHT on time, Meg and a young girl and a man who put Brad in mind of Paul Newman. Willie, who'd been resting on the soft grass bordering the flagstone patio off the kitchen, keeping an eye on his new master while he prepared the barbeque grill for action, gave a soft little woof.

Brad watched as Meg approached, thinking how delicious she looked in her jeans and lightweight, close-fitting sweater. She hadn't explained who her company was, but looking at them, Brad saw the girl's resemblance to Meg, and guessed the man to be the father she hadn't seen since she was a toddler.

He smiled.

The girl blushed and stared at him.

"Hey," he said, putting out a hand. "My name's Brad O'Ballivan."

"I know," the girl said.

"My sister, Carly," Meg told him. "And this is my— this is Ted Ledger."

Shyly, Carly slipped off her backpack, reached inside, took out a couple of beat-up CDs. "Meg said I could maybe get your autograph."

"No maybe about it," Brad answered. "I don't happen to have a pen on me at the moment, though."

Carly swallowed visibly. "That's okay," she said, her gaze straying to Willie, who was thumping his tail against the ground and grinning a goofy dog grin at her, hoping for friendship. "What happened to him?"

"He had a run-in with a pack of coyotes," Brad said. "He'll be all right, though. Just needs a little time to mend."

The girl crouched next to the dog, stroked him gently. "Hi," she said.

Meanwhile, Meg's father took a seat at the patio table. He looked bushed.

"I had to have stitches once," Carly told Willie. "Not as many as you've got, though."

"Brad's sister is a veterinarian," Meg said, finally finding her voice. "She fixed him right up."

"I'd like to be a veterinarian," Carly said.

"No reason you can't," Brad replied, turning his attention to Ted Ledger. "Can I get you a drink, Mr. Ledger?"

Ledger shook his head. "No, thanks," he said quietly. His gaze moved fondly between Meg and Carly, resting on one, then the other. "Good of you to have us over. I appreciate it. And I'd rather you called me Ted."

"Is there anything I can do to help?" Meg asked.

"I've got it under control," Brad told her. "Just relax."

Great advice, O'Ballivan, he thought. *Maybe you ought to take it.*

Meg went to greet Willie, who gave a whine of

greeting and tried to lick her face. She laughed, and Brad felt something open up inside him, at the sound. When he'd conceived the supper idea, he'd intended to ply her with good wine and a thick steak, then take her to bed. The extra guests precluded that plan, of course, but he didn't regret it. When it finally registered that his and Meg's child might have looked a lot like Carly, though, he felt bruised all over again.

"Any news about Ransom?" Meg asked, stepping up beside him when he turned his back to lay steaks on the grill, along with foil-wrapped baked potatoes that had been cooking for a while.

Brad shook his head, suddenly unable to look at her. If he did, she'd see all the things he felt, and he wasn't ready for that.

"According to the radio," Meg persisted, "the blizzard's passed, and the snow's melted."

Brad sighed. "I guess that means I'd better ride up and look for that stallion before Livie decides to do it by herself."

"I'd like to go with you," Meg said, sounding almost shy.

Brad thought about the baby who'd never had a chance to grow up. The baby Meg hadn't seen fit to tell him about. "We'll see," he answered noncommittally. "How do you like your steak?"

CHAPTER TEN

AFTER THE MEAL had been served and enjoyed, with Willie getting the occasional scrap, Brad signed the astounding succession of CDs Carly fished out of her backpack. Ted, who had eaten little, seemed content to watch the scene from a patio chair, and Meg insisted on cleaning up; since she'd had no part in the preparations, it only seemed fair.

As she carried in plates and glasses and silverware, rinsed them and put them into the oversize dishwasher, she reflected on Brad's mood change. He'd been warm to Ted, and chatted and joked with Carly, but when she'd mentioned that she'd like to accompany him when he went looking for Ransom again, it was as if a wall had slammed down between them.

She was just shutting the dishwasher and looking for the appropriate button to push when the screen door creaked open behind her. She turned, saw Brad hesitating on the threshold. It was past dusk—outside, the patio lights were burning brightly—but Meg hadn't bothered to flip a switch when she came in, so the kitchen was almost dark.

"Kid wants a T-shirt," he said, his face in shadow so she couldn't read his expression. "I think I have a few around here someplace."

Meg nodded, oddly stricken.

Brad didn't move right away, but simply stood there for a few long moments; she knew by the tilt of his head that he was watching her.

"You've gone out of your way to be kind to Carly," Meg managed, because the silence was unbearable. "Thank you."

He still didn't speak, or move.

Meg swallowed hard. "Well, it's getting late," she said awkwardly. "I guess we'd better be heading for home soon."

Brad reached out for a switch, and the overhead lights came on, seeming harsh after the previous cozy twilight in the room. His face looked bleak to Meg, his broad shoulders seemed to stoop a little.

"Seeing her—Carly, I mean—"

"I know," Meg said very softly. Of course Brad saw what she had, when he looked at Carly—the child who might have been.

"She's her own person," Brad said with an almost inaudible sigh. "It wouldn't be right to think of her in any other way. But it gave me a start, seeing her. She looks so much like you. So much like—"

"Yes."

"What's going on, Meg? You said you couldn't explain over the phone, and I figured out that Ledger had to be your dad. But there's more to this, isn't there?"

Meg bit her lower lip. "Ted is dying," she said. "And it turns out that Carly has no one else in the world except me."

Brad processed that, nodded. "Be careful," he told her quietly. "Carly is Carly. It would be all too easy—and completely unfair—to superimpose—"

"I wouldn't do that, Brad," Meg broke in, bristling. "I'm not pretending she's—she's our daughter."

"Guess I'll go rustle up that T-shirt," Brad said.

Meg didn't respond. For the time being, the conversation—at least as far as their lost child was concerned—was over.

Carly wore the T-shirt home—Brad's guitar-wielding profile was silhouetted on the front, along with the year of a recent tour and an impressive list of cities—practically bouncing in the car seat as she examined the showy signature on the face of each of her CDs.

"I bet he never trashed a single hotel room," she enthused, from the backseat of Meg's Blazer. "He's way too nice to do that."

Meg and Ted exchanged a look of weary amusement up front.

"It was quite an evening," Ted said. "Thanks, Meg."

"Brad did all the work," she replied.

"I like his dog, too," Carly bubbled. She seemed to have forgotten her situation, for the time being, and Meg could see that was a relief to Ted. "Brad said he'd change his name to Stitches, if he didn't already answer to Willie."

Meg smiled.

All the way home, it was Brad said this, Brad said that.

Once they'd reached the ranch house, Ted went inside, exhausted, while Carly and Meg headed for the barn to feed the horses. Despite her earlier condemnation of the entire equine species, Carly proved a fair hand with hay and grain.

"Is he your boyfriend?" Carly asked, keeping pace with Meg as they returned to the house.

"Is who my boyfriend?" Meg parried.

"You *know* I mean Brad," Carly said. "Is he?"

"He's a *friend*," Meg said. But a voice in her mind chided, *Right. And last night, you were rolling around on a mattress with him.*

"I may be twelve, but I'm not stupid," Carly remarked, as they reached the back door. "I saw the way he looked at you. Like he wanted to put his hands on you all the time."

Yeah, Meg thought wearily. *Specifically, around my throat.*

"You're imagining things."

"I'm very sophisticated for twelve," Carly argued.

"Maybe *too* sophisticated."

"If you think I'm going to act like some *kid,* just because I'm twelve, think again."

"That's exactly what I think. A twelve-year-old *is* a kid." Meg pushed open the kitchen door; Ted had turned on the lights as he entered, and the place glowed with homey warmth. "Go to bed."

"There's no TV in my room," Carly protested. "And I'm not sleepy."

"Tough it out," Meg replied. Crossing to the china cabinet on the far side of the room, she opened a drawer, found a notebook and a pen, and handed them to her little sister. "Here," she said. "Keep a journal. It's a tradition in the McKettrick family."

Carly hesitated, then accepted the offering. "I guess I could write about Brad O'Ballivan," she said. She held the notebook to her chest for a moment. "Are you going to read it?"

"No," Meg said, softening a little. "You can write anything you want to. Sometimes it helps to get feelings out of your head and onto paper. Then you can get some perspective."

Carly considered. "Okay," she said and started for the stairs, taking the notebook with her.

Meg, knowing she wouldn't sleep, tired as she was, headed for the study as soon as Carly disappeared, logged onto the Internet and resumed her research.

"You won't find him on that contraption," Angus told her.

She looked up to see him sitting in the big leather wingback chair by the fireplace. Like many other things in the house, the chair was a holdover from the Holt and Lorelei days.

"Josiah, I mean," Angus added, jawline hard again as he remembered the brother who had so disappointed him. "I told you he didn't use the McKettrick name." He gave a snort. "Sounded too Irish for him."

"Help me out, here," Meg said.

Angus remained silent.

Meg sighed and turned back to the screen. She'd been scrolling through names, intermittently, for days. And now, suddenly, she had a hit, more an instinct than anything specific.

"Creed, Josiah *McKettrick,*" she said excitedly, clicking on the link. "I must have passed right over him dozens of times."

Angus materialized at her elbow, stooping and staring at the screen, his heavy eyebrows pulled together in consternation and curiosity.

"Captain in the United States Army," Meg read aloud, and with a note of triumph in her voice. "Founder of 'the legendary Stillwater Springs Ranch,' in western Montana. Owner of the Stillwater Springs *Cou-*

rier, the first newspaper in that part of the territory. On the town council, two terms as mayor. Wife, four sons, active member of the Methodist Church." She stopped, looked up at Angus. "Doesn't sound like an anti-Irish pirate to me." She tapped at Josiah's solemn photograph on the home page. Bewhiskered, with a thick head of white hair, he looked dour and prosperous in his dark suit, the coat fastened with one button at his breastbone, in that curious nineteenth-century way. "There he is, Angus," she said. "Your brother, Josiah McKettrick Creed."

"I'll be hornswoggled," Angus said.

"Whatever that is," Meg replied, busily copying information onto a notepad. The Web site was obviously the work of a skillful amateur, probably a family member with a genealogical bent, and there was no "contact us" link, but the name of the town, and the ranch if it still existed, was information enough.

"Looks like you missed something," Angus said.

Meg peered at the screen, trying to see past Angus's big index finger, scattering a ring of pixels around its end.

She pushed his hand gently aside.

And saw a tiny link at the bottom of the page, printed in blue letters.

A press of a mouse button and she and Angus were looking at the masthead of Josiah's newspaper, the *Courier.*

The headline was printed in heavy type. *MURDER AND SCANDAL BESET STILLWATER SPRINGS RANCH.*

Something quivered in the pit of Meg's stomach, a peculiar combination of dread and fascination. The by-line was Josiah's own, and the brief obituary beneath it still pulsed with the staunch grief of an old man, bitterly determined to tell the unflinching truth.

> *Dawson James Creed, 21, youngest son of Josiah McKettrick Creed and Cora Dawson Creed, perished yesterday at the hand of his first cousin, Benjamin A. Dawson, who shot him dead over a game of cards and a woman. Both the shootist and the woman have since fled these parts. Services tomorrow at 2:00 p.m., at the First Street Methodist Church. Viewing this evening at the Creed home. Our boy will be sorely missed.*

"Creed," Angus repeated, musing. "That was my mother's name, before she and my pa hitched up."

"So maybe Josiah *wasn't* a McKettrick," Meg ventured. "Maybe your mother was married before, or—"

Angus stiffened. "Or nothing," he said pointedly. "Back in those days, women didn't go around having babies out of wedlock. Pa must have been her second husband."

Meg, feeling a little stung, didn't comment. Nor did she argue the point, which would have been easy to back up, that premarital pregnancies weren't as uncommon in "his day" as Angus liked to think.

"Where's that old Bible Georgia set such store by?" he asked now.

Georgia, his second wife, mother of Rafe, Kade and Jeb, had evidently been her generation's record-keeper and family historian. "I suppose Keegan has it," she answered, "since he lives in the main ranch house."

"Ma wrote all the begats in that book," Angus recalled. "I never thought to look at it."

"She never mentioned being married before?"

"No," Angus admitted. "But folks didn't talk about things like that much. It was a private matter and besides, they had their hands full just surviving from day to day. No time to sit around jawing about the past."

"I'll drop in on Keegan and Molly in the morning," Meg said. "Ask if I can borrow the Bible."

"I want to look at it *now*."

"Angus, it's late—"

He vanished.

Meg sighed. There were no more articles on the website—just that short, sad obituary notice—so she logged off the computer. She was brewing a cup of herbal tea in the microwave, hoping it would help her sleep, when Ted came down the backstairs, wearing an old plaid flannel bathrobe and scruffy slippers.

Lord, he wanted to talk.

Now, from the look on his face.

She wasn't ready, and that didn't matter.

The time had come.

Dragging back a chair at the table, Ted crumpled into it.

"Tea?" Meg asked, and immediately felt stupid.

"Sit down, Meg," Ted said gently.

She took the mug from the microwave, grateful for its citrusy steamy scent, and joined him, perching on the end of one of the benches.

"There's no money," Ted said.

"I gathered that," Meg replied, though not flippantly. And the dizzying thought came to her that maybe this was all some kind of con—a *Paper Moon* kind of thing,

Ted playing the Ryan O'Neal part, while Carly handled Tatum's role. But the idea fizzled almost as quickly as it had flared up in her mind—a scam would have been so much easier to take than the grim reality.

Ted ran a tremulous hand through his thinning hair. "I wish things had happened differently, Meg," he said. "I wanted to come back a hundred times, say I was sorry for everything that happened. I convinced myself I was being noble—you were a McKettrick, and you didn't need an ex-yardbird complicating your life. The truth gets harder to deny when you're toeing up to the pearly gates, though. I was a coward, that's all. I tried to make up for it by being the best father I could to Carly." He paused, chuckled ruefully. "I won't take any prizes for that, either. After Rose died, it was as if somebody had greased the bottom of my feet. I just couldn't stay put, and it was mostly downhill, a slippery slope, all the way. The worst part is, I dragged Carly right along with me. Last job I had, I stocked shelves in a discount store."

"You don't have to do this," Meg said, blinking back tears she didn't want him to see.

"Yes," Ted said, "I do. I loved your mother and she loved me. You need to know how happy we were when you were born—that you were welcome in this big old crazy world."

"Okay," Meg allowed. "You were happy." She swallowed. "Then you embezzled a lot of money and went to prison."

"Like most embezzlers," Ted answered, "I thought I could put it back before it was missed. It didn't happen that way. Your mother tried to cover for me at first, but there were other McKettricks on the board, and they weren't going to tolerate a thief."

"Why did you do it?" The question, more breathed than spoken, hovered in the otherwise silent room.

"Before I met Eve, I gambled. A lot. I still owed some people. I was ashamed to tell Eve—and I knew she'd divorce me—so I 'borrowed' what I needed and left as few tracks as possible. That got my creditors off my back—they were knee-breakers, Meg, and they wouldn't have stopped at hurting me. They'd have gone after you and Eve, too."

"So you stole the money to protect Mom and me?" Meg asked, not bothering to hide her skepticism.

"Partly. I was young and I was scared."

"You should have told Mom. She would have helped you."

"I know. But by the time I realized that, it was too late." He sighed. "Now it's too late for a lot of things."

"It's not too late for Carly," Meg said.

"Exactly my point. She's going to give you some trouble, Meg. She won't want to go to school, and she's used to being a loner. I'm all the family she's had since her mother was killed. Like I said before, I've got no right to ask you for anything. I don't expect sympathy. I know you won't grieve when I'm gone. But Carly *will,* and I'm hoping you're McKettrick enough to stand by her till she finds her balance. My worst fear is that she'll go down the same road I did, drifting from place to place, living by her wits, always on the outside looking in."

"I won't let that happen," Meg promised. "Not because of you, but because Carly is my sister. And because she's a child."

They'd been over this before, but Ted seemed to need a lot of reassurance. "I guess there is one other favor I could ask," he said.

Meg raised an eyebrow. Waited.

"Will you forgive me, Meg?"

"I stopped hating you a long time ago."

"That isn't the same as forgiving me," Ted replied.

She opened her mouth, closed it again. A glib, "Okay, I forgive you" died on her tongue.

Ted smiled sadly. "While you're at it, forgive your mother, too. We were both wrong, Eve and I, not to tell you the whole truth from the beginning. But she was trying to protect you, Meg. And it says a lot about the other McKettricks, that none of them ever let it slip that I was a thief doing time in a Texas prison while you were growing up. A lot of people would have found that secret too juicy to keep to themselves."

Meg wondered if Jesse, Rance and Keegan had known, and decided they hadn't. Their parents had, though, surely. All three of their fathers had been on the company board with Eve, back in those days. Meg thought of them as uncles—and they'd looked after her like a daughter, taken her under their powerful wings when she summered on the Triple M, and so had her "aunts." Stirred her right into the boisterous mix of loud cousins, remembered her birthdays and bought gifts at Christmas. All the while, they'd been conspiring to keep her in the dark about Ted Ledger, of course, but she couldn't resent them for it. Their intentions, like Eve's, had been good.

"Who are you, really?" Meg asked, remembering Carly's remark about changing last names so many times she was no longer sure what the real one was. And underlying the surface question was another.

Who am I?

Ted smiled, patted her hand. "When I married your mother, I was Ted Sullivan. I was born in Chicago, to Alice and Carl Sullivan. Alice was a homemaker, Carl was a finance manager at a used car dealership."

"No brothers or sisters?"

"I had a sister, Sarah. She died of meningitis when she was fifteen. I was nineteen at the time. Mom never recovered from Sarah's death—she was the promising child. I was the problem."

"How did you meet Mom?" She hadn't thought she needed, or even wanted, to know such things. But, suddenly, she did.

Ted grinned at the memory, and for just a moment, he looked young again, and well. "After I left home, I took college courses and worked nights as a hotel desk clerk. I moved around the country, and by the time I wound up in San Antonio, I was a manager. McKettrickCo owned the chain I worked for, and one of your uncles decided I was a bright young man with a future. Hired me to work in the home office. Where, of course, I saw Eve every day."

Meg imagined how it must have been, both Ted and Eve still young, and relatively mistake-free. "And you fell in love."

"Yes," Ted said. "The family accepted me, which was decent of them, considering they were rich and I had an old car and a couple of thousand dollars squirreled away in a low-interest savings account. The McKettricks are a lot of things, but they're not snobs."

Having money doesn't make us better than other

people, Eve had often said as Meg was growing up. *It just makes us luckier.*

"No," she agreed. "They're not snobs." She tried to smile and failed. "So I would have been Meg Sullivan, not Meg McKettrick—if things hadn't gone the way they did?"

Ted chuckled. "Not in a million years. You know the McKettrick women don't change their names when they marry. According to Eve, the custom goes all the way back to old Angus's only daughter."

"Katie," Meg said. Her mind did a time-warp thing—for about fifteen seconds, she was nineteen and pregnant, having her last argument with Brad before he got into his old truck and drove away. Late that night, he would board a bus for Nashville.

We'll get married when I get back, Brad had said. *I promise.*

You're not coming back, Meg had replied, in tears.

Yes, I am. You'll see—you'll be Meg O'Ballivan before you know it.

I'll never be Meg O'Ballivan. I'm not taking your name.

Have it your way, Ms. McKettrick. You always do.

"Meg?" Ted's voice brought her back to the kitchen on the Triple M. Her tea had grown cold, sitting on the tabletop in its heavy mug.

"You're not the first person who ever made a mistake," she told her father. "I hereby confer upon you my complete forgiveness."

He laughed, but his eyes were glossy with tears.

"You're tired," Meg said. "Get some rest."

"I want to hear your story, Meg. Eve sent me a few

pictures, the occasional copy of a report card, when I was on the inside. But there are a lot of gaps."

"Another time," Meg answered. But even as Ted stood to make his way back upstairs, and she disposed of her cold tea and put the mug into the dishwasher, she wondered if there would *be* another time.

PHIL WAS BACK.

Brad, accompanied to the barn by an adoring Willie, tossed the last flake of hay into the last feeder when he heard the distinctive purr of a limo engine and swore under his breath.

"This is getting old," he told Willie.

Willie whined in agreement and wagged his tail.

Phil was walking toward Brad, the stretch gleaming in the early morning light, when he and Willie stepped outside.

"Good news!" Phil cried, beaming. "I spoke to the Hollywood people, and they're willing to make the movie right here at Stone Creek!"

Brad stopped, facing off with Phil like a gunfighter on a windswept Western street. "No," he said.

Phil, being Phil, was undaunted. "Now, don't be too hasty," he counseled. "It would really give this town a boost. Why, the jobs alone—"

"Phil—"

Just then, Livie's ancient Suburban topped the hill, started down, dust billowing behind. Brad took a certain satisfaction in the sight when the rig screeched to a halt alongside Phil's limo, covering it in fine red dirt.

Livie sprang from the Suburban, smiling. "Good news," she called, unknowingly echoing Phil's opening line. "The Iversons' cattle aren't infected."

Phil nudged Brad in the ribs and said in a stage whisper, "She could be an extra. Bet your sister would like to be in a movie."

"In a what?" Livie asked, frowning. She crouched to examine Willie briefly, and accept a few face licks, before straightening and putting out a hand to Phil Meadowbrook. "Olivia O'Ballivan," she said. "You must be my brother's manager."

"*Former* manager," Brad said.

"But still with his best interests at heart," Phil added, placing splayed fingers over his avaricious little ticker and looking woebegone, long-suffering and misunderstood. "I'm offering him a chance to make a *feature film,* right here on the ranch. Just *look* at this place! It's perfect! John Ford would salivate—"

"Who's John Ford?" Livie asked.

"He made some John Wayne movies," Brad explained, beginning to feel cornered.

Livie's dusty face lit up. She had hay dust in her hair—probably acquired during an early morning visit to the Iversons' dairy barn. "Wait till I tell the twins," she burst out.

"Hold it," Brad said, raising both hands, palms out. "There isn't going to *be* any movie."

"Why not?" Livie asked, suddenly crestfallen.

"Because I'm retired," Brad reminded her patiently.

Phil huffed out a disgusted sigh.

"I don't see the problem if they made the movie right here," Livie said.

"At last," Phil interjected. "Another voice of reason, besides my own."

"Shut up, Phil," Brad said.

"You always talked about making a movie," Livie

went on, watching Brad with a mischievous light dancing in her eyes. "You even started a production company once."

"Cynthia got it in the divorce," Phil confided, as though Brad wasn't standing there. "The production company, I mean. I think that soured him."

"Will you stop acting as if I'm not here?" Brad snapped.

Willie whimpered, worried.

"See?" Phil was quick to say. "You're upsetting the dog." Another patented Phil Meadowbrook grin flashed. "Hey! He could be in the movie, too. People eat that animal stuff up. We might even be able to get Disney in on the project—"

"No," Brad said, exasperated. "No Disney. No dog. No petite veterinarian with hay in her hair. *I don't want to make a movie.*"

"You could build a library or a youth center or something with the money," Phil said, trailing after Brad as he broke from the group and strode toward the house, fully intending to slam the door on his way in.

"We could use an animal shelter," Livie said, scrambling along at his other side.

"Fine," Brad snapped, slowing down a little because he realized Willie was having trouble keeping up. "I'll have my accountant cut a check."

The limo driver gave the horn a discreet honk, then got out and tapped at his watch.

"Plane to catch," Phil said. "Big Hollywood meeting. I'll fax you the contract."

"Don't bother," Brad warned.

Livie caught at his arm, sounding a little breathless. "What is the *matter* with you?" she whispered. "That movie would be the biggest thing to happen in Stone Creek since that pack of outlaws robbed the bank in 1907!"

Brad stopped. Thrust his nose right up to Livie's. "I. Am. *Retired.*"

Livie set her hands on her skinny hips. She really needed to put some meat on those fragile little bones of hers. "I think you're chicken," she said.

Willie gave a cheery little yip.

"You stay out of this, Stitches," Brad told him.

"Chicken," Livie repeated, as the now-dusty limo made a wide turn and started swallowing up dirt road.

"Not," Brad argued.

"Then what?"

Brad shoved a hand through his hair as the answer to Livie's question settled over him, like the red dust that had showered the limo. He was making some headway with Meg, slowly but surely, but Meg and show business mixed about as well as oil and water. Deep down, she probably believed, as Livie had until this morning, that he'd go back to being that other Brad O'Ballivan, the one whose name was always written in capital letters, if the offer was good enough.

Too, if he agreed to do the movie, Phil would never get off his back. He'd be back, before the cameras stopped rolling, with another offer, another contract, another big idea.

"I used to be a performer," Brad said finally. "Now I'm a rancher. I can't keep going back and forth between the two."

"It's one movie, Brad, not a world concert tour. And you wanted to do a movie for so long. What happened?

Was it losing the production company to Cynthia, like your manager said?"

"No," Brad said. "This is a Pandora's box, Livie. It's the proverbial can of worms. One thing will lead to another—"

"And you'll leave again? For good, this time?"

He shook his head. "No."

"Then just think about it," Livie reasoned. "Making the movie, I mean. Think about the money it would bring into Stone Creek, and how excited the local people would be."

"And the animal shelter," Brad said, sighing.

"Small as Stone Creek is, there are a lot of strays," Livie said.

"Did you come out here for a reason?"

"Yes, to see my big brother and check up on Willie."

"Well, here I am, and Willie's fine. Go or stay, but I don't want to talk about that damn movie anymore, understood?"

Livie smirked. "Understood," she said sweetly.

At four-thirty that afternoon, the movie contract appeared in Brad's email.

He read it, signed it and emailed it back.

CHAPTER ELEVEN

CARLY SAT HUNCHED in the front passenger seat of the Blazer, arms folded, glowering as kids converged on Indian Rock Middle School, colorful clothes and backpacks still new, since class had only been in session for a little over a month. It was Monday morning and Ted was scheduled to enter the hospital in Flagstaff for "treatment" the following day. Meg's solemn promise to take Carly to visit him every afternoon, admittedly small comfort, was nonetheless all she had to offer.

"I don't want to go in there," Carly said. "They're going to give me some stupid test and put me with the little kids. I just know it."

Ted had homeschooled Carly, for the most part, and though she was obviously a very bright child, there was no telling what kind of curriculum he'd used, or if the process had involved books at all. Her scores would determine her placement, and she was understandably worried.

"Everything will be all right," Meg said.

"You keep saying that," Carly protested. "Everybody says that. *My dad is going to die.* How is that 'all right'?"

"It isn't. It totally bites."

"You could homeschool me."

Meg shook her head. "I'm not a teacher, Carly."

"Neither is my dad, and he did fine!"

That, Meg thought, *remains to be seen.* "More than anything in the world, your dad wants you to have a good life. And that means getting an education."

Tears brimmed in Carly's eyes. "*My* dad? He's *your* dad, too."

"Okay," Meg said.

"You hate him. You don't care if he dies!"

"I *don't* hate him, and if there was any way to keep him alive, I'd do it."

Carly's right hand went to the door handle; with her left, she gathered up the neon pink backpack Meg had bought for her over the weekend, along with some new clothes. "Well, not hating somebody isn't the same as *loving* them."

With that, she shoved open the car door, unfastened her seat belt and got out to stand on the sidewalk, facing the long brick schoolhouse, her small shoulders squared under more burdens than any child ought to have to carry.

Meg waited, her eyes scalding, until Carly disappeared into the building. Then she drove to Sierra's house, where she found her other sister on the front porch, deadheading the flowers in a large clay pot.

The bright October sunshine gilded Sierra's chestnut hair; she looked like Mother Nature herself in her floral print maternity dress.

Meg parked the Blazer in the driveway and approached, slinging her bag over her shoulder as she walked.

Sierra beamed, delighted, and straightened, one hand resting protectively on her enormous belly, the other shading her eyes. "I just made a fresh pot of coffee," she called. "Come in, and we'll catch up."

Meg smiled. She'd lived her life as an only child; now she had two sisters. She and Sierra had had time to bond, but establishing a relationship with Carly was going to be a major challenge.

"I suppose Mom told you the latest," Meg said, referring to Ted and Carly's arrival.

"Some of it. The gossip lasted about twenty minutes, though—you got beat out by the news that Brad O'Ballivan is making a movie over at Stone Creek. Everybody in the county wants to be an extra."

Meg stopped in the middle of the sidewalk. Brad hadn't called since the barbeque, and she hadn't heard about the movie. That hurt, and though she regained her composure quickly, Sierra was quicker.

"You didn't know?" she asked, holding the front door open and urging Meg through it.

Meg sighed, shook her head.

Sierra patted her shoulder. "Let's have that coffee," she said softly.

For the next hour, she and Meg sat in the sunny kitchen, catching up. Meg told her sister what she knew about Ted's condition, Carly, and *most* of what had happened between her and Brad.

Sierra chuckled at the account of Jesse and Keegan's helicopter rescue the day of the blizzard. Got tears in her eyes when Meg related Willie's story.

Although Sierra was one of the most grounded people Meg knew, her emotions had been mercurial since the beginning of her last trimester.

"So when is this baby going to show up, anyhow?"

Meg inquired cheerfully when she was through with the briefing. It was definitely time to change the subject.

"I was due a week ago," Sierra answered. "The nursery is all ready, and so am I. Apparently, the baby isn't."

Meg touched her sister's hand. "Are you scared?"

Sierra shook her head. "I'm past that. Mostly, I feel like a bowling-ball smuggler."

"You know," Meg teased, "if you'd spilled the beans about whether this kid is a boy or a girl, you wouldn't have gotten so many yellow layettes at your baby shower."

Sierra laughed, crying a little at the same time. "The sonogram was inconclusive," she said. "The little dickens drew one leg up and hid the evidence."

Meg sobered, looked away briefly. "Would you hate me if I admitted I'm a little envious? Because the baby's coming, I mean, and because you already have Liam, and Travis loves you so much?"

"You know I couldn't hate you," Sierra answered gently, but there was a worried expression in her blue eyes. Long ago, Meg and Travis had dated briefly, and they were still very good friends. While Sierra surely knew neither of them would deceive her, ever, she might think she'd stolen Travis's affections and broken Meg's heart in the process. "Truth time. Do you still have feelings for Travis?"

"The same kind of feelings I have for Jesse and Keegan and Rance," Meg replied honestly. She drew a deep breath and puffed it out. "Truth time? Here's the whole enchilada. I fell hard for Brad O'Ballivan when I was in high school, and I don't think I'm over it."

"Is that a bad thing?"

Meg remembered the way Brad had looked as they

stood in his kitchen, after the steak dinner on the patio. She'd seen sorrow, disappointment and a sense of betrayal in his eyes, and the set of his face and shoulders. "I'm not sure," she said. Then she stood, carried her empty cup and Sierra's to the sink. "I'd better get home. Ted's there alone, and he wasn't feeling well when I left to take Carly to school."

Sierra nodded, remaining in her chair, squirming a little and looking anxious.

"You're okay, right?" Meg asked, alarmed.

"Just a few twinges," Sierra said. "It's probably nothing."

Meg was glad she'd already set the cups down, because she'd have dropped them to the floor if she hadn't. *Just a few twinges?*

"Would you mind calling Travis?" Sierra asked. "And Mom?"

"Oh, my God," Meg said, grabbing her bag, scrabbling through it for her cell phone. "You've been sitting there listening to my tales of woe and all the time you've been *in labor?*"

"Not the whole time," Sierra said lamely. "I thought it was indigestion."

Meg speed-dialed Travis. "Come home," she said before he'd finished his hello. "Sierra's having the baby!"

"On my way," he replied, and hung up in her ear.

Next, she called Eve. "It's happening!" she blurted. "The baby—"

"For heaven's sake," Sierra protested good-naturedly, "you make it sound as though I'm giving birth on the kitchen floor."

"Margaret McKettrick," Eve instructed sternly,

"calm yourself. We have a plan. Travis will take Sierra to the hospital, and I will pick Liam up after school. I assume you're with Sierra right now?"

"I'm with her," Meg said, wondering if she'd have to deliver her niece or nephew before help arrived. She'd watched calves, puppies and colts coming into the world, but *this* was definitely in another league.

"Did you call Travis?" Eve wanted to know.

"Yes," Meg watched Sierra anxiously as she spoke.

"My water just broke," Sierra said.

"Oh, my God," Meg ranted. "Her water just broke!"

"Margaret," Eve said, "get a grip—and a towel. I'll be there in five minutes."

Travis showed up in four flat. He paused to bend and kiss Sierra soundly on the mouth, then dashed off, returning momentarily with a suitcase, presumably packed with things his wife would need at the hospital.

Meg sat at the table, with her head between her knees, feeling woozy.

"I think she's hyperventilating," Sierra told Travis. "Do we have any paper bags?"

Just then, Eve breezed in through the back door. She tsk-tsked Meg, but naturally, Sierra was her main concern. As her younger daughter stood, with some help from Travis, Eve cupped Sierra's face between her hands and kissed her on the forehead.

"Don't worry about a thing," she ordered. "I'll see to Liam."

Sierra nodded, gave Meg one last worried glance and allowed Travis to steer her out the back door.

"Shouldn't we have called an ambulance or some-thing?" Meg fretted.

"Oh, for heaven's sake," Eve replied. "You don't need an ambulance!"

"Not for *me,* Mother. For Sierra."

Eve soaked a cloth at the sink, wrung it out and slapped it onto the back of Meg's neck. "Breathe," she said.

BRAD WATCHED FROM a front window as Livie parked the Suburban, got out and headed for the barn. "Here we go," he told Willie, resigned. "She's on the hunt for Ransom again, and that means I'll have to go. You're going to have to stay behind, buddy."

Willie, curled up on a hooked rug in front of the living room fireplace, simply sighed and closed his eyes for a snooze, clearly unconcerned. Some of the advance people from the movie studio had already arrived in an RV, to scout the location, and the kid with the backward baseball cap was a dog-lover. If necessary, Brad would press him into service.

Brad had been up half the night going over the script, faxed by Phil, penning in the occasional dialogue change. For all his reluctance to get involved in the project, he liked the story, tentatively titled *The Showdown,* and he was looking forward to trying his hand at a little acting.

The truth was, though, he'd had to read and reread because his mind kept straying to Meg. He'd been so sure, right along, that they could make things work. But seeing Carly—a younger version of Meg, and most likely of the daughter they might have had—brought up a lot of conflicting feelings, ones he wasn't sure how to deal with.

It wasn't rational; he knew that. Meg's explanation

was believable, even if it stung, and her reasons for keeping the secret from him made sense. Still, a part of him was deeply resentful, even enraged.

Livie was saddling Cinnamon when he reached the barn.

"Where do you think you're going?" he asked.

She gave him a look. "Three guesses, genius," she said pleasantly. "And the first two don't count."

"I guess you didn't hear about the blizzard that blew up in about five minutes when Meg and I were up in the hills trying to find that damn horse?"

"I heard about it," Livie said. She put her shoulder to Cinnamon's belly and pulled hard to tighten the cinch. "I just want to check on him, that's all. Just take a look."

Brad leaned one shoulder against the door frame, arms folded, letting his body language say he wasn't above blocking the door.

Livie's expression said *she* wasn't above riding right over him.

"I'll see if I can talk one of Meg's cousins into taking you up in the helicopter," Brad said.

"Oh, right," Livie mocked. "And scare Ransom to death with the noise."

"Livie, will you listen to reason? That horse has survived all this time without a lick of help from you. What's different now?"

"Will you stop calling him 'that horse'? His name is Ransom and he's a *legend,* thank you very much."

"Being a legend," Brad drawled, "isn't all it's cracked up to be."

Livie led Cinnamon toward him; he moved into the center of the doorway and stood his ground.

"What's different, Livie?" he repeated.

She sighed, seemed even smaller and more fragile than usual. "You wouldn't believe me if I told you."

"Give it a shot," Brad said.

"Dreams," Livie said. "I have these dreams—"

"Dreams."

"I knew you wouldn't—"

"Hold it," Brad interrupted. "I'm listening."

"Just get out of my way, please."

Brad shook his head, shifted so his feet were a little farther apart, kept his arms folded. "Not gonna happen."

"He talks to me," Livie said, her voice small and exasperated and full of the O'Ballivan grit that was so much a part of her nature.

"A horse talks to you." He tried not to sound skeptical, but didn't quite succeed.

"In dreams," Livie said, flushing.

"Like Mr. Ed, in that old TV show?"

Livie's temper flared in her eyes, then her cheekbones. "No," she said. "Not 'like Mr. Ed in that old TV show'!"

"How, then?"

"I just hear him, that's all. He doesn't move his lips, for pity's sake!"

"Okay."

"You believe me?"

"I believe that you believe it, Liv. You have a lot of deep feelings where animals are concerned—sometimes I wish you liked people half as much—and you've been worried about that—about Ransom for a long time. It makes sense that he'd show up in your dreams."

Livie let Cinnamon's reins dangle and set her hands on her hips. "What did you do, take an online shrink course or something? Jungian analysis in ten easy lessons? Next, you'll be saying Ransom is a symbol with unconscious sexual connotations!"

Brad suppressed an urge to roll his eyes. "Is that really so far beyond the realm of possibility?"

"Yes!"

"Why?"

"Because Ransom isn't the only animal I dream about, that's why. And it isn't a recent phenomenon—it's been happening since I was little! Remember Simon, that old sheepdog we had when we were kids? He told me he was leaving—and three days later, he was hit by a car. I could go on, because there are a whole lot of other stories, but frankly, I don't have time. Ransom is in trouble."

Surprise was too mild a word for what Brad felt. Livie had always been crazy about animals, but she was stone practical, with a scientific turn of mind, not given to spooky stuff. And she'd never once confided that she got dream messages from four-legged friends.

"Why didn't you tell me? Did Big John know?"

"You'd have packed me off to a therapist. Big John had enough to worry about without Dr. Doolittle for a granddaughter. Now—will you please move?"

"No," Brad said. "I won't move, please or otherwise. Not until you tell me what's so urgent about tracking down a wild stallion on top of a damn mountain!"

Tears glistened in Livie's eyes, and Brad felt a stab to his conscience.

Livie's struggle was visible, and painful to see, but

she finally answered. "He's in pain. There's something wrong with his right foreleg."

"And you plan to do what when—and if—you find him? Shoot him with a tranquilizer gun? Livie, this is Stone Creek, Arizona, not the *Wild Kingdom*. And dream or no dream, that horse—" He raised both hands to forestall the impatience brewing in her face. "*Ransom* is not a character in a Disney movie. He's not going to let you walk up to him, examine his foreleg and give him a nice little shot. If you *did* get close, he'd probably stomp you down to bone fragments and a bloodstain!"

"He wouldn't," Livie said. "He knows I want to help him."

"Livie, suppose—just *suppose,* damn it—that you're wrong."

"I'm not wrong."

"Of *course* you're not wrong. You're a freaking O'Ballivan!" He paused, shoved a hand through his hair. Tried another tack. "There aren't that many hours of daylight left. You're not going up that mountain alone, little sister—not if I have to hog-tie you to keep you here."

"Then you can come with me."

"Oh, that's noble of you. I'd *love* to risk freezing to death in a freaking blizzard. Hell, I've got nothing *better* to do, besides nurse a wounded dog that *you* brought to me, and make a freaking *movie*—also your idea—"

Livie's mouth twitched at one corner. She fought the grin, but it came anyway. "Do you realize you've used the word 'freaking' three times in the last minute and a half? Have you considered switching to decaf?"

"Very funny," Brad said, but he couldn't help grinning back. He rested his hands on Livie's shoulders, squeezed lightly. "You're my little sister. I love you. If you insist on tracking a wild stallion all over the mountain, at least wait until morning. We'll saddle up at dawn."

Livie looked serious again. "You promise?"

"I promise."

"Okay," she said.

"Okay? That's it? You're giving up without a fight?"

"Don't be so suspicious. I said I'd wait until dawn, and I will."

Brad raised one eyebrow. "Shake on it?"

Livie put out a hand. "Shake," she said.

He had to be satisfied with that. In the O'Ballivan family, shaking hands on an agreement was like taking a blood oath—Big John had drilled that into them from childhood. "Since we're leaving so early, maybe you'd better spend the night here."

"I can do that," Livie said, turning to lead Cinnamon back to his stall. "But since I'm not going tonight, I might as well make my normal rounds first. I conned Dr. Summers into covering for me, but he wasn't too happy about it." Her eyes took on a mischievous twinkle as he approached, took over the process of unsaddling the horse. "How are things going with Meg?"

Brad didn't look at her. "Not all that well, actually."

"What's wrong?"

"I'm not sure I could put it into words."

Livie nudged him before pushing open the stall door to leave. "It's a long ride up the mountain," she said. "Plenty of time to talk."

"I might take you up on that," he answered.

"I'll just look in on Willie, then go make my rounds. See you later, alligator."

Brad's eyes burned. Like the handshake, "See you later, alligator" was a holdover from Big John. "In a while, crocodile," he answered on cue.

By the time he got back to the house, Livie had already examined Willie, climbed into the Suburban and driven off. A note stuck to the refrigerator door read, *Are you making supper, Mr. Movie Star? Or should I pick up a pizza?*

Brad chuckled and took a package of chicken out of the freezer.

The phone rang.

"Yea or nay on the double Hawaiian deluxe with extra ham, cheese and pineapple?" Livie asked.

"Forget the pizza," Brad replied. "I'm not eating anything you've handled. You stick your arm up cows' butts for a living, after all."

She laughed, said goodbye and hung up.

He started to replace the receiver, but Meg was still on his mind, so he punched in the digits. Funny, he reflected, how he remembered her number at the Triple M after all this time. He couldn't have recited the one he'd had in Nashville to save his life.

Voice mail picked up. "You've reached 555-7682," Meg said cheerily. "Leave a message and, if it's appropriate, I'll call you back."

Brad moved to disconnect, then put the receiver back to his ear. "It's Brad. I was just—a—calling to see how things are going with your dad and Carly—"

She came on the line, sounding a little breathless. "Brad?"

His heart did a slow backflip. "Yeah, it's me," he said.

"I hear you're making a movie in Stone Creek."

He closed his eyes. He'd blown it again—Meg

should have heard the news from him, not via the local grapevine. "I thought maybe Carly could be an extra," he said.

"She'd love that, I'm sure," Meg said with crisp formality.

"Meg? The movie thing—"

"It's all right, Brad. I'm happy for you. Really."

"You sound thrilled."

"You could have mentioned it. Not exactly an everyday occurrence, especially in the wilds of northern Arizona."

"I wanted to talk about it in person, Meg."

"You know where I live, and clearly, you know my telephone number."

"I know where your G-spot is, too," he said.

He heard her draw in a breath. "Dirty pool, O'Ballivan."

"All's fair in lust and war, McKettrick."

"Is that what this is? Lust?"

"You tell me."

"I'm not the one who took a step back," she reminded him.

He knew what she was talking about, of course. He'd been pretty cool to her the night of the steak dinner. "Livie and I are riding up the mountain again tomorrow, to look for Ransom. Do you still want to go?"

She sighed. He hoped she was thawing out, but with Meg, it could go either way. Ice or fire. "I wish I could. Ted's being admitted to the hospital tomorrow morning, and I promised to take Carly to visit him as soon as school lets out for the day."

"She's having a pretty rough time," he said. "If there's anything I can do to help—"

"The T-shirt was a hit. So is having your autograph

on all those CDs. Your kindness means a lot to her, Brad." A pause. "On a happier note, Sierra went into labor today. I'm expecting to be an aunt again at any moment."

"That is good news," Brad said, but he put one hand to his middle, as though he'd taken a fist to the stomach.

"Yeah," Meg said, and he knew by the catch in her voice that, somehow, she'd picked up on his reaction. "Well, anyway, congratulations on the movie, and thanks for getting in touch. Oh, and be careful on the mountain tomorrow."

The invisible fist moved from his solar plexus to his throat, squeezing hard. *Congratulations on the movie... thanks for getting in touch...so long, see you around.*

She'd hung up before he could get out a goodbye.

He thumbed the off button, leaned forward and rested his head against a cupboard door, eyes closed tight.

Willie nuzzled him in the thigh and gave a soft whine.

Two hours later, Livie returned, freshly showered and wearing a dress.

"Got a hot date?" Brad asked, trying to remember the last time he'd seen his sister in anything besides boots, ragbag jeans and one of Big John's old shirts.

She ignored the question and, with a flourish, pulled a bottle of wine from her tote bag and set it on the counter, sniffing the air appreciatively. "Fried chicken? Is there no end to your talents?"

"Not as far as I know," he joked.

Livie elbowed him. "We should have invited the

twins to join us. It would be like old times, all of us sitting down together in this kitchen."

Not quite like old times, Brad thought, missing Big John with a sudden, piercing ache, as fresh as if he'd just gotten the call announcing his grandfather's death.

Livie was way too good at reading him. She snatched a cucumber slice from the salad and nibbled at it, leaning back against the counter and studying his face. "You really miss Big John, don't you?"

He nodded, not quite trusting himself to speak.

"He was so proud of you, Brad."

He swallowed. Averted his eyes. "Keep your fingers out of the salad," he said.

Livie laid a hand on his arm. "I know you think you disappointed him at practically every turn. That you should have been here, instead of in Nashville or on the road or wherever, and maybe all of that's true, but he *was* proud. And he was grateful, too, for everything you did."

"He'd raise hell about this movie," Brad said hoarsely.

"He'd brag to everybody who would let him bend their ear," Livie replied.

"Do you know what I'd give to be able to talk to Big John just one more time? To say I'm sorry I didn't visit—call more often?"

"A lot, I guess. But you can still talk to him. He'll hear you." She stood on tiptoe, kissed Brad lightly on the cheek. "Tell me you've already fed the horses, because I'd hate to have to swap out this getup for barn gear."

Brad laughed. "I've fed them," he said. He turned, smiled down into her upturned face. "I never would have taken you for a mystic, Doc. Do you talk to Big John? Or just wild stallions and sheepdogs?"

"All the time," Livie said, plundering a drawer for a corkscrew, which Brad immediately took from her. "I don't think he's really gone. Most of the time, it feels as if he's in the next room, not some far-off heaven— sometimes, I even catch the scent of his pipe tobacco."

Since Brad had taken over opening the cabernet, Livie got out a couple of wineglasses. Willie poked his nose at her knee, angling for attention.

"Yes," she told the dog. "I know you're there."

"Does he talk to you, too?" Brad asked, only half kidding.

"Sure," Livie replied airily. "He likes you. You're a little awkward, but Willie thinks you have real potential as a dog owner."

Grinning, Brad sloshed wine into Livie's glass, then his. Raised it in a toast. "To Big John," he said, "and King's Ransom, and Stone Creek's own Dr. Doolittle. And Willie."

"To the movie and Meg McKettrick," Livie added, and clinked her glass against Brad's.

Brad hesitated before he drank. "To Meg," he said finally.

During supper, they chatted about Livie's preliminary plans for the promised animal shelter—it would be state of the art, offering free spaying and neutering, inoculations, etc.

They cleaned up the kitchen together afterward, as they had done when they were kids, then took Willie out for a brief walk. He was still sore, though the pain medication helped, and couldn't make it far, but he managed.

Since he hadn't slept much the night before, Brad crashed in the downstairs guest room early, leaving Livie sitting at the kitchen table, absorbed in his copy of the script.

Hours later, sleep-grogged and blinking in the harsh light of the bedside lamp, he awakened to find Livie standing over him, fully dressed—this time in the customary jeans—and practically vibrating with anxiety.

He yawned and dragged himself upright against the headboard, "Liv, it's the middle of the night."

"Ransom's cornered," Livie blurted. "We have to get to him, and quick. Call a McKettrick and borrow that helicopter!"

CHAPTER TWELVE

The whole thing was crazy.

It was two in the morning.

He'd have to swallow his pride to roust Jesse or Keegan at that hour, and ask for a monumental favor in the bargain. *My sister had this dream, involving a talking horse,* he imagined himself saying.

But the look of desperation in Livie's eyes made the difference.

"Here's a number," she said, shoving a bit of paper at him and handing him the cordless phone from the kitchen.

"Where did you get this?" Brad asked as Willie, curled at the foot of his bed, stood, made a tight circle and laid himself down again.

Livie answered from the doorway, plainly exasperated. "Jesse and I used to go out once in a while," she said. "Make the call and get dressed!"

She didn't give him a chance to suggest that *she* make the request, since she and Jesse had evidently been an item at one time, but hurried out.

As soon as the door shut behind her, Brad sat up, reached for his jeans, which had been in a heap on the floor, and got into them while he thumbed Jesse's number.

McKettrick answered on the second ring, growling, "This had better be good."

Brad closed his eyes for a moment, used one hand to button his fly while keeping the receiver propped between his ear and his right shoulder. "It's Brad O'Ballivan," he said. "Sorry to wake you up, but there's an emergency and—" He paused only briefly, for the last words had to be forced out. "I need some help."

Barely forty-five minutes later, the McKettrickCo helicopter landed, running lights glaring like something out of *Close Encounters of the Third Kind,* in the field directly behind the ranch house. Jesse was at the controls.

"Hey, Liv," he said with a Jesse-grin once she'd scrambled into the small rear seat and put on a pair of earphones.

"Hey," Livie replied. There was no stiffness about either of them—the dating scenario must have ended affably, or not been serious in the first place.

Brad sat up front, next to Jesse, with a rifle between his knees, dreading the moment when he'd have to explain what this moonlight odyssey was all about.

But Jesse didn't ask for an explanation. All he said was, "Where to?"

"Horse Thief Canyon," Livie answered. "On the eastern rim."

Jesse nodded, cast one sidelong glance at Brad's rifle, and lifted the copter off the ground.

I might have to get one of these things, Brad thought, still sleep-jangled.

Within fifteen minutes, they were high over the mountain, spot-lighting the canyon, so named for being the place where Sam O'Ballivan and some of his Ari-

zona Rangers had once cornered a band of horse rus-
tlers.

"There he is!" Livie shouted, fairly blowing out
Brad's eardrums. He leaned for a look and what he
saw made his heart swoop to his boot heels.

Ransom gleamed in the glare of the searchlight,
rearing and pawing the ground with his powerful forelegs. Behind him, against a rock face, were his mares—
Brad counted three, but it was hard to tell how many
others might be in the shadows—and before him, a
pack of nearly a dozen wolves was closing in. They
were hungry, focused on their cornered prey, and
they paid no attention whatsoever to the copter roar-
ing above their heads.

"Set this thing down!" Livie ordered. "Fast!"

Jesse worked the controls with one hand and hauled
a second rifle out from under the pilot's seat with the
other. Clearly, he'd spotted the wolves, too.

He landed the copter on what looked like a ledge,
too narrow for Brad's comfort. The wait for the blades
to slow seemed endless.

"Showtime," Jesse said, shoving open his door, rifle
in hand. "Keep your heads down. The updraft will be
pretty strong."

Brad nodded and pushed open the door, willing
Livie to stay behind, knowing she wouldn't.

Just fifty yards away, Ransom and the wolf pack
were still facing off. The mares screamed and snorted,
frantic with fear, their rolling eyes shining white in
the darkness.

With only the moon for light now, the scene was
eerie.

The small hairs rose on the back of Brad's neck and

one of the wolves turned and studied him with implacable amber eyes. His gray-white ruff shimmered in the silvery glow of cold, distant stars.

Some kind of weird connection sparked between man and beast. Brad was only vaguely aware of Jesse coming up behind him, of Livie already fiddling with her veterinary kit.

I'm a predator, the wolf told Brad. *This is what I do.*

Brad cocked the rifle. *I'm a predator, too,* he replied silently. *And you can't have these horses.*

The wolf pondered a moment, took a single stealthy step toward Ransom, the stallion bloody-legged and exhausted from holding off the pack.

Brad took aim. *Don't do it, Brother Wolf. This isn't a bluff.*

Tilting his massive head back, the wolf gave a chilling howl.

Ransom was stumbling a little by then, looking as though he'd go down. That, of course, was exactly what the pack was waiting for. Once the great steed was on the ground, they'd have him—and the mares. And the resultant carnage didn't bear considering.

Jesse stood at Brad's side, his own rifle ready. "I wouldn't have believed he was real," McKettrick said in a whisper, though whether he was referring to Ransom or the old wolf was anybody's guess, "if I hadn't seen him with my own eyes."

The wolf yowled again, the sound raising something primitive in Brad.

And then it was over.

The leader turned, moving back through the pack at a trot, and they rounded, one by one, with a lethal and hesitant grace, to follow.

Brad let out his breath, lowered his rifle. Jesse relaxed, too.

Livie, carrying her kit in one hand, headed straight for Ransom.

Brad moved to stop her, but Jesse put out his arm.

"Easy," he said. "This is no time to spook that horse."

It would be the supreme irony, Brad reflected grimly, if they had to shoot Ransom in the end, after going to all this trouble to save his hide. If the stallion made one aggressive move toward Livie, though, he'd do it.

"It's me, Olivia," Livie told the legendary wild stallion in a companionable tone. "I came as soon as I could."

Brad brought his rifle up quickly when Ransom butted Livie with his massive head, but Jesse forced the barrel down, murmuring, "Wait."

Ransom stood, lathered and shining with sweat and fresh blood, and allowed Livie to stroke his long neck, ruffle his mane. When she squatted to run her hands over his forelegs, he allowed that, too.

"I'll be damned," Jesse muttered.

The vision was surreal—Brad wasn't entirely convinced he wasn't dreaming at home in his bed.

"You're going to have to come in," Livie told the horse, "at least long enough for that leg to heal."

Unbelievably, Ransom nickered and tossed his head as though he were nodding in agreement.

"How the hell does she expect to drive a band of wild horses all the way down the mountain to Stone Creek Ranch?" Brad asked. He wasn't looking for an answer from Jesse—he was just thinking out loud.

Jesse whacked him on the shoulder. "You've been in the big city too long, O'Ballivan," he said. "You stay here, in case the wolves come back, and I'll go gather a roundup crew. It'll be a few hours before we get here, though—keep your eye out for the pack and pray for good weather. About the last thing we need is another of those blizzards."

By that time, Livie had produced a syringe from her kit, and was preparing to poke it through the hide on Ransom's neck.

Brad moved a step closer.

"Stay back," Livie said. "Ransom's calm enough, but these mares are stressed out. I'd rather not find myself at the center of an impromptu rodeo, if it's all the same to you."

Jesse chuckled, handed Brad his rifle, and turned to sprint back to the copter. Moments later, it was lifting off again, veering southwest.

Brad stood unmoving for a long time, still not sure he wasn't caught up in the aftermath of a nightmare, then leaned his and Jesse's rifles against the trunk of a nearby tree.

Ransom stood with his head down, dazed by the drug Livie had administered minutes before. The mares, still fitful but evidently aware that the worst danger had passed, fanned out to graze on the dry grass.

In the distance, the old wolf howled with piteous fury.

PINKISH-GOLD LIGHT RIMMED the eastern hills as Meg returned to the house, after feeding the horses, and the phone was ringing.

She dived for it, in case it was Travis calling to say Sierra had had the baby.

In case it was Brad.

It was Eve.

"You're an aunt again," Meg's mother announced, with brisk pride. "Sierra had a healthy baby boy at four-thirty this morning. I think they're going to call him Brody, for Travis's brother."

Joy fluttered inside Meg's heart, like something trying delicate wings, and tears smarted in her eyes. "She's okay? Sierra, I mean?"

"She's fine, by all reports," Eve answered. "Liam and I are heading for Flagstaff right after breakfast. He's beside himself."

After washing her hands at the kitchen sink, Meg poured herself a cup of hot coffee. By habit, she'd set it brewing before going out to the barn. Upstairs, she heard Ted's slow step as he moved along the corridor.

"Ted's checking in today," she said, keeping her voice down. "I'll stop by to see Sierra and the baby after I get him settled." She drew a breath, let it out softly. "Mother, Carly is not handling this well."

Eve sighed sadly. "I'm sure she isn't, the poor child," she said. "Why don't you keep her out of school for the day and let her come along with you and Ted?"

"I suggested that," Meg replied, as her father appeared on the back stairs, dressed, with a shaving kit in one hand.

Their gazes met.

"And?" Eve prompted.

"And Ted said he wants her to attend class and visit later, when school's out for the day."

Ted nodded. "Is that Eve?"

"Yes," Meg said.

He gestured for the phone, and Meg handed it to him.

"This is Ted," he told Meg's mother. While he explained that Carly needed to settle into as normal a life as possible, as soon as possible, Carly herself appeared on the stairs, looking glum and stubborn.

She wore jeans and the souvenir T-shirt Brad had given her, in spite of the fact that it reached almost to her knees. The expression in her eyes dared Meg to object to the outfit—or anything else in the known universe.

"Hungry?" Meg asked.

"No," Carly said.

"Too bad. In this house, we eat breakfast."

"I might puke."

"You might."

Ted cupped a hand over one end of the phone. "Carly," he said sternly, "you *will* eat."

Scowling, Carly swung a leg over the bench next to the table and plunked down, angrily bereft. Meg poured orange juice, carried the glass to the table, set it down in front of her sister.

It was a wonder the stuff didn't come to an instant boil, considering the heat of Carly's glare as she stared at it.

"This bites," she said.

"Okay, I'll pass the word," Ted told Eve. "See you later."

He hung up. "Eve's hoping you can have lunch with her and Liam after you visit Sierra and the baby."

Meg nodded, distracted.

"It bites," Carly repeated, watching Ted with thunderous eyes. "You're going to the *hospital,* and I have to go to that stupid school, where they'll probably put me in *kindergarten* or something. I'm *supposed* to be in seventh grade."

Meg had no idea how Carly had fared on the tests she'd taken the day before, but it seemed safe to say things probably wouldn't go as badly as all that.

She got a frown for her trouble.

"This time next week," Ted told his younger daughter, "you'll probably be a sophomore at Harvard. Drink your orange juice."

Carly took a reluctant sip and eyeballed Meg's jeans, which were covered with bits of hay. "Don't you have like a *job* or something?"

"Yeah," Meg said, putting a pan on the stove to boil water for oatmeal. "I'm a ranch hand. The work's hard, the pay is lousy, there's no retirement plan and you have to shovel a lot of manure, but I love it."

Breakfast was a dismal affair, one Carly did her best to drag out, but, finally, the time came to leave.

Meg remained in the house for a few extra minutes while Ted and Carly got into the Blazer, giving them time to talk privately.

When she joined them, Carly was in tears, and Ted looked weary to the center of his soul.

Meg gave him a sympathetic look, pushed the button to roll up the garage door and backed out.

When they reached the school, Ted climbed laboriously out of the Blazer and stood on the sidewalk with Carly. They spoke earnestly, though Meg couldn't hear what they said, and Carly dashed at her cheeks with the back of one hand before turning to march staunchly through the colorful herd of kids toward the entrance.

Ted had trouble getting back into the car, but when Meg moved to get out and come around to help him, he shook his head.

"Don't," he said.

She nodded, thick-throated and close to tears herself.

When they reached the hospital in Flagstaff, Eve was waiting in the admittance office.

"I'll take over from here," she told Meg, standing up extra-straight as she watched a nurse ease Ted into a waiting wheelchair. "You go upstairs and see your sister and your new nephew. Room 502."

Meg hesitated, nodded. Then, surprising even herself, she bent and kissed Ted on top of the head before walking purposefully toward the nearest elevator.

SIERRA GLOWED FROM the inside, as though she'd distilled sunlight to a golden potion and swallowed it down. The room was bedecked in flowers, splashes of watercolor pink, blue and yellow shimmered all around.

"Aunt Meg!" Liam cried delightedly, zooming out of the teary blur. "I've got a brand-new brother and his name is Brody Travis Reid!"

With a choked laugh, Meg hugged the little boy, almost displacing his Harry Potter glasses in the process. "Where *is* this Brody yahoo, anyhow?" she teased. "His legend looms large in this here town, but so far, I haven't seen hide nor hair of him."

"Silly," Liam said. "He's in the *nursery,* with all the other babies!"

Meg ruffled his hair. Went to give Sierra a kiss on the forehead.

"Congratulations, little sister," she said.

"He's so beautiful," Sierra whispered.

"Boys are supposed to be *handsome,* not beautiful," Liam protested, dragging a chair up on the other side of Sierra's bed and standing in the seat so he could be eye to eye with his mother. "Was I handsome?"

Sierra smiled, squeezed his small hand. "You're *still* handsome," she said gently. "And Dad and I are counting on you to be a really good big brother to Brody."

Liam turned to Meg, beaming. "Travis is going to adopt me. I'll be Liam McKettrick Reid, and Mom's changing her name, too."

Meg lifted her eyebrows slightly.

"Somebody had to break the tradition," Sierra said. "I've already told Eve."

Sierra would be the first McKettrick woman to take her husband's last name in generations.

"Mom's okay with that?" Meg asked.

Sierra grinned. "Timing is everything," she said. "If you want to break disturbing news to her, be sure to give birth first."

Meg chuckled. "You are a brave woman," she told Sierra. Then, turning to her nephew, she held out a hand. "How about showing me that brother of yours, Liam McKettrick Reid?"

JESSE RETURNED AT MIDMORNING, as promised, with a dozen mounted cowboys. To Brad, the bunch looked as though they'd ridden straight out of an old black-and-white movie, their clothes, gear and horses only taking on color as they drew within hailing distance.

Brad was bone-tired, and Livie, her doctoring completed for the time being, had fallen asleep under a tree, bundled in his coat as well as her own. He'd built a fire an hour or so before dawn, but he craved coffee something fierce, and he was chilled to his core.

Before bedding down in the wee small hours, Livie had cheerfully informed her brother that while he ought to keep watch for the wolf pack, he didn't need to worry that Ransom and the mares would run off. They knew, she assured him, that they were among friends.

He'd kept watch through what remained of the night, pondering the undeniable proof that his sister *had* received an SOS from Ransom.

Now, with riders approaching, Livie wakened and got up off the ground, smiling and dusting dried pine needles and dirt off her jeans.

Jesse, Keegan and Rance were in the lead, ropes coiled around the horns of their saddles, rifles in their scabbards.

Rance nodded to Brad, dismounted and walked over to Ransom. He checked the animal's legs as deftly as Livie had.

"Think he can make it down the mountain to the ranch?" Rance asked.

Livie nodded. "If we take it slowly," she said. Her smile took in the three McKettricks and the men they'd rallied to help. "Thanks, everybody."

Most of the cowboys stared at Ransom as though they expected him to sprout wings, like Pegasus, and take to the blue-gold morning sky. One rode forward, leading mounts for Livie and Brad.

Livie took off Brad's coat and handed it to him, then swung up into the saddle with an ease he couldn't hope to emulate. He kicked dirt over the last embers of the campfire while Rance handed up Livie's veterinary kit.

The ride down the mountain would be long and

hard, though thank God the weather had held. The sky was blue as Meg's eyes.

Brad took a deep breath, jabbed a foot into the stirrup and hauled himself onto the back of a pinto gelding. He was still pretty sore from the *last* trip up and down this mountain.

The cowboys went to work, starting Ransom and his mares along the trail with low whistles to urge them along.

Livie rode up beside Brad and grinned. "You look like hell," she said.

"Gosh, thanks," Brad grimaced, shifting in the saddle in a vain attempt to get comfortable.

She chuckled. "Think of it as getting into character for the movie."

SEEING BRODY FOR the first time was the high point of Meg's day, but from there, it was all downhill.

Ted's tests were invasive, and he was drugged.

Liam was hyper with excitement, and didn't sit still for a second during lunch, despite Eve's grandmotherly reprimands. The food in the cafeteria tasted like wood shavings, and she got a call from the police in Indian Rock on her way home.

Carly had ditched school, and Wyatt Terp, the town marshal, had picked her up along Highway 17. She'd been trying to hitchhike to Flagstaff.

Meg sped to the police station, screeched to a stop in the parking lot and stormed inside.

Carly sat forlornly in a chair near Wyatt's desk, looking even younger than twelve.

"I just wanted to see my dad," she said in a small voice, taking all the bluster out of Meg's sails.

Meg pulled up a chair alongside Carly's and sat down, taking a few deep breaths to center herself. Wyatt smiled and busied himself in another part of the station house.

"You could have been kidnapped, or hit by a car, or a thousand other things," Meg said carefully.

"Dad and I thumbed it lots of times," Carly said defensively, "when our car broke down."

Meg closed her eyes for a moment. Waited for a sensible reply to occur to her. When that didn't happen, she opened them again.

"Will you take me to see him now?" Carly asked.

Meg sighed. "Depends," she said. "Are you under arrest, or just being held for questioning?"

Carly relaxed a little. "I'm not busted," she answered seriously. "But Marshal Terp says if he catches me hitchhiking again, I'll probably do hard time."

"You pull any more stupid tricks like this one, kiddo," Meg said, "and *I'll* give you all the 'hard time' you can handle."

Wyatt approached, doing his best to look like a stern lawman, but the effect was more Andy-of-Mayberry. "You can go, young lady," he told Carly, "but I'd better not see you in this office again unless you're selling Girl Scout cookies or 4-H raffle tickets or something. Got it?"

"Got it," Carly said meekly, ducking her head slightly.

Meg stood, motioned for her sister to head for the door.

Carly didn't move until the lawman raised an eyebrow at her.

"Is it the badge that makes her mind?" she whispered to Wyatt, once Carly was out of earshot. "And if so, do you happen to have a spare?"

HE NEEDED TO see Meg.

It was seven-thirty that night before Ransom and his band were corralled at Stone Creek Ranch, and the McKettricks and their helpers had unsaddled all their horses, loaded them into trailers and driven off. Livie had greeted Willie, taken a hot shower and, bundled in one of Big John's ugly Indian-blanket bathrobes, gobbled down a bologna sandwich before climbing the stairs to her old room to sleep.

Brad was tired.

He was cold and he was hungry and he was saddle sore.

The only sensible thing to do was shower, eat and sleep like a dead man.

But he still needed to see Meg.

He settled for the shower and clean clothes.

Calling first would have been the polite thing to do, but he was past that. So he scrawled a note to Livie— *Feed the dog and the horses if I'm not back by morning*—and left.

The truck knew its way to the Triple M, which was a good thing, since he was in a daze.

Lights glowed warm and golden from Meg's windows, and his heart lifted at the sight, at the prospect of seeing her. The McKettricks, he recalled, tended to gather in kitchens. He parked the truck in the drive and walked around to the back of the house, knocked at the door.

Carly answered. She looked wan, as worn-out and used-up as Brad felt, but her face lit up when she saw him.

"I get to stay in seventh grade," she said. "According to my test scores, I'm gifted."

Brad rustled up a grin and resisted the urge to look past her, searching for Meg. "I could have told you that," he said as she stepped back to let him in.

"Meg's upstairs," Carly told him. "She has a sick headache and I'm supposed to leave her alone unless I'm bleeding or there's a national emergency."

Brad hid his disappointment. "Oh," he said, because nothing better came to him.

"I heard you were making a movie," Carly said. Clearly she was lonesome, needed somebody to talk to.

Brad could certainly identify. "Yeah," he answered, and this time the grin was a little easier to find.

"Can I be in it? I wouldn't have to have lines or anything. Just a costume."

"I'll see what I can do," Brad said. "My people will call your people."

Carly laughed, and the sound was good to hear.

He was about to excuse himself and leave when Meg appeared on the stairs wearing a cotton nightgown, with her hair all rumpled and shadows under her eyes.

"Rough day?" he asked, a feeling of bruised tenderness stealing up from his middle to his throat, like thick smoke from a smudge fire.

She tried to smile, pausing a moment on the stairs.

"Time for me to get lost," Carly said. "Can I use your computer, Meg?"

Meg nodded.

Carly left the room and Brad stood still, watching Meg.

"I guess I should have called first," he said.

"Sit down," Meg told him. "I'll make some coffee."

"I'll make the coffee," Brad replied. "*You* sit down."

For once, she didn't give him any back talk. She just padded over to the table and plunked into the big chair at the head of it.

"Did you find Ransom?" she asked, while Brad opened cupboard doors, scouting for a can of coffee.

"Yes," he said, pleased that she'd remembered, given everything else that was going on in her life. "He and the mares have the run of my best pasture." He told Meg the rest of the story, or most of it, leaving out the part about Livie's dreams, not because he was afraid of what she might think of his sister's strange talent, but because the tale was Livie's to tell or keep to herself.

Meg grinned as she listened, shaking her head. "Rance and Keegan and Jesse must have been in their element, driving wild horses down the mountain like they were back in the old West."

"Maybe," Brad agreed, leaning back against the counter as he waited for the coffee to brew. "As for me—if I never have to do that again, it'll be too soon."

Meg laughed, but her eyes misted over in the next moment. She'd looked away too late to keep him from seeing. "Sierra—my other sister—had a baby this morning. A boy. His name is Brody."

Brad ached inside. It had been hard for Meg to share that news, and it shouldn't have been. Given the way he'd shut her out after meeting Carly, he couldn't blame her for being wary.

He went to her, crouched beside her chair, took one of her hands in both of his. "I'm sorry about the other night, Meg. I was just—I don't know—a little rattled by Carly's age, and her resemblance to you."

"It's okay," Meg said, but a tear slipped down her cheek.

Brad brushed it away with the side of one thumb. "It isn't okay. I acted like a jerk."

She sniffled. Nodded. "A *major* jerk."

He chuckled, blinked a couple of times because his eyes burned. Rose to his full height again. "I was hoping to spend the night," he said. "Until I remembered Carly's living here now."

Meg bit her lip. "I have guest rooms," she told him.

She didn't want him to leave, then.

Brad's spirits rose a notch.

"But what about Willie, and your horses?"

"Livie's at the house," he said, moving away from her, getting mugs down out of a cupboard. If he'd stayed close, he'd have hauled her to her feet and laid a big sloppy one on her, complete with tongue, and with a twelve-year-old in practically the next room, that was out. "She'll take care of the livestock."

After that, they sat quietly at the venerable old McKettrick table and talked about ordinary things. It made him surprisingly happy, just being there with Meg, doing nothing in particular.

In fact, life seemed downright perfect to him.

Which just went to show what *he* knew.

CHAPTER THIRTEEN

BRAD BLINKED AWAKE, sprawled on his back on the big leather couch in Meg's study, fully dressed and covered with an old quilt.

Carly stood looking down at him, a curious expression on her face, probably surprised that he hadn't slept with Meg.

"What time is it?" he asked, yawning.

"Six-thirty," Carly answered. She was wearing jeans and the T-shirt he'd given her, and it looked a little the worse for wear. "Have you decided if I get to be in your movie?"

Brad chuckled, yawned again. "I haven't heard from your agent," he teased.

She frowned. "I don't have an agent," she replied. "Is that a problem?"

"No," he relented, smiling. "I can promise you a walk-on. Beyond that, it's out of my hands. Deal?"

"Deal!" Carly beamed. But then her face fell. "I hope my dad makes it long enough to see me on the big screen," she said.

Brad's heart slipped, caught itself with a lurch that was almost painful. "We could show him the rushes," he said after swallowing once. "Right in his hospital room."

"What are rushes?"

"Film clips. They're not edited, and there's no music—not even sound, sometimes. But he'd see you."

Meg appeared in the doorway of the study, clad in chore clothes.

"I get to be in the movie," Carly informed her excitedly. "Even though I don't have an agent."

"That's great," Meg said softly, her gaze resting with tender gratitude on Brad. "Coffee's on, if anybody's interested."

Brad threw back the quilt, sat upright, pulled on his boots. "Somebody's interested, all right," he said. "I'll feed the horses if you'll make breakfast."

"Sounds fair," Meg answered, turning her attention back to Carly. "Nix on the T-shirt, Ms. Streep. You've worn it for three days in a row now—it goes in the laundry."

On her way to certain stardom, Carly apparently figured she could give ground on the T-shirt edict. "Okay," she said, and headed out of the room, ostensibly to go upstairs and change clothes.

"Carly got arrested yesterday," Meg announced, looking wan.

Brad stood, surprised. And not surprised. "What happened?"

"She decided to cut school and hitchhike to Flagstaff to see Ted in the hospital. Thank God, Wyatt happened to be heading up Highway 17 and spotted her from his squad car."

Brad approached Meg, took her elbows gently into his hands. "Having doubts about being an instant mother, McKettrick?" he asked quietly. She seemed uncommonly fragile, and knowing she'd been flattened by a headache the night before worried him.

"Yes," she said after gnawing at her lower lip for a couple of seconds. "I've always wanted a child, more than anything, but I didn't expect it to happen this way."

He drew her close, held her, buried his face in her hair and breathed in the flower-and-summer-grass scent of it. "I know you don't think of Ted as a father," he said close to her ear, "but a reunion with him this late in the game, especially with a terminal diagnosis hanging over his head, has to be a serious blow. Maybe you need to acknowledge that Carly isn't the only one with some grieving to do."

She tilted her head back, her blue eyes shining with tears. "Damn him," she whispered. "Damn him for coming back here to die! Where was he when I took my first steps—lost my front teeth—broke my leg at horseback riding camp—graduated from high school and college? Where was he when you—"

"When I broke your heart?" Brad finished for her.

"Well—" Meg paused to sniffle once. "Yeah."

"I'd do anything to make that up to you, Meg. Anything for a do over. But the world doesn't work that way. Maybe besides finding a place for Carly, where he knows she'll be loved and she'll be safe, Ted's looking for the same thing I am. A second chance with you."

She looked taken aback. "Maybe," she agreed. "But he sure took his sweet time putting in an appearance, and so did you."

Brad gave her another hug. They were on tricky ground, and he knew it. Carly could be heard clattering down the stairs at the back of the house, into the kitchen.

They needed privacy to carry the conversation any further.

"I'll go feed the horses," he reiterated. "You make breakfast." He kissed her forehead, not wanting to let her go. "Once you've dropped Carly off at school, you could drop in at my place."

He held his breath, awaiting her answer. Both of them knew what would happen if he and Meg were alone at Stone Creek Ranch.

"I'll let you know," she said at long last.

He hesitated, nodded once and left her to feed the horses.

Breakfast turned out to be toaster waffles and microwave bacon.

"Next time," Brad told Meg, after they'd exchanged a light kiss next to her Blazer, with Carly watching avidly from the passenger seat, "I'll cook and *you* feed the horses."

He sang old Johnny Cash favorites all the way home, at the top of his lungs, with the truck windows rolled down.

But the song died in his throat when he topped the rise and saw a sleek white limo waiting in the driveway. Some gut instinct, as primitive as what he'd felt facing down the leader of the wolf pack up at Horse Thief Canyon, told him this wasn't Phil, or even a bunch of movie executives on an outing.

The chauffer got out, opened the rear right-hand door of the limo as Brad pulled to a stop next to it, buzzing up the truck windows and frowning.

A pair of long, shapely legs swung into view.

Brad swore and slammed out of the truck to stand like a gunfighter, his hands on his hips.

"I'd be perfect for the female lead in this movie," Cynthia Donnigan said, tottering toward him on spiked heels that sank into the dirt. Her short, stretchy skirt rode up on her gym-toned thighs, and she didn't bother to adjust it.

He stared at her in amazement and disbelief, literally speechless.

Cynthia lowered her expensive sunglasses and batted her lashes—as fake as her breasts—and her collagen-enhanced lips puckered into a pout. "Aren't you glad to see me?"

Her hair, black as Ransom's coat, was arranged in artfully careless tufts stiff enough to do damage if she decided to head butt somebody.

"What do you think?" he growled.

Luck, Big John had often said, was never so bad that it couldn't get worse. At that moment, Meg's Blazer came over the rise, dust spiraling behind it.

"I think you're not very forgiving," Cynthia said, following his gaze and then zeroing in on his face with a smug little twist of her mouth. "Bygones are bygones, baby. I'm ideal for the part and you know it."

Brad took a step back as she teetered a step forward. "Not a chance," he said, aware of Meg coming to a stop behind him, but not getting out of the Blazer.

Cynthia smiled and did a waggle-fingered wave in Meg's direction. "I've checked into a resort in Sedona," she said sweetly. "I can wait until you come to your senses and agree that the part of the lawman's widow was written for me."

Brad turned, approached the Blazer and met Meg's wide eyes through the glass of the driver's-side window. He opened the door and offered a hand to help her down.

"The second wife?" Meg asked, more mouthing the words than saying them.

Brad nodded shortly.

Meg peered around him as she got out of the Blazer. Then, with a big smile, she walked right up to Cynthia with her hand out. "I think I've seen you in several feminine hygiene product commercials," she said.

That made Brad chuckle to himself.

Cynthia simmered. "Hello," she responded, in a dangerous purr. "You must be the girl Brad left behind."

Meg had grown up rough-and-tumble, with a bunch of mischievous boy cousins, and served on the executive staff of a multinational corporation. She wasn't easy to intimidate. To Brad's relief—and amusement— she hooked an arm through his, smiled winningly and said, "It's sort of an on-again, off-again kind of thing with Brad and me. Right now, it's definitely on."

Cynthia blinked. She was strictly a B-grade celebrity, but as Brad's ex-wife and sole owner of an up-and-coming production company, she was used to deference of the Beverly Hills variety.

But this was Stone Creek, Arizona, not Beverly Hills.

And the word *deference* wasn't in Meg's vocabulary.

Temporarily stymied, Cynthia pushed her sunglasses back up her nose, minced back toward the waiting limo. The driver stood waiting, still holding her door open and staring off into space as though oblivious to everything going on in what was essentially the barnyard.

Brad followed. "If you manage to wangle your way into this movie," he said, "I'm out."

Cynthia plopped her scantily clad butt onto the leather seat, but didn't draw her killer legs inside. "Read your contract, Brad," she said. "You signed with Starglow Productions. *My* company."

The shock that made his stomach go into a free fall must have shown in his face, because his ex-wife smiled.

"Didn't I tell you I changed the name of the company?" she asked. "No me, no movie, cowboy."

"No movie," Brad said, feeling sick. The whole county was excited about the project—they'd have talked about it for years to come. Carly and a lot of other people would be disappointed—not least of all, himself.

"Back to Sedona," Cynthia told the driver, with a lofty gesture of one manicured hand.

"Yes, ma'am," he replied. But he gave Brad a sympathetic glance before getting behind the wheel.

Brad stood still, furious not only with Cynthia, and with Phil, who had to have known who owned Starglow Productions, but with himself. He'd been too quick to sign on the dotted line, swayed by his own desire to play big-screen cowboy, and by Livie's suggestion that he build an animal shelter with the proceeds. If he tried to back out of the deal now, Cynthia's lawyers would be all over him like fleas on an old hound dog, and he didn't even want to think of the potential publicity.

"So that's the second wife," Meg said, stepping up beside him and watching as the sleek car zipped away.

"That's her," he replied gloomily. "And I am royally, totally screwed."

She moved to stand in front of him, looking up into his face. "I was trying hard not to eavesdrop," she said, "but I couldn't help gathering that she wants to be in the movie."

"She *owns* the movie," Brad said.

"And this is so awful because—?"

"Because she's a first-class, card-carrying bitch. And because I can hardly stand to be in the same room with her, let alone on a movie set for three or four months."

Meg took his hand, gave him a gentle tug in the direction of the house. "Can't you break the contract?"

"Not without getting sued for everything I have, including this ranch, and bringing so many tabloid stringers to Stone Creek that they'll be swinging from the telephone poles."

"Then maybe you should just bite the proverbial bullet and make the movie."

"You haven't read the script," Brad said. "I have to kiss her. And there's a love scene—"

Meg's eyes twinkled. "You sound like a little boy, balking at being in the school play with a *girl*." She tugged him up the back steps, toward the kitchen door.

Willie met them on the other side, wagging cheerfully.

Brad let him out, scowling, and he and Meg waited on the porch while the dog attended to his duties.

"You have no idea what she's like," Brad said.

Meg gave him a light poke with her elbow. "I know you must have loved her once. After all, you married her."

"The truth is a lot less flattering than that," he replied, unable, for a long moment, to meet Meg's eyes.

What he had to say was going to upset her, for several reasons, and there was no way to avoid it. "We hooked up after a party. Six weeks later, she called and told me she was pregnant, and the baby was mine. I married her, because she said she was going to get an abortion if I didn't. I went on tour—she wanted to go along and I refused. Frankly, I wasn't ready to present Cynthia to the world as my adored bride. She called the press in, gave them pictures of the 'wedding.' And then, just to make sure I knew what it meant to cross her, she had the abortion anyway."

The pain was there in Meg's face—she had to be thinking that, had she told him about *their* baby, he'd have married her with the same singular lack of enthusiasm—but her words took him by surprise. "I'm sorry, Brad," she said softly. "You must have really wanted to be a dad."

He whistled for Willie, since speaking was beyond him for the moment, and the dog, obviously on the mend, made it up the porch steps with no help. "Yeah," he said.

"I have an idea," Meg said.

He glanced at her. "What?"

"We could rehearse your love scene. Just to be sure you get it right."

In spite of everything, he chuckled. The sound was raw and hurt his throat, but it was genuine. "Aren't you the least bit jealous?" he asked.

She looked honestly puzzled. "Of what?"

"I'm going to have to kiss Cynthia. Get naked with her on the silver screen. This doesn't bother you?"

"I'll cover my eyes during that part of the movie," she joked, with a little what-the-hell motion of her shoulders. Then her expression turned serious. "Of course, there's a fine line between hatred and passion. If you care for Cynthia, you need to tell me—now."

He laid his hands on her shoulders, remembered the satiny smoothness of her bare skin. "I care for *you,* Meg McKettrick," he said. "I tried hard—with Valerie, even with Cynthia—but it never worked. I was always thinking about you—reading about you in the business pages of newspapers, getting what news I could through my sisters, checking the McKettrickCo Web site. Whenever I read or heard your name, I got this sour ache in the pit of my stomach, because I was scared a wedding announcement would follow."

Meg stiffened slightly. "What would you have done if one had?"

"Stopped the wedding," he said. "Made a scene Indian Rock and Stone Creek would never forget." He smiled crookedly. "Kind of a sticky proposition, given that I could have been married at the time."

"Not to mention that my cousins would have thrown you bodily out of the church," Meg huffed, but there was a smile beginning in her eyes, already tugging at the corners of her mouth.

"I said it would have been an unforgettable scene," he reminded her, grinning. "I would have fought back, you see, and yelled your name, like Stanley yelling for Stella in *A Streetcar Named Desire.*"

She pretended to punch him in the stomach. "You're impossible."

"I'm also horny. And a lot more—though I'm not sure you're ready to hear that part."

"Try me."

"Okay. I love you, Meg McKettrick. I always have. I always will."

"You're right. I wasn't ready."

"Then I guess rehearsing the love scene is out?"

She smiled, stood on tiptoe and kissed the cleft in his chin. "I didn't say that. Hardworking actors should know their scenes cold."

He bent his head, nibbled at her delectable mouth. "Oh, I'll know the scene," he breathed. "But there won't be anything 'cold' about it."

MEG HAULED HERSELF up onto her elbows, out of a sated sleep, glanced at the clock on the table next to Brad's bed and screamed.

"What?" Brad asked, bolting awake.

"Look at the time!" Meg wailed. "Carly will be out of school in fifteen minutes!"

Calmly, Brad reached for the telephone receiver, handed it to her. "Call the school and tell them you've been detained and you'll be there soon."

"Detained?"

"Would you rather say you've been in bed with me all afternoon?"

"No," she admitted, and dialed 411, asking to be connected to Indian Rock Middle School.

When she arrived at the school forty-five minutes later, Carly was waiting glumly in the principal's office. Her expression softened, though, when she saw that Brad had come along.

"Oh, great," she said. "Brad O'Ballivan shows up at my school, *in person,* and nobody's around to see but the geek-wads in detention. Who'd believe a word *they* said?"

Brad laughed. "Did I ever tell you I was one of those 'geek-wads' once upon a time, always in detention?"

"Get out," Carly said, intrigued.

"Don't get the idea that being in detention is cool," Meg warned.

Carly rolled her eyes.

The three of them made the drive to Flagstaff in Brad's truck. Carly chattered nonstop for the first few miles, pointing out the place where she'd been "busted" for trying to hitch a ride, but as they drew nearer to their destination, she grew more and more subdued.

It didn't help that Ted was worse than he'd been the day before. He looked shrunken, lying there in his bed with tubes and monitors attached to every part of his body.

Looking at her father, it seemed to Meg that he'd used up the last of his personal resources to fling himself over an invisible finish line—getting Carly to her for safekeeping. For the first time it was actually real to Meg: he *was* dying.

Brad gave her a nudge toward the bed, an unspoken reminder of what he'd said about her having grieving to do, just as Carly did.

"How about a milk shake in the cafeteria?" Meg heard Brad say to Carly.

In the next moment, the two of them were gone, and Meg was alone with the man who had abandoned her so long ago that she didn't even remember him.

"That young man," Ted said, "is in love with you."

"He left me, too," Meg said without meaning to expose the rawest nerve in her psyche. "It's a pattern. First you, then Brad."

"Do yourself a favor and don't superimpose your

old man over him," Ted struggled to say. "And when Carly gets old enough, don't let her make that mistake, either. I don't have time to make it up to you, what I did and didn't do, but he does. You give him the chance."

Tears welled in Meg's eyes, thickened her throat. "I hate it that you're dying," she said.

Ted put out his left hand, an IV tube dangling from it. "Me, too," he ground out. "Come here, kid."

Meg let him pull her closer, lowered her forehead to rest against his.

She felt moisture in the gray stubble on his cheeks and didn't know if the tears were hers or her father's. Or both.

"If I could stay around a little longer, I'd find a way to prove that you're still my little girl and I've always loved you. Since I'm not going to get that chance, you'll have to take my word for it."

"It isn't fair," Meg protested, knowing the remark was childish.

"Not much is, in this life," Ted answered, as Meg raised her head so she could look into his face. "Know what I'd tell you if I'd been around all this time like a regular father, and had the right to say what's on my mind?"

Meg couldn't answer.

"I'd tell you not to let Brad O'Ballivan get away. Don't let your damnable McKettrick pride get in the way of what he's offering, Meg."

"He told me he loves me," she said.

"Do you believe him?"

"I don't know."

"All right, then, do you love him?"

Meg bit her lower lip, nodded.

"Have you told him?"

"Sort of," Meg said.

"Take it from me, kid," Ted countered, trying to smile. "'Sort of' ain't good enough." His faded eyes seemed to memorize Meg, take her in. "Get the nurse for me, will you? This pain medication isn't working."

Meg immediately rang for the nurse, and when help came, rushed to the elevators and punched the button for the cafeteria. By the time she got back with Carly and Brad, the room was full of people in scrubs.

Carly broke free and rushed to her dad's bedside, squirming through until she caught hold of his hand.

The medical team, in the midst of an emergency, would have pushed Carly aside if Brad hadn't spoken in a voice of calm but unmistakable authority.

"Let her stay," he said.

"Dad?" Carly whispered desperately. "Dad, don't go, okay? Don't go!"

A nurse eased Carly back from the bedside, and the work continued, but it was too late, and everyone knew it.

The heartbeat monitor blipped, then flatlined.

Carly turned, sobbing, not into Meg's arms, but into Brad's.

He held her and drew Meg close against his side at the same time.

After that, there were papers to sign. Meg would have to call her mother later, but at the moment, she simply couldn't say the words.

Carly seemed dazed, allowing herself to be led out of the hospital, back to Brad's truck. She'd been inconsolable in Ted's hospital room, but now she was dry-eyed and the only sound she made was the occasional hiccup.

Brad didn't take them back to the Triple M, but to his own ranch. There, he called Eve, then Jesse. Vaguely, as if from a great distance, Meg heard him ask her cousin to make sure her horses got fed.

There were other calls, too, but Meg wasn't tracking. She simply sat at the kitchen table, watching numbly while Carly knelt on the floor, both arms around a sympathetic Willie, her face buried in his fur.

Olivia arrived—Brad must have summoned her— and brought a stack of pizza boxes with her. She set the boxes on the counter, washed her hands at the sink and immediately started setting out plates and silverware.

"I'm not hungry," Carly said.

"Me, either," Meg echoed.

"Humor me," Olivia said.

The pizza tasted like cardboard, but it filled a hole, if only a physical one, and Meg was grateful. Following her example, Carly ate, too.

"Are we staying here tonight?" Carly asked Brad, her eyes enormous and hollow.

Olivia answered for him. "Yes," she said.

"Who are you?"

"I'm Livie—Brad's sister."

"The veterinarian?"

Olivia nodded.

"My dad died today."

Olivia's expressive eyes filled with tears. "I know."

Meg swallowed, but didn't speak. Next to her, Brad took her hand briefly, gave it a squeeze.

"Do you like being an animal doctor?" Carly asked. She'd said hardly a word to Meg or even Brad since they'd left the hospital, but for some reason, she was reaching out to Olivia O'Ballivan.

"I love it," Olivia said. "It's hard sometimes, though. When I try really hard to help an animal, and they don't get better."

"I kept thinking my dad would get well, but he didn't."

"Our dad died, too," Olivia said after a glance in Brad's direction. "He was struck by lightning during a roundup. I kept thinking there must have been a mistake—that he was just down in Phoenix at a cattle auction, or looking for strays up on the mountain."

Meg felt a quick tension in Brad, a singular alertness, gone again as soon as it came. Her guess was he hadn't known his sister, a child when the accident happened, had secretly believed their father would come home.

"Does it ever stop hurting?" Carly asked, her voice small and fragile.

Meg squeezed her eyes shut. Does *it ever stop hurting?* she wondered.

"You'll never forget your dad, if that's what you mean," Olivia said. "But it gets easier. Brad and our sisters and I, we were lucky. We had our grandfather, Big John. Like you've got Meg."

Brad pushed his chair back, left the table. Stood with his back to them all, as if gazing out the darkened window over the sink.

"Big John passed away, too," Olivia explained quietly. "But we were all grown up by then. He was there when it counted, and now we've got each other."

Carly turned imploring eyes on Meg. "You won't die, too? You won't die and leave me all alone?"

Meg got up, went to Carly, gathered her into her arms. "I'll be here," she promised. *"I'll be here."*

Carly clung to her for a long time, then, typically, pulled away. "Where am I going to sleep?" she asked.

"I thought maybe you'd like to stay in my room," Olivia said. "It has twin beds. You can have the one by the window, if you'd like."

"You're going to stay, too?"

"For tonight," Olivia answered.

Carly looked relieved. Maybe, for a child, it was a matter of safety in numbers—herself, Meg, Brad, Olivia and Willie, all huddled in the same house, somehow keeping the uncertain darkness at bay. "I think I'd like to sleep now," she said. "Can Willie come, too?"

"He'll need to go outside first, I think," Olivia said.

Brad took Willie out, without a word, returned and watched as the old dog climbed the stairs, Carly leading the way, Olivia bringing up the rear.

"Thanks," Meg said when she and Brad were alone. "You've been wonderful."

Brad began clearing the table, disposing of pizza boxes.

Meg caught his arm. "Brad, what—?"

"My grandfather," he said. "I just got to missing him. Regretting a lot of things."

She nodded. Waited.

"I'm sorry, Meg," he told her. "That your dad's gone, and you didn't get a chance to know him. That you've got a rough time ahead with Carly. And most of all, I'm sorry there's nothing I can do to make this better."

"You could hold me," Meg said.

He pulled her into an easy, gentle embrace. Kissed her forehead. "I could hold you," he confirmed.

She wanted to ask if he'd meant it, when—was it only a few hours ago?—he'd said he loved her. The problem was, she knew if he took the words back, or qualified them somehow, she wouldn't be able to bear it. Not now, while she was mourning the father she'd lost years ago.

They stood like that for a while, then, by tacit agreement, finished tidying up the kitchen. Before they started up the backstairs, Brad switched out the lights, and Meg stood waiting for him, blinded, not knowing her way around the house, but unafraid. As long as Brad was there, no gloom would have been deep enough to swallow her.

In his room upstairs, they undressed, got into bed together, lay enfolded in each other's arms.

I love you, Meg thought with stark clarity.

They didn't make love.

They didn't talk.

But Meg felt a bittersweet gratification just the same, a deep shift somewhere inside herself, where spirit and body met.

On the edge of sleep, just before she tumbled helplessly over the precipice, Angus crossed her mind, along with a whisper-thin wondering.

Where had he gone?

CHAPTER FOURTEEN

THE SNOWS CAME early that year, to the annoyance of the movie people, and Brad was away from the ranch a lot, filming scenes in a studio in Flagstaff. He'd grudgingly admitted that Cynthia had been right—she was perfect for the part of Sarah Jane Stone—and while Meg visited the set once or twice, she stayed away when the love scenes were on the schedule.

She had a lot of other things on her mind, as it happened. She and Carly were bonding, slowly but surely, but the process was rocky. With the help of a counselor, they felt their way toward each other—backed off—tried again.

When the day came for Carly's promised scene— she played a nameless character in calico and a bonnet who brought Brad a glass of punch at a party and solemnly offered it. She'd endlessly practiced her single line—a "you're welcome, mister" to his "thank you"—telling Meg very seriously that there were no small parts, only small actors.

The movie part gave Carly something to hold on to in the dark days after Ted's passing, and Meg was eternally grateful for that. Both she and Carly spent a lot of time at Brad's house, even when he wasn't around, looking after Willie and gradually becoming a part of the place itself.

Ransom and his mares occupied the main pasture at Stone Creek Ranch, and the job of driving hay out to them usually fell to Olivia and Meg, with Carly riding in the back of the truck, seated on the bales. During that time, Meg and Olivia became good friends.

In the spring, when there would be fresh grass in the high country, and no snow to impede their mobility, Ransom and the mares would be turned loose.

"You'll miss him," Meg said once, watching Olivia as she stood in the pickup bed, tossing bales of grass hay to the ground after Carly cut the twine that held them together.

Olivia swallowed visibly and nodded, admiring the stallion as he stood, head turned toward the mountain, sniffing the air for the scents of spring and freedom. On warmer days, he was especially restless, prancing back and forth along the farthest fence, tail high, mane flying in the breeze.

Meg knew there had been many opportunities to sell Ransom for staggering amounts of money, but neither Olivia nor Brad had even considered the idea. In their minds, Ransom wasn't theirs to sell—he belonged to himself, to the high country, to legend. With his wounds healed, he'd have been able to soar over any fence, but he seemed to know the time wasn't right. There in the O'Ballivans' pasture, he had plenty of feed and easily accessible water, hard to find in winter, especially up in the red peaks and canyons, and he'd be at a disadvantage with the wolves. Still, there was a palpable, restless air of yearning about him that bruised Meg's heart.

It would be a sad and wonderful day when the far gate was opened.

Olivia cheered herself, along with Meg and Carly, with the fact that Brad had decided to make the ranch a haven for displaced mules, donkeys and horses, including unwanted Thoroughbreds who hadn't made the grade as racers, studs or broodmares. At the first sign of spring, the adoptees would begin arriving, courtesy of the Bureau of Land Management and various animal-rescue groups.

In the meantime, the ranch, like the larger world, seemed to Meg to be hibernating, practically in suspended animation. Like Ransom, she longed for spring.

It was after one of their visits to Brad's, while they were attending to their own horses on the Triple M, that Carly brought up a subject Meg had been troubled by, but hadn't wanted to raise.

"Where do you suppose Angus is?" the child asked. "I haven't seen him around in a couple of months."

"Hard to know," Meg said carefully.

"Maybe he's busy on the other side," Carly suggested. "You know, showing my dad around and stuff."

"Could be," Meg allowed. Until his last visit—the night he'd been so anxious for a look at the McKettrick family Bible—Meg had seen and spoken to her illustrious ancestor almost every day of her life. She hadn't had so much as a glimpse of him since then, and while there had been countless times she'd wished Angus would stay where he belonged, so she could be a normal person, she missed him.

Surely he wouldn't have simply stopped visiting her without even saying goodbye. It appeared, though, that that was exactly what he'd done.

"I wish he'd come," Carly said somewhat wistfully. "I want to ask him if he's seen my dad."

Meg slipped an arm around her sister, held her close against her side for a second or two. "I'm sure your—our—dad is fine," she said softly.

Carly smiled, but sadness lingered in her eyes. "For a while, I hoped Dad would come back, the way Angus did. But I guess he's busy or something."

"Probably," Meg agreed. It went without saying that the Angus phenomenon was rare, but there were times when she wondered if that was really true. How many children, prattling about their imaginary playmates, were actually seeing someone real?

They started back toward the house, two sisters, walking close.

Inside, they both washed up—Meg at the kitchen sink, Carly in the downstairs powder room—and began preparing supper. After the meal, salad and a tamale pie from a recently acquired cookbook geared to the culinarily challenged, Meg cleared the table and loaded the dishwasher while Carly settled down to her homework.

Like most kids, she had a way of asking penetrating questions with no preamble. "Are you going to marry Brad O'Ballivan?" she inquired now, looking up from her math text. "We spend a lot of time at his place, and I know you sleep over when I'm visiting Eve. Or he comes here."

Things were good between Brad and Meg, probably because he was so busy with the movie that they rarely saw each other. When they *were* together, they took every opportunity to make love.

"He hasn't asked," Meg said lightly. "And you're in some pretty personal territory, here. Have I mentioned lately that you're twelve?"

"I might be twelve," Carly replied, "but I'm not stupid."

"You're definitely not stupid," Meg agreed good-naturedly, but on the inside, she was dancing to a different tune. Her period, always as regular as the orbit of the moon, was two weeks late. She'd bought a home pregnancy test at a drugstore in Flagstaff, not wanting word of the purchase to get around Indian Rock as it would have if she'd made the purchase locally, but she hadn't worked up the nerve to use it yet.

As much as she'd wanted a child, she almost hoped the results would be negative. She knew what would happen if the plus sign came up, instead of the minus. She'd tell Brad, he'd insist on marrying her, just as he'd done with both Valerie and Cynthia, and for the rest of her days, she'd wonder if he'd proposed out of honor, or because he actually loved her.

On the other hand, she wouldn't dare keep the knowledge from him, not after what had happened before, when they were teenagers. He'd never forgive her if something went wrong; even the truest, deepest kind of love between a man and a woman couldn't survive if there was no trust.

All of which left Meg in a state of suspecting she was carrying Brad's child, not knowing for sure, and being afraid to find out.

Carly, whose intuition seemed uncanny at times, blindsided her again. "I saw the pregnancy-test kit," she announced.

Meg, in the process of wiping out the sink, froze.

"I didn't mean to snoop," Carly said quickly. By turns, she was rebellious and paranoid, convinced on some level that living on the Triple M as a part of the McKettrick family was an interval of sorts, not a permanent arrangement. In her experience, everything was temporary. "I ran out of toothpaste, and I went into your bathroom to borrow some, and I saw the kit."

Sighing, Meg went to the table and sat down next to Carly, searching for words.

"Are you mad at me?" Carly asked.

"No," Meg said. "And I wouldn't send you away even if I was, Carly. You need to get clear on that."

"Okay," Carly said, but she didn't sound convinced. Meg guessed it would take time, maybe a very long time, for her little sister to feel secure. Her face brightened. "It would be so cool if you had a baby!" she spouted.

"Yes," Meg agreed, smiling. "It would."

"So what's the problem with finding out for sure?"

"Brad's really busy right now. I guess I'm looking for a chance to tell him."

Just then, as if by the hand of Providence, a rig drove up outside, a door slammed.

Carly rushed to the window, gave a yip of excitement. "He's here!" she crowed. "And Willie's with him!"

Meg closed her eyes. So much for procrastination.

Carly hurried to open the back door, and Brad and the dog blew in with a chilly wind.

"Here," Brad said, handing Carly a flash drive. "It's your big scene, complete with dialogue and music."

Carly grabbed the stick and fled to the study, fairly skipping and Willie, now almost wholly recovered from his injuries, dashed after her, barking happily.

Meg was conscious, in those moments, of everything that was at stake. The child and even the dog would suffer if the conversation she and Brad were about to have went sour.

"Sit down," she said, turning to watch Brad as he

shed his heavy coat and hung it from one of the pegs next to the door.

"Sounds serious," Brad mused. "Carly get into trouble at school again?"

"No," Meg answered, after swallowing hard.

Brad frowned and joined her at the table, sitting astraddle the bench while she occupied the chair at the end. "Meg, what's the trouble?" he asked worriedly.

"I bought a kit—" she began, immediately faltering.

His forehead crinkled. "A kit?" The light went on. "A *kit!*"

"I think I might be pregnant, Brad."

A smile spread across his face, shone in his eyes, giving her hope. But then he went solemn again. "You don't sound very happy about it," he said, looking wary. "When did you do the test?"

"That's just it. I haven't done it yet. Because I'm afraid."

"Afraid? Why?"

"Things have been so good between us, and—"

Gently, he took her hand. Turned it over to trace patterns on her palm with the pad of his thumb. "Go on," he said, his voice hoarse, obviously steeling himself against who knew what.

"I know you'll marry me," Meg forced herself to say. "If the test is positive, I mean. And I'll always wonder if you feel trapped, the way you did with Cynthia."

Brad considered her words, still caressing her palm. "All right," he said presently. "Then I guess we ought to get married *before* you take the pregnancy test. Because either way, Meg, I want you to be my wife. Baby or no baby."

She studied him. "Maybe we should live together for a while. See how it goes."

"No way, McKettrick," Brad replied instantly. "I know lots of good people share a house without benefit of a wedding these days, but when it comes down to it, I'm an old-fashioned guy."

"You'd really do that? Marry me without knowing the results of the test? What if it's negative?"

"Then we'd keep working on it." Brad grinned.

Meg bit her lower lip, thinking hard.

Finally, she stood and said, "Wait here."

But she only got as far as the middle of the back stairway before she returned.

"The McKettrick women don't change their names when they get married," she reminded him, though they both knew Sierra had already broken that tradition, and happily so.

"Call yourself whatever you want," Brad replied. "For a year. At the end of that time, if you're convinced we can make it, then you'll go by O'Ballivan. Deal?"

Meg pondered the question. "Deal," she said at long last.

She went upstairs, slipped into her bathroom and leaned against the closed door, her heart pounding. Her reflection in the long mirror over the double sink stared back at her.

"Pee on the stick, McKettrick," she told herself, "and get it over with."

Five minutes later, she was staring at the little plastic stick, filled with mixed emotion. There was happiness, but trepidation, too. *What-ifs* hammered at her from every side.

A light knock sounded at the door, and Brad came in.

"The suspense," he said, "is killing me."

Meg showed him the stick.

And his whoop of joy echoed off every wall in that venerable old house.

"I THINK I have a future in show business," Carly confided to Brad later that night when she came into the kitchen to say good-night. She'd watched her scene on the study TV at least fourteen times.

"I think you have a future in the eighth grade," Meg responded, smiling.

"What if I end up on the cutting-room floor?" Carly fretted. Clearly, she'd been doing some online research into the moviemaking process.

"I'll see that you don't," Brad promised. "Go to bed, Carly. A movie star needs her beauty sleep."

Carly nodded, then went upstairs, flash drive in hand. Willie, who had been following her all evening, sighed despondently and lay down at Brad's feet, muzzle resting on his forepaws.

Brad leaned down to stroke the dog's smooth, graying back. "Looks like Carly's already got one devoted fan," he remarked.

Meg chuckled. "More than one," she said. "I certainly qualify, and so do you. Eve spoils her, and Rance's and Keegan's girls think of her as the family celebrity."

Brad grinned. "Carly's a pro," he said. "But you're wise to steer her away from show business, at least for the time being. It's hard enough for adults to handle, and kids have it even worse."

The topics of the baby and marriage pulsed in the air between them, but they skirted them, went on talking

about other things. Brad was comfortable with that—
there would be time enough to make plans.

"According to her teachers," Meg said, "Carly has a
near-genius affinity for computers, or anything techni-
cal. Last week she actually got the clock on the DVD
player to stop blinking twelves. This, I might add, is a
skill that has eluded presidents."

"Lots of things elude presidents," Brad replied, finishing his coffee. "We're wrapping up the movie next
week," he added. "The indoor scenes, at least. We'll have
to do the stagecoach robbery and all the rest next spring.
Think you could pencil a wedding into your schedule?"

Meg's cheeks colored attractively, causing Brad to
wonder what *other* parts of her were turning pink. She
hesitated, then nodded, but as she looked at him, her
gaze switched to something just beyond his left shoulder.

Brad turned to look, but there was nothing there.

"I hate leaving you," he said, turning back, frowning a little. "But I've got an early call in the morning."
Neither of them were comfortable sleeping together
with Carly around, but that would change after they
were married.

"I understand," Meg said.

"Do you, Meg?" he asked very quietly. "I love you.
I want to marry you, and I would have, even if the test
had been negative."

She said them then, the words he'd been waiting for.
Before that, she'd spoken them only in the throes of passion.

"I love you right back, Brad O'Ballivan."

He stood, drew her to her feet and kissed her. It was
a lingering kiss, gentle but thorough.

"But there's still one thing I haven't told you," she choked out, when their mouths parted.

Brad braced himself. Waited, his mind scrambling over possibilities—there was another man out there somewhere after all, one with some emotional claim on her, or more she hadn't told him about the first pregnancy, or the miscarriage...

"Ever since I was a little girl," she said, "I've been seeing Angus McKettrick. In fact, he's here right now."

Brad recalled the glance she'd thrown over his shoulder a few minutes before, the odd expression in her eyes. First Livie, with her Dr. Doolittle act—now Meg claimed she could see the family patriarch, who had been dead for over a century.

He thrust out a sigh.

She waited, gnawing at her lip, her eyes wide and hopeful.

"If you say so," he said at last, "I believe you."

Joy suffused her face. "Really?"

"Really," he said, though the truth was more like: *I'm* trying *to believe you.* As with Livie, he would believe if it killed him, despite all the rational arguments crowding his mind.

She stood on tiptoe and kissed him. "I'd insist that you stay, since we're engaged," she whispered, "but Angus is even more old-fashioned than you are."

He laughed, said good-night and looked down at Willie.

The dog was standing, wagging his tail and grinning, looking up at someone who wasn't there.

There were indeed, Brad thought, as he and Willie made the lonely drive back to Stone Creek Ranch in his truck, more things in heaven and earth than this world dreams of.

"WHERE HAVE YOU BEEN?" Meg demanded, torn between relief at seeing Angus again, and complete exasperation.

"You always knew I wouldn't be around forever," Angus said. He looked older than he had the last time she'd seen him, even careworn, but somehow serene, too. "Things are winding down, girl. I figured you needed to start getting used to my being gone."

Meg blinked, surprised by the stab of pain she felt at the prospect of Angus's leaving for good. On the other hand, she *had* always known the last parting would come.

"I'm going to have a baby," she said, struggling not to cry. "I'll need you. The baby and Carly will need you."

Angus seldom touched her, but now he cupped one hand under her chin. His skin felt warm, not cold, and solid, not ethereal. "No," he said gruffly. "You only need yourselves and each other. Things are going to be fine from here on out, Meg. You'll see."

She swallowed, wanting to cling to him, knowing it wouldn't be right. He had a life to live, somewhere else, beyond some unseen border. There were others there, waiting for him.

"Why did you come?" she asked. "In the first place, I mean?"

"You needed me," he said simply.

"I did," she confirmed. For all the nannies and "aunts and uncles," she'd been a lost soul as a child, especially after Sierra was kidnapped and Eve fell apart in so many ways. She'd never blamed her mother, never harbored any resentment for the inevitable neglect she'd suffered, but she knew now that, without Angus, she would have been bereft.

He was carrying a hat in his left hand, and now he put it on, the gesture somehow final. "You say good-bye to Carly for me," he said. "And tell her that her pa's just fine where he is."

Meg nodded, unable to speak.

Angus leaned in, planted a light, awkward kiss on Meg's forehead. "When you get to the end of the trail," he said, "and that's a long ways off, I promise, I'll be there to say welcome."

Still, no words would come. Not even ones of farewell. So Meg merely nodded again.

Angus turned his back and, in the blink of an eye, he was gone.

She cried that night, for sorrow, for joy and for a thousand other reasons, but when the morning came, she knew Angus had been right.

She didn't need him anymore.

THE WEDDING WAS small and simple, with only family and a few friends present. Meg still considered the marriage provisional, and went on calling herself Meg McKettrick, although she and Carly moved in at Stone Creek Ranch right away. All the horses came with them, but Meg still paid regular visits to the Triple M, always hoping, on some level, for just one more glimpse of Angus.

It didn't happen, of course.

So she sorted old photos and journals when she was there, and with some help from Sierra, catalogued them into something resembling archives. Eve, tired of hotel living, planned on moving back in. A grandmother, she maintained, with Eve-logic, ought to live in the country. She ought to bake pies and cookies and shelter the children of the family under broad, sturdy branches, like an old oak tree.

Meg smiled every time she pictured her rich, sophisticated, well-traveled mother in an apron and sensible shoes, but she had to admit Eve had pulled off a spectacular country-style Christmas. There had been a massive tree, covered in lights and heirloom ornaments, bulging stockings for Carly and Liam and little Brody, and a complete turkey dinner, only partly catered.

She'd already taken over the master bedroom, and she'd brought her two champion jumpers from the stables in San Antonio, and installed them in the barn. She rode every chance she got, often with Brad and Carly and sometimes with Jesse, Rance and Keegan.

Meg, being pregnant and out of practice when it came to horseback riding, usually watched from a perch on the pasture fence. She didn't believe in being overly cautious—it wasn't the McKettrick way—but this baby was precious to her, and to Brad. She wasn't taking any chances.

Dusting off an old photograph of Holt and Lorelei, Meg stepped back to admire the way it looked on the study mantle. She heard her mother at the back of the house.

"Meg? Are you here?"

"In the study," Meg called back.

Eve tracked her down. "Feeling nostalgic?" she asked, eyeing the picture.

Meg sighed, sat down in a high-backed leather chair, facing the fireplace. "Maybe it's part of the pregnancy. Hormones, or something."

Eve, always practical, threw off her coat, draping it over the back of the sofa, marched to the fireplace and started a crackling, cheerful blaze. She let Meg's words hang, all that time, finally turning to study her daughter.

"Are you happy, Meg? With Brad, I mean?"

When it came to happiness, she and Brad were constantly charting fresh territory. Learning new things about each other, stumbling over surprises both profound and prosaic. For all of that, there was a sense of fragility to the relationship.

"I'm happy," she said.

"But?" Eve prompted. She stood with her back to the fireplace, looking very ungrandmotherly in her tailored slacks and silk sweater.

"It feels—well—too good to be true," Meg admitted.

Eve crossed to drag a chair closer to Meg's and sit beside her. "You're holding back a part of yourself, aren't you? From Brad, from the marriage?"

"I suppose I am," Meg said. "It's sort of like the first day we were allowed to swim in the pond, late in the spring, when Jesse and Rance and Keegan and I were kids. The water was always freezing. I'd stick a toe in and stand shivering on the bank while the boys cannonballed into the water, howling and whooping and trying to splash me. Finally, more out of shame than courage, I'd jump in." She shuddered. "I still remember that icy shock—it always knocked the wind out of me for a few minutes."

Eve smiled, probably remembering similar swimming fests from her own childhood, with another set of McKettrick cousins. "But then you got used to the temperature and had as much fun as the boys did."

Meg nodded.

"It's not smart to hold yourself apart from the shocks of life, Meg—the good ones or the bad. They're all part of the mix, and paradoxically, shying away from them only makes things harder."

Meg was quiet for a long time. Then she said quietly, "Angus is gone."

Eve waited.

"I miss him," Meg confessed. "When I was a teenager, especially, I used to wish he'd leave me alone. Now that he's gone—well—every day, the memories seem less and less real."

Eve took her hand, squeezed. "Sometimes," she said very softly, "just at twilight, I think I see them—Angus and his four sturdy, handsome sons—riding single-file along the creek bank. Just a glimpse, a heartbeat really, and then they're gone. It's odd, because they don't look like ghosts. Just men on horseback, going about their ordinary business. I could almost convince myself that, for a fraction of a moment, a curtain had opened between their time and ours."

"Rance told me the same thing once," Meg said. "He used different words, but he saw the riders, traveling one behind the other beside the creek, and he knew who they were."

The two women sat in thoughtful silence for a while.

"It's a strange thing, being a McKettrick," Meg finally said.

"You're an O'Ballivan now," Eve surprised her by saying. "And your baby will be an O'Ballivan, too."

Meg looked hard at her mother, startled. Eve had been miffed when Sierra took Travis's last name, and made a few remarks about tradition not being what it once was.

"What about the McKettrick way?" she asked.

"The McKettrick way," Eve said, giving Meg's hand another squeeze, "is living at full throttle, holding nothing back. It's taking life—and change—as they come. Anyway, lots of women keep their last names these days—taking their husbands' is the novelty now." She paused, studying Meg with loving, intelligent eyes. "It's what's standing in your way," she said decisively. "You're afraid that if you're not Meg McKettrick anymore, you'll lose some part of your identity, and have to get to know yourself as a new person."

Meg realized that she *was* a new person—though of course still herself in the most fundamental ways. She was a wife now, a mother-figure as well as a sister to Carly. When the baby came, there would be yet another new level to who she was.

"I've been hiding behind the McKettrick name," she mused, more to herself than Eve.

"It's a fine name," Eve said. "We take a lot of pride in it—maybe too much, sometimes."

"Would *you* take your husband's name, if you remarried?" Meg ventured.

Eve thought about her answer before shaking her head from side to side. "No," she said. "I don't think so. I've been a McKettrick for so long, I wouldn't know how to be anything else."

Meg smiled. "And you don't want me to follow in your footsteps?"

"I want you to be *happy*. Don't stand on the bank shivering, Meg. *Jump in. Get wet.*"

"Were *you* happy, Mom?" The reply to that question seemed terribly important; Meg held her breath to hear it.

"Most of the time, yes," Eve said. "When Hank took Sierra and vanished, I was shattered. I don't think I could have gone on if it hadn't been for you. Though I realize it probably didn't seem that way to you, that you were my main reason for living, you and the hope of getting Sierra back. I'm so sorry, Meg, for coming apart at the seams the way I did. For not being there for you."

"I've never resented that, Mom. As young as I was, I knew you loved me, and that the things that were happening didn't change that for a moment. Besides, I had Angus."

The clock on the mantelpiece ticked ponderously, marking off the hours, the minutes, the seconds, as it had been doing for over a hundred years. It had ticked and tocked through the lives of Holt and Lorelei and their children, and the generations to follow.

The sound reminded Meg of something she'd always known, at least unconsciously. Life seemed long, but it was finite, too. One day, some future McKettrick would sit listening to that same clock, and Meg herself would be a memory. An ancestor in a photo.

"Gotta go pick Carly up at school," she said, standing up.

Time to find Brad, she added silently, *and introduce him to his wife.*

"Hello," I'll say, as if we're meeting for the first time. "My name is Meg O'Ballivan."

CHAPTER FIFTEEN

THAT LATE MARCH day was blustery and cold, but there was a fresh, piney tinge to the air. Brad, Meg and Carly stood watching from a short distance as Olivia squared her shoulders, walked to the far gate, sprung the latch and opened the way for Ransom to go.

A part of Meg hoped he'd choose to stay, but it wasn't to be.

Ransom approached the path to freedom cautiously at first, the mares straggling behind him, still shaggy with their winter coats.

When the great stallion drew abreast of Olivia, he paused, nickered and tossed his magnificent head once, as if to bid her goodbye. Tears slipped down Olivia's cheeks, and she made no attempt to wipe them away. She'd arrived during breakfast that morning and said Ransom had told her it was time.

Meg, who had after all seen a ghost from childhood, didn't question her sister-in-law's ability to communicate with animals. Even Brad, quietly skeptical about such things, couldn't write it all off to coincidence.

Carly, her own face wet, leaned into Brad a little. Meg sniffled, trying to be brave and philosophical.

He put one arm around her shoulders and one around Carly's. Glancing up at him, Meg didn't see the sorrow she and Carly and Olivia were feeling, but an expression of almost transported wonder and awe.

Ransom walked through the gate, turned a little way beyond and reared onto his hind legs, a startlingly beautiful sight against the early-spring sky, summoning his mares with a loud whinny.

"I guess being in a couple of movie scenes went to his head," Brad joked, a rasp in his voice. "He thinks he's Flicka." The filming was over now, and things were settling down on the ranch, and around town. Local attention had turned to the new animal shelter, now under construction just off Main Street.

Meg's throat was so clogged with emotion, she couldn't speak. She rested her head against Brad's shoulder and watched, riveted, as Ransom shot off across the meadow, headed back up the mountain.

The mares followed, tails high.

Olivia watched them out of sight. Then, with a visible sigh and another squaring of her shoulders, she slowly closed the gate.

Meg started toward her, but Brad caught hold of her hand and held her back.

Olivia passed them by as if they were invisible, climbed agilely over the inside fence, and moved toward her perennially dusty Suburban.

"She'll be all right," Brad assured Meg quietly, watching his sister go.

Together, Brad, Carly and Meg returned to the house, saying little.

Life went on. Willie needed to go out. The phone was ringing. Business as usual, Meg thought, quietly happy, despite her sadness over the departure of Ransom and the mares. She knew, as Brad did, and certainly Olivia, that they might never see those horses again.

"I don't suppose I could stay home from school, just for today?" Carly ventured, as Brad answered the phone and Meg started a fresh pot of coffee.

Outside, the toot of a horn announced the arrival of the school bus, and Brad cocked a thumb in that direction and gave Carly a mock stern look.

She sighed dramatically, still angling for an Oscar, as Brad had once observed, but grabbed up her backpack and left the house.

"No, Phil," Brad said into the telephone receiver, "I'm *still* not doing that gig in Vegas. I don't *care* how good the buzz is about the movie—"

Meg smiled.

Brad rolled his eyes, listening. "I am so not over the way you stuck me with Cynthia for a leading lady," he went on. "You owe me for that one, big-time."

When the call was over, though, Brad found his guitar and settled into a chair in the living room, looking out over the land, playing soft thoughtful chords.

Meg knew, without being told, that he was writing a new song. She loved listening to him, loved being his wife. While he was still adamant about not doing concert tours, they'd been drawing up plans for weeks for a recording studio to be constructed out behind the house. Brad O'Ballivan was filled with music, and he had to have some outlet for it.

He didn't seem to long for the old life, though. First and foremost, he was a family man. He and Meg had legally adopted Carly, though he was still Brad to her, and Ted would always be Dad. He looked forward to the baby's birth as much as Meg did, and had even gone so far as to have the first sonogram framed.

Their son, McKettrick "Mac" O'Ballivan, was strong and sturdy within Meg's womb. He was due on the Fourth of July.

Meg paused by Brad's chair, bent to kiss the top of his head.

He looked up at her, grinned and went on strumming and murmuring lyrics.

When a knock came at the front door, Willie growled halfheartedly but didn't get up from his favorite lounging place, the thick rug in front of the fire.

Meg went to answer, and felt a strange shock of recognition as she gazed into the face of a stranger, somewhere in his midthirties.

His hair was dark, and so were his eyes, and yet he bore a striking resemblance to Jesse. Dressed casually in clean, good-quality Western clothes, he took off his hat and smiled, and only then did Meg remember Angus's prediction.

One of them's about to land on your doorstep, he'd said.

"Meg McKettrick?" the man asked, showing white teeth as he smiled.

"Meg O'Ballivan," she clarified. Brad was standing behind her now, clearly curious.

"My name is Logan Creed," said the cowboy. "And I believe you and I are kissin' cousins."

* * * * *

Books by B.J. Daniels

Harlequin Intrigue

Cardwell Cousins

Crime Scene at Cardwell Ranch
Justice at Cardwell Ranch
Cardwell Ranch Trespasser
Christmas at Cardwell Ranch

Rescue at Cardwell Ranch
Wedding at Cardwell Ranch
Deliverance at Cardwell Ranch
Reunion at Cardwell Ranch

HQN Books

The Montana Hamiltons

Wild Horses
Lone Rider
Lucky Shot

Beartooth, Montana

Mercy
Atonement
Forsaken
Redemption
Unforgiven

And don't miss

Hard Rain

MOUNTAIN SHERIFF

B.J. Daniels

This book is dedicated with much appreciation to JoAnn Brehm. Thank you for sharing your stories about life in Oregon and the long rainy season.

Oregon is a beautiful, diverse state and one I found both fascinating and a little mystifying. Especially in the deepest, darkest woods on the rain shadow side of the Cascades, where it takes little imagination to believe that Bigfoot watches from the shadows.

CHAPTER ONE

Tuesday, October 27

DARKNESS PRESSED AGAINST the window. Beyond the glass, something moved at the edge of the tangle of growth.

Under the glow of the desk lamp, Nina Monroe feathered the paint along one side of the wooden duck decoy.

She'd forgotten she was alone in the isolated Dennison Ducks decoy plant. Nor had she noticed how late it was. Her mind had been on her future.

For the first time in her twenty-seven years of life, her future looked good. Not just good. Dazzling. Almost blinding. Sometimes she had to pinch herself it was so hard to believe. Soon she would have everything she'd ever wanted. Soon she wouldn't be painting duck decoys in the middle of nowhere, that was for sure.

A voice in her head warned her not to count her chickens before they'd hatched. The voice was that of her old-maid aunt Harriet and she shut it out, just as she had all of her life. Aunt Harriet the doomsayer.

After tonight, Nina would finally have what she deserved. It had been a long time coming. She smiled at the thought of blowing this dinky boring town knowing she'd never look back, never even give Timber Falls,

Oregon, another thought. She felt dazed by the possibilities. And filled with righteous indignation that it had taken so long for justice to finally be done.

She'd picked Halloween. A perfect time to unmask the true villains. By Halloween, she'd be long gone—but not forgotten. She would have it all, the money—*and*—the revenge. Who said revenge wasn't sweet?

A noise at the window made her look up. From the darkness appeared a distorted face. It filled the window, the eyes like empty sockets.

She let out a strangled cry, dropping her paintbrush as she shoved back her chair and stumbled to her feet.

Just as suddenly as it had appeared, the face was gone. She snapped off the lamp, the only light in her corner of the decoy plant, and stood in the dark staring out at the night.

Beyond the glass was a jungle of ferns, vines, moss and trees that fought for space in the suffocating rain forest on the Pacific Ocean side of the Oregon Cascades. Sometimes she felt so closed in here she wanted to scream.

Like right now. The trees moved restlessly in the wind. Shadows flickered over the glass from what little moonlight pierced the forest.

She took a breath and tried to calm herself. There was no one out there. It had just been a trick of moonlight and shadows. Hadn't her life always been full of shadows? But not for much longer.

So close to finally getting everything she wanted, she felt nervous, jittery, excited and maybe a little spooked. Spooked because something could go wrong.

But she knew that was just her aunt Harriet talking. After all those years with the pessimistic old woman,

Nina could hear Harriet in her head. The voice of negativity. The voice of defeat.

She pushed all thoughts of Harriet away as she looked out the window again and saw nothing but the movement of trees and ferns in the faint moonlight.

Glancing at her watch, with its glowing dial, Nina saw that she had at least another hour to wait. She wanted to try to finish this duck decoy, hating to admit that over the past month, she'd come to enjoy the painting.

It required an exactness that appealed to her. She'd found she had a talent for it that surprised—and pleased—her.

From behind her, she heard a soft click. The sound of the door, on the other side of the building, opening?

She turned slowly. A single small bulb illuminated the employee entrance, casting the dark images of hundreds of ducks over her. Mallard and canvasback, pintail and greenwing, buffalohead and widgeon decoys filled the shelves from the floor to ceiling.

From where she stood, she couldn't see past the shelves covered with ducks. Had she imagined the sound, just as she'd imagined the face at the window?

"Sure, that's all it was," she could hear Aunt Harriet sneer. "Fool."

Something moved across the light on the other side of the building. A flicker of dark shadow followed by the soft scuff of a shoe on concrete. The scent of damp night air cut through the sweeter scent of freshly carved pine. She heard another click. The door closing?

It was too early. Unless there'd been a change in plans. But then, wouldn't she have gotten a call? After all, tonight was supposed to be the last time they would meet. Once she had the money…

She glanced up at Wade Dennison's second-story glassed-in office, half expecting to see the owner of the plant watching her as he so often did. But the office was dark, just as she knew it would be, and there was no one behind the glass.

Another soft scuff of a shoe, closer this time. She told herself it had to be one of the employees. No one else had a key to get in. Unless in her excitement she'd forgotten to lock the door.

Her heart lodged in her throat as she frantically tried to remember locking the door.

Maybe meeting here hadn't been such a good idea. But usually she had the place to herself, preferring to work at night. Her co-workers thought she worked late to impress the boss and resented her for it—as if she cared. But that was why meeting here had seemed ideal. No one ever came around at night and she didn't have to worry about her nosy old landlady eavesdropping.

"Who's there?" she called out, expecting an answer.

Silence.

She hadn't been afraid, hadn't had any reason to be afraid. Until now.

She heard Aunt Harriet snickering inside her head. "Told you this scheme would get you killed."

Nina hadn't considered how vulnerable she was, alone here in the plant. Dennison Ducks was ten miles from town and a good two miles from the nearest house, which was Wade Dennison's.

Another soft scuff of a shoe on the concrete. This one much closer. Her pulse jumped. Who was in the building with her? Someone who'd seen her car in the parking lot, known she was in here alone, maybe even knew exactly where she was in the building? Or one of the people she'd been expecting, only earlier? Either of them would have answered her. So who was in the building with her?

She could feel a presence on the other side of the row of ducks, someone moving slowly, purposefully, between the shelves toward her.

Panic filled her. She grabbed the duck off the table, smearing the wet paint. She could make a run for it around the opposite end of the shelves, dash for the door, but she knew it would be too easy for the person to cut her off before she got out—even if he didn't have a weapon.

She could hear breathing on the other side of the dense wall of carved ducks. It had to be someone who knew why she'd come to Timber Falls. Knew why she'd wanted to work at Dennison Ducks so badly. Someone who'd found out about her meeting here tonight. Someone who thought he could keep her from getting what she deserved. That narrowed it down considerably.

But which one was dumb enough to try to stop her? She thought she knew as she waited, clutching the large wooden duck in her fist, determined not to let anyone take what was rightfully hers. Not again.

She listened as the footsteps moved closer and closer—stopping at the end of the ceiling-high shelf filled with ducks nearest her.

Quietly she slipped to the end of the row and raised the duck over her head. *Come on. Just a few more steps...*

The figure came around the end of the wall of duck-filled shelves.

Nina stared in confusion. For an instant, she almost laughed she was so relieved. She lowered the duck. She had nothing to fear.

She couldn't have been more mistaken.

CHAPTER TWO

Wednesday, October 28

EARLY THE NEXT MORNING, an ill wind whirled through Timber Falls. It started at the north end of Main, down by the Ho Hum Motel. Just a breeze. But by the time it reached Betty's Café, it had picked up speed, dirt and dried leaves, stripping Lydia Abernathy's maple tree bare.

Now a dust devil, it reeled past the Spit Curl, the post office and the *Timber Falls Courier,* discarding leaves and dust like unwelcome offerings in each doorway of the small Oregon town.

By the time the dust devil swept past Harry's Hardware and the Duck-In bar, the sky was dark as mud.

As if sensing more than an ill wind had blown into town, Sheriff Mitch Tanner got up from his desk at Town Hall to close the window moments before the panes began to rattle. Dirt and debris clattered against the glass. The dense wall of rain forest surrounding the town shimmered in the dull light, a flickering of dark shadows from within.

Just as suddenly as it had begun, the wind died, the dust and debris settled, leaves floated gently to the ground and the first drops of rain *plinked* against the window.

The rainy season in Timber Falls had begun.

Mitch groaned. Trouble always seemed to accompany the rain. And he feared, this year both had come early. To make matters worse, Halloween was only days away and he'd heard that the Duck-In bar was hosting a costume party. He could figure on a long night of breaking up fights and trying to get locals home safely.

Behind him, Wade Dennison cleared his throat. "As I was saying, Sheriff…"

Mitch dragged his gaze from the rain-streaked window, trying to shake an ominous sense of dread as he turned his attention back to the man sitting across the desk from him.

Over sixty, his dark hair peppered with gray, Wade Dennison had a look of privilege about him.

"It just isn't like Nina not to show for work." Wade was a soft-spoken man, but a powerful one in this town. He owned Dennison Ducks, Timber Falls's claim to fame—and its main source of income.

Mitch nodded, wondering why Wade was in such a tizzy. This couldn't be the first employee who hadn't shown up for work.

"I called. Her landlady said she didn't come home last night," Wade was saying.

"She doesn't have a cell phone?"

Wade shook his head, worry in his gaze. Maybe more worry than was warranted? More worry than was appropriate for a young and attractive female employee?

"Could be she stayed over at a friend's or a boyfriend's," Mitch suggested. "Or maybe she's with family."

Wade shook his head. "She doesn't have any family. No boyfriend, either. Or friends."

Mitch raised a brow.

"At least not that I know of," Wade added. "She's only been in town a month."

A month was plenty long enough to make friends, let alone a boyfriend. But Mitch didn't say anything.

Wade shifted in his chair. "Nina's…shy. Keeps to herself. She's real serious, you know?"

He didn't. But he was curious about how Wade knew all this. Mitch had seen Nina Monroe only a few times around town and just in passing, but he remembered her as being attractive with long dark hair and dark eyes. "Serious how?"

"She's a good worker, always on time," Wade was saying. "In fact, she works late a lot, real serious about her job." The older man cleared his throat again. "That's why I'm worried something might have happened to her."

Mitch's radar clicked on. "Like what?"

Wade shook his head. "I'm just saying she would have called if she wasn't coming in."

A shadow filled the open office doorway. Town clerk Sissy Walker stood, hands on her ample hips, a look of irritation on her face. He knew the look only too well.

"Ms. Jenkins on line two," she said. "It's the *fifth* time she's called this morning. She says if you don't talk to her, she'll track you down like a dog."

Mitch groaned, knowing that was no idle threat. "Wade, I have the information on Nina that you gave me. Let me do some checking and get back to you."

Wade Dennison slowly rose to his feet. "You'll let me know as soon as you hear something."

It wasn't a question. "You know I will." After Wade closed the office door behind him, Mitch picked up the phone and hit line two. "Charity?" It was never good news when Charity Jenkins called.

"Hello, Mitch," she said, a hint of humor in her tone. No doubt because she'd managed to get him on the line—in more ways than one over the years.

"You know threatening a sheriff is against the law," he said, always surprised by what just the sound of her voice did to him.

She laughed. She had a great laugh. "You gonna lock me up?" She made it sound like something she wouldn't mind.

He tried to imagine Charity in one of his cells and shook his head at even the thought. "What's so important that you've got Sissy ticked off already this morning?"

"Sissy is always ticked off," Charity said. "I called about the latest news."

He wasn't sure what news that might be. Knowing Charity, she'd probably already gotten wind of Nina Monroe's alleged disappearance. The woman was a bloodhound.

Charity owned the local weekly, *Timber Falls Courier,* she'd started straight out of college, her journalism degree in her hot little hands. Mitch secretly believed she'd only started the newspaper as an excuse to butt into everyone's business—especially his. He was sure she couldn't make much money at it in a town the size of Timber Falls. But as he knew only too well, Charity loved a challenge.

"What news is that?" He hated to ask.

"Don't tell me you haven't heard! There's been a Bigfoot sighting on the edge of town. Frank, the Granny's bread deliveryman, saw it clear as day in his headlights last night. Practically ran off the road he was so upset."

Mitch swore under his breath. Bigfoot. Great. The news couldn't have been worse if an alien spaceship had landed at Dennison Ducks and abducted Nina Monroe. *Bigfoot.* This sort of thing only brought more wackos to town—as if Timber Falls needed that. And during the rainy season!

"I'm over at Betty's having breakfast," Charity said.

This was not anything new. He could imagine her sitting on her usual stool at the café. The sight was more than appealing. She'd be wearing jeans and a sweater that would hug her curves. Her burnished auburn hair would be pulled up into a ponytail. Or maybe down around her shoulders, falling in natural loose curls around her face, making her big brown eyes golden as summer sunshine.

"Everyone's talking about the sighting," she was saying. "I hear it's made all the big papers."

He groaned, hating to think how many people would drive up this way hoping to get a glimpse of the mythical creature. Just the way they did the last time. Damn.

"Betty made banana-cream pie," Charity said. She was making his mouth water and she knew it. The woman was relentless. "Have you had breakfast?"

Only Charity Jenkins would think pie was the "breakfast of champions." Not that he hadn't spent a good share of his mornings over the years on the stool next to her having pie for breakfast. The woman had corrupted him in ways he hated even to think about.

But not this morning. "As enticing as your offer is, I have to pass." Charity would do anything for a story, including tempt him with banana-cream pie. But he wasn't about to say something he would regret so she could print it.

Besides, he had to get on the Nina Monroe case, if there was a case, and the last thing he needed was to start the rainy season by spending time with Charity Jenkins. Hadn't he learned his lesson with that woman?

"Is there something going on I should know about?" she asked, always on alert.

"No," he said quickly. Probably too quickly. "I just don't want anything to do with this article. You know how I feel about these damned Bigfoot sightings. Fools seeing things that we all know don't exist and then shooting off their mouths."

"Can I quote you on that?"

"No! And speaking of fools, make sure there is no mention of my father and Bigfoot this time. I mean it, Charity."

She made a disgruntled sound. "You really are no fun."

"Yeah, so you keep telling me." She'd always said he had no imagination because he didn't buy into flying saucers, ghosts or marriage. If she hadn't already, she could add Bigfoot to that list.

"Well, all right, if you're sure. By the way," she said in that seductive soft tone of hers, "thanks for the present."

"Present?"

"The one you left on my doorstep?" She didn't sound very sure.

"Charity, I didn't leave you a present."

"Oh, I thought…"

He heard the disappointment in her voice. He hated hurting her. It was one of the reasons he would never have left her a present. "Sorry, it wasn't me."

She let out a small sigh as if she should have known. Just as she should have known not to set her heart on marrying him. But she had, anyway.

Despite his feelings for her, he couldn't marry her. Couldn't marry anyone. But especially Charity. Just the thought of mixing their genes made him break out in a cold sweat.

"I wonder who could have left the present, then?" she said more to herself than to him.

He wondered the same thing. Hadn't he known it was only a matter of time before some man swept Charity off her feet? Knowing it was one thing. Having it actually happen… It surprised him how much the idea of Charity with another man rattled him.

"I almost forgot," she said. "Didn't I just see Wade Dennison come out of your office a few minutes ago? Something going on at Dennison Ducks I should know about?"

This Charity he could deal with. "Not everything is a news story. Or any of your business."

Charity laughed. "We both know better than that."

He hung up and saw Sissy in the doorway again, giving him one of her why-don't-you-do-something-about-that-woman? looks. "Let me ask you something," he said before she could start to nag him about his personal life. "Do you think Wade Dennison is hand-some?"

"Not my type."

"No, I mean, do women find him...attractive?"

She snorted. "He's got money, so hell yes, women find him attractive."

Mitch shook his head, wondering why it was so hard to get a straight answer out of a woman. "Is it possible that Wade and a twenty-something woman might—"

"I see where you're going with this," she interrupted impatiently. "Would he be interested in a woman young enough to be his daughter?" Her brows shot up. "Wade Dennison is a man, isn't he?" With that she turned and marched back to her desk.

Mitch shook his head and looked at the information Wade had given him. But his thoughts veered off again to Charity and the "present" some secret admirer had left her. It bothered him that the man didn't have the guts to come forward and make his intentions known. He wondered who the guy was. And what his intentions were.

With a curse, he again looked at what Wade had given him, focusing on Nina Monroe's address. He groaned when he saw who her landlady was—Charity's Aunt Florie. This town was too damned small, and it only seemed to get smaller when the rainy season began.

CHARITY JENKINS TOOK a bite of the banana-cream pie, closed her eyes and instantly conjured up the image of Mitch Tanner. Something about the combination of sugar, cream and butter...

Of course, she'd been thinking about Mitch since

she was four, so it came pretty easy after twenty-two years.

It was odd, though, the way she saw him in her day-dreams. If she was eating something rich and wonderful, like banana-cream pie, then Mitch always appeared in snug-fitting worn jeans and a T-shirt that accentuated his broad muscled chest and shoulders. Without fail, he would be smiling at her, the sunlight on his tanned face, his eyes as blue as the Pacific.

Other foods, however, such as vegetables or anything low-fat, had Mitch in his sheriff's uniform, scowling at her in disapproval. For obvious reasons, she avoided those foods.

She took another bite of pie, closed her eyes and was startled when Mitch popped up in her daydream wearing a black tuxedo and standing at an altar.

Her eyes flew open, her heart pounding. *Her* wedding? The one she'd imagined and planned since age four?

On this, she was not mistaken. Mitch in a black tux, she in white satin. Or maybe white silk. Or lace. The imagined wedding changed, depending on her mood. But the groom never had.

"The pie all right?" Betty asked as she stopped on the other side of the counter.

"De-e-elicious," Charity said, closing her eyes again and licking her lips in true delight, hoping to see Mitch in that wedding tux again. No such luck. She opened her eyes as Betty refilled her diet cola.

Betty Garrett was a pleasingly plump bottled-blond on this side of fifty but who could pass for thirty-five in a pinch and had a talent for attracting the wrong men the way a white blouse attracts blackberry jam. She'd married and changed her last name so many times that most people in town couldn't tell you what it was at any given moment. Right now Betty was between men, but it wouldn't last long. It never did.

"I just put a couple of lemon-meringue pies in the oven in case you're interested," Betty said.

Interested? Lemon meringue was her second favorite.

"I figure this Bigfoot sighting will bring 'em in for sure. Did last time," the older woman said. "I decided I'd better make some extra pies."

Bigfoot sightings packed the town. The curious drove up to Timber Falls in hopes of seeing what some called the Hill Ghost or Sasquatch.

"I heard the No Vacancy sign is already on at the Ho Hum and a half-dozen campers are parked over by the old train depot," Betty was saying. Everyone wanted to see Bigfoot and prove the legendary creature's existence.

None as badly as Charity Jenkins, though. Every journalist dreamed of that one big story. The Pulitzer-prize winner. Charity yearned to write about something other than church dinners and wooden decoys. The truth was, she desperately needed one big story. It was the only way she could make everyone in this town see that she wasn't like the rest of her family, she was a normal levelheaded woman and a serious journalist. All right, she didn't care about everyone in town. She just wanted to prove it to Mitch.

She took the last bite of her pie, savoring it, eyes closed. No Mitch in jeans or a tux. She opened her eyes, disappointed.

"Where do you put it all?" Betty asked with a shake of her head as she took the empty plate.

Charity was blessed. Probably because she was a fidgeter. She couldn't sit still. Nor did she ever stop thinking. Like right now. Between planning how to play the Bigfoot sighting in tomorrow's paper, she was thinking about Mitch and if her banana-cream-pie fantasy had any credibility.

Just the thought of Mitch standing next to her at the altar was enough to burn up a whole day's worth of calories. She and Mitch had a history, an off-and-on-again attachment that went as far back as shared glue in kindergarten.

Right now they were at a slight lull in their relationship: he pretended he was a confirmed bachelor and she pretended she was going to let him stay that way.

This morning she'd been so excited when she'd seen the present on her doorstep. She'd been so sure it was from Mitch. Who else? But he'd sworn it hadn't been him. And why pretend he hadn't left it if he had? Then again, why pretend he wasn't wild about her when he obviously was? She'd never understand the man.

"Would you look at this place?" Betty said, shaking her head. The café was full, everyone talking about the Bigfoot sighting. "I can't believe these fools are still arguing over Bigfoot after all these years."

Charity glanced around the small café. It was the only place in town to sit down and eat, plus it was *the* place to get homemade pies and cinnamon rolls and the latest scuttlebutt.

As she picked up her diet cola, she had an eerie feeling that someone was watching her. It wasn't the first time, either. She turned and caught a flash of black on the street outside. Her breath caught as a black pickup drove by. It was the same black truck she'd seen last night by her house and again on her way to Betty's this morning. Both times she'd had the feeling the driver was watching her.

She shivered as she watched the truck disappear up Main Street. While she could only make out a large shape behind the dark-tinted windows, she could feel the driver watching her through the rain. Her stomach tightened, remembering the present she'd found on her doorstep this morning. Could one have anything to do with the other?

RAIN HAMMERED THE ROOF of the Sheriff's Department patrol car, mist rising ghostlike from the drenched pavement, as Mitch drove out to the address Wade had given him for Nina Monroe. A swollen gray sky hung low over the pines as if closing in the tiny town, limiting more than visibility.

Mitch dreaded another rainy season in Timber Falls, especially one that appeared to be starting a month early and could last until at least April. It wasn't just the endless rain or the dull overcast days. Without fail, the rainy season seemed to bring out the worst in the residents.

One year, Bud Harper hung himself from a beam in his garage just days before the sun shone. Another year, a local guy shot up the Duck-In bar when he caught his wife there with another man. And twenty-seven years ago, during the worst rainy season of all, Wade and Daisy Dennison's baby girl Angela disappeared from her crib, never to be found.

It was always during the rainy season that strange

and often horrible things happened in this small isolated town deep in the Cascades. It was as if the gloomy days, when the rain never stopped, did something to make the residents behave more oddly than usual. As if on those days, the only place to look was inward. And sometimes that was as dark as the day—and far more disturbing.

And if the rain wasn't bad enough, there was the forest that surrounded Timber Falls, imprisoned it, really, and constantly had to be fought back as if it was at war with the tiny town. As he drove past the city limits, the forest formed almost a canopy over the two-lane highway, a tunnel of green darkness over the only road out.

To the clack of the wipers, he turned off in front of a cottage-style house with a dozen smaller bungalows lined up behind it. Years ago, the place had been a motel. But not long after Wade Dennison started his decoy factory, Florence Jenkins had taken down the motel sign and started renting out the bungalows as apartments.

It was about the same time that Florence discovered her hidden powers. The sign out front now read: Madam Florie's. Under it was her Web site address. Nina Monroe had been renting from Charity's Aunt Florie, Timber Falls's self-proclaimed clairvoyant.

Mitch braced himself then climbed out of his patrol car and hurried through the pouring rain to the front door.

When an elderly woman opened the door, he tipped his hat, dreading this more than he'd imagined. "Mornin', Florie."

"Sheriff. I've been expecting you." She smiled

knowingly, her eyes twinkling in her lined face. "Saw that you'd be by in my coffee dregs this morning."

He nodded. If Florie could see the future in her coffee cup, more power to her. He just didn't want to hear about his own future. He wanted to be surprised.

She motioned him in with a dramatic sweep of her arm, reminding him of some exotic, brightly feathered bird. Florie was sixty if she was a day. Her dyed flame-red hair swirled around her head like a turban. She wore a flamboyant caftan, large gold hoop earrings, several dozen jangling bracelets and a thick layer of turquoise eye shadow.

Florie and her much younger sister Fredricka, Charity's mother, had been raised by hippies in a commune just outside of town. Freddie still lived on the old commune property with a dozen other people but seldom came into town. While Freddie raised organic vegetables, Florie predicted the future to tourists in the summer and locals during the rainy season—another reason Mitch had cause for concern during the rainy season.

The old motel office was painted black and had recessed lighting that illuminated the only piece of furniture in the room—a purple-velvet-covered table with a crystal ball at its center. Florie had had the ball shipped in from a store in Portland. It gleamed darkly, as if mirroring the weather outside.

"I suppose your coffee dregs also told you *why* I'm here," he said as he entered. "Or maybe Wade mentioned it when he called you about Nina Monroe not showing up for work?"

Florie gave him an annoyed look and pointed to a sign on the wall in the entry that read No Negative Thoughts. A series of other small signs advertised palm, tarot and crystal ball readings.

"I was concerned after what I saw in my cup this morning," she said, lifting one tweezed dyed-red brow as she waited for him to ask.

No way was he going there.

"It involved my niece Charity," she added, not a woman to give up easily, a trait she shared with her niece.

"I understand that Nina Monroe rents from you and she didn't come home last night," he said, cutting to the chase.

Florie nodded, obviously disappointed by his lack of curiosity about those telltale coffee dregs.

"How do you know she didn't come home last night and then leave again before you got up?" he asked.

"Because I was up until daylight." At his surprised look, she added, "My Internet business—horoscopes, tarot cards, psychic readings, all by e-mail. You really should get your chart done. I'm concerned about your aura."

He had worse things to worry about than his aura right now. "I need to see Nina's bungalow."

Florie stepped behind a dark-velvet curtain. She came back with a key attached to a round small cardboard tag.

When he reached for the key, she took his hand and turned it palm up.

"Ah, a long life line with a single marriage." She beamed and dropped the key into his palm.

He shook his head. His palm lied. His parents' marriage had more than convinced him what his future *didn't* hold—a wedding.

"'Aries'?" he asked, reading the lettering on the key's tag.

"I try to match my guests and their bungalows based on their horoscopes. Better karma."

"So Nina was an Aries?"

"No, the Aries bungalow just happened to be the only unit I had open when she showed up."

He reminded himself that Charity shared Florie's genes. All the more reason to keep Charity at arm's length. Several car lengths would be even better. "So what was Nina?"

Florie shrugged. "She wouldn't tell me her birth sign. Can you believe some people aren't interested in enlightenment?"

He could. "Nina rented the bungalow in September?"

"Drove up in that little red compact of hers looking for a room. September nineteenth. I remember because she didn't even have a job yet. But that very afternoon, she got one at Dennison Ducks. Kismet, I guess."

Or something like that. "No need for you to come out in the rain with me."

Florie took a bright purple raincoat from the closet and a pair of matching purple galoshes. "I wouldn't dream of letting you go alone. I've been picking up some really weird vibes from that girl," she said, and stepped past him and out the front door.

He followed her around back through the rain to the first of twelve bungalows, the one with the Aries symbol on the door.

Standing on the small porch, he felt a sudden chill as if someone had walked over his grave. Florie knocked, then cautiously unlocked the door.

"Oh, my!" she cried as the door swung open on the ransacked bungalow.

"Stay here," he ordered, and stepped inside to look for Nina Monroe's body in the mess.

CHAPTER THREE

"You all right?" Betty asked, looking concerned.

Charity turned back to the counter as the black pickup disappeared from view in the steady torrent of rain. "I just thought I saw..." She shook her head, catching herself. "Nothing."

She didn't want it all over town that she thought somebody in a black pickup was following her. Or that she'd found a present on her doorstep, a palm-size heart-shaped red stone in a small white box with a bright-red ribbon and a small card that read THINK-ING OF YOU in computer-generated letters. No name.

"Is it me or is the whole town on edge today?" Betty said. "Kind of gives you the creeps thinking that Frank might really have seen Bigfoot."

"Yeah." Charity turned again to look through the rain to the dense forest beyond the street. The foliage was so thick that not even light could get through in places. Who knew what lived there?

Charity shivered. "Frank's a pretty reliable witness," she said. "He saw *some*thing. Something he thought was Bigfoot, at least."

Betty nodded and moved away. Behind Charity, several other diners began arguing amongst themselves.

"All Frank saw was a bear," said one.

"A bear that walks on its hind legs?" said another.

"It was dark," a third put in. "Probably just saw a shadow move across the road."

"I say it's some ancient ancestor. You know, a former race of giants."

"Who just happens to live in the Timber Falls mountains and never comes out? Puh-leeze."

Charity had heard these arguments for years.

She went back to thinking about Mitch. No hardship there. She'd so hoped he'd left the present. Just as she hoped he'd change his mind about marriage. She knew he wanted her, but just not on her terms. If she'd settle for anything else...

Well, she wouldn't. Couldn't. No matter how tempted she was. She was the one in the family who was going to do it the right way, not like her mother, who had three daughters—Faith, Hope and, what else, Charity—and hadn't bothered to get married until all three were old enough to be bridesmaids.

It was embarrassing to come from a family of not just old hippies but screwballs. Was it any wonder Mitch was scared to death to marry her and have children, given her genes?

That was why she had to show him. He'd been surprised when she'd gotten her journalism degree and started her own newspaper. Now all she needed was a Pulitzer-prize-winning story. She would change the family's image, even if it killed her, by doing everything the way it should be—right down to the wedding in white.

"Charity, tell them," Betty called to her from across the café. "Tell them about all those Bigfoot sightings going years back and all over the world."

"It's true," Charity said, pulling herself away from

her daydream. "A creature like Bigfoot has been reported in every state except Hawaii and Rhode Island. More than two hundred sightings going back to ancient man and probably untold numbers of people who have seen something and kept it to themselves because they were afraid of being ridiculed."

"Yeah, then how come no one's ever found any Bigfoot bones?" another customer asked.

"Maybe they bury their dead," someone replied.

"Or the bodies decay too quickly in this kind of climate," someone else suggested.

"Or Bigfoot is nothing but a myth," still another said.

"Charity, you really believe Bigfoot exists, don't you?" Betty asked as she refilled her diet cola.

A woman who hung on to the belief that one day she'd get Mitch Tanner to marry her? Oh, yeah. "He not only exists, but one of these days I'm going to prove it."

"You do that!" Betty said, and shot an indignant look at the customers who laughed.

Charity could just imagine a photo of Bigfoot on the front page of her paper. Imagine the look on Mitch's face. He'd have to take her paper seriously then, wouldn't he? And her, as well.

But he'd also have to apologize to his father. Lee Tanner had become the laughingstock of Timber Falls a few years ago when he'd stumbled across a Bigfoot on his way home from the bar—and reported it. No one had taken him seriously because he'd been drunk. But Charity had seen the truth in his eyes. Lee had seen *some*thing out there that night. Something that scared the hell out of him.

"A confirmed Bigfoot sighting could really put Timber Falls on the map," said Twila Langsley.

Twila had put Timber Falls on the map six years back when Charity and Mitch had discovered some of Archibald Montgomery's mummified remains in the huge carpetbag Twila carried, the rest of him in a trunk at the end of her bed.

Archibald had been Twila's beau, and she, it seemed, had killed him more than fifty-odd years ago to keep him from running off with her best friend, Lorinda Nichols. Archie, the slick devil, had been romancing them both.

Twila did five years at the state pen. She got out on good behavior in time to celebrate her ninetieth birthday.

No one in town felt any ill will toward her. She just wasn't allowed to bring her old carpetbag into Betty's—even if all she carried in it now was her knitting.

"I don't think even Bigfoot could put Timber Falls on the map," Betty said.

"If there is a Bigfoot, it's got to be smart," one of the customers noted. "Smart enough to know we'd cage it or kill it if it came near us."

Betty laughed. "Smarter than my ex-husbands, then."

Charity thought about having another piece of pie, unable to get the image of Mitch Tanner in the tux out of her mind. Did she dare hope it meant what she thought it did?

She finished her soda and had started to leave when she saw the black pickup again. Her heart lodged in her throat as the pickup slowed. She could see the shadow of someone behind the tinted glass just before the driver sped away. One thing was certain. Whoever was driving that truck *was* following her.

"DID YOU FIND HER?" Florie asked from the doorway of the ransacked Aries bungalow.

Mitch shook his head. He didn't find a body, but he feared Wade was right about Nina Monroe's being in trouble.

"I told you I was picking up weird vibes," Florie said.

Mitch was picking up more than a few of his own.

The bungalow was tiny, just a living area, bedroom, bath and kitchenette, all furnished with garage-sale finds.

In the bedroom at the back sat a sagging double bed and a scarred chest of drawers beside an open closet door. The bath had a metal shower, sink and toilet. No storage.

It was obvious someone had searched the place, looking for something that was small enough to conceal under a couch cushion. Or in a toilet tank. Or at the back of a drawer. Drugs? It was Mitch's first thought.

"Any idea what they might have been looking for?" he asked Florie on the off chance she'd done more than pick up bad vibes.

She shook her head. "The girl didn't have much. I don't even think she owned a suitcase. The day she checked in here all she had was that old compact car and whatever she had stuffed into a large worn backpack."

He glanced through the open door of the bedroom. A stained and frayed navy nylon backpack lay on the floor, open and empty. "She talk to you about where she was from?"

"Didn't talk at all. I barely saw her. Got up early and came in late."

"Any friends stop by?" He knew Florie kept a pretty good eye on the comings and goings of her tenants. The crystal-ball business was fairly slow in a town the size of Timber Falls.

"There was a guy. A couple of nights ago."

Mitch's ears perked up. "What did he look like?"

"Didn't get a good look at him. It was too dark. She never used her porch light. But he was tall as you, wore dark clothing. I got the impression he didn't want to be seen."

"What did he drive?"

Again Florie shook her head. "He must have parked down the road," she said. "But they had one heck of a fight."

"About what?"

"That, I can't tell you. I could just hear the raised voices for a few moments, then nothing."

"You didn't recognize the man's voice?"

"That darn Kinsey had her stereo on too loud in the Aquarius bungalow next door," Florie said. "You know she's gone and dyed her hair cotton-candy pink. Like I'm going to let someone with pink hair cut my hair."

He nodded. Kinsey had come back from beautician school determined to make her mother's shop, the Spit Curl, hip.

Mitch moved to the bedroom, wondering who the man was Nina had been arguing with. Florie stayed in the bungalow doorway. Only a few items of clothing hung in the closet. Probably just what had fit into the backpack. Either Nina couldn't afford more or she hadn't brought all her belongings to Timber Falls.

A bell jangled outside. "It's my private line," Florie announced. "I'm going to have to take it. One of my clients needs me."

He could tell she hated to leave. This was probably the most excitement she'd had in years. But money was money. "I'll be here."

She nodded as the bell jangled again, then took off hunkered deep in her coat against the rain.

Mitch looked around the room, hoping to find an address book or some clue where Nina might be.

The room was bare except for the bed and four-drawer dresser. There were no knickknacks, no photos, no personal items other than clothing in here or in the living room.

All of the drawers in the dresser had been pulled out, the sparse contents dumped on the floor. All except the bottom drawer.

He moved to the dresser, squatted down and pulled on the stuck drawer. Empty. Still squatting, he glanced under the bed. Nothing but dust balls.

The lack of clothing bothered him. Even counting what Nina was last seen wearing, the woman had only about four days' worth of clothes.

That seemed odd to him. But if there were more belongings, where were they? And why did she leave them behind when she'd come to Timber Falls?

It made him wonder if this was only to be a short stay.

He started to get up, shoving the drawer back in as he rose. It stuck. He had to pull hard to get the drawer to slide out again. As he did, he heard a soft metallic clink.

Withdrawing the drawer completely, he turned it over, curious what had made the sound. There were several pieces of torn masking tape stuck to the bottom. Something had been taped there but had broken loose.

Setting the drawer aside, he crouched down and felt around under the dresser until his fingers touched something small, metallic and cold.

His heart leaped as he withdrew a tarnished-silver baby's spoon and saw that the handle was in the shape of a duck's head. The same shape that had made Dennison Ducks famous. Even through the tarnish, he could read the name engraved on the spoon's handle: Angela. He felt a chill spike up his spine.

He'd heard that Wade Dennison had hired a jeweler in Eugene to make specially designed silverware for each of his daughters. First for Desiree, then two years later for Angela. Could this be Angela Dennison's baby spoon? And if it was, what was Nina doing with it twenty-seven years after the baby had disappeared from her crib?

CHARITY RAN THROUGH the rain to her old VW bug parked in front of Betty's and sat for a moment with the heater running as she tried to shake off her chill.

She'd seen the black truck again and there was no doubt in her mind that it was following her. Worse, she thought, looking at the small white box with the bright red ribbon sitting on her passenger seat, she suspected the driver had left her the present.

She stared at the box for a long moment before picking it up. There was no writing on it, not even a store logo. She opened the lid again and parted the white tissue paper.

Earlier all that had registered was that the stone was heart-shaped. She'd been so excited about getting a present from Mitch that she hadn't noticed that the stone was also blood-red and cold to the touch. She shivered as she turned the stone over.

There was nothing on it. No lettering. No artist's imprint. Nothing. The shiny surface seemed to capture what little light the gloomy day afforded, absorbing it deep within, as if harboring it like a secret.

She pulled out the tissue paper to make sure there wasn't something inside the box that she'd missed. Like a clue as to who had left it for her. Earlier it had seemed like a gift. Now it felt more like a threat.

She stuffed the heart back into the box, hurriedly closing the lid. The defroster had finally cleared enough of her windshield that she could drive the two blocks to the post office. But as she started to pull out, she caught a glimpse of a black pickup one street over.

She shifted into gear and took off after it. As she reached the corner, she half expected the truck to be gone. But there it was, creeping along as if the driver was lost. Or sightseeing. Could she be wrong about it following her?

There was only one way to find out, she thought, as she floored the gas, roared past the pickup and then hit her brakes, skidding sideways to block the street.

She leaped from her car into the pouring rain, ran up to the driver's side of the pickup and jerked the door open.

A startled gray-haired man stared out at her. Beside

him, a younger woman with blond hair clasped both hands over her chest as if she was having a heart attack.

Too late Charity noticed that the windows on the pickup weren't tinted. This wasn't the black truck she'd seen earlier, the one she was sure had been following her. On closer inspection this pickup was a much newer model. Worse, she knew the driver.

"Charity?" the elderly man gasped.

She groaned. "Mr. Sawyer, I'm so sorry. I thought you were someone else." He'd left Timber Falls about ten years ago after his wife died, but he'd kept the old Victorian house at the edge of town that had been in his family for generations.

"What in heaven's name were you thinking?" the blonde next to him demanded.

"It's all right, Emily," Liam said to the woman. "It's just Charity Jenkins. She's a good friend of my daughter Roz's." He turned to Charity. "This is my wife, Emily. I've moved back home."

He'd remarried? And come back to Timber Falls? Charity had noticed someone painting the old place just the other day, but never dreamed Liam Sawyer would return.

"Congratulations," she said, trying to hide her surprise and embarrassment. "I hope that means Rozalyn will be coming up to visit." She hadn't seen her friend for several years now.

Liam smiled ruefully. "She's awfully busy. You know she's a famous photographer now."

Charity nodded, the rain dripping off the front of her hood. "I have all her books."

"Could we get going?" Emily asked Liam.

"I'm sorry," Charity said again, realizing the rain was getting into the pickup. Liam seemed oblivious to it, though. "I'll move my car."

He smiled at her. "It is good to see you, Charity. Please stop by and visit."

"Tell her to wait until we get settled," Emily said. "The place is a disaster. It's going to take months to get it into any shape at all."

Charity sprinted back to her car and hurriedly pulled away, thinking about Roz as she drove to the post office to pick up her mail. She and Roz had been inseparable as kids. Of course Roz would be coming to visit her father, no matter how busy she was. It would be good to see her again.

Postmistress Sarah Bridges looked up as Charity came into the small post office. "Just got all the mail out," Sarah said from behind the caged opening on the left. To the right was a row of mailboxes.

"Anything good in mine?" Charity asked as she walked down to her box and, using her key, opened it to see a stack of bills.

"You know I never pay any attention to who gets what," Sarah called from behind the wall of boxes.

Uh-huh. Charity flipped through the stack as she walked back to where Sarah stood. Sarah was a good source of gossip.

"So what's new?" she asked Sarah.

"Liam Sawyer's remarried and back in town."

Darn. Charity hoped she had the jump on that story. No such luck. "I know. I just saw them."

Sarah shot her a look. "What do you think of the new wife?"

Charity might have shared her thoughts on Emily Sawyer if it hadn't been for an old loyalty to Roz. "I only saw her for a minute."

Sarah nodded, lips pursed, eyeing her as if she was holding out. "Well, you have a good day."

Charity doubted that, given how the day had gone so far. She pushed open the door and made a run for her car through the rain. She hadn't gone but a few steps when she caught a movement from the alley between the post office and bank.

An instant later she was hit by what felt like a freight train. Her mail went flying as she was knocked down in the mud by someone wearing a large dark raincoat. The cloaked figure stopped, back turned to her and knelt to hurriedly scoop up her mail from the wet ground.

She pushed herself up into a sitting position, too stunned to stand—until she realized the person in the dark raincoat wasn't picking up her mail to give her, but going through it!

"Hey!" Charity cried.

The dark raincoat didn't turn. Behind her Charity heard Sarah come out of the post office. "Charity?"

The figure dropped the mail and took off at a run down the alley.

"What in the world?" Sarah demanded, charging out to scoop up the wet mail and help Charity to her feet as the dark raincoat disappeared around the corner.

Charity took the mail from Sarah, her gaze still on the street where the figure had vanished. She heard an engine start in the distance. A few seconds later, a black pickup with tinted windows roared off two blocks away.

MITCH TUCKED THE baby spoon in his pocket as Florie swept back into the bungalow on a gust of wind and rain.

"How's the client?" he asked, trying to cover the fact that she'd startled him.

"Problems of the heart," she said with a wave of her hand. "She's going to call me back. Have you figured out where Nina has gone?"

He shook his head. "When she arrived she didn't have a job, you said."

Florie nodded. "She asked me about a bungalow, I said I had one, she said she'd take it and then she asked me how to get to Dennison Ducks."

So Nina had been confident she was going to get a job at the decoy plant. It *was* the biggest business in town, and maybe Nina had experience that made her confident she'd be hired. But Mitch also knew jobs at the plant were hard to come by. Nor were there many openings, because wages and benefits were good and with so few jobs in Timber Falls, employees tended to stay.

"What kind of paperwork did you get her to fill out before you rented her the bungalow?" Mitch asked, hoping for a clue as to Nina Monroe's life before she showed up here.

"None, other than her name," Florie said with a shake of her head. "I just go by whatever vibe I pick up."

"Vibes, instead of a former address or references?" he asked, unable to hide his disbelief.

"I'll have you know vibes are much more reliable than references."

He sighed. "But you told me her vibes were bad."

Florie flushed. "Actually, no, I said they were weird. I remember thinking she was awfully nervous. From her aura I could tell she had man trouble. But with women that's usually the case, isn't it?"

"But you rented to her, anyway?"

"She had cash," Florie said with an embarrassed shrug.

He counted to ten. "She get any phone calls while she was here?"

"Just one. From some woman. Sounded old. Maybe her mother, or grandmother. Nina didn't want to the take the call but finally did. I heard a little of it. Nina said, 'How did you find me? I told you to leave me alone.' She paused, then said, 'Right, you're worried about me. That's a laugh. Don't call here again. You're just going to mess things up.'"

Not bad for hearing only a "little" of a one-sided conversation. "The woman ever call again?"

Florie shook her head. "And before you ask, the number was blocked. You know, on my caller ID. I only checked because I didn't like the vibes I got from the caller. Just like what I'm picking up now about Nina. Worse vibes than before, you know?"

He knew, thinking of the missing woman and the baby spoon in his pocket.

CHAPTER FOUR

BACK AT HIS OFFICE, Mitch closed the door and went straight to his computer. He typed in Nina Monroe's name and her social security number Wade had given him—not surprised by the results.

Nina Monroe had lied about not only her social security number, but her name, as well.

"I'm going to get some doughnuts," Sissy said, sticking her head in the door.

"Lemon-filled?"

She nodded and smiled. "You need anything before I go?"

He shook his head and waited until he heard her leave before he went down to the basement where the old files were kept.

He dug out Angela Dennison's file, dusted it off and took it back upstairs.

Sheriff Bill "Hud" Hudson had been like a father to Mitch, as well as a mentor and friend. Hud had also been a first-rate sheriff and the reason Mitch had taken the same career path, instead of following his father's example and becoming a drunk.

Hud had been sheriff at the time of Angela's disappearance. At first, it was believed that the baby had been kidnapped. But no ransom demand was ever made and no body was ever found.

Not far into the file, Mitch started seeing a pattern, one he didn't like. In these types of cases, the parents are usually the first suspects, and Wade and Daisy Dennison were no exceptions.

In Sheriff Hudson's interview with Daisy, she testified that she didn't recall seeing Wade until the baby was discovered missing the next morning. She'd said she'd gone to bed early and didn't know when Wade had gotten home.

Wade, however, said he returned home at his usual time to find that Daisy had been drinking. They'd argued. She'd gone to bed. He'd slept in the den until he was wakened by the nanny early the next morning screaming that the baby was gone.

The nanny, Alma Bromdale, said she'd put the baby to bed about eight that night and gone to bed early herself. She'd taken some cold medicine that made her drowsy and thought that was why she hadn't heard anything in the adjacent room where the baby was sleeping.

That meant none of the three had an alibi.

Alma Bromdale. Mitch wrote down the name in his notebook. The nanny had been with the Dennisons for more than two years. She'd been hired just before the Dennisons first daughter, Desiree, was born. Alma was twenty-five at the time, from Coos Bay and had listed her job experience as one previous nanny job, babysitting and a nanny course through the adult-education program at the high school. She must be about fifty-two now.

Alma had been fired the day after the presumed kidnapping and had left Timber Falls. Mitch checked the telephone directory online. There was only one Bromdale in Coos Bay—Harriet Bromdale. A relative? He wrote down that name, as well, wondering what in the hell he was doing.

So he found an old baby's spoon with a Dennison duck head and "Angela" engraved on it. And so Nina Monroe was the right age and was now missing. Did he really think Nina might be the missing Angela?

He looked down at the file again, shaking his head. He didn't know what to think. Hud had noted in his interview with Alma that she'd seemed scared and upset, both natural for someone who'd just learned that the baby she was responsible for had been stolen—and from the adjacent room.

Alma had admitted that Wade and Daisy fought and, yes, she'd overheard them arguing about the paternity of the baby. Wade didn't think it was his.

Mitch swore under his breath.

The alleged kidnapper had climbed the trellis to the second-story room, but was believed to have taken the baby down the back stairs and out through a rear door on the first floor. Unfortunately, Sheriff Hudson had noted Wade had initiated a search of the area, using a few Dennison Duck employees, before calling the sheriff, and they'd tracked all over and destroyed any evidence there might have been outside the baby's bedroom window.

Baby Angela had been wearing a pink nightshirt. The only other item taken from the room was the quilt from her bed. Nothing else. No baby spoon, but Mitch knew that the spoon could have easily been overlooked.

He continued down the list of suspects to the live-in housekeeper who'd been fired a week before the abduction, a woman by the name of Georgette Bonners.

Georgette had been angry and, like Alma, had nothing good to say about the Dennisons. She had also alluded to the fighting and the question of the baby's paternity.

On the night of the abduction, Georgette said she was with her husband, Tim. He confirmed it. Both were now deceased.

Mitch closed the file, telling himself he was probably barking up the wrong tree. But there was that damned spoon. And Nina Monroe was missing. He put the file in his drawer and locked it.

As Sissy came in with the doughnuts, he grabbed his coat and headed for the door, taking the lemon-filled doughnut she shoved at him on his way out with a grin and a thanks.

The road to Dennison Ducks was narrow and dark, ten miles carved through the forest. Today, with the rain beating down, the road was even darker, gloomy somehow.

Or maybe it was just his mood, which hadn't been helped by the thought of that damned present someone had left for Charity. She'd sounded so excited. He wondered now what the gift had been.

Dennison Ducks was Timber Falls's claim to fame. Of course, if Wade Dennison had his way, the town would be renamed Dennison. Or even Dennison Ducks. Fortunately Wade didn't have his way *all* the time.

The decoys were sold in a small outlet store in town next to the *Timber Falls Courier* office, from mid-April to mid-October. But few people knew where the ducks were actually carved, since none were sold on site at the plant. There wasn't even a Dennison Ducks sign on the large metal building, just a small sign at the gravel parking lot that read Employees Only.

There was no gate. No security guard. And since no one lived on the premises, no one had seen Nina Monroe arrive or leave last night, according to Wade.

This morning there were a half-dozen cars in the lot. Mitch had called on the way to make sure Wade was in his office. He was and had told Mitch he could talk to any of the workers he needed to. Earlier Mitch had suspected Wade hadn't been telling him everything. Now, after seeing Nina's ransacked bungalow, he was convinced of it. He parked and rang the bell at the employee entrance. The door was opened by Bud Farnsworth, the production manager.

Mitch was assaulted by the heavy scent of freshly cut pine as he entered the building. From deep inside came the drone of band saws, carving machines and sanders. Ducks in various stages of production lined the tall metal shelves that ran the length of the room.

"Wade said you'd be coming by." Bud didn't sound happy about that. "You know this is our busiest time of the year, gearing up for Christmas." He was a burly fifty-something man with receding dark hair and small dark eyes that always seemed to be squinted in a frown. Like most of the employees, he'd started working at the decoy plant in high school and had worked his way up.

Bud drank on his time off and it showed in his ruddy complexion, as well as in his cranky demeanor, probably the result of a hangover. "Before you bother to ask, I don't know anything about Nina Monroe. She didn't work for me. Never said two words to her." Bud's crankiness verged on hostility. "Paint department's down there." He pointed between the shelves of ducks.

"If you think of anything that might help, give me a call," Mitch said to the man's retreating back.

Bud gave no sign he'd heard.

Mitch rounded the end of the last shelf to what was obviously the paint department. Three artists were seated at a large wooden table next to a window. Both the table and the floor around them were covered in dried paint. One of the four chairs at the table was empty. Nina Monroe's.

Mitch made his way to the painters, recognizing all three women. The thing about living in a small town like Timber Falls was that everyone knows everyone else—and their business. For most people, that was a curse. For the town sheriff, it was a mixed blessing.

Sheryl Bends didn't look up as he dragged out the empty chair next to her and sat down. He'd gone to school with Sheryl, even kissed her once in junior high. She was divorced from Fred Bends, a local logger, had worked at Dennison Ducks since high school and spent most evenings at the Duck-In Bar.

She had a narrow face with strong features and wide pale-green eyes, and wore her brown hair in a single braid that fell to the middle of her back. She often invited him over for dinner at her place. He'd never accepted, although he'd been tempted on occasion—usually when he just couldn't get Charity off his mind. But he'd never been tempted enough to actually accept.

Sheryl wore her usual outfit—a Western shirt, jeans, moccasins and long beaded earrings. Both the shirt and jeans seemed to be fighting to keep her ample breasts and bottom from bursting out.

"Hello, Sheriff," Sheryl said, giving him one of her slow sexy smiles.

"Sheryl." He felt his face warm a little.

From across the table, Tracy Shank seemed amused to see him flustered. Tracy was thirty-something with cropped brown hair and close-set eyes. She gave him a nod and kept working.

Next to her sat Pat Ames. She was fiftyish with a head of gray curly hair and a small delicate frame.

"Sheriff," Pat said, and kept painting the drake decoy in front of her.

He turned his attention to Nina's workspace, hoping to find some personal item that might give him a clue as to her whereabouts. But while the other women had photos of husbands or boyfriends or kids, there was nothing personal at Nina's end.

Mitch watched the women work for a moment, wondering if he should talk to them separately. He hoped they'd be more honest as a group. Also, he was still expecting Nina to turn up. It wasn't as if he had a murder investigation on his hands.

"I suppose you heard I'm looking for Nina Monroe."

They had. He went through his questions with Pat and Tracy, who told him what they knew, with Sheryl nodding in agreement. According to the women, Nina stayed to herself, didn't talk much, didn't socialize with her fellow workers, didn't even eat her brown-bag lunch with them.

"Where'd she eat lunch?" he asked, having noticed what looked like a coffee-break room on his way in.

The women shrugged. "She'd leave the building," Pat said quietly as she carefully painted a patch of Mallard green on her duck decoy.

"She ate outside?" he asked.

Pat shrugged and whispered, "Wade usually left

for lunch right after her." Pat didn't look at him, just kept working.

"You think there was something going on between them?" he asked, keeping his voice down, too.

No answer.

Sheryl glanced past his shoulder. He followed her gaze to the large plate-glass window of Wade's office on the second floor. The office was situated so that it overlooked the plant floor, giving him a view of the entire production area. Wade stood at the window, watching.

Mitch shoved back his chair, stood and thanked the women before heading upstairs.

Wade was still standing at the glass looking down when Mitch stepped into his office. He turned, not looking happy. But then, he seldom did.

"Have you found out anything?" he demanded.

"Not much. I'd like to see Nina's employment file."

"I don't know what help it'll be." Wade motioned for Mitch to draw up a chair in front of his desk as he stepped into the reception area outside his office, opened a large file cabinet and pulled out a file folder. His secretary's desk was empty, Mitch noted.

On a high shelf that ran the circumference of the office were samples of every decoy ever made at Dennison Ducks, all painted, all different sizes, shapes and types of ducks. The light made the dozens of eyes glitter as if watching him.

Wade handed Mitch the file and returned to his big black leather chair on the other side of the desk.

The folder had little in it. The Dennison Ducks employment application was one page. Under Former Employers, Nina had named a craft shop in Lincoln City called Doodles and a restaurant called The Cove in North Bend along the coast where she'd been a waitress. Not exactly great references for decoy painting, which he'd always heard took a great deal of artistic talent. So why had Nina been hired so quickly at Dennison Ducks?

Nina had left the phone numbers of her past employers blank. Under the space for her former address, she'd just put Lincoln City and the name of a motel or apartment building there, Seashore Views. No address. No phone number.

"There isn't much here," Mitch agreed. "And it doesn't look like she had any experience as a painter."

"She'd done some painting at the craft shop where she worked." Wade sounded defensive. "She just didn't put it down."

Uh-huh. There was *nothing* about painting experience on her application. Nor was there anything under next of kin or a number to call in case of emergency. "What do you know about her personally?"

Wade looked surprised. "Personally? I don't know anything about her."

"You must have talked to her," Mitch said.

"I might have complimented her on a couple of the designs she came to me with, but nothing other than that. I let my group leaders or my secretary handle all personnel problems."

"Were there problems with Nina?" Mitch had to ask.

"None that I know of." Wade seemed to avoid his gaze.

Mitch didn't like the feeling he was getting. "You told me earlier that she didn't have any family or friends or boyfriends."

"That's just what I heard." He straightened several items on his desk, obviously nervous.

"Who is the group leader in the paint department?"

"Sheryl Bends." Sheryl who hadn't said squat the whole time Mitch had asked questions.

"Do you have a photograph of Nina?"

Wade seemed startled by the question. "Why would I have a photo of her?"

"I thought maybe you had some sort of employee card with her photo on it or possibly a photo that was taken at some Dennison Duck function," he suggested.

Wade shook his head. He was perspiring, although the office was quite cool. There were large patches of sweat darkening the underarms of his shirt. "Nina had only worked here a month. She missed the company summer picnic."

Mitch asked for a copy of the one-page application and a W-9 form she had filled out stating only one deduction, everything that had been in her file. Wade made the copies himself on a small copier just outside his office.

"Where's Ethel?" Mitch asked, wondering where Wade's secretary was today.

Wade blinked as if he'd been a thousand miles away. "She's off sick." He handed him the copies, his fingers shaking as he did.

The man was awfully upset about an employee he'd hardly known and who'd only worked for him a month.

"Wade," he said folding the copies and putting them into his coat pocket, "I need you to be honest with me. If there's something more going on with Nina—"

Wade waved him off. "I've got a lot on my mind today, some personal things I need to tend to. I'm just concerned about her, that's all. I don't want anything to have happened to her."

"Why do you think something has happened to her?" Mitch asked. Wade didn't know about Nina's ransacked bungalow. Or did he? Wade knew something. That much was clear.

"I just think about Desiree…" Wade broke off, shook his head and looked away. "You know, if she was the one missing…"

"How *is* Desiree?" Mitch inquired, pretty sure he already knew the answer. Desiree was twenty-nine and pretty wild.

"Fine," Wade said quickly. "Desiree is fine."

Mitch studied him for a moment. "Okay," he said, and got to his feet, thinking about the baby spoon in his pocket, wondering how to ask about it, deciding now wasn't the time. "If you hear anything…"

Wade glanced at his phone. "I'll call you," he said, seeming anxious to get Mitch out of his office.

As Mitch passed the secretary's desk on his way out, he wondered if Ethel Whiting had ever missed a day of work in her life. Ethel had been with Wade since day one. She probably knew the family better than anyone in town.

Coincidence that she'd called in sick on the day Nina Monroe had gone missing?

The phone rang in Wade's office as Mitch started down the stairs. "It's about time you called," Wade snapped, making Mitch pause on the steps. "Listen to me, Desiree. I've always bailed you out of trouble, but this time you've gone too far. You know damned well what I'm talking about—" The office door closed, cutting off anything further.

Mitch could only imagine what sort of behavior Wade had been referring to. He'd heard stories about Desiree Dennison and her wild antics. Who hadn't? Mitch had picked her up for speeding in that little red sports car on several occasions. Recently she'd reportedly run Sissy's brother T.C. off the road. T.C. made furniture at his small shop outside of town.

Fortunately for Desiree, T.C. hadn't wanted to press charges, but it was obvious that Desiree had purposely forced T.C.'s old pickup off the road because he'd been going too slowly.

Maybe what had Wade upset and concerned this morning was really Desiree, not Nina Monroe. Wade *should* be concerned about Desiree. The woman was headed for trouble, sure as hell.

It was still raining, coming down in sheets, as Mitch stepped outside to find decoy painter Tracy Shank having a cigarette under the overhang of the roof. She glanced around when she saw him as if she thought someone might be watching her and stubbed out the cigarette.

"Did you find out anything?" she asked.

He shook his head. "Nothing more than I already knew."

Tracy lit another cigarette, took a drag and blew the smoke out into the rain. "There's something going on. Something…odd."

"With Nina?"

"With Nina, with Wade, with this place," she said, and glanced over her shoulder. "Nina was no painter. She just showed up one day and Wade hired her. She acted like all she wanted was to learn how to paint decoys. That's why she worked late all the time."

"You don't think that was the case?" he asked.

She let out an oath and shook her head.

"Then why work late?"

"I don't know. The plant is deserted after six. She'd have the whole place to herself. Painters are pretty much allowed to work their own hours, but something else was going on with that girl."

"You think she was meeting someone here? Having an affair? Wouldn't that make more sense at her apartment?" he asked.

"She was living at Florie's," Tracy pointed out. Everyone in town knew how Florie was about minding everyone else's business. It ran in the family. "If she didn't want anyone to know, the plant would be the perfect place."

"No one checks after hours?"

Tracy shook her head. "Doubt Wade's ever needed to. The place is locked up so only employees have access. What employee would be stupid enough to steal a duck? Wouldn't be worth it if you lost your job—plus, we get all the decoys we want at cost. Not that anyone who works here wants to even look at a damned duck after a whole day with them." She took another long drag on her cigarette.

"If Nina was using the plant, who do you think she was meeting here? Wade?"

Tracy made a face. "He's old enough to be her father."

Yeah, that was just what worried Mitch.

"Is there anyone else she might have been romantically involved with?"

Tracy snorted. "Have you seen the guys who work

here? The ones who aren't married are all like Bud. Enough said?"

He nodded. "You didn't like Nina."

Tracy looked startled. "I didn't have anything to do with her disappearance, if that's what you're thinking."

He said nothing, waiting.

Tracy finished her cigarette, stubbed out the butt on the concrete and crossed her arms. She looked cold and he realized she'd come outside without her coat, but she didn't appear ready to go back in yet. "I suppose you'll hear about this sooner or later," she said. "Nina and I hung out for a while after she first came to work here."

That surprised him, but he said nothing.

"She befriended *me* and she dropped me as soon as I was no longer useful."

"Useful?"

"She wanted to know a lot of stuff about Dennison Ducks and Wade and the family and everyone who worked here—you know, the good gossip."

He nodded.

"Okay, I screwed up. She and I would have a few beers and I probably talked too much. Hell, I thought she was my friend, all right? How was I to know she would use everything I told her against me?"

Tracy had just given herself a motive if Nina turned up dead, and she must have realized it. "Look, no one liked her. What she did to me was minor compared to the crap she pulled on other people here. She was a user. It made you sick to watch her. Especially the way she played up to Wade."

"She got special treatment?"

Tracy rolled her eyes. "I'll say."

"Why, if Wade wasn't romantically involved with her?"

Tracy shifted her feet and looked out at the rain for a moment. "It was more like Nina had something on him, you know? He treated her with kid gloves. So did Bud. But you know Bud—he does whatever Wade tells him to."

Mitch noticed that Tracy was talking about Nina in the past tense. "You make it sound like you don't think Nina will be back."

"It would be like her to up and leave town. I always got the feeling that she wasn't planning to stay long, anyway." She glanced at her watch. "I've got to get back in. I need this job."

"Thanks for your help. Call me if you think of anything else."

She nodded, but he could tell she was already regretting talking to him. He wouldn't be hearing from *her*.

After she disappeared back into the building, he stood for a moment watching the rain before he sprinted to his patrol car. Once inside, he pulled the papers Wade had given him from his coat pocket, his fingers brushing the baby spoon.

Slowly, he reached into his pocket and palmed the spoon. It felt cold and oddly heavy, a weight he desperately wanted to shed.

He'd almost asked Wade about it. But the timing had felt wrong. There had to be way to find out if it was indeed Angela Dennison's baby spoon, why Nina Monroe had it hidden under her bureau drawer and finally what, if anything, the spoon might have to do with Nina's disappearance.

Unfortunately all that would have to wait, he thought

as a yellow VW bug whipped in behind his patrol car, blocking his exit. He dropped the baby spoon back into his pocket as Charity Jenkins in a hooded clear plastic raincoat with bright red ladybugs on it jumped out and ran through the rain toward his car.

He groaned, struck as always with both desire and worry. What was Charity up to now?

CHAPTER FIVE

CHARITY SAW THE frown on Mitch's face she associated with broccoli as he opened his door and climbed out into the pouring rain to walk toward her.

"I was just mugged at the post office," she blurted out. So much for her plan to remain calm, not to act hysterical, to keep that wonderful control she associated with normal.

"Mugged?" After all, this *was* Timber Falls.

She pointed at the mud on one side of her jeans as irrefutable evidence she'd been knocked down.

He looked at her jeans, then at her.

She could tell he was struggling with her story. "Someone knocked me down and tried to steal my mail!"

"Is this a joke?" He smiled, making those little crinkles she loved around his incredible sky-blue eyes and those deep Tanner dimples. Rain dripped from his hat and his raincoat. As annoyed as she was, she wished he'd take her in his arms and hold her. For a moment she thought he might.

But then he said, "Let's get out of the rain. Climb in the patrol car and you can tell me what happened."

Brushing a wet lock of hair back under her raincoat hood, she stepped around to the passenger side, opened the door and slid in, steeling herself. Whenever she got within two feet of the man, sparks flew—one way or another.

It was exactly as she knew it would be inside his patrol car. Warm, dry and intimate, with just the hint of his scent, a mixture of soap, rain and maleness. Lots of maleness.

She took a deep breath and let it out slowly, trying to keep her equilibrium. This man was like a washing machine's spin cycle.

He climbed in and started the engine, kicking up the heater. "Okay, you say someone took your mail?"

"Someone knocked me down and then started going through the mail I'd dropped as if he was looking for something." It sounded so improbable to her she couldn't imagine Mitch believing it, which he obviously didn't, judging from his expression.

Which made her all the more determined to make him believe her. "Sarah saw it. She came running out and he took off!"

"With your mail?"

"No," she said. "He dropped it."

"You're sure he was going through it? He wasn't just picking it up and the two of you scared him? There wasn't any yelling or screaming involved, was there?"

He knew her too well. "You know Sarah. She yelled at him. But he *was* going through my mail looking for something." Mitch was starting to irritate her. "That isn't all. I'm pretty sure he took off in a black pickup—the same black pickup that's been following me."

"A black pickup's been *following* you? Since when?"

"I saw it the first time last night just before I went to bed. It followed me to Betty's this morning. And while I was there, it came by twice more, real slow, and I could feel the driver staring at me."

"You *saw* the driver?"

"Well, no. The truck has dark-tinted windows, but I could feel him looking at me."

Kind of the way Mitch was right now. Only Mitch was frowning, too. "Charity," he said with obvious patience, "there are a lot of strangers in town because of this Bigfoot thing, people just driving around, looking around."

There was no convincing him. Worse, she wondered now if he could be right. But then, that would make her wrong. "The truck was definitely following me."

"Charity, how can you be sure if you didn't even see his face? He could have been looking for someone in the café. Someone other than you."

"Right. And he was looking for that same person in front of my house last night? Why is it so hard for you to believe me?" she demanded, annoyed with him, annoyed even more that her story did sound hard to believe, now that she'd said it out loud. Not that she would admit it to him. "The driver of the pickup was *following* me and then he attacked me outside the post office."

Mitch sighed. "You said you *thought* the man who knocked you down got into a black pickup?"

"I didn't see him get in it, no. But I saw a black pickup down the street a few moments later."

He raised a brow and she wondered if someone had told him about her earlier mistaken encounter with the *wrong* black pickup. Liam wouldn't tell on her. But that Emily would.

"Fine. Don't believe me. But I think the driver is the same person who left the present on my doorstep."

"I thought you were convinced I left it."

"Well, you obviously didn't, so now I think it was the guy in the black truck."

"You noticed this pickup last night, you say? But you didn't bother to mention any of this when we talked earlier this morning. Maybe the present was left on your doorstep by mistake."

Oh, that was so like him. "You just can't believe that I might have a…a…secret admirer, can you?"

"That's not it," he said.

She opened the passenger-side door. "I thought you might want to find this black pickup before he does more than mug me and try to steal my mail, but since you don't believe me—"

"Hold on," Mitch said, his voice low and soft and sexy as ever. "Give me a description of the person who knocked you down at the post office."

"*Mugged* me. He was big or at least his raincoat was big. He had his back to me and his hood up, so I never saw his face or his body really."

"It was a man? Not some kid?"

"Yes, it was a man. A big man. Or a really big woman."

Mitch groaned. "Were there any checks or money orders in your mail?"

"I don't know. I just glanced at it. I didn't see anything interesting. I'm pretty sure it was all bills."

He nodded, obviously wondering why anyone would steal her bills. Good question. "So he looked through your mail."

"He dropped it when Sarah came out." She knew what Mitch was thinking. That the person hadn't meant to knock her down, that it was just an accident.

But that didn't explain the black pickup following her. "Just forget it." She shoved open the door and propelled herself out into the pouring rain. "I'll find the truck myself." She slammed the door and stomped toward her car.

"Charity!" he called after her.

She heard his door open, but she didn't turn. She climbed into her VW, her hands shaking with anger as she fumbled for the key. That man was impossible. Worse, she feared she'd done it again. Acted irrationally and confirmed Mitch's suspicions that she was a flake just like the rest of her family.

Was it possible that the truck wasn't following her? That the man at the post office had accidentally knocked her down and was only picking up her mail when she and Sarah yelled at him? Was it possible she, Charity Jenkins, had overreacted?

"Charity." Mitch was at her side window looking down at her, water pouring off his hat, his expression pained. "Roll down your window. Please," he said through the drumming rain.

She finally found the key and turned it. The VW engine started. She wanted to throw the car into reverse and go racing out of there, but she rolled down her window.

"I'm sorry," he said, then looked past her to the passenger-side seat. "Is that the present?"

"Yes."

"Let me see it."

She carefully handed the box with the stone heart in it to him and he stuck it inside his coat.

"Did you handle the stone?" he asked, then looked

at her and groaned as if he knew she had. "Well, there might be other prints."

Rain was coming in the window but she hardly noticed. "Yeah, maybe." She was touched that he was at least acting as if he was taking her seriously. That was something, right? Even if he was just humoring her?

"Can you think of any reason someone would be following you? Have an interest in your mail? Or leave you this?"

"No."

"What does this black pickup look like?"

"Older model, black with dark-tinted windows. I didn't see the plate. There was too much mud on it."

He looked at her and she could feel that old chemistry bubbling between them and knew he could, too. But chemistry wasn't the problem. It was the M-word: marriage. She had to hold out for it. No matter how strong the pull. She couldn't let Mitch talk her into anything short of holy matrimony. But right now, just the thought of being snuggled in his arms…

"If you see this pickup again, try to get a license-plate number for me. Or a description of the driver. But don't take any chances. Call me at once."

She nodded, then remembered Wade Dennison had been seen coming out of Mitch's office earlier. Wade, according to her source, had looked upset, and Mitch was up here at the plant. Now why was that?

"Something's going on with Wade Dennison, isn't it?" she asked, and saw his expression change ever so slightly. Oh, she did love it when she was right. Something *was* up! Her journalistic nose for news smelled a story. "What's going on?"

"How did you know I was out here?" he asked, frowning through the rain.

"I can't reveal my sources. Pretend I followed you."

"Speaking of being followed by a dangerous person…" He shook his head as if he'd finally figured out that lecturing her was a waste of breath, but the corners of his mouth turned up a little. His warm fingers squeezed her shoulder. "Call me if you see the truck," he said, and trotted back to his patrol car.

Charity drove back into town, warmed all over even though still muddy and wet from being attacked at the post office—and sitting with her window down talking to Mitch. His touch always sent sparks shooting through her body and a warmth better than her VW heater.

She had interviewed Frank, the Granny's bread deliveryman late last night, but she hadn't written the story yet. She reminded herself that she had a paper to put out, but first she needed to change into some dry clothes. Then she could worry about what Mitch was doing at Dennison Ducks.

Meanwhile, she kept an eye out for the black pickup. There was always the chance she wasn't overreacting.

MITCH WATCHED CHARITY drive away, remembering what she'd said about the person who'd knocked her down outside the post office. It had to have been an accident. This was Timber Falls. People didn't get mugged.

But as he glanced over at the red heart-shaped stone in the package on the seat next to him, he couldn't shake the bad feeling he had. Charity in some sort of trouble? What were the chances?

He started the patrol car and followed her at an inconspicuous distance back into town. She went straight home. Since he lived just next door, he pulled into his own driveway and waited until she was safely inside her house. But even then he couldn't bring himself to leave and kept watching the street behind him for a black pickup.

Fifteen minutes later, she emerged in clean jeans, climbed into her VW and drove to her office uptown. If she noticed him, which she must have, she didn't let on.

He figured she'd be safe at her office since she was only down the block. He needed to find out more about Nina Monroe.

Back at his own office, he double-checked Nina Monroe's social security number from her Dennison Ducks employment application. Same as the invalid one Wade had given him earlier.

He called her references. The manager of Doodles, the craft shop where she said she'd worked, had never heard of her. Nor did the woman recognize the description Mitch gave him. The same with The Cove in North Bend and Seashore Views apartment complex in Lincoln City. He hung up, wishing he had a photograph. But he doubted it would have done any good. Obviously all the information on Nina's application was bogus. So who *was* she?

He hated to think.

After he'd exhausted all law-enforcement avenues, he put on his coat again and headed for the door, knowing the one person who might be able to help him.

WADE DENNISON'S SECRETARY lived in a big old Victorian at the end of Main. Ethel Whiting's roots could be traced back to before Timber Falls was even a town, when it was nothing more than a logging camp. Her father had been one of the town's founders. He'd married well, but brought only one child into the world, a daughter, Ethel. His only heir.

Ethel still lived in the house where she was born. In fact, she'd never left. Right after high school, she'd gone to work and taken care of her aging parents, until both passed on.

Now in her early seventies, Ethel didn't need to work—at least not for the money. She was probably the richest woman in town. It was rumored she'd helped Wade Dennison start the decoy plant years ago. Others swore it had been Wade's new bride, Daisy, who'd footed the bill. Either way, Ethel had been a permanent fixture at Dennison Ducks ever since.

The decoy business had grown and so had the town as the demand for decoys grew and Dennison Ducks became famous.

Mitch hurried through the rain to the front door of the well-kept Victorian, rang the bell and waited. If Ethel really was sick...

She opened the door immediately. Almost as if she'd been expecting him. "Mitchell," she said. She was the only person besides his mother who'd ever called him that. "Do come in."

He stepped into the cool darkness of the house. It smelled of furniture polish and fresh-perked coffee. As Ethel motioned him into the parlor, he caught the hint of lilac perfume.

She wore a blue cotton dress, sensible shoes and a white cardigan with tiny blue-and-white flowers on it. Her gray hair was neatly pulled back in a bun from her heart-shaped face. It was obvious she'd once been a real beauty.

"Would you care for a cup of coffee?" she asked after offering him one of the antique chairs in the dark and austere parlor. He doubted the decor had changed since her parents' day.

"I'd love a cup, if it's not too much trouble."

"I just made a pot. Please make yourself comfortable."

It surprised him that she lived alone. She'd never married or hired a companion or any help. She was much too independent and self-sufficient for that. He thought it too bad more women weren't like her—then he thought of Charity and that overconfidence and irritating independence of hers. Maybe it was better more women didn't have it.

"You don't take cream or sugar, as I recall," Ethel said, putting down a silver tray. She poured the coffee, handing him a fine china cup and saucer.

"You have a good memory." He took a sip, the china feeling fragile in his big hands. "I'd forgotten how good perked coffee tastes."

"Did you stop by to compliment my coffee?"

"No, I'm here for the same reason you made a fresh pot. You knew I'd be asking you about Nina Monroe."

She nodded. "I understand she's missing?"

He nodded. "Tell me about her."

Ethel raised a brow. "She's only been employed at Dennison Ducks for a little over a month."

"And caused a lot of trouble during that time."

"You are well-informed."

"Is there any truth to it?" he asked.

"Truth to what?"

Age didn't seem to matter when it came to getting straight answers from women, he thought. "That Nina could easily be Wade Dennison's downfall?"

"You're asking if Nina had some kind of hold on him...." Her blue eyes darkened and she nodded. "I saw it and tried to warn Wade about her." She sighed and picked up her cup and saucer to take a dainty sip of her coffee.

He noticed that her hands were shaking. "Wade didn't take kindly to your concern?"

"He reminded me yesterday that I was only his secretary."

Mitch was surprised. If there was any truth to the rumor that she'd helped Wade start the business, she must have been furious. And hurt. "I'm surprised he'd say that to you."

"I was, too." She paused. "I'm very concerned for him."

"Not for Nina?"

"Nina, it seems, can take care of herself."

"You didn't like her."

Ethel's only response was a tight smile.

"I've never known you to miss a day of work."

"I've never known you not to say what's on your mind, Mitchell."

"You aren't sick."

"No, I resigned yesterday."

He was shocked. "After you spoke to Wade about Nina?" And before Nina's disappearance, he thought.

She nodded. "I should have retired a long time ago. Wade just helped me realize that the time was right."

"Was Wade's attitude toward Nina the only reason?"

She put down her cup and saucer and folded her hands in her lap. "It was time."

"Ethel, I need to ask you something and I'm not sure how. You've been close to the Dennisons for years."

"I've known Wade all my life."

"You probably remember when Desiree was born." She nodded and he continued, "Wade had special silverware designed for her. Then another set made when Angela was born two years later. Ones with duck's heads on them?"

"A spoon and a fork engraved with each girl's name. Hart's Jewelry in Eugene made them just for Wade."

"Then Daisy probably still has them."

Ethel shook her head. "Wade ordered everything of Angela's to be discarded. He couldn't bear to see anything that reminded him of his daughter."

"When was this?" Mitch asked.

"A few weeks after the baby disappeared. By that time, he was convinced Angela wouldn't be returned, and every time Daisy saw something of the baby's, she became upset."

Wade's compassion for his wife surprised Mitch. Especially if the rumors were true and baby Angela hadn't even been Wade's. Whatever the case, Daisy had been a recluse, hiding in that big old house for the past twenty-seven years, ever since her daughter's disappearance.

"Wade didn't keep even Angela's baby silver?"

She shook her head. "Not as far as I know. He took everything of the baby's to the dump and buried it himself. I remember the day all too well. I'd never seen Wade so...devastated." Her eyes shone with tears and her cheeks were heightened with color.

Mitch stared at Ethel, wondering why he'd never seen it before. She was in love with Wade! Ethel was a good five years older than Wade. Not that the age difference mattered when it came to love. Mitch wondered if Wade knew. According to Sissy, men could be dense as tree stumps when it came to this sort of thing.

"You don't think Daisy squirreled away something of Angela's?" he asked. "Or maybe Wade did at the last moment?"

Ethel shook her head. "Why are you asking about this now?"

"I found what I believe is Angela's baby spoon. It was in Nina's bungalow, taped under a dresser drawer."

She took in a sharp breath, her eyes suddenly hard and cold. "I haven't heard Angela's name even whispered in years, and now this."

"Is it possible Nina is Angela?" If he'd expected Ethel to be surprised by the question, he would have been wrong.

She didn't even blink. "It is possible Wade *believed* it. Or wished it were true."

"You don't believe she's Angela?"

Ethel smiled. "It really doesn't matter what I believe, does it, Mitchell?"

"It does to me."

She straightened and took a breath, her gaze steely. "If Nina Monroe is the baby who was stolen from her crib at the Dennison house twenty-seven years ago, then it's best if we never know it."

"I don't understand."

"Nina Monroe is…flawed. Maybe she was born that way. Maybe life made her that way. It doesn't matter really. Either way, if she is Angela Dennison, then it's a dark day for the Dennison family."

"Flawed how?"

"I believe she is capable of doing *anything* to get what she wants. No matter who she hurts. She is a dangerous woman who won't stop until she destroys herself and anyone who gets in her path."

He felt a chill curl around his neck. "What does she want?"

"Money, position. Everything she's been denied."

He stared at her. "She wants to be… Angela Dennison?"

Ethel raised a brow. "If it gets her what she feels she deserves."

He didn't like what he was hearing. If Ethel was right and Nina wanted to be Angela Dennison—might actually be Angela—who in town would try to stop her?

Ethel Whiting for one, he thought. She would do whatever it took to protect Wade, he realized with a start.

He'd learned a long time ago to leave the hard questions until last. That way if he got thrown out, he'd at least have some answers.

"I took a look at the old case file on Angela Dennison's disappearance," he said carefully. "Wade was a suspect. It seems there was a rumor circulating that Angela wasn't his and he knew it."

Ethel got to her feet and drew herself up to her full height. "Wade Dennison can be a fool, he's proved that. But he wouldn't have hurt that baby. Even if it wasn't his."

"Was it his?"

"Were either of them his? I guess that's something you'd have to ask his wife." She met his gaze, making one thing perfectly clear: there was no love lost between Ethel and Daisy.

"Thanks for the coffee. It was wonderful. I'd appreciate it if you didn't…"

"I wouldn't dream of carrying this conversation outside these walls," Ethel said primly.

"Sorry, it's habit. But if you should think of anyone who might know something about Nina…"

"I wouldn't rule out Nina staging her own disappearance," Ethel said. "Or using Charity to get what she wants."

"Charity?"

"Yes. She was asking questions about Nina at the plant yesterday."

He was stunned. Charity had been asking questions about Nina Monroe the day she disappeared? "What kind of questions?"

Ethel shook her head. "She didn't talk to me. I think she knows I would never talk about Dennison Duck business with a reporter. You'll have to ask her."

He turned to leave, anxious to find Charity and do just that.

"Mitchell."

He felt Ethel's fingers dig into his arm.

"Whatever you do, don't underestimate Nina—or what she's capable of." Ethel's words vibrated with emotion. "Be careful. Very careful."

He nodded, surprised by the concern he heard in her voice.

"You know where you can find me if you should…
need to," she said, and released his arm, appearing almost embarrassed by her little outburst as she turned
away.

CHAPTER SIX

CHARITY LOOKED UP from her computer, surprised to see Mitch come through the newspaper-office door. He appeared upset.

"You found the black pickup?" she cried, getting to her feet. Or did his visit have something to do with that stupid present?

"Why were you asking questions about Nina Monroe?" he demanded.

She stared at him. "What?"

"It's true, isn't it?"

Where had he heard that? And more important, why was he so upset? "Unless I'm mistaken, you and I don't talk about much of anything anymore. And you certainly haven't shown any interest in my newspaper articles."

"You were doing an article on Nina?"

He wasn't going to tell her that there really was a story there, was he? "Why do you care?"

He pulled off his hat, raked a hand through his hair and groaned. "I just found out that you were asking questions about her the day she disappeared."

Charity blinked. *"Disappeared?"* Holy moly, maybe there really was a story.

"Nina didn't show up for work this morning, and Wade is worried that something's happened to her."

Charity lowered herself into a chair, her mind reeling. "I'd heard rumors about the new painter at the plant but—"

"What kind of rumors?"

She looked up at him. "Rumors that something was going on between her and Wade."

"And?"

"And nothing. I asked a few questions, didn't get any answers." Had she missed something? Obviously. "I was going to do a feature on her. She'd promised to write down a few things for me and get back to me."

"Charity, if you know anything about Nina Monroe's disappearance, now is the time to tell me."

She wished she did. "I haven't a clue, really."

He sighed, eyeing her suspiciously. "It just seems odd that you would be asking questions about her on the day she was last seen."

Yes, it did. She glanced at her watch.

"What?" he demanded.

"I was just thinking." Her stomach rumbled.

"About food?" He sounded incredulous.

She smiled. "You know me *so* well."

"Charity, I don't have time for even a late lunch."

"I had Betty put back two pieces of lemon-meringue pie." She gave him her most seductive smile, hoping that, combined with lemon-meringue pie, she'd be irresistible.

"You were that sure we'd be having lunch together?"

"I guess some things are destined, Mitch, especially if you want to continue this discussion," she said, and went to get her raincoat before he could argue the point.

Mitch told himself that he had to eat. Also, he knew he'd get more answers out of her on a full stomach—

hers, not his. And there was something about Nina Monroe she wasn't telling him.

BECAUSE IT WAS the middle of the afternoon, Betty's Café was relatively empty. Everyone was probably out looking for Bigfoot.

He and Charity took a booth at the back and ordered their usual: cheeseburgers, loaded, and French fries, the kind that were hot and greasy and made from potatoes that still had their skins on when they hit the boiling grease.

It reminded him of when they were in high school. Those were good memories. In fact, when he thought about it, he could call up lots of good memories with Charity. But they were before she'd become the town reporter and he'd become the sheriff, before he'd realized that marrying her would be nothing less than disastrous given their families and their genes.

"All right, let's hear it," he said, after he'd watched Charity put away most of her burger and fries.

With her fingers, she dragged a long greasy French fry through a pool of ketchup and took a bite, closing her eyes as if eating for her was an erotic experience. He had a feeling it probably was. Just watching her definitely did something to him.

She smiled as her eyes opened, focusing on him in a way that made him more than a little uneasy.

"Nina," he reminded her quietly. Betty was busy helping the cook finish up the dinner special and so was out of earshot. But this *was* Timber Falls. And Betty had amazing hearing.

Charity swallowed the bite, putting down the French fry to wipe her hands on her napkin.

He reached across the table to whisk away the drop of ketchup at the corner of her mouth. She did have the most wonderful mouth, bow-shaped lips full and luscious.

He shook himself mentally, knowing where thinking like that would get him. A cold shower. How many times had Charity made it abundantly clear: marriage or nothing. Nothing but frustration.

She gave him a smile now and licked the spot where he'd touched her lips. The woman was incorrigible.

"Charity."

"I already told you. I heard rumors about Nina and Wade, about her not being too popular out at the plant, and I decided to do a story on her."

"And?"

Charity picked up another fry and eyed him, smiling. "Your turn. Tell me what you've found out."

"It doesn't work that way and you know it."

"It should." She took a bite.

He groaned. "Her bungalow at your aunt's was ransacked." He figured Florie would tell Charity, anyway. "Your turn. Was Wade having an affair with Nina?"

"I don't think so, and frankly, most of what I heard about Nina sounded like sour grapes among a few employees trying to make trouble for her and Wade, especially Sheryl. She'd be my first suspect if Nina really is missing."

He wished now he hadn't said anything. All he'd done was alert Charity to a possible story. But then again, Nina had done that by disappearing. He was reminded of what Ethel had said. Was this just a way for Nina to call attention to herself? Had she ransacked her own bungalow, leaving the baby spoon for him to find, knowing Wade would involve the sheriff when she didn't show up for work? And maybe she'd helped along the rumors about her and Wade just to get Charity involved. Ethel had said Nina might be using Charity. Nina had agreed to an interview. If Nina was Angela Dennison, maybe Nina hoped Charity would break the story.

He frowned. "You said Nina was going to write something down for you? Like what?"

Charity shrugged. "She said she'd had an interesting life. *Everybody* thinks their life would make a good book. What would make Wade think Nina met with foul play?"

He shrugged.

She wasn't buying it. "Maybe there *was* something going on between them."

"I don't think so." He tried to think of something to change the subject.

Charity looked disappointed but not deterred. "It would explain why Wade hired her without any experience and so quickly, why he seemed to think she could do no wrong, even why he's so worried about her now, huh?"

Yeah, that was one explanation all right.

"But then there's the gun she bought for protection," Charity said.

"Gun?" It wasn't registered to Nina Monroe or it would have come up on the computer. And why had she thought she needed protection?

"She showed it to Hank Bridges one night at the Duck-In."

"She showed it to the *bartender?*" He definitely didn't like the sound of this.

"I guess she'd had quite a lot to drink—she was the last to leave the bar. Hank was worried about her getting home safely. She told him she could take care of herself, then opened her purse and showed him the gun."

"What kind of gun?"

"You know Hank." She rolled her eyes. Hank Bridges still lived with his parents. His mother, Sarah, was Timber Falls's postmistress, and Buzz, his father, was a carver out at Dennison Ducks. His younger brother, Blaine, was still in high school and worked part-time for Charity. Neither young man was what you'd call manly. Hank, especially, was scared to death of guns and spiders and, well, most everything outdoors.

"Hank didn't know what kind of gun it was."

Charity nodded. "Just said it was small but lethal-looking."

"When was this?"

"Saturday night."

"What if Nina did write something down and mailed it to me?" she cried.

He stared at her. "Like what?"

"Her life history. Or maybe why she was carrying a gun for protection?" Charity suggested.

"Sounds like a long shot."

"But it's a theory, anyway."

Charity and her theories.

He swore under his breath. Just a few nights before Nina disappeared she'd been at the Duck-In drinking too much and waving around a firearm? She'd also had an argument with some man at her bungalow earlier Tuesday evening, according to Florie. "She happen to mention to Hank why she thought she needed protection?"

Charity wagged her head. "Hank didn't *want* to know."

"That's everything you know about Nina?"

She nodded.

He studied her. Why did he get the feeling she still wasn't telling him everything? Because she was Charity.

"You can't really keep me from doing this story, you know," she said.

He knew. It would soon be public knowledge that one of Dennison Ducks painters had gone missing. He couldn't keep Charity from printing that.

What worried him now was that Charity would go after the story like the bloodhound she was. He groaned at the thought, remembering what Ethel had said.

"This could be dangerous," he warned.

Charity arched a brow. "I'm a journalist. We don't back off from a story because it might be dangerous. It would be like you refusing to do your job for the same reason."

Right. "Okay, how are your sisters?" he asked, knowing he wasn't going to change her mind. Not Charity. And the harder he pushed, the more determined she would become.

"Why are you asking about my sisters?" she questioned suspiciously. "Is one of them missing, too?"

"No, I just…" He wished now he'd simply eaten his pie and said nothing. "I was just curious. I saw Hope a while back, that's all."

Charity was still eyeing him as if he'd only brought up her family as an example of why the two of them were so wrong for each other. Her crazy family. Not to mention his own. And all he'd wanted to do was change the subject. "Hope told me she split up with her boyfriend."

Charity made a face. "Good riddance. She deserved better."

"You've seen her, then?" he asked, surprised. He got the impression that Charity tried to distance herself from her family—as if that would change her DNA.

"Hope drove up one night last week, brought a bottle of wine and a pizza from the Duck-In. We both got a little tipsy and giggly." She smiled in memory.

He wished he'd seen that. He could just imagine Charity's full lips stained red with wine. Damn, but he missed kissing her.

Charity pulled her piece of lemon-meringue pie close enough so she could get a fork into it. She gazed down at the bite with nothing short of worship. "Her boyfriend turned out to be a real bastard." She put the bite in her mouth, closed her lips on the tines and shut her eyes as she slowly withdrew the fork from between her lips.

He groaned inwardly as he watched her and tried damned hard not to remember a time he'd been responsible for putting that look on her face. "How was he a bastard?"

She opened her eyes, grimaced as if disappointed.

"Tart?" he asked.

Her eyes widened. "You say the sweetest things."

"I meant the pie."

She smiled and took another bite, obviously knowing only too well what he meant. She didn't close her eyes this time. "I think her boyfriend took advantage of her."

Mitch felt himself squirm. "In what way?"

She looked over at him, her gaze locking with his. Her eyes were warm honey, flecked with equal amounts sunbeams and mischief. "He wanted her—just not badly enough to marry her."

"The *bastard,*" Mitch said.

"Funny." She took another bite of pie.

Speaking of boyfriends… "Do you know if Nina was seeing anyone?"

Charity shook her head.

Damn. He could see the wheels turning. He'd given her something else to go after, and Charity was amazing at finding out information. "If you should learn anything more about Nina or her disappearance…"

She smiled at him. "I have your number."

Yeah. He glanced at his watch, then at her. Time to go. But he hesitated. That stupid red heart-shaped stone bothered him, as did Charity's story about the black pickup and the man who'd knocked her down at the post office.

Mitch feared that the black pickup and the man at the post office were somehow tied in with Nina's disappearance. If Nina really had disappeared. He was still holding out hope that she'd show up before dark.

"Also, if you see that black pickup or get any more gifts…" He couldn't help but worry about Charity, especially given that she'd been asking questions about Nina the day the painter had disappeared. Except what could he do? Lock Charity up? Not let her out of his sight? "You're going back to your office?"

She nodded.

"Is Blaine coming in to help put the paper together tonight?"

Charity smiled at his concern, eating it up like pie. "I won't be alone, if that's what you're worried about."

He started to deny that he worried about her, but saved his breath as he picked up his hat from the seat beside him, settled it on his head and looked at her. "Lunch was a good idea."

"Lunch is always a good idea," she said, and smiled up at him as he slid from the booth. She had a killer smile. It had nearly done him in more times than he wanted to remember.

He stood for a moment just looking at her, tempted. Tempted to ask her to the community-center dance next weekend. Tempted to see what she was doing for dinner tonight. Just plain tempted.

But then the strangest thing happened. He heard wedding bells. It was only the old bell ringing down at the church signaling school was out, but the effect was like a cold shower.

"See ya," he said, and tried not to run as he left.

Charity let out a long sigh and fought to slow her pounding pulse. The man had no idea what he did to her. Thank heaven. If she showed even the slightest weakness, she'd be a goner.

"How was it?" Betty asked, sliding into the seat Mitch had just vacated. She wasn't asking about the food.

Charity couldn't help grinning at the older woman. "Nice. Sweet. I think I'm getting to him."

Betty laughed and shook her head. "I would have given up on that man years ago."

"Can't."

"Hell, girl, there's dozens of men who could curl your toes if you'd just let them." Betty gave her a sympathetic look. "Some men just aren't the marrying kind, hon. Mitch thinks he's...damaged goods because of his folks. You know that. Marriage scares him. Maybe especially with you."

Charity nodded. She knew only too well how Mitch felt. "Then I guess I'll be an old maid."

Betty howled at that, sliding out of the booth as a group of out-of-towners came in the door. They shook off raindrops as they inquired about the blue plate special and where exactly Frank, the bread deliveryman, had seen Bigfoot.

Charity sat for a moment, seriously considering the idea of being an old maid. It didn't have much appeal. But it would be *all* Mitch's fault. That was some consolation.

As she started to leave, she saw the black pickup. It cruised by slowly, then took off as if the driver had seen her watching him.

She made a dash for her car, parked down the block in front of the newspaper. Her hands were shaking as she leaped behind the wheel. The engine turned over immediately and she whipped out into the street.

She could see the black truck turn right at the end of Main onto Mill Creek Road. She took off in pursuit, fumbling to dial the Sheriff's Department number on her cell phone as she did.

"Sheriff's Department," Sissy said, sounding half-asleep.

"Where's Mitch?" Charity demanded, heart pounding.

Sissy sighed her Oh-it's-you-again sigh. "Out on patrol." Mitch could have been in the john or even dead and Sissy still would have said that.

Charity swung a right just past the Spit Curl. The pickup was already past town, headed out the narrow road that led to Dennison Ducks and beyond.

"Get word to Mitch that I found the pickup. He'll know what I'm talking about. I'm chasing it. We're headed east toward the plant. Tell him to hurry!"

That's when she saw the second present. It was stuck to the passenger seat of her car by one long sharp thorn. A bright red rose.

"WHAT THE HELL is that woman thinking?" Mitch demanded when he got the call over the radio a few minutes later.

"We're talking Charity here," Sissy retorted.

Mitch swore as he found a place to turn around. He'd stopped by the post office and talked to Sarah Bridges. She hadn't gotten a look at the person who'd knocked Charity down in the parking lot. In fact, like Charity, she couldn't even be sure it was a man. Just someone in a big dark hooded raincoat.

After that, he'd driven around town, thinking he might come across Nina's red compact. Wade didn't have a plate number. Just a description of the vehicle. And without Nina's real name...

But Mitch hadn't seen the car. Or a black pickup. Or anyone walking down the highway in a dark raincoat and looking suspicious.

He had, however, been counting the reasons he should stay clear of Charity Jenkins. There were many. At the top of the list was the fact that the woman lacked good sense and, worse, stole his reason, as well. When he was around her, it was as if she'd drugged him, his desire for her a lethal dose that would kill him eventually if he wasn't careful.

He reached the turnoff and headed toward Dennison Ducks as he tried to calculate how far behind Charity he was. He knew that if she chased the pickup past the plant, she could be in real trouble. The area was isolated, the logging road narrow and seldom used. A person could get lost just a few feet off the road up there, the vegetation was so thick.

Didn't she realize how dangerous this was? Chasing a vehicle and driver she thought was following her? What kind of sense did that make?

What worried him the most was that Charity would be acting on impulse—after all it *was* Charity—and not even considering that the pickup might be leading her into a trap. If the driver of the black pickup had some reason to get Charity on an isolated road alone, she'd just played right into his hands.

Just before he reached Dennison Ducks, he tried her cell-phone number. Either out of the calling area. Or turned off. Great.

Sissy had told him that she'd heard Charity had accosted Liam Sawyer earlier. Liam's new wife had called to complain. Maybe Charity was now chasing Liam.

But that didn't explain the red heart-shaped stone that someone had left for her or the note: THINKING OF YOU. Both worried him.

Charity was in trouble. He could feel it.

As he passed the Dennison Ducks parking lot, he looked to see if either rig was there. No black truck. No yellow VW bug. He swore and kept going, driving as fast as he could, considering the rain was making the narrow muddy road even more treacherous.

He tried not to think about what would happen if Charity caught up with the truck and driver. She wouldn't have thought that far ahead, knowing her. Damn, why did she always have to be so impulsive and take matters into her own hands?

He felt a stab of guilt. It wasn't just her screwball genes. He hadn't really bought her story and she knew it. He'd had a rational explanation for the present, the attack at the post office, the mysterious black truck she said was following her.

Now, knowing Charity, she was dead set on proving to him that she was right—even if it killed her.

He hoped to hell she was wrong this time, though. If the black pickup really had been following her...

He came around a corner in the road and hit his brakes. The VW bug was sitting sideways in the middle of the road, the driver's-side door hanging open, the interior light on, but even from here, he could see that the car was empty.

Dear Lord, where was Charity?

CHAPTER SEVEN

CHARITY BAILED OFF the mountainside on foot, clutching her camera to her breast, pretty sure she'd lost her mind.

Not far up the road, she'd realized—belatedly—that there was a good chance the driver of the pickup was leading her into a trap. He'd left the red rose in her car. Had he also made sure she saw him? Because he wanted her to chase him?

It definitely looked that way. He'd taken a road that was seldom used, and while it eventually wound back around and came out on the highway into Timber Falls, there was a lot of remote country between here and there.

He was drawing her deeper into that country. The truth was, he could have lost her easily since he was driving a vehicle that could go faster than hers.

But at the same time, she desperately wanted to find out who he was—and prove to Mitch the man in the black pickup existed.

That was when the desperate idea had struck her. As the truck disappeared around a curve in the road ahead, she slammed on her brakes, grabbed her camera from the case, got out of her car and dropped over the side of the road down through the thick tangle of underbrush and trees.

The plan was simple. She would cut off the pickup on foot. The truck would soon reach a hairpin curve and loop back directly below the spot where she'd left the VW.

All she had to do was drop straight down the mountainside on foot, push through the jungle of growth, keep from killing herself and reach the road below before the pickup did. Then she could hide in the bushes and get a shot of the pickup—and driver—as both went by.

She'd come this far and she was going to get a photograph of the truck to show Mitch, or die trying.

The idea had seemed inspired at the time.

Now, committed in more ways than one, more out of control than in, trying to protect the camera and save her own life, she crashed down the steep mountainside through the soaking wet foliage, ready to admit it had been a less-than-brilliant plan.

"Eek!" she squealed when, too late, she saw the huge spider web and pretty much fell through it. Frantically she brushed at the silken threads on her face and hair, her raincoat hood falling back, as she continued her downward plunge through the wet ferns and pine boughs, with no chance of stopping. All she could hope was to stay on her feet in the rotting maple leaves.

Sometimes she scared herself with her harebrained ideas. At these moments, she could kind of see why the thought of marriage to her scared Mitch.

In the distance, she thought she heard the pickup's engine. Soon it would be on the road directly below her. She couldn't see the road yet. Then again, she couldn't see five feet in front of her because of the forest, but she knew she had to be getting close.

She just hoped she didn't come crashing out of the trees and dense brush only to be run down by the truck. Regrettably it appeared she might reach the road at the same time as the black pickup.

And at some point she'd thought this plan was inspired? She was about to find out the driver's intentions—and in the worst possible place. That was if she didn't break her neck before she reached the road. And he didn't run over her.

That was when she heard it. Something crashing through the trees and brush just below her on the mountain. Something *big*. She caught a glimpse of brown fur.

Her breath caught in her throat as she grabbed at tree branches, trying to stop her descent, thoughts of the black pickup replaced by the terrifying thought of colliding with a bear.

Unfortunately she was moving too fast down the precipitous slope to decelerate at all.

Suddenly she broke through the thick cover, bursting out of the trees in a flurry of fern fronds, pine needles and dried leaves, arms and legs flailing. She crashed down in the middle of the road, somehow managing to stay on her feet as she stumbled to a stop. Then she heard the sound of the pickup truck's engine coming closer.

In that instant, something large and dark streaked across the road just inches in front of the pickup's chrome grill. She didn't even realize that she'd jerked the camera up, could barely hear the sound of its motor drive over the thunder of her heart and the screech of the pickup's brakes. Between her and the pickup's grill was something big, dark and furry.

The pickup skidded on the wet muddy road, the grill coming closer and closer and closer to where Charity stood. *Snap, snap, snap.*

At the very last moment, she dove into the dense growth below the road, hugging the camera protectively to her chest as she tumbled a half-dozen yards down the mountainside, disappearing in the dense greenery. When she finally stopped, she lay very still.

Above her, she heard the pickup come to a stop a few yards past where she'd bailed out. Heard the truck door open with a groan. Heard the slap of footsteps through the mud puddles. The sound of heavy breathing. A limb snapped directly above her at the edge of the road, and she knew the driver was standing up there looking down at the spot where she lay hidden in the ferns. At least she hoped she was hidden.

MITCH LEAPED FROM his patrol car, weapon drawn, as he rushed to Charity's VW. The car was indeed empty, and the keys were still in the ignition.

Whatever had happened here, Charity hadn't had time to even grab her purse. It was on the seat next to— His heart stuck in his throat as he saw the red rose speared to the passenger seat.

"Oh, God," he breathed. "Charity?" His voice cracked. *"Charity!"*

A blue jay answered from the dripping trees overhead. Rain fell through the lush green canopy and pattered on the forest floor. Over it, he heard what sounded like a car door slam, then the roar of an engine below him on the mountain. Damn. "Charity!"

He hurriedly climbed into the VW, started the engine and pulled the car out of the way, then he rushed back to his patrol car and took off down the road after the sound of the retreating engine.

Not far past the hairpin curve, he spotted her. A small soaked figure in a dirt-covered ladybug-printed raincoat walking up the road toward him. She was hunched forward, clutching her chest.

He threw on his brakes and was out of the patrol car, running toward her before he even realized it.

She looked like a drowned rat, her long auburn hair plastered to her face, her hood thrown back.

As he approached her, he saw that her hair was full of wet leaves and twigs, her ladybug plastic raincoat in tatters and her face scratched and bleeding.

His heart jerked in his chest at the sight of her, and all he wanted to do was take her in his arms.

"Are you all right?" He barely got the words out before he saw what she had clutched to her chest. Her camera. He'd been wrong back at her car. She'd managed to grab at least one thing before she left the car.

She nodded at him, lifting the camera, her lips turning up in a grin. "I got a photo of the black pickup."

He stopped short of her, just short of gathering her in his arms and crushing her to him. *"You what?"*

"I got a photo of the truck that was following me. I had to cut down the mountain through the brush to get the shot, but I did it," she said triumphantly.

He fought the urge to turn her over his knee and spank her. "Have you completely lost your mind?" he demanded.

She brushed a lock of wet hair from her eyes. "What did you expect me to do?"

"With you, Charity, I never know what to expect." He shook his head. She could have been killed. Coming down that mountainside on foot was dangerous enough, but actually getting a photo of the pickup she thought had been following her?

"When you yelled for me, you scared him off," she said. "And just in time." She shivered and looked away. "Thanks."

He took several deep breaths and counted to ten, still so angry he wanted to throttle her. She was all right. Safe. Wasn't that what mattered?

The only sound for long moments was the sound of the rain.

"You could have been killed," he said finally, still angry with her, still scared. "This was a stupid stunt."

"I got the photo." She stepped past him, head high, her wet leaf-strewn hair flipped to one side and her eyes bright with more than defiance. She was scared, too. She'd actually scared herself. Too bad she never learned from these kinds of experiences.

He watched her start up the road and swore under his breath, wishing she didn't do foolish things like this, wishing things were different between them, wishing she wasn't the only one who held out hope for the two of them, wishing he didn't want this woman so damned badly.

What was it his mother used to say? If wishes were horses, everyone would ride.

"Look," he said, going after her. Why did she always have to be so... Charity? But even as he thought it, he couldn't imagine her any other way. The thought surprised him, given how he felt about marriage and the mere mention of mixing their genes.

"Charity, I'm sorry I didn't—"

"—believe me?" she snapped.

"When I was looking for Nina's car, I was also keeping an eye out for your black pickup. If you'd just given me a chance—"

"You still don't believe the truck was following me, do you," she said, stopping in her tracks. "He left me another present. A rose. It was stuck to the passenger seat of my car when I left Betty's."

"I know. I saw it." Someone had put it in her car parked in front of the newspaper office while they were having a late lunch. The person had been that bold, and it scared the hell out of him. He wanted to be there the next time and catch the guy.

"You don't think it's the man in the black truck, do you." She shook her head as if disgusted with him. "Well, as soon as I develop this roll, you'll see."

He hoped so. "You have a photo of the driver?" He saw the flicker of uncertainty.

"You'll just see," she said, and continued up the road.

He pulled off his hat, raked his fingers through his damp hair, the rain feeling good on his face. "Get in. I'll give you a ride," he called after her.

She glared at him over her shoulder. It would be just like her to walk all the way back up the road in the rain to her car just to show him she didn't need him.

"Charity, come on. Let me give you a ride."

To his surprise, she stopped and came back to climb into the passenger side of the patrol car, although with obvious reluctance.

He got behind the wheel, found a wide spot to turn around and drove back up the road to her car, all the while trying to think of something to say. He was still angry with her. And she with him. Silence seemed safest.

The moment he slowed, she threw open the door and was out, headed for her car.

"Let me know when you get the photos developed," he said to her retreating back.

She didn't answer.

He waited until she turned the VW around, then followed her back down the road to the newspaper office. The blinds were up, the lights on inside the small building, and he could see her assistant, high-school student Blaine Bridges, inside working.

Charity parked out front and stomped into the newspaper office with her camera bag. She didn't give Mitch so much as a sideways glance.

He waited until she was safely inside before he drove down to his office. While he wasn't about to tell Charity, a photo of the pickup wasn't going to prove that the driver had been following her—or leaving her any presents. Neither would a shot of the driver. Even if the driver had left her the heart-shaped stone and the rose, there was no law against it.

The photograph she'd just risked her damned life for was worth nothing. All it would prove was that there was a black pickup in town with tinted windows and someone driving it.

But it *might* give Mitch a face, a license number, maybe, and possibly a name. And maybe a reason—if the truck really had been following her.

He left the patrol car and started through the rain toward Town Hall, where the Sheriff's Department shared the right half of the building.

A thought struck him. What had made Charity so

sure the pickup was following her in the first place? Did she have some reason she hadn't told him about? Was she involved in something he was unaware of? What was the chance of that? Ha. About the same as the chance of rain.

What worried him was the possibility that it had something to do with Nina's disappearance and the questions Charity had been asking about her. But then, there was that damned baby spoon he'd found in Nina's bungalow. If Nina had been planning to blow the whistle on someone in town, then using Charity and the newspaper would be the best way to do it.

"Well?" Sissy demanded as Mitch walked into the Sheriff's Department office shaking off raindrops. She had that What's-Charity-done-now? look on her face.

"Do you know anyone who drives a black pickup with tinted windows?" he asked.

Sissy narrowed her eyes. "Not anyone in Timber Falls."

He nodded and walked into his office.

"Wade Dennison called. Wants an update," Sissy hollered after him. "Said you were to call the moment you walked in the—"

The last word was cut off as Mitch closed his office door. Damn Charity. He didn't want to admit just how much she'd scared him. He hung up his coat and sat down, still shaken.

He scrubbed his hands over his face, elbows on his desk. Maybe he *didn't* take Charity seriously enough. Except for her determination to get him to the altar. He took that damned seriously.

His intercom buzzed and he groaned. Surely Charity hadn't had enough time to develop the film already. "Yes?"

"Wade Dennison on line one. I told him you were heading for your desk as he called. You *owe* me."

There were too many women in his life, Mitch thought as he picked up line one. "Hello, Wade."

"What have you found out?"

Just enough to give myself a headache. "I've been looking for Nina, asking everyone who knew her where she might be, searching for her car. So far—" he hated to admit this "—I haven't turned up much."

"She didn't just vanish!" Wade snapped, then let out an irritated sigh.

"These kinds of investigations take time," Mitch said.

"Every hour that goes by is time lost."

"I know that, but in big cities, law enforcement doesn't even start a search until the person has been missing for at least forty-eight hours."

"This is not a big city," Wade said.

"No, it isn't, and that's why I've been looking for her and will continue looking for her. Wade, my other line's going. I gotta answer. I'll get back to you."

Mitch disconnected, shaking his head. Wade had sounded even more upset than he had earlier. What the hell had Wade's relationship been with the woman who called herself Nina Monroe?

Tracy Shank at Dennison Ducks thought Nina had something on Wade. Blackmail?

But people being blackmailed rarely got upset when the blackmailer suddenly disappeared.

Was it possible Wade and Nina had been romantically involved and that was why he was so upset?

That just didn't feel right to Mitch, either.

Maybe Wade had found out about the woman's lies.

But then Wade wouldn't have come to Mitch pretending he didn't know anything about her, would he?

And there was that damned spoon, Mitch thought, remembering it in his jacket pocket.

If Nina Monroe was Angela Dennison, then that would certainly explain a lot of things—like Wade's odd behavior. But Mitch couldn't see Wade keeping something like that a secret. Quite the opposite. Unless there was some reason Wade wouldn't want anyone to know that Angela had been found.

Mitch's head was killing him. He reached into his drawer, took out the bottle of aspirin, spilled two into his hand and downed them with the cold coffee in his mug on the desk. He shuddered at the bitter taste.

His door opened. "I'm leaving," Sissy announced as if she thought he might argue with her. "It's after five."

He glanced at the clock, surprised how quickly the day had gone. He'd hoped to find Nina before the day was out. He still had until midnight, but it would be dark soon, which would only make searching for her car more difficult.

"Have a nice evening," he said to Sissy.

She stayed in the doorway. "Are you all right?"

"Why?"

"You don't even have anything smart to say to me before I leave?" Sissy sounded disappointed.

"I used it all up on Charity."

Sissy laughed. "Good night, boss."

CHARITY COULDN'T WAIT to see what she'd gotten on film. She'd headed straight for the darkroom with her camera bag.

"Want anything from Betty's?" Blaine had asked. "I was just going to get some dinner."

"No thanks. I had a late lunch." Not even food could distract her right now. Once she had the roll of film developed...well, that was another story. "Take your time. I won't need you for a while." Right now she just had to see what she'd shot, and she didn't want any distractions.

"I'll return all those books to the shelves when I come back." A huge stack of books was sitting on the floor near the door to the storage room. Blaine had insisted on putting the books in alphabetical order by author. The boy just couldn't help himself.

As Blaine left, he locked the door behind him, and Charity stepped into the darkroom, shed her ripped-up raincoat and pulled her camera from the bag.

She was chilled to the bone, clothes drenched, teeth chattering. Her fingers shook as she tried to remove the film—and finally gave up. She kept an old sweatshirt and a pair of jeans at the office for "grunge" work. She stripped and changed into the dry clothing, including her favorite old red sneakers, then removed the film and began the developing process.

Most newspapers had gone to digital cameras, but she liked the old-fashioned darkroom process. There was something much more satisfying about it. But right now she would have loved to just zap the photos into a computer and see what she had.

The strip of negatives came out of the processor and she hung it up to dry. There looked to be a great shot of the front of the pickup and quite possibly the driver, although he was in shadow.

The same went for the dark furry animal that had

run in front of the truck. It was only a blur off to one side, but it appeared to be nothing more than a bear. No Bigfoot.

However, there was good light on the front of the pickup. In fact, she could make out the last four figures of the license plate—4 AKS. She couldn't wait to take a closer look when the negatives finally dried and she could blow up the shot.

From what she'd seen quickly scanning the strip of negatives, she had all the shots she needed for this week's paper. Shots of Frank, the Granny's bread deliveryman, standing by the road where he'd reportedly seen Bigfoot looked as if it would work for page one.

She was thinking about how she'd lay out the page when she heard a thump outside the darkroom door. She turned, frowning.

"Did you forget something?" she called out, knowing it had to be Blaine. The doors were locked and he was the only one with a key.

No answer. He must have already left again.

It had almost sounded as if he'd collided with one of the desks, she thought. What was he doing?

Another soft thump, this one closer to the darkroom. She froze as the knob on the darkroom door began to turn. The light was still on outside and Blaine knew better than to open the door while she was developing film.

The door opened. But even before she glimpsed the face distorted by a nylon stocking, she knew it wasn't Blaine.

MITCH GLANCED AT the clock, surprised by how much time had passed. Even more surprised Charity hadn't called. She would have had the film developed by now. Maybe she hadn't gotten a clear shot of the pickup, after all. He couldn't imagine any other reason she wouldn't have contacted him otherwise.

He got up from his desk, stretched and realized he was hungry. That meant Charity must be starving. Maybe he could make amends by taking her to Betty's. The special tonight was stuffed pork chops, mashed potatoes with gravy, applesauce and double chocolate cake.

He got his coat and headed out the door, locking it behind him. The rain had let up. Temporarily. Fog hovered over the town like a bad omen.

As he walked down the block, he was unable to shake his uneasiness. Charity worked too many late nights at the newspaper. It was the nature of the business, but still, he didn't like her being there alone so often. Why couldn't that woman have gotten a normal job?

But as hard as he tried, he couldn't imagine Charity doing anything else. As a reporter she got to butt into people's business—and get paid for it. Journalism was obviously her true calling.

The blinds were drawn and the newspaper office was dark except for two faint lights he could make out through a crack in the blinds at the back of the building. A small glow to the left and the red light outside the darkroom across from it.

He couldn't see either Charity or Blaine. Was Charity still in the darkroom developing the film? Or had she gone to Betty's for dinner? The thought surprised—and worried—him. Charity had been so excited about what she was sure would be on the film. She wouldn't have left. That meant she had to be blowing up the photos in the darkroom now. Playing detective. Now that sounded like Charity.

He tried the front door. Locked. He knocked, waited, knocked harder. No answer. The newspaper was housed in a small narrow one-story brick building on a corner. Next door was a T-shirt shop that was closed. Behind it was an empty lot, overgrown with encroaching vegetation, a dirt alley separating the two.

As he walked around to the rear of the building, he was surprised how dark it was back there. Charity needed some sort of security light. He'd mention that to her, for all the good it would do.

As he neared the back, he saw that the door was ajar, a sliver of light spilling out onto the ground.

Maybe Charity had left the door open for some reason. He stepped closer and saw the telltale marks. The lock had been jimmied.

Heart in his throat, he drew his weapon and pushed open the door with his foot as he slipped through. The single light glowing off to the right was coming from the bathroom. It was empty, just like the office appeared to be. He moved to the darkroom door. The door opened at the turn of the knob and he caught a glimpse of something red on the floor just inside the door.

His blood thrummed in his ears. The darkroom was empty. Except for one of Charity's red sneakers, the white laces still tied, lying on its side on the floor.

CHAPTER EIGHT

CHARITY. MITCH'S STOMACH cramped with fear as he took in her wet clothing hanging over a rod in the corner of the darkroom, and below them, the shoes she'd been wearing when she'd chased the black pickup.

There were empty film canisters scattered on the darkroom floor, and the contents of the camera bag was strewn over the counter. But no negative strips had been hung to dry. No photos pinned overhead.

He turned and moved through the small office: the layout area, photo light table, three desks, a copy machine in the corner.

In only a few seconds, he took it all in. The in-mail box turned upside down on the first desk. All the mail spread across the desktop, some on the floor, as if someone had gone through it. All three desktops a mess. The drawers open, contents obviously searched.

Like Nina's apartment. The burglar had been looking for something in particular.

But where was Charity? She would have been in the darkroom working. She wouldn't have heard anyone at the back door. Or heard anyone come in...until it was too late.

Mitch felt sick. Was it possible the burglar had taken Charity with him? A terrifying thought.

He froze, listening. He thought he heard something.

There it was again. A muffled moan. It seemed to be coming from behind a bank of reference books stacked in the corner. It looked as if someone had been cleaning off the bookcase against the wall and been interrupted.

On the other side of the stack of books, Mitch spotted a door. This had to lead to a storage area of some kind.

Silently he moved toward it, aware that the intruders could be inside there with a knife to Charity's throat.

At the door, he stopped, listened. Another soft moan. The burglar could have his hand over Charity's mouth. Mitch tried to imagine that scenario and couldn't. Charity wouldn't have stood still for that. Especially if she thought someone was outside the door looking for her.

Mitch reached for the doorknob and turned it as quietly as possible. Locked. Another muffled moan.

He looked around for something to break the lock. A large petrified-wood paperweight sat on a nearby desk. He took it in one hand, his weapon in the other, and prayed as he brought the paperweight down hard on the doorknob. The metal knob thumped to the floor.

He jerked the door open, weapon ready.

It was pitch-black inside what was indeed a small storage closet. He could make out boxes of paper stacked high in the tight quarters. No room for a man to be holding a woman.

Fumbling, he found the light switch, flipped it and blinked as a bright bulb came on overhead.

For a moment, he didn't see her. Bound with wrapping tape, Charity was wedged in the corner between the stacks of paper boxes.

She blinked, blinded for an instant by the light. He

saw relief swell in her brown eyes, but it was nothing compared to his. She made another muffled sound as she tried to speak through the tape over her lips.

He reached in and grabbed an end of the tape, jerking it off quickly to lessen the pain.

She let out a cry, but it sounded more like frustration and fear than real pain.

"Are you all right?" he asked as he moved a few of the boxes to get her out of her prison. Then he lifted her out and set her down gently on her feet. Her hands were bound with tape behind her, her ankles also wrapped tightly. She was fully clothed except for the one sneaker and didn't seem to be bleeding or injured as far as he could tell.

With his pocketknife he cut the tape, freeing her ankles and wrists. She wriggled as if to get the blood flowing again to her extremities, but he could see that she was trembling.

"Charity?" he asked, worried about her since she hadn't said a word yet and she'd seemed so anxious to have the tape off her mouth. He'd expected her to be talking a mile a minute. It scared him when she didn't.

He lifted her chin with his finger to look into her eyes and saw the unshed tears glittering there. She was shaking, her teeth chattering. He'd never seen her this frightened. Not even earlier when she'd scared herself falling down a mountainside in pursuit of a black pickup.

He drew her into his arms and held her tightly. "It's okay," he whispered against her hair. "You're fine." She smelled like paper stock.

She nodded against his chest and took several big gulps of air before pulling back to look at him. She seemed as if she was about to say something. Her lips puckered and several tears spilled soundlessly down one cheek.

Kissing her right then seemed as natural as breathing. He cupped her face in his palms. Her pulse jumped under his fingertips. He dropped his mouth to hers, wanting to kiss away all her hurt and fear. Wanting desperately to assure himself she really was all right.

Her mouth was pure nectar. Her lips parted, opening to him like a flower to a bee. He pulled her closer and deepened the kiss, his blood thundering in his ears.

At first she felt small and fragile in his arms. But soon his body became acutely aware of her wonderfully lush curves. Charity was all woman, rounded in all the right places. He felt that familiar and yet always shocking chemistry fire through him, warming him to his toes.

Her arms came up to loop around his neck. She pulled him more deeply into the kiss. Yes, she was just fine.

Her kiss was a potent elixir, as addictive as any drug, and he couldn't get enough of her. Oh, how he'd missed kissing her, holding her. He could never get enough of her. Never.

He felt dizzy and off balance and then, suddenly, he was falling. Dropping like dead weight off a bottomless cliff. Completely out of control.

He jerked back, disengaging his lips from hers. It always ended like this. With that horrible sensation of falling helplessly whenever he got too close to her. Even in his dreams at night about her. He would bolt upright in bed, heart pounding, and realize he'd just had a close call.

He felt that way right now as he cleared his throat and unhooked her arms from around her neck to hold her at arm's length.

Disappointment flickered across her features, then amusement, as if she thought him a fool for fighting the chemistry between them, because he could never win. It scared the hell out of him that she might be right.

He breathed deeply, trying to restore his equilibrium. "Sorry about that. I just wanted to see if you were all right."

"Uh-huh." Charity licked her lips, the kiss still lingering there, and grinned. He didn't really expect her to believe that, did he? "So am I all right?"

"Fine." He stepped back. Did he really think putting distance between them was going to help?

She'd seen how frightened he'd been and how relieved to find her. And that kiss…that kiss was no mistake. It was one honest-to-goodness kiss. She was trembling, but it had nothing to do with the intruder now.

But she could see from Mitch's expression that he was afraid the kiss would give her the wrong idea. He didn't want her to think that he might want her as badly as she did him. Or that he was finally coming around or that it was just a matter of time before she got him to the altar.

"It was just a kiss," she said. Uh-huh.

"Right." But he gave her a funny look as if to say the kiss had been a hell of a lot more than that.

Her head began to clear as she glanced toward the darkroom. "The bastard took the negatives, didn't he." She stormed past Mitch. She heard him swear under his breath, then follow her.

"You saw him?" Mitch asked.

She shook her head. "He was wearing a nylon stocking over his head. But I did get in one good kick." She glanced over her shoulder at Mitch. "From the sound he made, he was definitely male."

Mitch winced. Who said he didn't have a good imagination? "Did you see what was on the negatives before he took them?"

Again she had to shake her head. "But it *was* on there. The truck and maybe the driver."

"I should have believed you about the truck. I should also have come back here with you to develop the film."

"You can't protect me 24/7. Anyway, I never expected the guy to break in. I'm glad Blaine wasn't here." Who knows what that fool kid would have done. Or her burglar.

"Where *is* Blaine?"

She glanced at her watch. "He should have been back by now. Oh, Mitch, you don't think—"

"Where did he go?"

"To Betty's to get some food."

"Stay here," Mitch ordered. "Lock the door behind me and put a chair against the back door." He had his no-arguments face on. "I'll be right back."

She nodded, worried about Blaine.

Mitch was good as his word. "Blaine's fine," he said when she opened the door and let him in again a few minutes later. "Someone jumped him just this side of Betty's. He was bound up with tape in the alley. I sent him home to his mother."

"You're sure he's all right?"

"He's fine. His ego's a little battered, but he wasn't hurt. He was worried about you." Mitch held up his hand. "I told him you were fine. I didn't get into what happened."

She sighed with relief. Blaine was a sweet kid. She didn't want him worrying. Nor did she want this all over town—everyone knew what a gossip his mother, Sarah, was. "I did see something on the negatives. Part of the truck's license plate number 4AKS. Sorry, that's all I got."

"Coupled with a description of the pickup, that might be enough to narrow it down," Mitch said, sounding excited. "You think it was the man driving the black pickup who broke in?"

"Who else?" She hadn't even been sure the driver of the black pickup had realized she'd taken his photo. He'd been busy trying to keep from hitting the furry beast that had crossed the road in front of his truck— probably a large bear. And she'd been well behind the animal when she'd taken the shots.

The driver must have seen her, though. He'd stopped his truck and looked down over the edge of the road— until he heard Mitch calling for her. Then he'd taken off fast. Which he wouldn't have done if he'd been looking down the mountainside for the bear. Or Bigfoot. Right?

So the burglar had to be the driver of the black truck. He'd seen her taking pictures and he'd come after the film. He must really not want her to know who he was.

"You're sure the back door was locked?" Mitch asked.

She nodded.

"It doesn't look like a professional job."

That was supposed to make her feel better? She'd had the truck, possibly even the driver's face on film. She might have been able to make an identification once she'd blown up the shot and maybe, just maybe, a blurred shot of Bigfoot. Or a large bear. Now she would never know. Now that she wasn't afraid, she was mad.

"What else was on that roll?"

"Just all the photographs I'd taken for this week's edition." She had to fight back tears of anger and frustration. She'd have to reshoot all of her lead photos. That meant the paper would be late this week. Some journalist she was.

"I'm sorry," Mitch said behind her.

She turned to face him. He *looked* sorry. He also looked worried. And it was obvious he didn't know what to say. Men. Right now would have been a great time to kiss her again and tell her he loved her. Even telling her he liked her a little would help.

"I can try to get fingerprints—"

"He wore gloves."

Mitch nodded and shifted his feet. Any hope of him declaring his love was quickly slipping away, along with any chance that he would kiss her again. He looked like a man who was dying to get away. Nothing new there.

"How long will it take you to figure out what was stolen?" he asked.

She shook her head as she looked at the mess the burglar had made on the desks. "My latest strip of negatives for starters." She suspected that's what he was after. So why ransack the office? Had he been looking for something else? Or had he just wanted her to think he had?

Mitch was staring at her, that lawman look on his handsome face.

She felt a prickle of worry.

"I don't want you going to your house alone tonight," he said.

Music to her ears. She smiled. "So what did you have in mind?"

He pulled out his cell phone and she watched him start to tap in a number.

"What are you doing?" she asked, afraid she already knew.

"I'm calling your aunt Florie."

"You wouldn't!" She grabbed for the cell phone, but he was too quick for her as he pulled it back out of her reach.

"Charity, I'd feel a whole lot better if you were at your aunt's tonight."

"Maybe *you'd* feel better…"

"Come on, one night. How bad can it be?"

Charity groaned, just imagining. "You live right next door to me. How much safer could I be?"

He was shaking his head, still dialing. "Or I can call your mother."

The ultimate threat. "Just shoot me now." Her mother would go ballistic, then load up the van with her commune family and drive into town with a plan to take her back to the farm. No way.

"Or I can lock you up in jail for your own protection. Sissy always comes in early. Her face will be the first thing you see in the morning and her voice the first thing you hear."

"You wouldn't." The only face Charity wanted to see first thing in the morning was Mitch's. But that offer didn't appear to be forthcoming.

She started to argue that she would be perfectly safe at home, the thief had gotten what he wanted, so why come after her again? But perusing the office, she wasn't sure that was true. Could the burglar be the same person who'd attacked her outside the post office, followed her and left her presents?

Also, she could see the determined set of Mitch's stubbled jaw and the pure steel in those wonderful blue eyes of his. He'd make good on *one* of his threats. She was trying to figure out which was the least of the three evils when she had one of her inspired ideas.

"What about my cat?" she demanded. "I have to be home to feed him."

"You have a cat?" Mitch asked, surprised.

Didn't every old maid? After all, at twenty-six, she was on the downhill slide to thirty.

Mitch was frowning. "Why can't I see you with a cat? What's his name?"

His name? "Winky."

"Winky?"

"Winky hates being left alone at night, and you'll be right next door if I need you," she said. "I can just yell." She picked up her purse from the floor, shoving everything back inside it. As far as she could tell, nothing was missing. Not even her twelve dollars in cash.

His frown deepened. He hit the last several numbers he'd been dialing. "Florie," he said, his gaze meeting Charity's glare. "Charity needs you to come stay with her tonight."

Charity crossed her fingers that Florie would be too busy telling Crystal from Evansville, Indiana, or Roberta from Spokane, Washington, about the position of her stars.

"Great!" Mitch said enthusiastically.

Damn. Her luck really stunk.

"Tell her not to bring the tarot cards," Charity said. But it was too late. Mitch had already hung up.

"She's meeting us at your house in five minutes."

Charity gave him her I'll-get-even-with-you-even-if-it-kills-me smile.

"Add it to that long list of things you'll never forgive me for," he suggested, as if she wouldn't. "I'll follow you home."

"You don't trust me to go by myself?"

"Not for an instant," he said, and motioned to the door. "I'll turn out the lights and lock up behind you. I suggest you get dead bolts installed tomorrow and a security light out back."

The man was impossible. And his lack of trust appalled her. But she did like his company and she *was* still shaken up. Not that she would admit it to Mitch. She couldn't stand the thought of him thinking she was one of those helpless females.

Aunt Florie came rushing into the house on a gust of wind only minutes later, her wizard-print caftan billowing around her small frame, her arms full.

"This really isn't necessary," Charity said, spotting what looked like one of her aunt's casseroles. Oh, no, this was going to be worse than she'd thought.

"It's no trouble at all," her aunt said. "I go where I'm needed." Florie charged into the kitchen and put her armload on the table, then threw her arms around Charity. "Tell me everything."

Mitch filled Florie in as Charity groaned inwardly, knowing her aunt was almost as bad as Sarah Bridges about spreading gossip.

"Oh, you must have been frightened out of your

skin!" Florie cried, and hugged her again. "But not to worry. I'm here now. You'll be safe with me."

Mitch looked skeptical, but then, he did live next door.

"Where's your cat?" he asked looking around.

"He must be hiding," Charity said.

"You have a cat?" Florie asked.

"Winky?" Mitch called. "I don't see a litter box."

"He's trained to go in the toilet," Charity said.

"Really?"

"Why can't I see you with a cat?" Florie was saying.

Mitch carried Florie's huge suitcase upstairs to the guest bedroom. Charity caught him looking around for the cat. But Mitch was gone like a shot the moment Florie offered him some of the tofu-zucchini-eggplant casserole she'd taken out of the freezer for dinner.

"This person who broke in," Florie said as she put the casserole in Charity's microwave when they were alone. "I don't like the vibrations I'm picking up. We'll have to consult the tarot."

Oh, damn, she *had* brought the tarot cards!

When Charity was younger, she'd gotten a kick out of Florie's predictions. Even Charity's best friend, Roz, loved to have her cards read. The two would stay up half the night laughing and talking about their futures.

Now, with thirty drawing ever closer, Charity would have preferred an aunt who didn't really "know" things.

At one time, Charity had believed her aunt really did know—right up until the point where the cards started suggesting Charity might not end up with Mitch.

"You know what I think? I'll bet your stars are out of whack," Florie said now, studying her through squinted eyes. "We must do your chart soon. I sense that trouble is brewing on your horizon."

Trouble was often brewing on her horizon.

Charity opted to take a hot shower while her aunt unpacked and the casserole nuked. The two-story house was small, with a nice-size living room decorated with furniture Charity had reupholstered herself.

She'd also done all the painting and put up the wallpaper in the kitchen and the tiny dining room. There was a half bath downstairs with a laundry room. She'd made a small room off the living room into a home office. Upstairs were two bedrooms and a bath.

Charity had bought the house because it was affordable, just the right size, on a quiet dead-end street at the edge of town and next door to Mitch's house. Theirs were the only two houses on that side of the block, with the town starting one street over.

"See, your aura is already improving," Florie said when Charity emerged a while later. Florie had her huge suitcase open. A flannel nightgown, a wooden baseball bat, candles and other paraphernalia, including a well-worn deck of tarot cards, covered the bed.

Florie hefted the baseball bat and smiled. "You're safe now, sweetie." What Florie lacked in stature, she more than made up for in attitude.

Mitch had always said that it was that indomitable attitude, along with a screwball wackiness, that was Charity's legacy. As if it was hereditary.

"Ready for dinner? You look like you could use a good meal."

Charity groaned. She *could* use a good meal and wished she'd conned Mitch into dinner at Betty's. She'd kill for a cheeseburger, loaded, a side of fries and a piece of pie.

"Don't look so worried," Florie said as she started down the stairs. "The cards will know what's going on in your life."

Which was why Charity hated the cards and this whole prediction thing. She couldn't stand the thought that her future was already written somewhere—especially if it didn't read the way she wanted it to.

"Where do you keep your cat food?" Florie called up from the kitchen. "I'll feed your cat."

"I don't have a cat," she called back.

"But I thought Mitch said—"

"What does Mitch know?" Charity pulled on jeans and a sweater for dinner, muttering under her breath, "I'm perfectly safe. Or at least I would have been without my aunt. If I get up to go to the bathroom tonight, she'll probably slug me with that damned bat."

She tried to convince herself that the thief had gotten what he'd broken in for at the newspaper. The negatives. But it still nagged at her that he'd taken the time to ransack her office. What had he been looking for? Something valuable to pawn?

No, she thought with certainty. He'd been looking for something in her mail—just as he had at the post office earlier when he'd knocked her down.

CHAPTER NINE

MITCH TYPED THE partial license plate and description of the black pickup into the computer and crossed his fingers.

The match came up in a matter of minutes. A pickup with a license plate ending with 4AKS and matching Charity's description of the truck belonged to a Kyle L. Rogers Investigations of Portland.

Mitch checked the listing for Kyle L. Rogers Investigations in Portland and dialed the number. An answering machine picked up the call and informed him that Mr. Rogers was out of the office until next week. Mitch didn't leave a message. A private investigator?

He closed up the office and drove to Charity's.

She rushed to open the door in a pair of yellow-and-black penguin-print flannel pajamas. Her skin looked freshly scrubbed, a little flushed. Her hair was pulled up in a ponytail, the short curly hair at the nape of her neck still damp. And she smelled heavenly.

She threw herself into his arms excitedly.

It happened so fast he couldn't even be sure he initiated the kiss. Fortunately he disengaged himself from her lips as quickly as possible.

Her eyes were round as pie plates and she was smiling at him, that darned smile that said she'd get him to the altar yet.

"Don't just open the door to anyone who knocks," he chastised her, irritated with himself for kissing her.

She made a face. "Florie told me you were at the door."

"What did she do? Look in her crystal ball?" He knew why he was so annoyed. He was scared. Scared she was in danger. Scared she was getting to him.

"I saw your patrol car pull up," Florie said from upstairs.

He groaned inwardly.

"I have something important to tell you."

Charity looked as if she might pop. "You found the letter from Nina. I was right. The guy in the black pickup. That's why he knocked me down at the post office. That's why he broke into the newspaper and ransacked my office."

Mitch shook his head. "I did check your mailbox but there was no letter from Nina."

She looked disappointed but only for a moment. "But you have news. You found out who owns the pickup."

His expression must have given him away. *Was* Florie clairvoyant and *was* the "gift" in the Jenkins genes? It was a frightening thought.

"Yes, I do have a match on the pickup that was following you."

She looked as pleased as if he'd just slain a dragon for her.

"It's registered to Kyle L. Rogers Investigations out of Portland. Know him?"

She shook her head. "Should I?"

"Know any reason someone would put a private investigator on you?"

"No. You think someone up here hired him?"

Mitch thought about Charity's theory that Nina had not only written something down—she'd mailed it to Charity. Is that what Rogers was looking for? Then were was the letter?

He didn't know what to think. "Maybe. Maybe he's up here looking for Bigfoot."

He hoped knowing that the driver of the pickup was a private investigator would relieve her mind some. It had his. He didn't think this Rogers guy had come up here to harm Charity. Nor did he believe the P.I. was leaving her the presents. But he'd still be keeping a close eye on Charity tonight.

He moved toward the door. "If you see the truck again or need me…"

She nodded and smiled as she followed him to the door. "Glad you stopped by."

"Sure you don't want some vegetarian casserole?" Florie asked as she came downstairs.

"No thanks." He grimaced where only Charity could see.

"I will get you for this," she whispered, and then he was gone out the door as fast as he could go. As he drove away, he saw Florie signal from the doorway that all was well with a baseball bat. Great.

As he drove down Main Street past the *Timber Falls Courier* office, he tried to concentrate, but he kept thinking about yellow-and-black penguin pajamas. And worrying that Charity wouldn't be safe, maybe especially with her aunt and that baseball bat.

He touched his tongue to his upper lip. He could still taste her, the feel of her mouth branded on his lips. What kind of fool was he to have kissed her? Not once, but twice today? It was the rainy season. It made people crazy.

He vowed once again to keep her at arm's length. Distance was the only thing that would save him. And even as he thought it, he wondered how the hell he'd ever be able to keep away from Charity—even if she'd let him.

As he passed the Duck-In bar, he spotted Sheryl Bend's little blue car parked on the side. Earlier at the decoy plant he'd gotten the impression she'd wanted to talk, but feared retaliation from Wade.

He swung the patrol car into the lot, still hoping he'd find Nina Monroe before midnight.

As he pushed open the door, he wasn't surprised to see Sheryl sitting on her usual stool alone, staring down into her glass of beer. A country song played on the jukebox as he moved through the smoky din.

"Hey," Hank Bridges said as he slid a napkin in front of him. "What'll ya have, Sheriff?"

Sheryl swung her gaze from her beer to Mitch. She smiled, her eyes shiny with alcohol and invitation.

"A soda," Mitch told Frank, and pulled up a stool beside Sheryl.

"Haven't seen you in here in ages," she said, and took a sip of her beer, licking the foam from her lips.

He glanced around the bar, noting the regulars and a few faces he didn't recognize at several of the booths.

Out-of-towners were rare this time of year. Except when there'd been a Bigfoot sighting.

He turned back to the bar and Sheryl, glad he didn't see his father among the clientele. In the mirror behind the bar he caught the reflection of two people on the dance floor, both married, but not to each other.

That was another thing about the rainy season. It often led to affairs—and consequently divorces come spring. Former sheriff Hudson used to joke that Timber Falls held a roundup each spring to swap back wives and divide up the children.

"I wanted to talk to you," Mitch said to Sheryl after Hank slid an icy glass of cola in front of him and left. Mitch took a sip. He steered clear of alcohol. His father had drunk enough for both of them in his lifetime.

"Let me guess. You wanna talk about Nina," Sheryl said, sounding disappointed. "How come you never ask me out? How come you never take me up on dinner at my place?"

He smiled as he shook his head. He often wondered the same thing. But it seemed they both knew the answer.

"It's that damned Charity Jenkins, isn't it," she said.

He couldn't deny it. But he hadn't come here to talk about his love life. His nonexistent love life. "I got the feeling this morning talking to you that there was something you wanted to tell me about Nina but were maybe afraid to say anything with Wade up there... watching."

Sheryl sipped her beer, her eyes narrowing as she looked in the mirror over the back bar. "Nina was a back-stabbing bitch."

Mitch raised a brow. "Is that the beer talking?"

She swung her gaze to him. "That's the truth talking. The woman didn't care who she walked on to get what she wanted."

He took a wild guess. "She walked on you."

"She befriended me—just long enough to steal some of my duck designs, which she passed off as her own."

Mitch knew a little about painters at the plant getting royalties for new designs. "What did you do about it?"

"I went to Wade." She drained her glass and set it down a little too hard on the bar. Hank came over at once and twisted off the cap on another bottle of beer for her, sliding her a new frosted glass onto a fresh cocktail napkin before disappearing again down the bar.

"That son of a bitch Wade got mad at *me*. Said I was trying to take credit for Nina's work and warned me if there was any more trouble I'd be put on notice." She narrowed her eyes at Mitch. "Do you believe that? I've been there ten years. Ten friggin' years. And that... bitch was there, what? A month?"

"How'd she get so close to Wade so quickly?" Mitch asked. Even if they had been romantically involved, it seemed damned sudden. Not to mention the age difference between the two.

Sheryl was shaking her head. "It was like maybe he'd known her before. I mean, he hired her just like that." She snapped her fingers. "Treated her like—" she waved a hand "—like he had to walk on eggshells around her. She had him by the you-know-whats." Sheryl sounded close to tears.

"Did Nina tell you anything about her past during the time you were friendly with each other?"

Sheryl shrugged and took a drink of her beer. "It wasn't for long, but she did mention an aunt once. Auntie Em. I swear to God that's what she called her. Like in *The Wizard of Oz*. She said she never knew her parents and couldn't stand her aunt."

"Sounds like she might have had a tough life," he

said. The story could fit, if Nina Monroe was Angela Dennison—or wanted people to think she was.

"Probably every word of it was a lie." Sheryl took another long swallow of beer, licked the foam off her lips and stared down at the amber liquid miserably. "She still missing?"

"Yep."

"I hope to hell she stays that way."

Mitch had himself another suspect if Nina really had met with foul play, he thought as finished his soda. Now he hoped to leave before his father or Dennison Ducks production manager Bud Farnsworth showed up.

Unfortunately he was too late. Bud pushed through the door and they exchanged a look. Bud strode on past to the other end of the bar. That man was guilty of something, Mitch thought as he left.

In the patrol car again, Mitch cruised slowly by Charity's. All the lights were on, and through the thin curtains, he could see two figures sitting at the kitchen table. Just the thought of Charity eating tofu-zucchini-eggplant casserole brightened his mood.

He drove around town, making a loop by Florie's. Still no red compact parked in front of the Aries bungalow. He'd held out some hope that Nina had just bagged work and driven to Eugene for a day of shopping. If that was the case, then she had yet to return home. But it didn't explain the ransacked bungalow. Or Wade's anxiety.

The Ho Hum's No Vacancy light blinked bright red above the cars parked in front of the seven motel units. No black pickup. No compact. He wondered where Rogers might be staying. Probably down in Oakridge, twenty miles south.

At the *Courier* office, he checked the locks and windows. No one seemed to have come back. The town was quiet except for an occasional note or two drifting down from the jukebox at the Duck-In. Sheryl's car was still parked out front. So was Bud's pickup. Betty's Café was closed. Only the neon still glowed at the gas station.

Restless, Mitch drove out of town, not even realizing where he was going until he'd pulled the patrol car over to the side of the road and turned off his headlights.

The old place sat back from the road, the roof etched black against the trees. A light glowed inside, but he saw no movement. His father had probably taken off on foot through the woods to the Duck-In for his nightly drinking binge.

Just the sight of the house where Mitch had grown up made him aware of the painful void within him. He closed his eyes, trying to remember his mother's face, her voice, her touch, the part of his life he thought of as good, above reproach. Anything that would fill that awful hollow part of him.

But there was nothing of her left in him. It was spoiled by his bitterness toward his father.

Mitch opened his eyes and started to pull way. He shouldn't have come out here. Normally he avoided it at all costs.

But as his hand touched the gearshift, he saw him. A large dark silhouette against the light inside the house. His father stood at the edge of the covered porch, his huge hands gripping the rail, his head turned in Mitch's direction as if waiting.

Mitch shifted into first, snapped on the headlights, and got the patrol car moving. When he glanced back as he drove past, he saw that his father was still standing there, watching him run away just as he had watched Mitch's mother run away. Calling neither of them back.

AT FIRST IT was just part of the dream. The creak of a floorboard, the soft rustle of fabric, movement, then a deadly cold silence. It was the silence that dragged her up from dreamy sleep to wake to the terrifying knowledge that she was no longer alone.

Charity's eyes flew open. The blackness was complete—outside and in. No light anywhere. But she knew. Someone was standing just past the end of her bed. Realization stole the air from her lungs and sent her heart hammering.

She tried to convince herself it was just Aunt Florie. But the shape was too large, too solid. Too male. She couldn't see him, but she could feel him, hear him breathing, feel his gaze on her. How long had he been standing there watching her? The thought whizzed past in an instant of realization and horror, in the time it took her to breathe—and scream.

She lunged for the bedside table drawer where she kept her Derringer and pepper spray. The dark shadow at the end of her bed sprang to life. She thought he'd lunge at her, stop her before her hand could grasp the Derringer, swing and fire.

Her hand closed over the weapon. She swung. She hadn't heard his retreating footfalls over the percussion of her heart—or her scream. But she knew he was gone even before she heard the front door slam.

A light came on in the hallway. Her aunt appeared silhouetted in the doorway in a long flannel nightgown gripping the baseball bat.

IT WAS NOT long after two, after the Duck-In had closed and Timber Falls resembled a ghost town, when Mitch went home. He'd driven around for hours and finally given up any hope of finding Nina or her car.

He heated himself a can of tomato soup and fell asleep fully clothed on the couch after making sure that everything next door seemed normal.

As usual, he dreamed of Charity. At first the scream was part of the dream.

He came awake with a jerk, knowing even before his feet hit the floor where the sound had come from. Diving out the door, he sprinted next door, weapon drawn.

When he reached the front steps, though, he froze at the sight of Florie with a baseball bat in her hands and Charity holding what looked like a gun. Both women were standing on the porch, looking scared—and scary.

"There was a man in the house!" Charity cried.

"Did you see which way he went?"

They both pointed across the street toward town.

"Get back inside. Lock the door. And put that gun away."

The street was empty. He took off running in the direction the women had indicated down a narrow alley. He hadn't gone far when he spotted a dark figure walking ahead of him. Not running. Just walking in long strides toward Main Street.

"Freeze!" Mitch leveled his weapon at the retreating back.

The man stopped but didn't turn around. He was tall, about Mitch's height, and strong-looking. He wore a biker's black leather jacket, jeans and biker boots.

Mitch moved quickly down the alley, keeping the weapon leveled at the man's back. "Put your hands behind your head." The light from a street lamp at the other end of the alley barely reached down here, so he still couldn't see who the man was.

Slowly, almost contemptuously, the man raised his hands, elbows out as he locked his fingers behind his head in a stance that was obviously familiar to him.

His hair was dark, long and pulled back into a pony-tail. An earring glittered in his left lobe, and he wore a ring of thick gold on his right hand. It reflected the dim light as Mitch advanced.

But it was his stance that put Mitch on guard. He was used to bikers occasionally coming through town in the summer. Most were doctors or lawyers or computer whizzes, the kind of people who could afford a big motorcycle and the leather clothing that went with it, so there was never much trouble.

Seldom did Mitch see a biker this time of year. And this guy was no doctor or lawyer. Worse, there was something familiar about the way he moved.

"Turn around. Slowly," Mitch ordered, weapon still trained on him.

The man emitted a deep chuckle, then turned very, very slowly, grinning as he did. In the dim light, Mitch saw that his face was tanned and lean, his features strong. A woman, any woman, would have found him damned handsome. Many had. "Evenin', Sheriff."

Mitch had been right about one thing. This was no doctor. No lawyer. And certainly no computer whiz kid. Mitch shook his head and lowered his weapon. "Jesse."

"Hey, bro," Jesse Tanner said, dropping his arms and holding out his hand.

Mitch holstered his gun and reluctantly took his

brother's hand. Jesse didn't seem to notice his reluctance as he threw his arms around him, slapping Mitch on the back. "Great to see you again, man."

Mitch stepped back from the embrace. It had been a long time and Jesse hadn't left under the best of circumstances. "What are you doing here?" he asked, telling himself it couldn't have been Jesse who'd been in Charity's house a few minutes ago.

"This is home, remember?"

"I remember you saying it would be a cold day in hell before you'd ever come back here," Mitch said.

Jesse shrugged and smiled, flexing those Tanner dimples. "People change."

Not Jesse, Mitch thought. Not his older brother, the hellion. "Someone just scared the living daylights out of Charity Jenkins. Were you in her house?"

His brother lifted a brow. "Already looking to bust me again?"

"You just happened to be in the neighborhood?"

"I was just seeing how much the town had changed." Jesse grinned. "It hasn't."

"Checking out the town at four in the morning?"

"I like the quiet."

Mitch stared at his brother, surprised how much he wanted to believe him. "How long have you been back?"

"Three days. I'm staying out at the house," he added, knowing that was going to be Mitch's next question.

He'd gotten back Saturday or Sunday? Odd that no one had mentioned seeing Jesse back after almost five years. Also, he was staying with their father.

"How *is* Charity, little brother?"

Mitch felt his stomach tighten.

"I hear she hasn't changed a damn bit. Still cute as a bug's ear and all spit and vinegar. She always was something. Too bad she's been hung up on the wrong brother for so long."

Mitch could remember all too well a time when Jesse had tried his best to steal Charity's heart—without any luck. Jesse had left town shortly after that—in handcuffs. He'd gotten into trouble with the law as usual, but Mitch remembered how upset Charity had been.

"So what are you driving now?" Mitch asked, thinking about the black pickup Charity thought had been following her.

"Got me a bike. A Harley."

"Know anyone who drives a black pickup?"

"I know a lot of people who drive black pickups."

"This one has dark-tinted windows."

Jesse seemed to think about that for a minute, then shook his head. "Doesn't ring any bells. Sorry."

Mitch couldn't be positive that the black pickup Charity had seen was Kyle L. Rogers's. She might not have gotten the plate number right. And mostly, he couldn't imagine his brother hiring a private detective to spy on her, but then, he'd never understood his brother. And the truth and Jesse seldom crossed paths.

"Someone in a black pickup's been following Charity, and the newspaper office was broken into earlier tonight," Mitch said.

He *could* imagine Jesse breaking into the newspaper to steal a strip of negatives. Jesse had left Timber Falls after being acquitted of burglary only because the old man had given Jesse an alibi that Mitch knew damned well was a lie but couldn't prove it.

But Mitch couldn't see his brother attacking Charity. If Jesse had wanted those negatives, he would have tried to sweet-talk Charity out of them. He wouldn't have had to bind her with tape and put her in a storage room.

Or maybe Mitch just didn't want to believe Jesse was capable of doing anything like that. Especially to Charity. "The thief locked Charity in a storage closet."

Jesse frowned. "Sounds like you got a regular crime spree going on here. Any other unsolved crimes you'd like to pin on me?"

At least Jesse hadn't lost that chip on his shoulder, Mitch thought. "I guess I'm just wondering what you're doing in Timber Falls."

"Isn't it possible I got homesick?"

"No."

Jesse laughed softly. "I told you, bro, people change."

But for the better?

"Okay, I'll level with you," Jesse said, and grinned. Like Mitch, he had the Tanner dimples. "I was down in Mexico and I started thinking about Charity. I figured she was probably damned tired of carrying a torch for my brother by now, and I knew you sure as hell wouldn't have done anything like marry her, so I thought, Jesse, why don't you get on your bike and go see Charity? I thought she might want to run off with me." Jesse's laugh filled the alley. "You don't have a problem with that, do you, little brother?"

Mitch gritted his teeth.

"I didn't think so," Jesse said. Then he sobered. "I got homesick, Mitch. Plain and simple. I knew our old man wasn't getting any younger and I wasn't proud of the way I left things between you and me." His dark eyes were serious and he sounded so damned sincere. "You should come out and see Dad. He'd like that."

"But *I* wouldn't," Mitch said.

"Still carrying all that, are you?" Jesse shook his head. "It's been years, man. And he's changed."

"Yeah, everyone's changed. But I haven't."

"Maybe that's the problem." Jesse shook his head again. The grin returned. "Tell Charity hello for me. I won't kid you, man. I'm looking forward to seeing her." He turned and sauntered down the alley. "See ya 'round."

Mitch watched him stop in a deep shadow. The rumble of a big motorcycle echoed down the alley. A few seconds later Jesse roared off toward the place Mitch had once called home, the streetlight glaring off his helmet and shield, completely hiding his face.

Jesse was back in town, and just at the start of the rainy season. Mitch doubted it was because Jesse had gotten homesick, or that there was any chance Charity would just climb on the back of his bike and take off for parts unknown. She wouldn't, would she?

Mitch swore as he started toward her house. How *was* Charity going to take having Jesse back in town? Mitch hated to think that his brother could be right. Not that Mitch could blame Charity for getting tired of waiting around for him. But the last person he wanted to see Charity with was his brother!

CHAPTER TEN

Thursday, October 29

CHARITY AWOKE THE next morning after hardly sleeping a wink all night. Mitch had come back and insisted on sleeping on the couch downstairs. Just knowing he was downstairs, only yards away, had made sleep impossible.

Worse, he'd come back in a horrible mood, hardly saying two words. He'd found a back window that had been broken into but no sign of the intruder except for some shuffled papers on her desk.

Maybe that was why he was so upset. He was obviously worried about her. She was starting to get worried herself. What had the person been looking for? A letter? That was the only thing that made any sense.

Charity realized she must have dozed off at some point toward daybreak because she awoke to the sound of pots and pans rattling in the kitchen below her bedroom. She jumped into the shower, made herself as presentable as possible and rushed downstairs. Breakfast with Mitch would make eating whatever her aunt was cooking worth it.

"Where's Mitch?" she asked when she didn't see his lanky frame at the kitchen table.

"He was gone when I got up," Florie said. "He sure

seemed in a foul mood last night, and I didn't like the look of his aura this morning one bit."

Just then the doorbell rang. Charity smiled, letting her imagination off its leash. She imagined Mitch standing on the porch, looking sheepish and apologetic, holding a bouquet of flowers—no, not flowers, a pie, a banana-cream pie from Betty's.

She swung open the door, her imagination so powerful she thought she could smell bananas.

Mitch wasn't standing on her porch.

And there was no pie.

"Jesse?" He was a darker version of his younger brother but had the same dimples. And right now his grin was all dimples.

Before she could utter another word, he dropped his bike helmet, picked her up and swung her around in a hug. "Damn, it's good to see you!" Still grinning, he set her down.

"What are you doing here?" His leather jacket was damp and cold with rain, and beyond him, she could see his motorcycle parked out front in the drizzling rain.

"I got lonesome for you," he said.

She ignored that. "Does Mitch know you're back in town?"

"Ran into him last night not far from here." He grinned again. "He didn't seem happy to see me."

"Not far from here?" she cried, latching on to his words. "You!" She swatted at him a couple of times in quick succession. "You were in my bedroom last night! It was you!"

He ducked out of her reach. "Whoa. If I'd been in your bedroom last night, you'd have damned well known it. In fact, I'd probably still be there this morning—" his grin broadened "—and so would you."

"Are you telling me you haven't been following me?"

He shook his head, the grin gone. "Mitch told me someone in a black pickup's been following you?"

She nodded. "Leaving me presents, too."

"Really?" He was grinning again.

"It *was* you!" She cuffed him again.

"Hey, you liked them, didn't you, sweetheart?"

"No, and don't call me that. What are you doing here?"

"I came back for you."

She stared at him. "No, seriously."

He flashed those Tanner dimples again, reminding her too much of Mitch. "Run away with me."

"Are you high on something?"

He laughed. "I just drove two thousand miles to see you. The least you could do is invite me in."

"I'm not sure you haven't already *been* in," she said, eyeing him suspiciously. But she moved back to allow him entrance.

"I've missed you like crazy, Charity," he said as he stepped into her living room. "I've even missed Timber Falls and Mitch. Can you believe it?"

"No," Charity said, closing the door.

"Jesse Tanner?" Aunt Florie cried from the kitchen doorway, a wire whisk in her hand.

"Florie!" In two strides, Jesse reached her, picked her up and swung her around, making her squeal.

Her cheeks were flushed and her eyes were shiny when he put her back down. "You're a sight for sore eyes, young man." Jesse had always been Florie's favorite.

"It's nice that *some*one is happy to have me back," he said, shooting a glance at Charity.

"I was just whipping up breakfast," Florie said. "Come have some with us."

Charity could not imagine what her aunt had whipped up.

"I'd love to have breakfast with you," Jesse said. "That is, if Charity doesn't mind." He gave her a wink.

"Not in the least." She was already reaching for her purse and car keys. "Wish I could stay, but I have to get to work," she said over her aunt's protests as she backed toward the front door.

She left Florie and Jesse and headed toward the newspaper office, which she drove right past when she saw Mitch's patrol car parked in front of Betty's.

MITCH WAS SITTING at the counter in his usual spot when Charity stormed in. She marched over and sat down on the stool next to him.

Too busy to stop and talk, Betty set a diet cola in front of her, a fork and a piece of butterscotch-cream pie, then bustled off.

"Why didn't you tell me Jesse was back in town?" Charity demanded, keeping her voice down.

Mitch looked over at her, pretending surprise that she was next to him. "Good morning to you, too. How do you know about Jesse?" He took a sip of his coffee as if his brother being back wasn't big news.

"He came by for breakfast."

Mitch cursed under his breath. "I figured you'd find

out soon enough, since he says he's here because of you."

"And you believe him?"

Mitch looked over at her again. "Don't you?"

She made a face at him. "Some professional investigator you are." She took a sip of her diet cola. It calmed her a little. "He's been leaving the presents."

"He admitted that?"

She nodded. "And I think he was in my room last night, though he denies it. I just felt a presence there, looking at me in the dark."

Mitch stared at her. "But you can't be sure."

She shook her head.

"One of your back windows had been jimmied open," Mitch said and frowned, obviously thinking the same thing she was.

"Why would Jesse break into my house?"

"Why does Jesse do half the things he does?"

"Did he say how long he's been back in town?"

"Three days."

"So what's he been doing? Hiding out? Or hiding behind tinted pickup windows and keeping to the cover of darkness?"

"You make him sound like a vampire," Mitch said. "He's been staying out at the old man's."

Charity raised a brow. "And until last night, no one had seen him?"

Mitch rolled his eyes. Charity could be so dramatic. But she had a point. In a town the size of Timber Falls, news of Jesse's being back would have spread faster than a wildfire. Yet, other than their father, Mitch had been the first to see him last night. Or maybe Charity, if it really had been Jesse in her room. Sneaking into Charity's bedroom, though, sounded very unlike Jesse.

"Well, it definitely wasn't Jesse who broke into the newspaper office. He had no reason to want the negatives," she said. "But his timing bothers me."

Mitch couldn't agree more. After five years away, Jesse had come back to town the night before Nina Monroe disappeared and Charity had seen the black pickup following her.

He watched Charity take a bite of pie and close her eyes, savoring it. A small smile curled her irresistible lips. She opened her eyes and looked right at him, a satisfied gleam in her eyes that made him nervous, as if she knew something he didn't.

Normally one of his greatest pleasures was watching her eat since that was the *only* pleasure the two of them shared, but this morning he had other things on his mind.

Her eyes met his. He looked into those warm honey-brown depths and felt his body leaning of its own accord toward her. He could already taste her mouth on his.

The café phone rang. "It's for you, Sheriff," Betty called.

He blinked and jerked back. Charity had that damned knowing look on her face again. He got up and walked stiffly to the phone, afraid of who'd tracked him down at Betty's. He had a pretty good idea, but maybe it would be good news. Like Nina Monroe had shown up for work today.

"How's the pie?" Betty asked, coming up to lean against the counter. It was obvious from her expression that she had some good gossip.

"Amazing," Charity said, and watched Mitch on the phone across the room. He'd almost kissed her, she was positive. "I think I like butterscotch pie better than banana-cream." When she'd taken a bite, she'd seen it, clear as day. Mitch in a tux standing beside her at the altar.

"What's this I hear about the paper being broken into and you being hog-tied?" Betty asked.

"Where did you hear *that?*"

"Twila told me that Kinsey told her that Shirley told her that Lydia told her after Florie told her," Betty said.

Charity groaned. "Florie." Sure as the devil Mitch would think it was her fault Florie had blabbed.

In truth, she did blame herself. She'd let Mitch see how frightened she'd been. Big mistake. Now he'd want Florie to stay with her until this thing with the black pickup was resolved.

Not that she wasn't spooked by everything that had happened. Which was why from now on, or at least until she felt safe again, she'd be more careful—and carry her fear insurance with her. She had the small gun in her purse, along with the pepper spray and some handcuffs.

She'd also taken Mitch's advice and was having dead bolts and a back door security light installed at the newspaper office.

"So tell me *everything,*" Betty said, salivating for the whole story. Charity could almost hear the hum of the grapevine. That was the problem with this town. No one ever waited for the paper to come out.

Charity stalled, took another bite of her pie and closed her eyes. All she saw this time was darkness, accompanied by the smell of cleaning supplies and newsprint. That damned storage room. It had freaked her out more than she wanted to admit.

She opened her eyes. Betty was waiting and Mitch was watching her from across the room.

"It's just like you heard," Charity confirmed, and added enough details to thrill Betty, then asked, "Did you hear if Nina Monroe's been found yet?" If anyone would know, Betty would. And probably sooner than Mitch.

"No one's seen hide nor hair of her," Betty said. "Odd, isn't it, and at the same time as a Bigfoot sighting." She hummed the theme from *The Twilight Zone*.

Charity groaned. "You aren't suggesting the two are somehow linked, are you?" Ridiculous. But it would make for a great headline: Bigfoot Abducts Local Duck Painter.

Betty leaned toward her. "Remember that little boy who disappeared in the Cascades south of Portland? Lost for days in the mountains. No one thought he'd be found alive, not with the temperature dropping at night and no food or water." She straightened and nodded. "And what happened?"

Charity knew the story. It was the fabric from which legends were woven. "They found the boy alive and well."

"And when they asked him how he'd managed," Betty said, finishing up the story with her I-told-you-so look, "he said a nice monster took care of him." She broke into *The Twilight Zone* theme song again. "Nina could do worse," she said, and took off with a pot of coffee in each hand.

Charity wondered if that was true, Nina doing worse than being abducted by Bigfoot.

The café was busy, what with the regulars and all the visitors the Bigfoot sighting had brought to town. The Halloween weekend ahead would be worse. Especially if there was another Bigfoot sighting.

Charity thought about the blur of brown fur she'd caught on film. Had it just been a big bear?

Losing those photos hurt worse than being bound and gagged and stuffed between boxes of paper in a storage closet. Almost. She had to reshoot and get the newspaper ready to go.

But this thing with Nina had become a better story than Bigfoot—unless the call Mitch had taken was someone telling him that Nina was no longer missing. And if the black truck that had been following her really was just some private eye...

But why had someone stolen her film? A chill skittered up her spine. There had to have been something incriminating on that roll of film. Something more incriminating than a photo of a black truck.

But who else would be interested in the photographs? She tried to remember everything that had been on that roll.

That's when it hit her. Nina Monroe. *She'd taken a photo of Nina.* And that wasn't even the worst of it. She remembered now who might have seen her do it.

HANGING UP THE PHONE after listening to a resident rant and rave about a barking dog, Mitch returned to his pie and coffee—and Charity. He never dreamed he could get hooked on pie for breakfast, and all because of a woman. But he had to admit as he slid onto the stool next to her, pie beat the hell out of oatmeal.

Charity had ruined him for any other breakfast.

Just the way she'd apparently ruined him for any other woman, he thought grimly. Still, he couldn't believe he'd almost kissed her. Again. And in Betty's. And it was only the *beginning* of the rainy season. Hell, he could be married to Charity by spring the way he was going.

"Mitch," Charity said excitedly, "let's get out of here! There's something I have to tell you."

"Florie read something disturbing in your coffee grounds this morning?"

She pushed her pie away and stood.

Mitch looked from the unfinished butterscotch pie to Charity. "Are you sick?"

"Funny. My stars are out of alignment and there is trouble on my celestial and terrestrial planes. I won't even tell you what else the tarot cards had to say."

"Good." It was pouring rain outside, but he figured he was going to need the fresh air. He downed most of his coffee, left enough money for it and Charity's breakfast and a tip, grabbed his coat and hat, and followed her outside.

Rain drummed on the roof overhead and poured in a sheet off all but one side. He hunkered down in his fleece-lined county-issue jacket, chilled more by the look on Charity's face than the weather.

She took a breath and let it out on a puff of white. "The guy from the black truck might not have been the one who took the strip of negatives. I remembered who else I'd shot on that roll of film—Nina."

"*Nina?* You shot a photograph of Nina and you just now remembered?" Since Charity might have had the *only* photograph of Nina, he found it hard to believe she'd forgotten until now.

"Get in the patrol car," he ordered.

Charity couldn't believe it. "You're going to arrest me?"

His look said it would be prudent if she got into the patrol car without making a scene in front of Betty's.

Good thinking.

She dashed through the rain to where the patrol car was parked on Main Street and climbed in the passenger side as he slid behind the wheel.

Without a word he started the engine, but didn't drive away. He turned on the heater. The windows began to clear.

It was cozy in here, nice to be out of the cold and wet. The rain made a pleasant sound on the roof, and she could smell Mitch's subtle aftershave, along with a warm maleness.

She breathed it in and closed her eyes, and for just an instant, she saw herself dressed all in white and next to her—

"Charity."

Her eyes flew open. "I'd forgotten I took a candid shot of Nina when I was at Dennison Ducks. After I talked to her about an interview I staked out the parking lot since I'd heard Wade often left right after Nina at lunchtime."

"And?"

"She came out, but she didn't go to her car. She walked toward the back of the building, stopped and was arguing with someone."

"Did you see who?"

She shook her head. "I couldn't hear the words, either. She had her back to me. But I could tell she was mad about something."

"I'll take your word for it."

"She stomped to her car, got in and drove off. I took a shot of her right before she took off."

"That was it?"

"Not exactly. I ducked down behind the trees again, put my camera away and started back to where I'd left my car parked down the road and… I ran into Wade."

Mitch let out a low whistle. "Did he see you take Nina's photograph?"

"Maybe. He couldn't have been the person she was arguing with, though. He came from the wrong direction, *through* the trees." There was an old bridle path behind the plant that lead to town and the Dennison mansion.

"His car wasn't in the lot?"

She shook her head. "I think Wade was spying on Nina."

"It makes more sense than them having an affair."

She chewed on a nail for a moment. "You're going to think I'm crazy, but I have this theory." She could tell Mitch didn't want to hear it. "Nina is the right age, the right coloring and given the way Wade treated her…" She met his gaze. "I think she's Angela."

He tried to appear shocked, but he couldn't fool her. "Nina *is* Angela!"

"Whoa! I didn't say a word," he protested.

"You, as the most cynical person on earth, wouldn't think Nina was Angela unless…unless you had proof! You found proof?"

"Stop. You're impossible." He rubbed his forehead as if he had a headache.

"Oh, I love it when I'm right! Tell me. You have to tell me. That's why you've been so worried about me. You know something. But what does it have to do with me?"

"Charity, I don't know what it has to do with you. That's why I have to tell you. But it's strictly off the record. It could be evidence in a murder case."

She hated anything being off the record, but she was dying to know what he'd found out. "Fine."

He told her about the silver baby spoon he found in Nina's bungalow.

"It's Angela Dennison's?"

"Looks that way, but I need to show it to the jeweler in Eugene who made it before I'll know for sure."

This was better than she'd hoped and the possibilities made her head spin. "The kidnapper could have taken the spoon, Nina found it and was blackmailing the kidnapper."

"Why would the kidnapper take the spoon?"

She shrugged. "Could have seen it by the bed. Took it because it was solid silver. Or because it represented the Dennisons' wealth."

He nodded. "You mean someone jealous of a baby born with a silver spoon in her mouth?"

She smiled. "Exactly. Since no ransom was ever demanded for Angela, he must have sold the baby or... been paid to take it." She could see that Mitch had already considered that possibility. "Or with the baby spoon, Nina could pass herself off as Angela. Or she really is Angela."

"The reason I told you about the baby spoon was so you'd understand how dangerous this could be. Especially for a nosy newspaperwoman who took a photo of Nina *one day* just before she disappeared."

"I wish I *had* that photo. Florie might be right about my stars being out of whack."

"I could have told you that without even looking at your stars." His gaze softened. He reached across the seat and took her hand, cupping it in his, sending a satisfying jolt through her. "I'm serious. I'm worried that you're in danger. I don't want you doing this story. At least not yet."

She was too lost in the feel of his warm fingers tracing over her skin to argue—at least for the moment.

A loud tap on the window behind Mitch's head made her jump.

Wade Dennison peered through the rain-streaked glass. He was looking past Mitch straight at her. "Charity Jenkins! You damn meddling woman," Wade bellowed. "I'm going to kill you!"

CHAPTER ELEVEN

SISSY SHOT MITCH a what-now look as he and Wade burst into the Sheriff's Department, raindrops puddling at their feet and Wade bellowing, "I want that woman locked up!"

It was clear Sissy knew what woman Wade was referring to and was in full agreement.

Mitch marched Wade into his office and closed the door.

"What the hell is Charity doing asking about Nina?" Wade demanded before the door closed. "Did you know she talked to some of my people? Asked a bunch of personal questions? You have to do something about her."

"Sit down, Wade." Wade didn't. Mitch walked around behind his desk and dropped into his chair, counting to ten before saying, "In the first place, Wade, I can't do anything about Charity because she hasn't broken any laws. But if you threaten to kill her again, you could end up behind bars. Being the local press, she has certain rights," he hurried on before Wade could argue. "Rights protected under the First Amendment."

"That allows her to butt into other people's business?" Wade demanded, slamming his fist down on the desk.

"Yes, actually, it does."

Wade slowly lowered himself into a chair. "The woman's a menace."

Mitch couldn't argue that. He was worried as hell about her. But he couldn't stop her from pursuing this story any more than he could get Wade Dennison to tell him the truth.

He studied the man across the desk from him. When Wade had shaved this morning, he'd missed a patch of gray whiskers on one side of his jaw, and his eyes were bloodshot, the skin under them baggy and dark as if he hadn't slept.

Still, Wade carried himself with an air that said he could make or break this town if he didn't get his way. In that sense alone Wade Dennison was dangerous.

What worried Mitch was the chance that Wade was more dangerous than any of them knew. He'd been in a rage outside Betty's a few minutes ago, threatening Charity. Mitch wondered if Wade was capable of violence and if Nina Monroe had been the first to find out. Or if Angela Dennison had been.

"Wade, it's time you told me what the hell is really going on."

CHARITY COULD ALMOST feel her ears burning. She would have loved to know what was being said about her over at the Sheriff's Department.

But she had work to do. And it wasn't as if Mitch had invited her to tag along with him and Wade. She probably didn't want to hear it, anyway.

She couldn't believe Wade had actually threatened to kill her, and in front of the sheriff. Was it possible that Wade had been the man who'd broken into the newspaper, stolen her negatives and bound and gagged her in the storage room? Wade might be in his sixties, but he was strong as an ox, and even if he hadn't been wearing a nylon stocking over his head, she'd never gotten a good look at the man who'd attacked her. Nor at the one who'd been in her bedroom.

A few days ago, she would have scoffed at the idea of Wade Dennison as her assailant and intruder. But seeing Wade's rage this morning, she wasn't so sure. The man seemed out of control. And all because of Nina Monroe. Now why was that?

She drove to her office in time to pay the handyman who'd installed her dead bolts and a security light out back, then locked up and, using her ladybug umbrella, walked down Main Street to the Busy Bee antique shop.

She couldn't still her excitement. She'd only asked a couple of people she knew who worked out at Dennison Ducks about Nina, and now Wade was in a murderous rage. There was definitely a story there. Nina Monroe might actually *be* Angela Dennison.

But wouldn't Wade have been delighted to have Angela back? Wouldn't he have told everyone? His behavior didn't make any sense and made her all the more determined to find out what was going on.

A tiny bell tinkled as Charity pushed open the door to the antique shop and was instantly assaulted with the wonderful smell of antiques—and peppermint tea.

The Busy Bee was anything but busy. The owner, Lydia Abernathy, smiled and waved from the back. She was a tiny woman, her hair a white downy halo around her head, her blue eyes a bright twinkle in her wrinkled face.

"You're just in time for tea, dear, and I have your favorite sugar cookies."

"The ones with the sprinkles on top?" Charity asked as she made her way through the antiques to the back.

"Of course." Lydia zipped over to the hot plate in her motorized wheelchair to get the teapot. She already had another cup and saucer out.

"You must have known I'd be stopping by," Charity said, dragging up a chair.

Lydia laughed. "Yup. As soon as I heard about my brother's behavior outside Betty's this morning. Everyone in town heard Wade hollering." She clasped her hands together in obvious delight. "Do tell me what you did to tick Wade off."

WHEN MITCH GOT TIRED of Wade's threats and obvious avoidance of the truth, he gave up and asked him to leave.

Wade stood and seemed to hesitate. "I'm telling you I don't know what happened to Nina."

Mitch nodded impatiently. "Why don't you tell me why you're so protective of her?"

"I'm protective of all my people."

"Dammit, Wade, you didn't even check her references. She never worked at any of those places she put down on her application." Wade started to interrupt, but Mitch cut him off, raising his voice. "You didn't check her social security number, either, or any other identification. Her name isn't even Nina Monroe."

Mitch hadn't planned to tell Wade that. At least not yet. But now that he had, he waited for a reaction and wasn't surprised when Wade didn't even flinch. "So you already knew that. Okay. Who is she?"

Wade just looked at the floor and shook his head.

"Is there any chance the reason you're so upset is because the woman who called herself Nina Monroe is actually Angela Dennison?"

Wade's head snapped up. "That's ridiculous. You get that from that so-called reporter girlfriend of yours?"

Mitch could almost see Sissy straining to listen on the other side of the wall. "I asked you a question. Just answer it. Is there even a chance that Nina is Angela?"

"Hell, no."

"Hell, no, you won't answer. Or hell, no, she wasn't Angela?"

"Just plain hell, no." Wade stormed over to the door and flung it open. "Do your damned job. Find Nina. I have to go out of town. I'll call you when I get back this evening." He slammed the front door on his way out.

Sissy stuck her head in the open doorway of Mitch's office as Wade's car roared away. "You want coffee? Colombian roast."

Sissy never got him coffee. Always said his legs worked just fine. So what was this about? Plain old nosiness, he decided. This town had more of it per capita than any town in the country, he'd swear. "No, and close the door."

"Ouch!" Sissy said, unperturbed as she shut the door.

Mitch tried to calm down, but couldn't. He unlocked his drawer and pulled out the Angela Dennison file again.

If someone in the house had abducted the baby and tried to make it look like a kidnapping, what would they have done with her? Killed her? Buried her in the backyard or the woods? Left her on a doorstep? Sold her?

Is that what he thought Wade had done? Gotten rid of Angela? And Nina had found out and was blackmailing him? Or Nina *was* Angela.

Mitch flipped through the interviews Sheriff Hudson had done after the abduction, fearing this old case was the key to Nina Monroe's disappearance. Jotted in the margins was a note. A name jumped out at him. He flipped back and stared down in disbelief. Ruth Anne Tanner. His mother? The sheriff had tried to reach Ruth Tanner to question her about her visit to the Dennison house earlier on the day of the kidnapping twenty-seven years ago?

"Where can I reach you?" Sissy asked as Mitch stormed out.

"The Dennison house."

"Oh."

Mitch couldn't have been more shocked as he drove out of town. Why would his mother go to see Daisy—the woman who'd been having an affair with Ruth Tanner's husband?

Mitch tossed his hat on the seat beside him and raked his hand through his hair. His head ached and he couldn't shake the bad feeling at the pit of his stomach.

His mother had dropped by for a visit with Daisy? Not bloody likely. She must have gone over to the house to confront Daisy about the affair, demand Daisy leave her husband alone.

He'd only been six but he remembered that day like it was yesterday. He'd come home from school to find not only his mother gone, but all her things. She hadn't even left a note. She was just gone. He'd found his father sitting on the deck facing the road. He'd told Mitch that he didn't know why she'd left, but they'd both known. They'd never heard from her again.

Years later, Mitch had tried to find her but to no avail. She'd probably changed her name. She obviously didn't want to be found for she'd left no trail.

So what had happened at the Dennisons that day? Had Daisy refused to break off the affair? Is that why his mother had left the way she had?

Mitch shook his head at his mother's timing. She had gone over to see Daisy just hours before the woman's baby was stolen—and before she herself disappeared without a trace.

The two couldn't have anything to do with each other. Dear God, he hoped not.

THE DENNISON HOUSE was pretentious at best, a huge plantation-style home with white pillars, porticos and a sweeping lawn completely out of place in the middle of the mountains of Oregon.

Out back was an indoor pool and recreation room. Beyond that, stables and corrals, where Daisy Dennison had once raised expensive horses.

Mitch parked the patrol car in the woods a couple of hundred yards from the house, checked his watch and waited, knowing there was no turning back once he knocked on the Dennisons' front door.

A few minutes later he saw the housekeeper leave. Anyone could have set a clock by her schedule. She drove into town the same time every day to do the shopping.

He figured Desiree would still be in bed this early, and Daisy would be forced to answer the door. He rang the bell a dozen times before she finally did.

She looked furious. He wasn't surprised, given their past. Or his persistence.

Her appearance, though, startled him, and he tried to remember the last time he'd seen her. She didn't come into town anymore, not that she'd ever embraced the locals. Most worked for her husband and so were beneath her.

Her implicit snobbery and her former legendary shopping trips to New York and Paris, among other things, had made Daisy Dennison the talk of Betty's for years. Back then, she'd dressed to kill, driven the most expensive cars, ridden the best horses money could buy and done whatever she damn well pleased, all the time rubbing it in everyone's faces, including her husband's.

That was until Angela's kidnapping. After that, Daisy had become a recluse, which started its own round of gossip. But even that had died down over the years, due to a lack of fresh dirt.

As far as Mitch knew, Daisy Dennison was seldom seen by anyone except her immediate family and their housekeeper, a tight-lipped German named Zinnia.

Zinnia did all the shopping, but spoke only broken English and didn't gossip, a crushing blow to Betty's crowd.

So Mitch was taken aback by how much Daisy had aged. Wade had shocked the town when he'd brought his new mystery bride home to Timber Falls. Daisy, a dark-haired beauty, was nineteen at the time, Wade forty. Great gossip down at Betty's for weeks.

Now Daisy, who wasn't even fifty, looked older than her husband, who was hugging seventy. She was far too thin. Her once gorgeous hair was dull and gray-ing and pulled severely back from her face. Her clothing was equally stark—baggy black sweats and worn black slippers.

There was no color in her face, no light in her eyes, not like the way she'd looked the summers she'd ridden her horse on the trail behind his house. Mitch had been just a kid, but he still recalled his father disappearing into the woods on those sunlit mornings and coming back in the late afternoon smelling of wine and perfume.

Mitch shoved aside the memory the way he did most thoughts of his father. Always better not to go there.

"Mrs. Dennison. Sorry to bother you, but I'm working on a missing person's case and I need to ask you a few questions."

Her look berated him for not calling first.

But they both knew why he hadn't.

"It will only take a few minutes."

She glanced at her watch as if trying to come up with an excuse. She didn't need an excuse not to talk to him and they both knew it. With an irritated sigh, she stepped back and let him enter.

He wondered about her life as she led him into a large living room to one side of the house. Long windows ran the perimeter of the room on three sides, providing views of the front, side and back yards and the deep green of the encroaching wilderness beyond—if the blinds hadn't been closed. The room was as dark and gloomy as the weather outside and the woman in it.

What did Daisy Dennison do in this huge house all day? And why had she closed herself up here all these years? He wondered what it must be like for her daughter Desiree, who still lived at home. Or maybe that was why Desiree stayed here—for her mother.

"What is it you want?" Daisy asked impatiently, motioning to a chair, making it clear he wouldn't be sitting long.

"One of the decoy painters is missing. Nina Monroe." He waited for a reaction and got none. Hadn't Wade told her about Nina? Obviously not. By just coming here, he was treading on thin ice. He decided to dive in and get it over with. "Wade is worried Nina might have met with foul play."

"I've no interest in the decoy business." Her tone made it clear she never had.

"Even if your husband and Nina have a relationship?"

The smile was bitter. "Especially if that's the case." She started to get up. "You should have called. I could have saved you the trip."

"Why did my mother come to see you the day Angela was abducted?"

Daisy Dennison lowered herself slowly back onto the chair, her face stony. "She wanted money to leave town. She thought she could blackmail me."

"That's a lie." The words were out before he could stop them.

She arched a brow. "You obviously didn't know your mother. How old were you—six when she left? I threw her out and never saw her again."

"What about my father? Did you see him again?"

Her gaze softened. "No. Not after I lost Angela. I doubt you'll believe this, either, but I loved your father."

He got to his feet. "I'd like a word with Desiree."

It was her first genuine emotion. Fear. "Desiree doesn't know about your father and me."

"But she might know about Nina Monroe," he said.

Daisy couldn't keep him from talking to her, though she might try.

"Nothing can change the past," Daisy said, her voice sounding like an old woman's, weak and shaky, all that confidence and bravado gone. "Can't you leave it buried for all our sakes?"

"I wish I could, but I'm afraid some things just won't stay buried."

Her dark eyes glinted with tears. She walked to the back wall. He thought for a moment she was calling someone to have him thrown out.

But instead, the blinds on the windows there groaned upward. She pointed toward the indoor pool, then reached for the phone, dismissing him.

He listened to her dial. She was calling her husband, sure as hell. Wade would be furious. Not that it mattered. It had been more than thirty-six hours since Nina was last seen. Mitch couldn't shake the feeling he was now investigating a homicide.

"OH, THESE COOKIES," Charity moaned with pleasure.

"Better than sex?" Lydia asked with a wink.

"If I ever have sex, I'll let you know."

Lydia laughed, then leaned forward in her wheelchair. "So tell me. Why are my brother's shorts in a bunch over this decoy painter?"

"I was hoping you could tell *me*. No one seems to know anything about her. Have you ever seen Wade this crazy before?"

"Just once," the older woman said. "When Angela was taken."

Charity nodded, counting on that answer. "You remember anything about that time?" she asked as she took another cookie.

"Like it was yesterday," Lydia said.

WARM MIST ROSE off the turquoise-blue water to fog the glass windows. Through the mist, Mitch saw Desiree Dennison lying on a lounger by the pool wearing a pale-pink one-piece. The suit was wet, her tanned skin covered with tiny droplets of water, the room hot as a sauna.

She glanced up as he approached. She reminded him of a sixteen-year-old. Not only because she was young-looking, but because she acted young. He found it hard to believe she was three years older than Charity.

"Sheriff Tanner?" Desiree sounded surprised. Was it possible she hadn't heard Nina Monroe was missing? Or maybe she couldn't have cared less, just like her mother.

"Is there someplace less…damp we could talk?"

She groaned and covered her eyes with one slim arm. "I have a bitch of a hangover and I'm in no mood for a lecture."

"I didn't come here to lecture you."

She lifted her arm and gazed up at him. "Did I break one of your laws?"

Probably a half dozen. "They aren't my laws. Would you mind putting something on?"

She looked down at her tanning-bed tanned full-figured body, then up at him and smiled teasingly. "Sure, Sheriff, if that's what you want."

He looked away as she slowly rose from the lounger and slipped into a large long-sleeved man's shirt. He wondered whose shirt it was. Definitely not her father's taste.

"Want something to drink?" she asked as she led him from the pool area into the game room, complete with dozens of commercial-size video games.

"Beer? Soda? Bottled water?" she asked as she went behind a bar and opened a small fridge.

"Nothing. Thanks."

She shrugged as she twisted the top off a bottle of beer, careful not to break her long lacquered nails.

"Come on, Daddy asked you to talk to me about... what? The evils of alcohol? Drugs? Speeding?" She grinned. "Sex?"

"I'm here about Nina Monroe's disappearance."

"Who?"

"The decoy painter at your father's plant everyone's talking about," he said patiently.

Desiree grinned. "I might have heard something about her at the Duck-In last night, but why ask me about her?"

"You never met her?"

She wrinkled her nose. "I don't hang out with people from the plant."

"Never ran into her at the Duck-In?"

She shrugged. "I guess not."

"Your father thinks Nina might have met with foul play."

"You mean like someone *murdered* her?" She made it sound as if Timber Falls could never be *that* interesting. He wondered why she'd stayed here. Was it the pool, the stocked fridge, the free ride on Daddy's money? Or was she afraid to leave her mother alone in this big old house?

She took another drink.

"One more question," he said, tired of the Dennison women. "What would happen if Angela came back?"

Desiree choked. "The precious younger child I've never been able to live up to because I'm still *alive?*" She made a disgusted sound. "Why would you even ask that? You don't think Nina—"

"Just curious."

She studied him for a moment, obviously battling with the idea. "My parents would stone her to death because how could she possibly live up to the perfect lost child they've canonized for twenty-seven years?" She looked at him, bitterness souring her gaze. "But you know, even if she wasn't the perfect daughter, she'd still make me look bad, wouldn't she?"

CHAPTER TWELVE

As MITCH DROVE AWAY from the Dennison house, the radio squawked and Sissy came on.

"I think one of your Bigfoot fanatics might have found something you've been looking for," she said.

"Go to the security channel."

A moment later, "You there?"

"Go ahead."

"Just got an anonymous call from some guy who says he spotted an older red compact in a ravine. He says he thinks there's someone in the car. Too steep to go down there. He called to the person a few times, but got no answer. So he drove out to report it. Didn't want to get involved, so he declined to give a name. Called from the pay phone outside the Duck-In."

Mitch muttered an oath. Wasn't this what he'd feared all morning?

"Where'd he see the car?"

"Just past Lost Creek Falls."

Seven miles out of town. "I'm on my way." He reached Main Street and started south on the highway. No lights. No siren. Watching his speed. He didn't want to add to the rumors already whizzing around town.

Suddenly a figure in a bright-red rain slicker rushed out into the street, arms waving. All he caught was a flash of red before he hit the brakes. The patrol car skidded on the wet pavement, coming to a stop just inches short of catastrophe.

Charity grinned at him from under her hood and stepped around to the passenger side to open the door.

"Have you lost your mind? I almost hit you," he hollered, his voice betraying just how close he'd come. Wade was right. The woman was a menace.

"You would never run me over," she said as she calmly climbed in and buckled her seat belt. "You might want to—" there was a smile in her voice "—but you wouldn't."

"What do you think you're doing?" he asked.

"I thought you might want to have some lunch," she said. "Betty made coconut-cream pie and I've found out a few things you're going to want to hear, such as Wade and Daisy had a huge fight the night Angela disappeared."

He hoped this fight had nothing to do with his mother. All these years he'd believed that no one knew about the affair between his father and Daisy Dennison. Was he only kidding himself?

Charity glanced into the rearview mirror. "You realize you're blocking traffic?"

He started to tell her he didn't have time for food or gossip, but if Nina's body was in her car in a ravine, then leaving Charity alone in town was too dangerous, given everything that had happened lately.

Mitch was only one of a half dozen sheriffs who covered remote areas of Oregon alone. When he needed help, he could call the state for backup—or deputize locally. Most of the time, though, he handled things just fine on his own. Having Charity where he could keep an eye on her would be the safest thing for her. As for him...well, that was another story.

He shifted into drive and got moving.

"Betty's is back that way," she said as he passed Florie's and left the city limits.

"I'm taking you into protective custody."

"Protective custody?" She seemed to like the sound of that. "Although unnecessary." She opened her purse and pulled out the small gun he'd seen the night before, a can of pepper spray and a set of handcuffs.

He groaned. "What the hell do you plan to do with the cuffs?"

"I might have to detain someone until you can get there to save me." She grinned. "Unless you can think of something else to do with them."

"Don't make me sorry I didn't just lock you up at the jail."

"Where are we going?"

"To check on an anonymous call about a red compact in a ravine."

She looked over at him in surprise. "Nina?"

"Maybe."

She shivered and looked out at the highway ahead. "We still don't know who she is, right?"

"No." He drove out of town to the hypnotic sounds of the falling rain, the hum of the heater and the rhythmic sweep of the wipers, trying to ignore Charity's warm tantalizing scent.

Charity took off her rain jacket and tossed it in the back, making him too aware of the way her rust-colored turtleneck sweater brought out the gold in her eyes, not to mention how it hugged her full breasts.

He cracked his window open to let in a little of the

cool damp air. Charity smiled as if she not only knew exactly what she did to him, but also enjoyed every minute of it.

Fog hung in the trees on both sides of the road like cotton ticking. A thin white mist swirled restlessly on the blacktop ahead of them. Not far out of town, they lost all traffic. This part of the state was isolated. Nothing but a narrow stretch of secondary two-lane highway hemmed in by dense coastal growth. The closest town, Oakridge, was a twenty-mile drive.

Unfortunately there were only a couple more hours of daylight left. Between that and the rain, the day was dark and gloomy enough without going looking for a dead body.

"So tell me about this alleged fight between Wade and Daisy," he said to keep his mind off what was up the road.

He didn't really mind having company on the drive to break the monotony. And as long as he kept pretending he wasn't susceptible to Charity's charms, he'd be fine.

"Wade and Daisy fought all the time, but this night it was huge."

"According to...?"

"You know I can't reveal my sources."

"Of course not."

"The nanny, Alma Bromdale, told my source in strictest confidence that she put Angela to bed, then went down to get the cold medicine she'd left in the kitchen."

The cold pills that had knocked Alma out and the reason she hadn't heard someone break into the house and take the baby, he thought remembering Alma's statement.

"Daisy was in the den just down the hall from the kitchen with Wade. Alma heard Wade tell Daisy that if Angela turned out not to be his, he'd throw her and the baby out without a cent, put her back on the street where he'd found her, and she'd never see Desiree again."

"What?"

"It's true. My source found out that Daisy's family was dirt poor. It was all an act, her being from money. She only married Wade for his."

That was no surprise, Mitch thought. But if Daisy was poor and Angela was another man's baby... All he could think about was what Daisy had told him earlier. That she'd loved his father. "If Wade wasn't the father, who was?" he asked, his stomach tightening. Was it possible Angela had been his half sister?

Charity shook her head. "I haven't been able to find out."

Knowing Charity, it wouldn't be long. "How was Alma able to hear all this? Wouldn't Wade and Daisy try to keep this sort of thing to themselves?"

"When it got really heated, Wade closed the den door, but Alma opened the dumbwaiter and could hear just fine."

He shook his head, wondering how any secrets were ever kept in this world. "If any of this is true, then why did it take so long to come out?"

"Daisy supposedly fired Alma. However, right after that, Alma came into a bunch of money and disappeared. My source stayed in touch with her through a friend. The only reason my source is talking now is that Alma is dead. Died of cancer the middle of September in Washington."

Damn, he'd hoped to talk to Alma about the baby spoon. "So there's no way to prove any of this?"

Charity smiled. "Alma has a sister, Harriet Bromdale, and she still lives in Coos Bay."

The only Bromdale in the Coos Bay phone book was Alma's sister? And leave it to Charity to come up with that nugget of information.

"I think Daisy paid Alma to keep quiet," Charity said.

"About some fight they had?"

She shook her head. "About the kidnapping."

He laughed. "Let me guess? You have a theory."

"Daisy couldn't let Wade find out that Angela wasn't his. She'd lose Desiree, and she and Angela would be out on the street. So Daisy hired someone to steal Angela. That's why Daisy's been a recluse all these years. She had to give up one child to save the other and has had trouble living with the bargain she made with the devil." Charity said all this as if she knew it for a fact. "Why else has Daisy locked herself up in that house?"

He glanced over at her. Sometimes her imagination amazed him. "It's as good a theory as any I've come up with."

She smiled that killer smile of hers.

"But if Nina is Angela, what does that do to your theory? Wouldn't Daisy be delighted to see her daughter after all these years?"

Charity shook her head. "Not if it would expose her affair. Also not if her daughter was blackmailing her."

He felt a sliver of ice run the length of his spine as he stared at Charity. It was one hell of a theory. What bothered him most was that it made a morbid kind of sense.

"Of course, I have a counter-theory," Charity said. "Wade got rid of the baby. Daisy knows it but can't prove it. So now she's living in seclusion with a monster she created. If she hadn't flaunted her affair, Angela would be alive. So she holds herself responsible for what happened to Angela. But at least she has Desiree—and she's still Mrs. Wade Dennison—and still living in the big house with all his money."

He smiled over at her. "A counter-theory, huh? Either way makes Daisy sound pretty callous. What if Angela was Wade's?"

"Even better," Charity said. "He got rid of his own child. Imagine how that must weigh on her. The irony. And she has only herself to blame."

"Oh, I think Daisy would see Wade behind bars if she really believed he'd abducted her baby," Mitch said, but both of Charity's theories were as plausible as any he'd come up with.

The Lost Creek Falls sign suddenly appeared in the patrol car's headlights and he slowed, sorry he hadn't locked Charity up in jail, rather than bring her along. He hadn't seen another car in miles and he didn't like the bad feeling he was getting.

As he turned off onto the paved road to the falls, the fog grew thicker. The paved road ended a few miles later in a small parking lot at the top of the falls.

Mitch stopped at the end of the paved road, rolled down his window and looked out.

There were two sets of tracks in the muddy road past the falls. A motorcycle had gone in and come back out. And a truck by the look of the tread. If Nina's car was down here, then it had been driven in before the rains began.

As he looked down the road into the darkness of the rain and forest, he could see his breath in the chilly air. His brother, Jesse, wasn't the only one who owned a motorcycle, he told himself.

He rolled up his window, suddenly sick with worry as he started up the muddy narrow logging road.

"What a great place to dispose of a car," Charity whispered as limbs scraped the top of the patrol car and the tires kicked mud up under the wheel wells. "Or a body."

"Perfect place for an ambush, too," Mitch said.

Charity shot him a look, then locked her side of the car, making him smile. Sometimes the woman showed enough sense to endear her to him.

The headlights cut a swath through the darkness. The only sound was the *whap, whap* of the wipers and the rain pounding the roof.

Half a mile in, the headlights picked up something through the rain. The shine of a chrome bumper. He felt Charity tense beside him as he slowed.

The red car had gone down a steep slope, ending up at the bottom of the ravine, partially hidden under the limbs of a large pine.

Mitch slowed to a stop, put on the emergency brake and pulled his binoculars from the glove compartment. He opened his door and stepped out into the rain and growing darkness. The car had torn through the thick vegetation along the slope to come to a crashing halt against the large pine.

He wiped moisture from the binocular lens and looked again, trying to decide if he should go down there now, with so little daylight left. He didn't like the idea of leaving Charity alone, and he knew that the compact had been driven in here days ago, before the rain. That meant Tuesday, the night Nina had disappeared, or early the next morning before the rain began. Could Nina still be alive if she'd survived the crash?

He didn't know. But it was the reason he couldn't put off going down there until morning.

THROUGH THE RAIN, Charity could see the rear of the red car where it had come to rest under the tree. Hugging herself, she looked over at Mitch as he got back into the car. "You're going to think I'm as deluded as Florie, but I'm picking up really bad vibes here."

He smiled reassuringly at her, his gaze meeting hers. "I won't be long."

"And if I never see you again?"

"The patrol car is four-wheel drive. If you go slowly, you'll be able to get out of here—if I don't come back."

"You're scaring me."

"I'm just covering all the bases." He climbed out again and went around to the back of the patrol car.

Against her better judgment, she climbed out, too, and watched as he pulled on a pair of overalls he'd taken from the back, along with a pair hiking boots.

"Shouldn't you call for backup?" she asked. It was getting dark and she couldn't shake the feeling that someone was watching them.

"We'd have to drive out to the highway to get the radio to work. And it would take several hours for the state police to get here. We only have about an hour left of daylight as it is. I'm not even sure it's Nina's car or I would have you drive out and call for backup."

She hated it when he was so logical. She glanced tentatively over the side of the steep ravine. It made her dizzy and sick to think he was actually about to go down there.

"Don't worry, I'll walk around to where it isn't so steep. It could take me a while, though. I want you to stay in the car and lock the doors. Give me until half an hour past dark. If I'm not back by then, drive out until the radio works and call for help."

He swung a backpack over one shoulder and looked at her as if he was afraid to leave her alone. That made two of them.

"I have my gun and pepper spray," she said.

"Oh, yeah." He made it sound like she had a poisonous snake in her purse. "And handcuffs. Don't forget those."

"You aren't making fun of me, are you?"

"You know me better than that."

"You should be glad I'm armed and can protect myself."

He didn't seem to take comfort in that. "We'll discuss the legality of carrying a concealed weapon without a permit when I get back."

"It will give us something to talk about on the ride back to town," she said sarcastically.

He pointed to the patrol car, apparently waiting for her to get in it before he left.

She marched to the driver's side, opened the door and slid in, then locked the doors. As he started past to head up the road, he hesitated as if he might stop and say something more to her. It was one of those times that "I have always loved you" would have been appropriate.

Instead, he continued up the road, his back to her.

Impulsively she rolled down her window and yelled after him, "In case you never come back—" he slowed, his back still to her "—I'll miss you!"

He continued walking as if he hadn't heard her. But she knew he had. Why hadn't she said that she loved him?

Because that wasn't what he wanted to hear, she told herself as she rolled up her window and settled in for a long wait. She put the loaded Derringer on the seat beside her, the pepper spray within reach. The keys were in the ignition.

It began to rain harder. The windows fogged up instantly. She thought about starting the car, letting the heater run, clearing the windows, but feared using up the gas. She might need it more later.

It made her nervous, not being able to see what was just outside the car. She wiped at the fogged-over glass, and the surface instantly skimmed over again with condensation. When she looked at her watch, she realized Mitch had only been gone five minutes.

MITCH WALKED DOWN the road until he found a game trail that dropped down the steep wet slope. He cautiously descended, then worked his way through the wet slick vegetation.

It was getting dark fast and the rain wasn't letting up. Thick fog began to fill the ravine. He tried to move faster, thinking of Charity up on the road waiting for him, worried what she might do. He hadn't wanted to leave her alone, but then, he should never have brought her. Maybe she would have been safer back in town. With Charity, it really was a toss-up.

Ahead, he thought he caught a glimpse of chrome. He pulled the flashlight from his backpack and shone it into the dense foliage. It flickered off a piece of chrome trim.

He worked his way closer, his breath coming out in white puffs. The fog was growing denser, the slit of sky overhead darker.

A chill crept up his spine as he shone the flashlight through the branches and saw the red compact.

The car had come to rest at an odd angle at the base of a pine tree among the rocks. The front end was tilted down, the rear barely visible beneath the limbs of the pine tree.

He wondered again how the anonymous caller had found the car, fearing the only person who knew where Nina's vehicle was the one responsible for its being there. He recalled the motorcycle tracks in the muddy road.

As he neared the rear of the car, he could see that the trunk was open—and empty. The branches of the tree completely blocked the driver's side of the car. He worked his way a little more deeply into the ravine and climbed under the pine boughs on the passenger side. By standing on a rock, he was the same height as the passenger-side window.

He shone the light into the car, bracing himself.

The driver's seat was empty.

But there was something on the floor. He pulled himself up to get a closer look. In the beam of his flashlight he saw a Dennison duck decoy. The duck had been only partially painted; the rest appeared to be covered in dried blood and bits of human tissue.

He shone his flashlight into the back seat, already knowing what he'd find. Nina Monroe's bludgeoned body.

CHAPTER THIRTEEN

Friday, October 30

IT WAS MORNING by the time the state police were able to get Nina's body into the coroner's van and secure the area. The forensics team arrived at first light to go over Nina's car.

From the car's registration in the glove compartment, the body was identified as Nina Bromdale. The same last name as the woman who'd been Angela Dennison's nanny twenty-seven years ago.

Mitch could feel the pieces coming together. According to Charity, Alma Bromdale had died in mid-September. Right after that, Nina had showed up in Timber Falls and gotten a job painting decoys at Dennison Ducks.

He glanced over at Charity as they passed Lost Creek Falls. She looked tired and pale, the night's events taking a toll on her, but incredibly beautiful. He knew she must be starving. He'd offered to drive her home but she'd wanted to stay with him—and he hadn't wanted to leave the crime scene unprotected.

"I'll buy you breakfast in Oakridge," he said.

She shot him a look. "We're going to Coos Bay to talk to Alma Bromdale's sister."

He'd seen the wheels turning in her head from the moment he'd told her Nina's real last name.

As they neared the highway, he saw a car pull up next to the deputy's vehicle blocking the road. Wade Dennison got out of the car and approached the deputy.

Wade looked up as Mitch stopped the patrol car and got out. "Stay here, okay?" he said to Charity.

She was looking at Wade. Mitch saw her shiver. "No problem."

"What the hell is going on?" Wade yelled through the rain the moment he saw Mitch coming toward him. "This damned deputy won't tell me a thing."

"Let's talk in your car," Mitch said as he walked to Wade's Lincoln and got in. The engine was running, the inside of the vehicle warm and spacious.

Wade climbed behind the wheel, breathing hard from the fury he had going. And maybe from fear, Mitch thought.

"We found Nina's car," he said.

Wade's head jerked around. It was clear he'd feared that was the case.

"Nina was inside. She's dead, Wade." He wasn't sure what reaction he'd been expecting. Certainly not the one he got.

"No." It came out a wail. Wade fell over the steering wheel, his head on his arms, his body racked with sobs.

Mitch waited until Wade got himself under control again. "Nina wasn't just your employee."

Wade wiped his eyes. "I can't talk about this now." His voice sounded hoarse, raspy.

"Wade—"

"Get out of my car. Please, Mitch. I can't just now, all right?" Wade had never called him by his first name.

It was always Tanner. Or Sheriff. And Wade sure as hell had never said please.

Mitch could see that he wasn't going to get anywhere with Wade right now. He got out, then watched as Wade took off, driving too fast. Headed for Timber Falls.

Mitch turned and walked back to the patrol car and Charity.

"What kind of reaction was that?" she asked, no longer looking tired or scared as the reporter in her came out.

"Odd."

"Did he tell you what was up with him and Nina?"

Mitch shook his head. He didn't even want to admit to himself just how scared he was that Nina's death had started a chain reaction of events that would change Timber Falls forever.

He looked over at Charity, studying her as if he'd never seen her clearly before. The rain had stopped. Droplets glistened in the sunlight all around them. The flecks in Charity's eyes shone golden, her hair a wild flame of color.

She wasn't just beautiful. There was something so alive about her. So filled with energy and excitement and life. He realized he was glad right now that she was so... Charity.

"What?" she asked.

He shook his head and smiled. "I was just wondering if we're going to be able to get pie in Oakridge."

HARRIET BROMDALE LIVED in an old farmhouse just outside Coos Bay. The house had once been white just like the picket fence, but the sea air had turned it gray over the years. Several pots of petunias still bloomed on the sidewalk beside the door as Charity waited beside Mitch for someone to answer his knock.

He'd been acting strangely all morning and she still couldn't believe he'd let her tag along. He hadn't even said the words "off the record" once.

An elderly woman wearing a striped waitress's uniform and worn white shoes answered the door. Her hair was pulled back from a face wrinkled and lined. She looked too old even to be Alma's older sister.

"Whatever you're selling, I'm not buying." She started to close the door.

"I'm Sheriff Mitch Tanner from Timber Falls," Mitch said, flashing his badge.

"Timber Falls?" Harriet shook her head. "What's she done now?"

"I beg your pardon?"

"Nina." She squinted at them. "That is why you're here, isn't it?"

"Then you do know Nina," he said.

"Know her?" The woman let out a harsh laugh. "I raised her. Not that she listened to anything I ever had to say."

"So you're her…"

"Aunt." She squinted at him. "Isn't that what you wanted to talk to me about?"

"Yes. I also wanted to ask about your sister, Alma."

Harriet pursed her lips. "Like mother, like daughter."

Charity felt Mitch's gaze on her. "Nina was Alma's daughter?" Charity asked.

The older woman looked at her, then Mitch. "Isn't that what I just said?"

"Would you mind if we came in for a few minutes?" Mitch asked.

Harriet hesitated, eyes small and hooded like a snake's as she looked at him. "I have to get to work soon."

"We won't take up any more of your time than we have to," he said, and she stepped back to let them in.

The house was dark inside and had that old closed-up smell, heightened by the odor of stale cigarette smoke. Harriet led them into a living room, motioning to a broken-down couch covered in what looked like the original plastic from when it was purchased probably fifty years ago.

Harriet sat in a threadbare recliner across from them, shook a cigarette from the pack in her uniform pocket and touched the flame of a lighter to the end. She took a deep drag, exhaled and squinted at the two of them through the smoke. "So what's Nina done now?"

Mitch had taken off his hat and now held it in his hands. "I'm sorry to have to tell you that she's dead. Apparent homicide."

The older woman let out a snort. "I'm not surprised. The boyfriend do it?"

"What boyfriend would that be?"

Harriet shrugged. "Some no-account. She sure could pick 'em. They never lasted long enough for me to get their names."

"When was the last time you saw Nina?"

"A month ago. I told her not to go to Timber Falls. Look what happened to her mother up there."

Charity figured Harriet was referring to Angela

Dennison's abduction—and Alma's subsequent firing, but Harriet added, "Ended up pregnant."

"Alma was pregnant when she returned from Timber Falls?"

"Dropped off a baby for me to raise," Harriet said.

"You're sure it was her baby?" Charity had to ask, thinking of Angela. She could feel Mitch's gaze and belatedly remembered her promise just to sit quietly and let him do the talking.

The old woman frowned. "Of course it was her baby."

"You said you raised Nina? Do you have her birth certificate?" Mitch asked.

"I got a copy. You're wondering who the father is, right? Well, it wasn't on the birth certificate, and Alma would never tell. He was married. Why else would he give her all that money unless it was to keep her mouth shut?"

Charity shot Mitch an I-told-you-so look.

"Alma ran off right after dropping that bawling baby off, leaving me to raise the brat," Harriet was saying. "You think it's easy raising a kid by yourself? Did Nina appreciate the sacrifices I made? Ha. She always thought she deserved better."

"Could I see that copy of her birth certificate?" Mitch asked.

Harriet glanced at her watch, made an unpleasant face and pushed herself out of the recliner, then left the room. Charity could hear her rummaging around in a nearby room. The old woman returned after a few minutes and handed Mitch an Oregon birth certificate for Nina Ann Bromdale. Charity leaned close enough to read it. Nina was born in March—just two months after Angela Dennison, then three months old, had been taken from her crib in Timber Falls.

"How old was the baby when Alma left her with you?" Charity just had to ask.

Harriet shrugged. "Six, eight months old." It was obvious it made no difference to her.

"Do you mind if I take this?" Mitch asked, holding up the certificate.

"Keep it. I don't want it," Harriet said. "I imagine you'll want me to bury her. Just got through burying her mother in September. Cancer." The woman nodded as if Alma had brought the cancer on herself.

"Alma say anything about Nina's father before she died?" Mitch asked.

Harriett glared down at the cigarette between her fingers. "I didn't even hear she was dead until Nina came back from Mexico and told me. On her deathbed she had someone track down Nina, just had to tell Nina a bunch of stuff that she knew would set the girl off."

"Like what?" Charity asked.

"Maybe about the girl's father. Alma wasn't even cold in her grave before Nina took off for Timber Falls, saying she was going to finally get what she deserved. Guess she did."

"I don't think anyone deserves to be murdered," Mitch said.

Harriet barked a laugh. "You didn't know Nina now, did you."

"So Nina went to Timber Falls to see her father?"

"See him?" Harriet let out another sarcastic bark. "She hated him. Blamed him for everything. She went up there to blackmail every last cent out of him, then make him pay. That's what she said, 'make him damned sorry.'"

"Did Alma ever talk about the baby that was abducted while she was a nanny in Timber Falls?" Mitch asked.

Harriet took a puff on her cigarette. "Those rich people's baby? They fired Alma over it."

"What was her side of the story?" Mitch asked.

"She said she didn't know nothin'." Harriet rolled her eyes. "I wouldn't be surprised if Alma had something to do with that baby disappearing."

"Why do you say that?" Mitch asked.

"All that money she supposedly got from her baby's father," Harriet said. "What man would do that?"

Charity looked at Mitch.

"Didn't you ever wonder if maybe the baby your sister brought you was the Dennison's missing baby?" he asked.

"I'm no fool," Harriet said, sounding angry. "But I also know when to keep my mouth shut. Didn't have nothin' to do with me."

Charity watched Mitch rake his hand through his hair in frustration. "Have you ever seen this?" Mitch said as he pulled the baby spoon out of his pocket.

Harriett started to reach for it, but then pulled her hand back. "That belonged to that baby, didn't it?"

He nodded. "Did Alma ever show it to you?"

She shook her head violently.

"Nina had this spoon," he said.

Harriett got to her feet a little unsteadily. "I have to get to work."

Mitch and Charity got to their feet, as well. "If you think of anything else…" Mitch handed Harriet his card.

She took it reluctantly, as if she thought it might contaminate her. "It's that town. It's evil."

MITCH COULD TELL that Charity was bursting at the seams to say something. "Nina Ann Bromdale could have been Angela," she said the moment they were in the patrol car. "Even if the birth certificate is real, Harriet had no idea how old Nina was when she got her."

He nodded. "But nothing is definite without DNA testing, and I'm not sure Wade will agree to it."

"That's crazy. If Nina was Angela... You don't think Wade would kill his own daughter?"

Mitch shook his head, remembering Wade's reaction. "I think there's more to the story and I'm not convinced Nina *was* Angela."

Charity was quiet for a few miles. "The town isn't evil."

"It's the rain," he said. "The rain and the isolation, the dark days trapped inside. It makes people in Timber Falls crazy."

She looked over at him. "So why do you stay?"

The question took him by surprise. He frowned, unable to answer.

Charity was smiling smugly as if she thought she knew the reason. He'd only left long enough to graduate from college. She'd left only long enough to get her journalism degree. Did she think he only stayed because she was there?

"I want to talk to the jeweler in Eugene who made the baby spoon," he said, changing the subject. "But I would imagine you're hungry again, aren't you?"

They ate in a small café overlooking the water. Charity had fried oysters, French fries and coleslaw, followed by a piece of coconut-cream pie. He had the red snapper, but he hardly tasted it. He couldn't quit thinking about Nina and Wade and Angela, and those damned motorcycle tracks in the mud. Or what Harriet had said about Nina coming back from Mexico to see her mother. Mexico.

"This pie isn't as good as Betty's," Charity said, and smiled at him.

Why did he stay in Timber Falls? He had a bad feeling it was because of the woman across the table from him. And an even worse feeling that she knew it.

A NICELY DRESSED gray-haired woman looked up from behind the counter at Hart's Jewelry as they entered.

The woman's face brightened at the sight of them. "Good afternoon. Let me guess. You're looking for an engagement ring. I can always tell."

Mitch saw Charity's face redden with embarrassment. His own stomach tightened. "We're here on official business," he said, and flashed his badge.

"I'm sorry, I just… What can I help you with, Sheriff? I'm Lois Hart, the owner."

Charity wandered over to a display case. He watched her admire a silver bracelet as he took the baby spoon from his pocket and set it gingerly on the glass counter.

The clerk picked it up, seeming to recognize it.

"I understand this spoon was made here, designed especially for Wade Dennison of Dennison Ducks," Mitch said, watching her face.

"My husband made it." Her voice broke and Mitch knew what was coming: "He died four years ago."

"I'm sorry. How many of these did your husband make?"

"Two sets. One for the first baby, engraved with that baby's name, and a second for the new baby. Mr. Dennison was very explicit. He made my husband promise never to make another set like them. Of course my husband never did."

"You're sure this is your husband's work?"

"Oh, yes," she said with a soft smile.

"No one ever requested he make another set?"

She shook her head. "We were just sick when we heard about what happened, someone stealing that baby. Was she ever found?"

He shook his head.

She held out the baby spoon to him as if she no longer liked holding it. "What kind of monster would do that?"

Mitch wished he knew. "Well, thank you for your time," he said as he took the spoon and pocketed it again. Charity was still at the display counter looking at the silver bracelet again. "Here is my card if you think of anything else."

"Sorry about that mix-up back there," he said as he and Charity headed for his patrol car.

She gave him a small smile. "I've pretty much accepted that I'm going to be an old maid."

He laughed. "I can't see you as an old maid." He hated the thought of Charity not being loved and cherished and cared for. She deserved more. But he also hated the thought of her with another man. "But then, you already have the cat."

She made a face. "Where to now?"

He pulled his keys out of his pocket as they reached the patrol car. "I just remembered something I forgot to ask Mrs. Hart. Wait for me in the car for a minute?"

She nodded and took the keys.

He trotted back to the store. Lois Hart looked up in surprise. "There's a silver bracelet my friend was looking at." He pointed to the one Charity hadn't been able to take her eyes off. "Would you wrap it? I'd like to buy it."

Lois Hart smiled. "So I *was* right about the two of you."

Mitch didn't bother to correct her. As he walked back to the patrol car and Charity, he felt the small wrapped jewelry box in his pocket and wondered what had possessed him. He couldn't give it to her. She'd get the wrong impression, and that would only make things worse between them.

He cursed his moment of weakness. He hadn't thought. He'd just wanted her to have the bracelet.

"Did you ask her the question you forgot?" Charity inquired as he climbed behind the wheel.

"Yeah." He turned on the ignition, the small package in his pocket feeling as weighty as the silver spoon.

On the way back to Timber Falls, Charity gave up trying to draw him into conversation and finally curled up and slept.

Mitch got the call just outside of town. "Nina Bromdale's got a sheet on her," the trooper from the state police informed him. He rattled off a series of arrests for shoplifting, misdemeanor theft and driving while under the influence. "Her last arrest was in San Diego. She and her boyfriend were both picked up after a city cop pulled her over. The boyfriend was driving. He got a DUI. She got thirty days for resisting arrest and disorderly conduct."

"Boyfriend?"

"Let me check here. Yeah. Name's Jesse Tanner. Tanner. Any relation?"

"Afraid so." Jesse hadn't just known Nina, he'd shared the back seat of a cop car with her. Mitch felt sick. So much for his brother's coming back to Timber Falls because he was homesick—or to steal Charity. Jesse had come back because of Nina. But what worried Mitch were the motorcycle tracks on the road into where Nina's car—and body—were found.

Charity was snuggled against the passenger-side door sound asleep when he pulled up in front of his house. When he went around and opened the passenger-side door, she practically tumbled into his arms, stirring just long enough to wrap her arms around his neck.

As he carried her into the house, she sighed against his neck and smiled in her sleep, murmuring something that sounded...like banana cream?

By the time he lowered her to the bed in the spare room, she was snoring softly. He smiled to himself as he slipped off her boots and drew the quilt over her. Then he stood for a moment just looking down at her.

How was he going to protect her from herself?

That was when he remembered her cat. He called her house. Florie had gone home it seemed. He dug a can of tuna out of his kitchen cabinet and walked next door with Charity's house key from her purse.

"Winky? Winky?" In the kitchen he opened the tuna. Still no cat. Didn't most cats come running when they heard the can opener? Leave it to Charity to have a cat that was the exception to the rule.

He put the can of tuna on the floor and glanced around. No cat. Why was he surprised she even had a cat? He locked up behind him and hurried back to his house.

Charity was still fast asleep. He shook his head, smiling to himself, then stretched out, fully clothed, on the couch in the next room. She was safe. At least for tonight. He closed his eyes, listening to the sound of her breathing on the other side of the wall, no longer kidding himself.

He stayed in Timber Falls because of Charity.

CHAPTER FOURTEEN

Halloween

CHARITY OPENED HER EYES, the remnants of the dream still clinging and the blinding daylight coming through the window. She didn't want to leave the dream—and Mitch, who was wearing that black tuxedo again and looked so handsome....

She blinked. Why were the curtains open? Why were there no curtains at all? She blinked again. Because it wasn't her bedroom. It wasn't her bed. It wasn't even her house!

She sat up with a start, not sure for a moment where she was. Then she saw Mitch's uniform hat on a bureau by the door and through the open doorway, spotted his boots off the end of the couch.

She pulled down the quilt, disappointed to see that she was fully dressed. Darn. Slipping her legs over the side of the bed, she got up and tiptoed into the living room, trying to piece together last night.

Something told her nothing had happened between her and Mitch. Nothing at all. The man either had the strength of will of a saint or she wasn't as irresistible as she'd hoped. That was an awful thought.

Then she reminded herself she was holding out for marriage. Right.

Mitch was sound asleep on the couch. He looked wonderful. She leaned closer to study his handsome face. Suddenly he grabbed her, flipped her over on the couch and was on top of her before she knew what was happening.

"NEVER SNEAK UP on a man of the law," he growled down at her. "I could have shot you."

She smiled. "You would never shoot me. You might want to but—"

He silenced her with a kiss, drawing her into his arms without even thinking. She was still warm from sleep, soft in all the right places, her mouth so absolutely perfect. He could have kissed her until Christmas—

He jerked back at the sound of someone banging on his front door. Past Charity, he could see Wade Dennison's large frame through the bamboo blinds. Damn. Mitch looked at Charity. Desire burned bright in her eyes, making him weak in the knees. This woman would be the death of him. But the pounding on the door was too insistent to ignore.

"I need to talk to Wade," he said as rolled off her. Wade had saved him. So why wasn't he happy about that?

"I need to go to the paper," Charity said. "You aren't going to try to stop me from doing the story on Nina's murder, are you?"

He heard the challenge in her voice. "I'm no fool." That, of course, was debatable. He couldn't keep her from doing the story any more than he could keep her with him 24/7, and they both knew it.

"But you're taking a deputy with you," he said. "No

arguments." He picked up his cell phone and made the call as he tried to calm down physically before opening the door.

She didn't argue as she sashayed into the spare bedroom for her shoes. Mitch went to the front door and opened it.

"I have to talk to you." Wade shot a look at Charity as she swept past him, but had the good sense not to say anything. The moment the door closed behind Charity, Wade crossed to a chair and slumped into it.

"Nina was my daughter," Wade said, and put his head in his hands.

Mitch sat down. "Angela?"

"Angela?" Wade raised his head and frowned. "Not Angela. Nina. Aren't you listening to me? Do I have to spell it out for you? I had an affair with Alma."

Mitch stared at him. "Alma? Alma was pregnant with your baby?"

He nodded. "Daisy was pregnant and driving me crazy. There were rumors that the baby wasn't mine…" He waved a hand. "Alma overheard us arguing one night and…comforted me after Daisy went to bed…." He stopped and looked up.

"Alma got pregnant?"

Wade nodded.

"How much money did you give her to keep quiet?"

"Quiet?" Wade shook his head, his brow furrowing. "No, I gave her money to take care of our baby."

Mitch decided not to argue the point. "Wade, I know Nina came to Timber Falls to blackmail you."

"It wasn't like that. She was my daughter. Of course I'd give her money. I just wanted to help her."

"How much *help* was Nina demanding?"

Wade shot up out of the chair. "This is exactly why I didn't tell you," he said angrily. "I knew you'd try to make more out of this than it was. Nina wanted to do something with her life. I offered to help. I gave her a job. I offered her money."

Mitch took a deep breath. "Wade, if she was your daughter, then why keep it a secret?"

The older man closed his eyes and wagged his large head as he sank back down again. "I couldn't do that to Daisy. You know how she's been since Angela disappeared. I couldn't spring this daughter on her. Daisy and I spent years trying to find Angela, following up every lead only to reach another dead end. Nina understood that I couldn't tell Daisy. In fact, she insisted we keep it between the two of us. She didn't want to destroy my life. She just needed a little help to realize her dreams."

The Nina everyone described wouldn't have let Wade off that easily. "What was the price of those dreams?"

Wade's gaze narrowed, and anger sparked again in his eyes. "You're one cynical bastard, aren't you, Tanner."

Mitch waited.

"A million." He held up a hand. "It was money I'd put away for Angela twenty-seven years ago. I got lucky in a couple of investments." He shrugged.

He had given Nina Angela's money? Mitch wondered how Daisy would have taken that if she'd found out. "A million dollars is a lot of dreams. What if Angela turned up?" Or was Wade sure she never would?

"Nina was my daughter," Wade said defensively.

"You know that for sure?" Mitch had to ask.

"Alma was a virgin the night… I know, okay?" He shook his head. "Don't you believe anything anyone tells you?"

"Not really. So when were you going to give her the money?"

"I'd already put it in an account for her. I was to meet her at the plant Tuesday night to give her all the paperwork, but she wasn't there. Then when I didn't hear from her or she didn't show up at the plant…."

"What time were you to meet her?"

"Ten. I got there, but there was no sign of her."

Mitch rubbed his forehead. "Why were you so sure she'd come to harm?"

Wade sighed. "She wouldn't have walked away from the money, all right?" He sounded tired, defeated, a broken man.

Mitch could only imagine how Nina had worn him down until he promised to give her a million dollars. "Did you hire a private investigator to follow Charity?"

Wade frowned. "Why would I do that?"

"Just a day ago you threatened to kill her."

"I was angry and upset. But I certainly didn't hire anyone to follow her." He was still frowning, and Mitch wondered if he was worrying that Daisy might have hired the P.I.

"Did you ever employ a private investigator named Kyle L. Rogers out of Portland?" He could see that Wade had.

"If you're thinking that Daisy…"

"I'm just asking questions, Wade. That's what I do. I follow any lead I get and see where it goes." Mitch raked a hand through his hair. His head hurt. "Nina make any enemies that you know of?"

"She didn't get along with people all that well." No kidding. "She had trouble with the other painters, but I can't believe any of them—"

"Anyone else?"

Wade sighed. "I saw her arguing with Bud once, but everyone argues with Bud."

Mitch couldn't disagree with that. "Know what they argued about?"

Wade shrugged. "You'd have to ask Bud."

Bud had said they'd never spoken two words. "Where was this and when?"

"Outside the plant Monday afternoon."

So that's who Nina had been arguing with when Charity had seen her and taken her photo.

"Look, Wade, I know you were spying on Nina. Charity saw you in the trees. Why?"

"I was afraid she'd get in some sort of trouble before she left town."

"Or were you afraid she'd renege on your deal and tell everyone the truth?" What if there really was a letter from Nina to Charity? Maybe Wade just *feared* there was.

Wade got to his feet, his face turning bright red. "Maybe Nina would have been different if she'd had a father growing up."

Or maybe not. "I'm sorry about your daughter, but my job now is to find her killer. Did either Daisy or Desiree know about this financial arrangement you had with Nina?"

"Leave my family out of this."

"This is a murder investigation, Wade. Tell your family before I have to."

CHARITY WENT RIGHT to work on her stories, first writing about the Bigfoot sighting, which was starting to feel like old news, then the story about Nina Bromdale's murder.

She wished she had more information. But unfortunately Wade thwarted her attempts to talk to anyone who worked at Dennison Ducks. It seemed he'd told his staff that anyone who talked to the press would be fired.

She also couldn't print anything about the possibility of Nina being Angela Dennison. Not without proof. But how was she going to get proof?

As she sat down at her computer, she felt anxious—even with the Derringer, pepper spray and handcuffs in her purse and a deputy sitting in the corner. Nina had been murdered and the killer was still out there.

Worse, she knew Mitch wouldn't have put a deputy on her unless he thought she was in danger. That had to mean he bought her theory about the letter. He hardly ever bought her theories—and he'd kissed her three times in the past two days. That had to mean something, too, right?

She'd gone to her house, showered and changed before coming to the newspaper office, all the time knowing a deputy was not far away, but she still kept looking over her shoulder. As she went back over the past few days, she tried to imagine how all the pieces fit together. That was the problem. They didn't.

Worse, she didn't really have enough facts to do a story on the murder for this week. If only Nina really had written down her life story for Charity and—mailed it—and there really *was* a letter.

She looked up as the door opened. The deputy was already on his feet, hand on his revolver. "It's all right," she said, waving him back into his seat. "It's my assistant, Blaine."

Blaine didn't look any the worse for wear since being bound and left in an alley. In fact, he looked downright cheerful as he came in. She noticed he had a sketchbook in his hand. "I drew you something."

She made room on her desk for the book.

"I heard you lost your photo of Nina Monroe. I saw her a few times when I took papers up to Dennison Ducks. So…" He flipped open the sketchbook.

Charity gasped as she stared down at a perfect likeness of Nina Bromdale, aka Monroe.

AFTER WADE LEFT, and with Charity gone, Mitch noticed how empty his house seemed. He stood in the middle of the room, his senses assaulted by her. He could still smell the light scent of her perfume. Still taste her on his lips.

He should have known that having Charity here even for one night was going to change the way he felt about a lot of things—including this house.

He couldn't imagine opening the door without feeling as if something was missing once her scent had faded and the cool quiet had settled back in.

As if he didn't have enough trouble, he noticed jack-o'-lanterns on porches and cardboard goblins taped in windows as he drove through town. Halloween. He'd almost forgotten. All he needed now was a full moon. Every weirdo in town would be going crazy tonight—and there was already a killer on the loose.

His first stop was the post office to check Charity's mailbox. More than ever he wondered if Charity wasn't right about Nina writing a letter to the paper. But had the woman just been planning to expose her father? He couldn't forget the baby spoon he'd carried around in his jacket pocket.

Also from what he'd been told about Nina, he couldn't imagine that she'd just take the money and run. She'd wanted revenge. And a letter to the local paper gave credibility to Charity's attack at the post office.

But there was no letter from Nina in the newspaper post-office box. Charity would be disappointed that her theory wasn't panning out. No more disappointed than he was.

He wanted this case over and done with as quickly as possible. Letter or no letter Charity was in danger. He felt it, just a nagging feeling he couldn't shake.

He stopped by her office and gave her the mail from her post-office box, relieved to see she was busy at her computer with the deputy watching over her.

"No letter," Charity said seeing his face.

He shook his head. "If she'd mailed it before she was killed, it would have been here by now."

She nodded, then said, "Look what Blaine drew," she said excitedly.

He looked at the eerie likeness of Nina Bromdale on the computer screen next to the headline Quest to Find Father Ends in Murder. Under the sketch of Nina was the cutline "Who is this woman really?"

"Can we talk in the darkroom?" Mitch asked.

Charity smiled at him as if she thought it was just

a ploy so he could kiss her again. She got to her feet and led the way to the darkroom. He closed the door behind them.

"I need to tell you something," he said.

"Let me guess. Off the record? See, I'm getting where I can read your mind."

He hoped not. "Wade was Nina's father."

"So she *was* Angela!"

"No. It seems he had an affair with Alma."

"Get out of here."

"All we have is Alma's word that the baby was even his. Until we run the DNA, I'm still skeptical," Mitch said. "But Wade believed it. He was planning to give Nina money the night she disappeared."

"How much?"

"A cool million."

Charity let out a whistle. "If Wade really is Nina's father, then he paid Alma to keep quiet about it and now Nina. Or at least claims he was going to pay her off before she was killed."

Mitch did love Charity's mind sometimes. She could have been a cop.

"You don't think Wade…"

"Killed her?" He shook his head. "I don't know. Nina sounds like she was pretty coldhearted. Wade had to know that when she went through that million she'd be back demanding more."

"You think there's more to the story, don't you," Charity said. "Angela's baby spoon."

He nodded. "I think maybe there was more black-mail involved than just her paternity. I think she might have known who kidnapped Angela."

Charity nodded. "That's exactly what I think."

Yeah. Mitch thought. Maybe the two of them were getting where they could read each other's mind. Now, that *was* a scary idea.

He stepped to the darkroom door. It was too tight in here, too intimate. "I have to go. If you need me, call."

She laughed softly. "I might take you up on that."

Outside again, he started the patrol car, her words echoing in his head. She'd always held out for marriage, and that had kept him safe. He didn't want to think of what would happen if Charity changed her mind.

He headed out of town, dreading what he had to do. He wasn't looking forward to confronting his brother Jesse. And the last thing he wanted to do was see his father. Maybe he'd luck out and the old man would be at the bar. *Huh,* he thought. *First time I've ever wished that.*

He hadn't seen his father in months and only then in passing. He couldn't remember the last time they'd spoken. When he'd left home at eighteen, it had been for good. He'd never been back.

Lee Tanner opened the door at Mitch's knock almost as if he'd been expecting him. Lee was a big man, handsome to a fault, and from old family money. The latter had proved to be a curse since it afforded his father too much time to drink. He wasn't a mean drunk. Mitch couldn't remember his father ever raising his voice. He was just a drunk.

"I need to see Jesse," Mitch said, looking past his father. The house was neat as a pin. That surprised him. Nor did he pick up the smell of alcohol when his father said, "Jesse will be back shortly. Come on in, son."

The "son" grated, but Mitch didn't say anything. He hadn't come here to fight, just to try to get the truth out of Jesse. Who was he kidding? That would take a fight for sure, and even then Mitch couldn't trust that his brother would be truthful.

"It's good to see you," Lee said. "Can I offer you something to drink?"

"I don't drink."

Lee smiled. "I was thinking maybe a soda or a glass of iced tea. I have both."

Iced tea in this house? He'd believe it when he saw it. "Iced tea, then."

Lee walked into the kitchen, which was open to the living room, and took down two glasses before opening the fridge and pulling out a pitcher of iced tea. How about that? His father had definitely been expecting him. This had to be some kind of show.

Mitch glanced around the place, rather than watch his father fill the glasses. Lee had designed the house himself. At one time, he'd been an architect in Seattle. Then he'd married Ruth Marks, built this house and had two sons.

His father handed him a glass and took the other.

"Thanks." Mitch couldn't remember his father ever drinking iced tea.

"Have a seat. Jesse should be back soon."

"I'd rather stand."

His father took a sip of the tea and didn't even grimace at the taste. Maybe he'd put a little something in his.

"How long has Jesse been staying with you?" Mitch asked.

"Are you asking as a brother or a cop?"

"Does it matter?"

Lee smiled again. "Since late Saturday night. He'd

called to say he was coming home and asked if he could stay here for a while." Lee looked up, meeting Mitch's gaze. "It sure is nice to have the company. I'm trying to talk him into staying longer."

"Is he thinking about leaving?" If Jesse left now, he'd only look all the more guilty.

"He wants a place of his own. He's considering buying the old Kramer land outside of town. I'm surprised, too. But I think he missed his home. I know he missed you. He's hoping to mend a few fences. He's changed, Mitch."

Mitch stared at his father, not believing a word of it. "Yeah, he says you've changed, too." He hadn't meant to sound so cynical.

Lee chuckled. "Hard to believe, huh."

"Next to impossible."

His father's smile never wavered. "Stranger things have happened."

"What would Jesse do in Timber Falls?"

"Didn't he tell you about his paintings? Your brother's quite the artist."

The back door slammed and Mitch heard the sound of approaching footsteps. Jesse used to draw some when they were kids, but since when had he become an artist? And since when had their father become so naive?

Lee Tanner turned toward Jesse as he came through the kitchen. "Mitch is here. Why don't the two of you go out on the deck for some privacy?" He downed the rest of his iced tea, then took the glass into the kitchen to rinse it out.

"Yeah, let's talk outside," Mitch said, putting his unfinished iced tea on the kitchen counter.

Jesse shrugged and opened the front door. They stepped out onto the covered deck that ran the length of the front of the house.

"So, little bro," Jesse said. "Glad to see you took my advice and came out."

"Tell me about Nina Bromdale."

Jesse walked to the railing and leaned against it. "I wondered how long it would take you."

"She was your girlfriend."

"*Was* is the key word here."

"She's why you came back to Timber Falls."

Jesse shook his head. "It's a lot more complicated than that. You ever meet her?"

Mitch shook his head.

"Lucky you."

"She's dead," Mitch said. "Murdered, but I think you already know that. I saw your bike tracks on the road where Nina's car was found."

Jesse didn't say anything. "You going to arrest me for her murder?"

Mitch hoped he'd never have to. "Did you kill her?"

"No, but what are the chances of you believing that?"

"Why don't you try telling me the truth?"

"I wasn't lying about missing you and Dad."

"And Charity?" Mitch had gotten a print off the stone heart.

Jesse's.

He smiled. "I admit I gave her the presents. Maybe I thought if she had a secret admirer, you might wake up and admit how you feel about her. Maybe I'd hoped she was available." He shrugged and grinned.

The latter sounded more like it. "It was you in her house the other night, wasn't it."

Jesse nodded. "I saw someone go around the back of her house. I scared him off, but the back window had been pried open."

Mitch had found that when he'd investigated the break-in, but that didn't mean Jesse hadn't been the one to do it. "So you just climbed in?"

"I wanted to make sure there wasn't anyone else in the house."

Mitch shook his head. "You always have an answer, don't you."

"Maybe it's just the truth," Jesse said.

"When was the last time you saw Nina?"

"Monday."

The day before she disappeared.

"I don't expect you to believe me, but I thought I could stop her."

"Stop her from what?"

Jesse rubbed his jaw. "Getting herself killed."

"You knew what she was doing here?"

"I knew Nina had this thing about finding her father and making him pay."

Making him pay. Just as Harriet had said. Just as Charity had theorized. "She tell you who her father was?"

Jesse shook his head. "She didn't know. Then she got this message from her mother. Next thing I heard she was in Timber Falls."

"You said you saw her Monday. Where?"

Jesse sighed. "At her bungalow. She told me to get lost."

"Come on, Jesse. You didn't just come up here to try to save Nina."

His brother smiled. "Okay, she ripped me off when she left. She took some things of mine." He saw Mitch's expression. "Some canvases, if you must know. I'd been painting down in Mexico. Sold a few. She ripped me off when she left to go see her mother. I wanted the canvases back."

"Did you get them?"

"She'd already sold them. I was pissed. We argued. That was the last time I saw her." He paused. "You don't believe me."

"How did you know where her car was?"

Jesse sighed. "You told me that a black pickup had been following Charity. I followed one out of town. It led me to the car."

"You were the one who called it in?" Mitch asked in surprise.

Jesse nodded.

"Why didn't you give Sissy your name?"

He shrugged. "Never did like talking to cops."

"What about the truck?"

"I lost it. Or it lost me."

Mitch took off his hat and raked a hand through his hair. "Any chance forensics is going to find your prints in that car?"

"I'd be surprised if they didn't. Nina and I spent the past four months together down south."

"How *did* you hear that Nina was in Timber Falls?"

"Dad saw her and recognized her from a photo of the two of us in Mexico I'd sent him."

Mitch stared at his brother for a moment, then turned to go. "Don't leave town."

"Aren't you going to tell Dad goodbye?" Jesse asked. "He's been on the wagon."

"Right."

"Cut him some slack, little bro. He's trying damned hard and all because of you."

"Me?"

"That's right. He feels bad about the years he drowned himself in a bottle after our mother left."

"He should. His running around is why she left us."

"Like hell it is."

Mitch started to leave again. "I don't want to hear this."

"Well, you're going to," Jesse said, grabbing his sleeve and jerking him around to face him. "All these years you've blamed Dad because she left us. It's time you heard the truth. She left because she never loved him or us. She married him because he had money and because the man she really loved had married someone else."

"That's a lie!" Mitch snapped, jerking free. "He was drinking and having an affair with Daisy Dennison."

Jesse shook his head. "I was older than you. I remember the night she told him she'd never loved him, never wanted us, would rather be dead than stay with him. He loved her, man, and he was devastated. She demanded money so she could leave. He refused to let her go."

"So he had an affair."

"I know you were only six, but don't you remember how she was with us?" Jesse asked. "All the mornings she stayed in bed, didn't even get up to see us off to school."

Her disinterest was because of their father's unfaithfulness. He could remember well their father standing at the stove frying bacon, the quiet in the house so loud it was deafening. "She was depressed because she was married to a cheating drunk."

"Dad finally gave her the money she needed to leave. I followed Dad into the woods that day." Jesse's throat moved as if the words were stones he could barely swallow. "He fell to the ground and... I've never seen anyone cry like that."

Mitch stared at his brother, the weight on his chest unbearable. He wanted to defend their mother, but nothing came out. His memories of the past that had once been so clear now felt so damaged that he couldn't make sense of them. His father putting an arm around his mother's shoulders. Her shrugging it off. The hurt in his father's eyes, the pain.

"She wasn't any good—"

"Don't," their father said from the doorway. "Your mother loved you both. She wanted to take you, but she wasn't strong enough to raise two boys on her own."

The lie hung in the air.

Mitch met Jesse's gaze, the truth like an arrow through his heart. He glanced at the doorway, but his father was gone.

Jesse stepped to Mitch and hugged him tightly. Tears in his eyes, he let go, turned and walked back toward the front door, leaving Mitch standing on the deck alone.

Mitch felt sick. Was it possible he'd been wrong about everything he'd believed? All these years, why hadn't his father said something? But he knew the answer to that. No one had wanted to admit just what kind of mother Mitch had really had.

His cell phone rang. "Yes?"

"Thought you'd want this right away," said the head of forensics. "We got two matches on that decoy we found in the victim's car. Her prints and an Ethel Whiting's."

CHAPTER FIFTEEN

IT WAS LATE AFTERNOON and the rain was making the day even darker when Ethel Whiting opened her front door.

"I wondered when you'd be back." She motioned Mitch into the parlor.

"Your fingerprints were found on the decoy that was used to kill Nina Bromdale," he said as followed her into her sitting room.

Ethel lowered herself into a chair. "Bromdale?"

"It seems she might be the nanny's daughter," Mitch said. "Alma and Wade's daughter."

Ethel's face seemed to crumble. "She wasn't Angela?"

"No." It was obvious she'd wanted to believe that Nina was Daisy's and some other man's besides Wade. "I think you should call your lawyer, Ethel."

She shook her head. "I would have told you yesterday, but I thought Nina was still alive when her body wasn't found at Dennison Ducks. I didn't go to the plant Tuesday night planning to kill her. At least I don't think so. I didn't know who she was, just that she posed a danger to Wade. I thought I could scare her into leaving him alone." She laughed softly. "Nothing could scare that young woman. I could see that there wasn't enough money in the world to buy her off, either. We argued. She'd put down the duck she'd been painting. I hardly remember picking it up and hitting her."

"Was she dead?"

She looked up. "I thought so. I didn't check her pulse. I just dropped the decoy next to her body. I assumed as soon as you found her body and the murder weapon…"

"You knew your fingerprints were it?"

"Of course. And that they'd be on file. My parents had me fingerprinted as a child. They worried that because of their affluence, someone might kidnap me," Ethel said. "Ironic, isn't it."

"You didn't put Nina in her car and drive it into a ravine south of town?"

She gave him a sympathetic look. "I am not a deceitful woman, Mitchell. I did nothing to cover my crime. I had some things I wanted to get in order and I preferred spending what days I had left here in the house. I've been waiting for you to arrest me."

"What time did you go to the plant?" he asked.

"A little before nine. Her car was in the lot. I knew she worked late a lot. Whatever that woman had on Wade, I could see what it was doing to him. I had to stop her."

She'd done this for Wade. Mitch shook his head, remembering that Wade said he went to the plant at ten and Nina was gone. "Either Nina wasn't dead, or someone moved her body."

"Why would they do that?" Ethel asked.

"Is it possible Wade saw you leaving the plant Tuesday night? He found Nina's body and tried to cover for you?"

She shook her head. "Wade has made a lot of poor

decisions in his life, but he would never cover up a murder."

Ethel had a lot more faith in Wade than Mitch did. But then, love was blind, wasn't it?

"I'll have someone come over to take you in."

She gave him a reproachful look. "I'll be right here, Mitchell."

As he was about to call headquarters, he got another call. This one from the state police. Private investigator Kyle L. Rogers's body had just been found in a motel room in Oakridge. He'd been shot at close range with a small-caliber weapon. His black pickup was nowhere to be found. "I'm on my way."

CHARITY HAD HER latest edition out and on the streets by late afternoon. It was going to be her best-selling newspaper by all accounts. Blaine was out delivering papers. The deputy Mitch had guarding her was sitting in the corner, thumbing through a magazine.

She'd finished all her work and was thinking about Mitch when he walked through the door. She knew something was wrong the moment she saw him.

"Kyle Rogers's body had been found in a motel in Oakridge. Homicide," Mitch told her and the deputy.

"I want you to go home, Charity. I've already called Florie. She's meeting you at the house."

"Okay." He'd obviously expected her to argue and seemed surprised when she didn't. And pleased. Was it this easy to please the man?

"I have to run down to Oakridge, then I'll come by the house. I won't be long."

"Don't worry about me," she told Mitch. "I'm sure Florie will bring her baseball bat and I have an armed deputy. What more could a girl want?" She wanted Mitch's strong arms around her. This being independent all the time was getting old.

"Promise me you'll put the gun and pepper spray away with all the kids out trick-or-treating tonight."

She nodded. "As soon as I get home."

He glanced at the deputy. "You'll stay with her?"

"Sure thing."

Mitch walked her out to the deputy's car. The rain had stopped temporarily, but low-hunkering clouds cast an eerie glow over the town. Fog drifted out of the woods like ghosts to haunt the narrow streets.

Jack-o'-lanterns flickered in front of several businesses. With everything that had been happening, Charity realized she'd forgotten to buy treats for the kids. She'd have to stop on the way home.

"Be careful?" Mitch said.

It was another one of those moments when a kiss would have been nice. But she couldn't see Mitch kissing her in front of the deputy. "I will," she said, then watched him drive away.

"We need to stop by the grocery store on the way home," she told the deputy once they were in his car. "I have to pick up some candy for the trick-or-treaters. My Aunt Florie will bring things like carob cookies or tofu popcorn balls. I really don't want to get my windows soaped and egged."

She thought he might argue with her. Or maybe she just expected all men to argue with her the way Mitch did. So she was a little perplexed when he just laughed.

Little ghosts and goblins were already out trick-or-treating. Halloween was a big deal in Timber Falls. Everyone got into the act at a huge costume party at the

Duck-In. As the deputy drove her home from the grocery, they passed groups of children and adults dressed as vampires and zombies, aliens and witches.

Charity couldn't help but shiver. There was a killer out there, maybe closer than any of them thought.

A group of costumed kids skittered across the street in front of them, squealing and shrieking as the deputy pulled up in front of her house.

The kids clambered up the steps to the porch. A moment later Florie opened the door and began dispensing something from a large bowl. Nothing good, Charity was sure of that.

She got out of the car with the huge bag of candy she'd bought at the store. She turned at the sound of another vehicle. A UPS truck lumbered to a stop beside her. "Got a package for you," Chuck the UPS man called down to her from his truck.

The deputy had climbed out and come around to her side of the car. "Here," she said, shoving the bag of candy at the deputy. "Get up there on the porch and save my windows."

The deputy took the bag and hurried up the steps as Chuck held out his clipboard. "Need your signature right there, Charity."

She signed and he handed her a large cardboard envelope. Wishing her a happy Halloween, he hopped back into the truck and took off down the street as the first drops of rain began to fall again.

It wasn't until then that she looked at what he'd given her. Even in the dim light, she could read the sender's name: Nina Monroe. Charity's hands began to shake as she tore the parcel open to find a small white envelope inside with her name on it.

Rain fell harder and she started to open the purse hanging from her shoulder to stuff the letter inside. Unfortunately she had way too much in her purse already—gun, pepper spray, handcuffs—so she quickly shoved the letter into her jacket and zipped it closed.

She'd gotten a letter from a dead woman. The letter someone had been looking for? She couldn't wait to get inside and open it, even though she knew she should wait until Mitch got there.

Behind her on the porch children chattered, and more were coming up the street. As she turned toward the house, she caught movement in the trees next to her. Her heart leaped to her throat as a huge dark object came flying out of the trees like a giant bat.

But it was only a person in a hooded black cape, the face a grotesque rubbery mask. Her first thought was that it was one of the parents taking his kids trick-or-treating, someone she knew, someone just trying to scare her.

But she was too scared to speak when he grabbed her and tried to rip her coat open. It took her only an instant to realize that he was after the letter.

She screamed and fought him off, managing to break free. She could see the deputy trying to get through the cluster of kids to her.

But another cluster of kids had just started up the stairs to the porch, and the caped man was on her again. She fought him, clawing at his eyes, managing to pull his mask away for an instant. Just long enough to see his face. Bud Farnsworth! The foreman at Dennison Ducks.

She opened her mouth to scream again, but he clamped his gloved hand over her mouth and, lifting her, ran into the trees and darkness as the rain began to fall in a torrent.

Only a few yards into the forest, Charity looked back and couldn't see the house. Or anyone chasing them. They'd disappeared from view. She could hear the deputy behind them. But without a flashlight, he couldn't see her. She tried to scream but was prevented by the thick glove over her mouth. She heard the deputy on his radio calling Mitch. But how would Mitch ever be able to find her?

She struggled to free herself, but Bud was much stronger than she was, and now that she'd seen his face, she knew he'd never let her go.

He burst out of the trees onto a side road and carried her toward a black pickup. *The* black pickup. Jerking open the driver's side, he threw her in, then climbed in after her. Her purse strap broke, and several of the lighter items in it spilled across the seat. He grabbed the purse and threw it behind the seat, then hit the automatic door locks as she lunged for the opposite-side door handle. Trapped, she screamed bloody murder.

"Stupid bitch," he snarled, and backhanded her so hard she saw stars. The pickup engine roared to life. He hit the gas and tore off, tires screaming. In the side mirror, she thought she glimpsed the deputy run out into the street a block away, but Bud quickly turned and sped down the road toward Dennison Ducks.

"Give me the letter," he ordered, and ripped the mask from his face, throwing it to the floor. "Now." He backhanded her again when she didn't respond.

She cowered as close to her door as she could, crossing her arms over chest, the feel of the letter against her breast.

"Just give me the letter," he growled. "Don't make me take it from you."

Something deep inside her told her he would kill her once he got the letter. Whatever Nina had written was incriminating enough that it had cost at least one other person his life. If Charity gave Bud the letter, he would get away with murder. If she didn't, she had no doubt he would take it. Either way she was a dead woman unless she could get away from him.

Ahead she saw the turnoff for Dennison Ducks. She knew that if he took her past there, he would have her in an isolated area where she wouldn't stand a chance. In the side mirror, she saw that there were no lights in pursuit.

She was on her own.

She lunged for the steering wheel and jerked it toward the right. She heard his curse and felt the pickup swerve before he swung at her. She ducked back and felt something bite into her hip.

When her shoulder bag had spilled across the seat, the heavy items, like her gun and pepper spray, had stayed in the purse. Just her luck. Right now the handcuffs were digging into her hip. Why couldn't something useful have fallen out of her purse?

Bud fought to keep the pickup on the slippery muddy road, got it back under control and tromped down on the gas. "I was going to wait until we were farther up the road but…" He unlocked the doors and reached across her, grabbing the door handle. The door swung open and she saw what he planned to do. Throw her out! And at this speed, she was toast.

She reached under her hip for the handcuffs.

He grabbed the front of her jacket, trying to get the letter. Once he did…

"I'll give you the letter!" she cried, knocking his hands away.

He shifted his gaze back and forth between her and the road, not slowing down, but keeping his hands to himself. Did he think she didn't realize he still planned to throw her out the moment she handed him the letter?

A less-than-inspired plan leaped to mind. Amazing what the mind can come up with when you're totally panicked and fighting for your life.

It was suicidal. Her craziest plan yet. She reached into her jacket and then pretended to be jostled by the road. She fell toward him.

He grabbed the steering wheel with both hands, obviously thinking she was going to try to wrest it from his grip again. She reached over her head and snapped one cuff to his right wrist, planning to snap the other to the steering wheel.

The original plan had been simple, wreck the pickup and run. If she could run. And if he didn't run after her too quickly. This improved plan was even better. Bud wouldn't be able to run after her because he would be handcuffed to the steering wheel.

Bud was going ballistic, screaming at the sight of the handcuff dangling from his wrist and trying to hit her. But she had hold of the other cuff and was hanging on for dear life.

She grabbed the steering wheel, trying to hook the other cuff to it. The pickup began to swerve.

Bud knocked her away, breaking her hold on the other cuff. The pickup was skidding sideways in the mud. Bud was fighting to keep it on the road.

With both his hands busy, she tried again, only to have him grab her by the hair and hold her down with one hand as he tried to right the pickup.

From her position facedown on the seat between the two of them, she couldn't reach the steering wheel. Her inspired plan took on a new twist, this one truly suicidal, but she'd run out of options and knew after this Bud would kill her and take the letter, then dump her body along the road and Mitch would find her in some ditch.

She snapped the other cuff to her own wrist—just an instant before the pickup careened off the road and came to a bone-jarring stop. Her head smacked the gearshift and the lights went out.

CHARITY AWOKE AWARE that she was being carried, the ground uneven, then flat. She opened her eyes. Rain fell on her face. There was no light at first. Then she saw the small glow at the employee entrance of Dennison Ducks. He was taking her to the plant.

At the door, he stopped to set her down, sweating from the effort of hauling her. "I should kill you right now," he said, waving a gun at her with his free hand. "Nina was much easier to kill than you. But then, Ethel had already coldcocked her good with a decoy."

She could tell he wanted to shoot her, but he was already winded from carrying her. He needed her to walk to wherever they were going. Otherwise, she'd already be dead.

He dug out his key, cursing her, then opened the door and shoved her through it. The handcuff chaffed her wrist painfully as she stumbled inside and he jerked her back to him.

She looked around for a weapon. Her purse was in the pickup and she could see nothing within reach that she could use as he dragged her back through the shelves of ducks, never letting her get close enough to grab one. It grew darker and darker as they moved away from the light near the entrance.

At the back of the building, Bud turned on a small lamp over a workbench, picked up a hacksaw and, with the sweep of his free arm, cleared off everything within her reach.

When he turned to look at her, his face was distorted in anger. "I can't believe you did something so stupid," he spat at her as he dragged her closer to the workbench. Dropping the hacksaw, he grabbed the front of her jacket and jerked her to him. He ripped the jacket apart and the letter fell to the floor.

He stared down at it for a moment as if surprised Nina had really written it. Or maybe just surprised at what he'd had to go through to get it.

Pulling Charity down with him, he retrieved the letter from the floor. She watched him open it, dying to see what was inside. What could be in the letter that was worth killing over? Surely not Nina's true paternity. Who cared after twenty-seven years?

It had to have something to do with Angela's kidnapping. "*You* kidnapped Angela!"

"Prove it." Bud curled a lip at her, then pulled a lighter from his pocket, flicked it on and touched the flame to the paper without even a glance in her direction.

"No!" she cried, grabbing for the letter. But it was too late. The paper caught fire in an instant, and as he dropped it to the floor, the flame turned what was left of the letter to ash.

She wanted to cry. But she had much worse problems. Bud had disposed of the letter. Now all he had to do was dispose of her. No one would suspect him, after all. The deputy who'd seen him grab her had only seen a man in a mask and cape driving a black pickup. Even with Rogers dead, no one would know it had been Bud behind the wheel.

Bud was going to get away not only with Angela's kidnapping but with two murders.

She told herself that Mitch would get here. The deputy had called him. Mitch would find the black pickup in the ditch. He would find her. Eventually.

Bud picked up the hacksaw and seemed to realize he couldn't both cut with the saw and hold the gun on her. He moved the gun out of her reach, shifted the hacksaw to his left hand and clumsily began to saw on the metal between the two cuffs, cursing a blue streak as he did.

Her mind raced. She knew that once he got the cuffs apart that would be it for her. She could try to run, but there was no doubt in her mind he would shoot her down. And what were the chances of anyone's coming here on Halloween night? She couldn't depend on Mitch's getting here in time, either.

She listened to the grating of the saw, horrified to see how quickly the blade was cutting through the metal. Must have been cheap handcuffs.

"You know you're not going to get away with this," she said.

He shot her a look that said that line only worked in movies. Of course he was going to get away with it.

Over the rasp of the saw, she thought she heard a

sound, a soft *whoosh* like a door opening. Mitch? No. If it really was the door opening, then it had to be someone with a key.

Something moved at the window next to her. A shadow. She glanced out of the corner of her eye, but saw only a tree limb brush against the glass. Just her imagination. Just like the sound of a door opening?

Bud was working at the handcuff. A few more moments and he would be free of her. She needed to make her move the second the cuffs came apart....

That was when she smelled wet night air. Someone *had* come in through the employee door. Bud didn't seem to have noticed.

She couldn't see who'd entered the plant because of the fully stocked shelves.

The saw cut through the link of metal that connected them. In that instant, Charity lunged for one of the decoys on the shelves off to her left and her hand closed around a drake's neck. She stepped back toward Bud and swung, catching him in the temple before he could pick up the gun. The gun fell, skittering across the concrete and sliding under one of the shelves.

He stumbled back and she turned to run, only to find herself staring into the business end of another gun. Holding it was the last person she'd expected to see.

"Daisy?"

Her theory about Daisy hiring someone to get rid of Angela suddenly came back to her in a rush.

"Don't move," Daisy ordered, pointing the gun at Bud now. Daisy's gaze moved to the ashes on the floor at his feet. "So you got to the letter and destroyed it." Her gaze was hard as stones.

Charity held her breath, not sure Daisy wouldn't

kill her if she moved. If Daisy really had hired Bud to kidnap Angela, then why was she pointing the gun at him? Unless she planned to kill him to keep him quiet. With Nina dead and the letter gone...

"Nina told me she knew who kidnapped Angela," Daisy was saying. "I thought she was bluffing. She said lucky for me she loved revenge even more than money and that she'd written a letter to the newspaper. Charity would get it on Halloween and the masks would be off. I guess the mask is off, Bud."

Bud licked his lips and looked nervously around.

"Where is the private investigator I hired?" Daisy asked. "I saw his truck..."

"He's dead," Charity offered. "Bud was driving the truck. He was getting ready to kill me when you came in."

Daisy didn't seem to hear. She narrowed her gaze at Bud and said, "Where is my daughter?" Her eerie calm made the hair stand up on the back of Charity's neck. "Oh God, I should have known it would be you who took my daughter. You'd do anything for money. Where is Angela?"

"I don't know, I swear to God, Daisy." Bud was leaning against the workbench as if his knees wouldn't hold him. "I sold her to some lawyer. He never gave me his name."

Bud glanced behind Daisy as if he saw something in the darkness by the decoy shelves. Or someone. Fear distorted his face. He was shaking his head as if suddenly more afraid.

Charity saw what he planned to do. She opened her mouth, but it happened too fast. Bud dived for his gun, which had slid under a decoy shelf.

He came up with it, rolling and firing at Daisy. The air boomed with gunfire and the smell of gunpowder met Charity's nostrils.

Charity saw Daisy stagger, her shoulder blooming with red as she crumpled to the floor. Then she heard Bud cry out as another shot exploded.

In the same instant, the window shattered behind her, showering her with glass. She was knocked to the floor and Mitch was there.

Then Charity was in Mitch's arms and he was holding her close and she was crying as he stroked her hair and whispered, "It's okay, baby. It's okay."

And Wade was there, rushing to Daisy's side, a gun in his hand. Charity was the only one to see Bud's expression. He was looking at Wade and trying to speak, but no words came out as he clutched his chest where he'd been shot, and died.

EPILOGUE

IN THE DAYS that followed, the talk at Betty's was about nothing but the murders—and the twenty-seven-year-old kidnapping. Another Bigfoot sighting on the edge of town went by barely noticed.

Mitch had pieced the story together as best he could for Charity. Nina had been planning to meet Wade at the decoy plant Tuesday night, but instead, Ethel Whiting had shown up. They'd fought and Ethel had hit Nina, knocking her unconscious.

Bud had been outside, planning to kill Nina. He'd found her, killed her and dumped her and her car in the ravine. The problem was, he wouldn't have been able to do that without help. Maybe his wife had driven the second car. She wasn't talking. In fact, she was packing, moving away from Timber Falls. Or maybe it had been someone else in town. Charity wondered if they would ever know the truth.

Bud had killed Nina to keep her from exposing his part in Angela's kidnapping. At least that was the theory. Charity had one of her own. If Bud had kidnapped Angela for money, then he could have killed Nina for the person behind the kidnapping.

Or there could have been no conspiracy at all, Mitch reminded her. Maybe along with Wade, Nina had been blackmailing Bud. Only, Bud was never planning to pay.

Daisy was recovering from a gunshot wound to her shoulder at a hospital in Eugene. When Charity went down to visit her, the room was full of flowers from residents of Timber Falls. Shooting Bud Farnsworth had gotten her back into the town's good graces, it seemed. People were willing to give her another chance.

"Did you see the letter before he burned it?" Daisy asked her.

Charity had to tell her she didn't. "I don't think Nina knew where Angela was." She wasn't sure if that had been the case, but she thought it would make things easier for Daisy, who'd hired Kyle Rogers to get the letter—if Nina really had written a letter to get her revenge like she'd told Daisy she planned to do. But all Rogers had gotten was killed for it. And no one would ever know now what Nina had written Charity about the kidnapping or Bud Farnsworth.

DNA tests had confirmed that Wade was indeed Nina's father. Charity had heard that Desiree hadn't taken it well. It was hard to say how Daisy took the news. She still seemed too calm to Charity, like a woman on the edge, barely hanging on.

When Wade entered the hospital room, Charity left. She couldn't forget Bud's fear just before he'd gone for his gun. Or his attempt to speak to Wade at the very end of his life. She still had nightmares.

Mitch had been sleeping on her couch in the weeks since. She'd decided it was all right to show a man that she needed him. At least for a while.

Ethel hadn't gone back to work at Dennison Ducks even after Wade apologized to her and she was released on bond, trial pending. No one thought she would get any jail time. Wade was advertising for a new secretary. Charity's newspaper circulation had increased and she was actually showing a pretty good profit. But she had realized something. Mitch didn't care if she wrote a Pulitzer prize-winning story or not. How about that?

On her way back from visiting Daisy at the hospital in Eugene, she drove into town in time for a late breakfast at Betty's Café.

Betty slid a piece of banana-cream pie and a diet cola in front of her as she took her usual stool.

"See that guy over there?" Betty whispered.

Charity turned to see a dark-haired man in his thirties sitting in the far booth poring over a stack of papers. He wasn't bad-looking. But he was no Mitch Tanner.

"He looks too stodgy for you," Charity said, turning back to her pie. "Anyway, I thought you were seeing that new bartender at the Duck-In."

Betty blushed. "Bruno? Who told you that?"

Charity just laughed. "Don't tell me that's Bruno over there."

"No, he's that scientist—the one who did that horrible article on Liam Sawyer. Said the photos Liam took all those years ago of Bigfoot were just part of an elaborate hoax."

Ford Lancaster. Charity glanced over her shoulder at him. "So what's he doing in town?"

"That's just it," Betty said. "No one knows. I guess it's probably this latest Bigfoot sighting, but I wonder if it could have anything to do with Liam being back in town."

Charity certainly hoped not. She didn't want to see her friend Roz hurt anymore by all that old stuff about her father. "So tell me about your latest heartache in blue jeans."

The bell over the door tinkled.

"Speaking of heartache," Betty said under her breath, then called out, "Good mornin', Sheriff. Saved you a piece of banana-cream."

"No pie for me this morning, Betty." Mitch slid onto the stool next to Charity, and Betty placed a cup of black coffee in front of him before disappearing discreetly into the back.

"GOOD MORNING, CHARITY." Mitch looked over at her and felt his heart leap at just the sight of her. It was overcast outside, clouds low and gray, rain threatening again. But it was like there was sunlight all around her. Her auburn hair seemed on fire this morning, and her face seemed to light up like springtime.

He told himself it was the banana-cream pie, not him.

"Morning, Sheriff." She took a bite of pie, closed her eyes and smiled. He hadn't seen her smile in days and felt a rush of pure pleasure just watching her.

She opened her eyes. "Care for a bite?"

Oh, he was tempted. But not by banana-cream pie. In the days since he'd crashed through a glass window to save Charity, he'd thought a lot about the two of them. He didn't know how he felt about anything— just that he couldn't stay away from her. Didn't want to.

Not that he wasn't still scared. Last night he'd had dinner with his father and Jesse. It hadn't been all that bad. He was trying to see the man that Jesse had always known. It would take time.

But he wasn't as afraid of himself. He'd always worried he was too much like his father. Now he wasn't so sure that was a bad thing.

As for Charity... "I was wondering..." His mouth

was dry as cotton. He took a sip of coffee. "Do you have any plans for this weekend?"

She raised a brow in surprise.

"Saturday night. I was thinking…" That old voice in his head tried to stop him, but he wasn't listening anymore. "Maybe you'd like to go to the community-center dance. We could have dinner first."

Charity was speechless. It was always something to behold. "Are you asking me for a…date?"

"I believe I am."

She grinned. "Well, you're in luck. I just happen to be free Saturday."

He reached into his pocket, feeling bashful, as he set the box with the bracelet on the counter. "I thought you might want to wear this."

Her eyes were big as pie plates when she saw the bracelet she'd eyed at the Eugene jewelry store. "Oh, Mitch." Tears welled in those eyes and she bit her lower lip. Then she kissed him.

He felt himself falling, out of control, falling, only this time it didn't seem quite so frightening. But then he saw himself clear as day in a black tuxedo standing at an altar, and next to him—

"It's just a dance," he said when the kiss ended.

Charity smiled that secret smile of hers. "Whatever you say, Mitch."

* * * * *

We hope you enjoyed reading

THE M^cKETTRICK WAY

by *New York Times* bestselling author

LINDA LAEL MILLER and

MOUNTAIN SHERIFF

by *New York Times* bestselling author

B.J. DANIELS

Both were originally
Harlequin® Special Edition and
Harlequin® Intrigue series stories!

Discover more heartfelt tales of family, friendship
and love from the **Harlequin Special Edition**
series. Romance is for life, and these stories
show that every chapter in a relationship has
its challenges and delights, and that love can be
renewed with each turn of the page!

◆HARLEQUIN®

SPECIAL EDITION

Life, Love and Family

When you're with family, you're home!

Look for six *new* romances every month
from **Harlequin Special Edition!**

Available wherever books are sold.

www.Harlequin.com

SPECIAL EXCERPT FROM

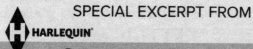

HARLEQUIN®

SPECIAL EDITION

*Obstetrician Avery Wallace treats pregnant patients,
but now she's sporting her own baby bump, thanks to
one passionate night with Dr. Justin Garrett. The good
doctor is eager to put his playboy ways in the past.
But can the daddy-to-be convince Avery to make their
instant family a reality?*

Read on for a sneak preview of
TWO DOCTORS & A BABY, the latest book in
Brenda Harlen's *fan-favorite series,*
THOSE ENGAGING GARRETTS!

"Thank you for tonight," she said as she walked him to
the door. "I was planning on leftovers when I got home—
this was better."

"I thought so, too." He settled his hands on her hips
and drew her toward him.

She put her hands on his chest, determined to hold him
at a distance. "What are you doing?"

"I'm going to kiss you goodbye."

"No, you're not," she said, a slight note of panic in
her voice.

"It's just a kiss, Avery." He held her gaze as his hand
slid up her back to the nape of her neck. "And hardly our
first."

Then he lowered his head slowly, the focused
intensity of those green eyes holding her captive as his
mouth settled on hers. Warm and firm and deliciously

intoxicating. Her own eyes drifted shut as a soft sigh whispered between her lips.

He kept the kiss gentle, patiently coaxing a response. She wanted to resist, but she had no defenses against the masterful seduction of his mouth. She arched against him, opened for him. And the first touch of his tongue to hers was like a lighted match to a candle wick—suddenly she was on fire, burning with desire.

It was like New Year's Eve all over again, but this time she didn't even have the excuse of adrenaline pulsing through her system. This time, it was all about Justin.

Or maybe it was the pregnancy.

Yes, that made sense. Her system was flooded with hormones as a result of the pregnancy, a common side effect of which was increased arousal. It wasn't that she was pathetically weak or even that he was so temptingly irresistible. It wasn't about Justin at all—it was a basic chemical reaction that was overriding her common sense and self-respect. Because even though she knew that he was wrong for her in so many ways, being with him, being in his arms, felt so right.

Don't miss
TWO DOCTORS & A BABY
by Brenda Harlen,
available April 2016 wherever
Harlequin® Special Edition books and ebooks are sold.

www.Harlequin.com

H HARLEQUIN®

SPECIAL EDITION

Life, Love and Family

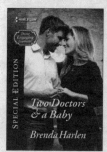

Use this coupon to save

$1.00

on the purchase of any
Harlequin® Special Edition book.

Available wherever books are sold, including
most bookstores, supermarkets, drugstores
and discount stores.

✂

Save $1.00

on the purchase of any Harlequin® Special Edition book.

Coupon valid until May 31, 2016.
Redeemable at participating outlets in the U.S. and Canada only.
Not redeemable at Barnes & Noble stores. Limit one coupon per customer.

52613500

Canadian Retailers: Harlequin Enterprises Limited will pay the face value of this coupon plus 10.25¢ if submitted by customer for this product only. Any other use constitutes fraud. Coupon is nonassignable. Void if taxed, prohibited or restricted by law. Consumer must pay any government taxes. Void if copied. Inmar Promotional Services ("IPS") customers submit coupons and proof of sales to Harlequin Enterprises Limited, P.O. Box 3000, Saint John, NB E2L 4L3, Canada. Non-IPS retailer—for reimbursement submit coupons and proof of sales directly to Harlequin Enterprises Limited, Retail Marketing Department, 225 Duncan Mill Rd., Don Mills, ON M3B 3K9, Canada.

5 65373 00076 2   (8100)0 12143

U.S. Retailers: Harlequin Enterprises Limited will pay the face value of this coupon plus 8¢ if submitted by customer for this product only. Any other use constitutes fraud. Coupon is nonassignable. Void if taxed, prohibited or restricted by law. Consumer must pay any government taxes. Void if copied. For reimbursement submit coupons and proof of sales directly to Harlequin Enterprises Limited, P.O. Box 880478, El Paso, TX 88588-0478, U.S.A. Cash value 1/100 cents.

® and ™ are trademarks owned and used by the trademark owner and/or its licensee.

© 2016 Harlequin Enterprises Limited

NYTCOUP0316

Meet the Carsons of Mustang Creek: three men who embody the West and define what it means to be a rancher, a cowboy and a hero in this brand-new series from *New York Times* bestselling author

LINDA LAEL MILLER

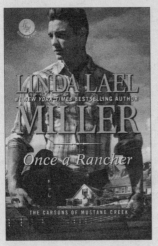

Slater Carson might be a filmmaker by trade, but he's still a cowboy at heart—and he knows the value of a hard day's work under the hot Wyoming sun. So when he sees troubled teen Ryder heading down a dangerous path, he offers the boy a job on the ranch he shares with his two younger brothers. And since Ryder's guardian is the gorgeous new Mustang Creek resort manager, Grace Emery, Slater figures it can't hurt to keep a closer eye on her, as well…

Grace Emery doesn't have time for romance. Between settling into her new job and caring for her ex-husband's rebellious son, her attraction to larger-than-life Slater is a distraction she can't afford. But when an unexpected threat emerges, she'll discover just how far Slater will go to protect what matters most—and that love is always worth fighting for.

Pick up your copy today!

Be sure to connect with us at:

Harlequin.com/Newsletters
Facebook.com/HarlequinBooks
Twitter.com/HQNBooks

31901060150663

HQN™
www.HQNBooks.com

PHLLM968